Barry Kir

The Eden Paradox

Summertime Publications Inc.

PARIS - SCOTTSDALE

THE EDEN PARADOX

English edition published
by Summertime Publications (USA) in 2011

copyright BARRY KIRWAN 2011

Summertime Publications

Summertime Publications Inc.
7502 E. Berridge Lane, Scottsdale, AZ 85250
All Rights Reserved
Isbn:978-0-9823698-4-5

for Lisa

Acknowledgements

I would like to thank all my fellow Parisian writers for their critique and support over the years, in particular Chris Vanier and Dimitri Keramitas who have been with me throughout this journey, as well as Jen Dick, Laurel Zuckerman, and Mary Ellen Gallagher. Thanks also to literary consultants Cornerstones and Writers Workshop, and SF author Gary Gibson, SF agent John Jarrold, and my former agent Robert Brown who first got me published with Ampichellis. Last but not least I'd like to thank my four readers, Veronique Begault, Andy Kilner, Anna Wennerberg and Kjersti Disen for their encouragement and enthusiasm for the novel.

The Eden Trilogy

The Eden Paradox

Eden's Trial

Eden's Revenge

Table of Contents

Part One : Journey to Eden

Part Two : Eden

Part Three

PART ONE

JOURNEY TO EDEN

Chapter 1

Assassin

People rarely search for bodies in ceilings, Gabriel O'Donnell reminded himself. He should have a couple of hours before anyone discovered his latest victim. Slipping unseen from the side door, he dissolved into the amoebic mass of dignitaries arriving for the fund-raiser at Eden Mission Control. He itched to shed his tuxedo and starched shirt, but he needed the camouflage – along with the stolen emotion-ID that had required a messy killing – to secure entry. He blended in with the wealthy entourage decked in stark designer suits and power dresses. He didn't speak to anyone, didn't sip from the champagne glass he occasionally raised to his lips. He let his eyes glaze over as if he, too, were rich enough to forget what was outside, an Earth maimed by War, near collapse from heat exhaustion.

Somewhere here was his target, but as yet he didn't know who. He slowed his breathing and sharpened his senses, filtering out the bass hum of the aircon and the drone of conversation. He suppressed the cocktail of cologne and perfume the crowd wore to mask residual traces of sweat from their journey through the early evening LA heat-haze. He glanced at his wristcom, switched to privacy mode so only he could read it – no message yet confirming his mark's identity. The display did tell him it was a cool nineteen degrees Celsius, compared to forty-five out in the open, and way below the 2061 climate control mandate for public buildings. Nothing new, he thought: the rich make laws for others to follow.

The idea flickered across his mind that if he dispatched ten or twenty of the moguls here tonight, instead of just one, a lot more mouths would find food. But only for a while. The latest vidcast from his mentor had confirmed what he'd already suspected – the holocaust was mere days away. When he found the right target, maybe he could delay its onset, and save millions.

Maybe.

A fanfare of horns sliced through the banter, announcing the holorium was open: the Eden show awaited them. He swept forward with the elite mob, a spider hiding amongst flies.

As the alcohol-rouged gathering rounded a corner, he glimpsed the twin Stentons bordering the corridor: floor-to-ceiling carbon-black monoliths. State-of-the-art security gear. He focused his mind, careful not to tense his body. A few surreptitious glances verified what the memorised floor plans had told him – this was the only access point. Six heavily-armed security guards manned the station, eyeing people as they passed through. The two in the front used an age-old technique called the *fence*, an unblinking stare-down subduing those passing through, ruffling a few of the male celebrities in the process. The middle two checked people and bags, but this was more for show – the Stentons did the real work. The final two guards scanned the assembly using peripheral vision – letting their right brains detect any unusual behaviour patterns of the swarm. Not bad, he thought. He knew he could take down all six if necessary, but then his mission would fail.

He had to get past them.

The Stentons were top of their class – a biometric system based on psychological finger-printing, using subliminal stimuli to trigger minute fear responses. The monoliths were especially good at picking out kamikaze terrorists, whose fear response had a singular signature, and experienced assassins like Gabriel, who had none. Earlier, he'd had to instil panic into the day's first victim before terminating him, while downloading the visceral feedback. Gabriel now had those terror responses primed in the neural net embedded in his scalp – they would match the dead man's E-ID card Gabriel held in his left palm. He'd actually apologised to the corpse afterward, taking rather more care than usual with the body. He was a Sentinel assassin, not a psychopath.

Slowing to an amble, he let one or two suits rub past him as he weighed his options. He laughed at a nearby joke as if he were part of that particular gang. But his insides felt hollow: too much was riding on tonight's mission. Watching the shuffling pack tighten toward the checkpoint scanners, he decided he needed an extra edge. Distraction was also an assassin's tool.

As they herded like cloned beef toward the final security check, he surveyed the audience and picked out a busty woman in her thirties, sporting an emerald halter neck dress of gossamer-thin silk. Most of the middle-aged men pretended a little too hard not to notice her. As he mingled behind the woman and her escort in the funnelling queue, he casually reached into his pocket. He extracted the sliver of acid-coated razor-wire from its sheath. He coughed as he approached the twin security columns. His right hand, en route to cover his mouth, grazed the material of the woman's halter with the filament, depositing a trace of acid. He let the hair-like strand drop to the floor, crushing it underfoot. Holding up his E-ID pass, he stared as required towards one of the monoliths, the under-dressed woman behind him. He held his breath.

Whoops and guffaws erupted as her halter snapped. Gabriel turned around, feigning surprise and interest, and the guards manhandled him through the full-scan checkpoint without serious attention. Once past he walked to the empty restroom and located the locked stall marked *Out of Order*. His fingers rapped in the entry digicode, and he stepped inside. He found what he expected, a small black rucksack, and checked the contents: gravitics, stiletto knife, and slimline S&W pulse gun with night-sighter. All he required now was his target's name, but his wristcom stayed quiet. His handler didn't usually leave it this late.

He zipped up the bag. As he headed out, he checked his reflection in the restroom mirror, and paused. He searched for any trace of the young man he'd been before the War, before becoming a killing machine, before losing her. Eyes black and remorseless as a shark's stared back at him; hers had been green, forgiving. She would have been twenty-seven today. He slung the rucksack over his shoulder. Happy birthday, Jenny. He broke off his gaze, stole through the door, and entered the holorium.

* * *

Despite the aircon maintaining the room at a fresh fifteen degrees Celsius to optimise the technology's performance, Micah was sweating.

"You won't make it, not this time," Rudi said, leering beneath a wavy moustache. He anchored his feet against the chrome desk, tilting the recliner back further, hands linked behind matted black curls.

You could have helped. Micah's silver gloves were a blur as he worked at the holo-bench. Its data columns and networking filaments resembled a complex city of skyscrapers: sapphire flying buttresses connecting golden spires and towers. He grimaced at the writhing red sores leaching energy from four of the amber columns, defects he had to remove for the program to run.

"Let me work, Rudi. I'm almost there."

Rudi persisted. "Why'd you agree to do this in the first place? Thought you'd get a chance to work with our resident Slovakian princess in Comms, eh?"

Micah dropped a filament and felt a stab of dread as it tumbled down inside the cylinder, ricocheting off several columns towards the central golden nexus. He caught it just in time with his left hand, without disturbing the overall structure. *That was close!* No time to wipe the beads of sweat building on his brow.

"Nice catch," Rudi muttered. "So is she, but out of your league. You know that, right?"

Micah ignored him, suspecting it wouldn't make any difference.

Rudi stretched his hands forward, framing Micah between thumbs and indexes as if taking a holopic. "I mean, look at you. The basics are okay – no hunchback, all your own teeth, body parts in the usual places. But the wiry fuzz on your head, the bulging eyes – is that a thyroid thing, by the way? And as for dress sense..." Rudi's hands returned to their habitual position, clasped behind his head. "Does your Mom still buy your clothes, or what? No style. That's the problem, Micah. She's class, you're not."

Micah braved a shrug, but he knew Rudi was right: unlike Rudi, he had an abysmal record with women. He glanced at the countdown: 3:08. Any second, he'd get the call. His fingers, wrapped in second-skin holo-transducers, felt the subtle vibrations in the digitised information, like pulsating ice cubes covered in Braille. This part of his job at Eden Mission Control still gave him a buzz. He threaded the teraquad info-strands into place with a precision and purpose he rarely knew in the rest of his life.

On cue, the screen switched on. A red-faced, balding man glared at him. Micah didn't stop. Seconds mattered.

"Sanderson. Tell me it's ready."

"Yes, Mr Vastra, Sir. Almost ready. It'll be on time."

"Better be." The screen blanked.

Rudi chuckled. "You're in deep shit. Three minutes till lights out."

Micah dismissed the remark and flipped back into the zone, holding his breath, rapt in concentration. All sound ceased in his mind, like a frozen waterfall. As he slotted the final filament into place, the reds vanished. The resultant data harmonic sent a tingling rush through his gloves into his arms and spine, making him gasp. He snapped his right forefinger and thumb together, transmitting the program.

"Done!" The display shimmered and was gone. He peeled off the gloves, threw them onto the work bench, and slumped into his chair.

Rudi sighed. "Why didn't you just re-use the last vid – why does each one have to be different? Why make work for yourself? These shitheads don't care. You'll get no credit. And meanwhile, *she* doesn't even know you exist!"

Micah grinned. This one was going to be good. It would move the audience, he just knew it. "You wouldn't understand, Rudi. It's… art. Besides, some of the Hi-creds here today have been to the show before – they'll be impressed when they realise it changes each time."

Rudi shook his head. "No hope whatsoever."

Micah snatched up the remote-ball and squeezed it to select the holorium viewscreen on his macro display, then pressed harder to show feeds from all eight cameras. He scanned the views, zooming in and out on the audience about to see his production. The stock-straight profile of the Eden Mission Director, Keiji Kane, was easy to pick out from the crowd, greeting indistinguishable men in dark suits with expandable waistlines. The younger women in the audience were strikingly dressed in angular flow-suits, the older ones decked out in more classic elegant outfits.

He watched Kane's acerbic assistant Sandy march up to him and whisper something in his ear, her hand touching his waist as she bent forward. Kane nodded, and headed over to his front row pew. People followed his lead and took their seats for the show, a prelude to a tour of Eden Mission Control, the first step in eliciting continued financial support from the ultra-rich. Micah wasn't keen on the fact they had to do this every month, but it was vital to keeping alive the four astronauts on their way to Eden.

He zoomed back out when someone unusual caught his eye – a tanned, slim man floating through the crowd like a dancer – all in black, no jacket, just a small back-pack. No one seemed to notice him as he headed toward the rear exit, cutting through the flood of people vying for the best places. Micah leant forward, intrigued by his effortless movements, like a dolphin swimming through the current. He lost him, though, as he moved out of camera range. Plain-clothes security, he assumed.

Rudi was right about one thing, though. This wasn't his real job. They were both full-time telemetry analysts, poring over sensor information slip-streaming back from Earth's only faster-than-light ship, the Ulysses. Comms was haphazard at best, involving unpredictable and still barely-understood tachyon fields, coupled with an increasing delay as Ulysses got farther from Earth. He didn't fully understand the theory, but he and Rudi were two of the people disentangling the data and making sense of it. Still, he had a modest talent for holo-vidding – not enough to give up his day job – but he enjoyed watching people's reactions, and it made a break from the drudgery of endless analysis of signals traversing incomprehensible distances across the void, telling everyone that all was *still* well on the mission to Eden.

Reluctantly, he had to admit that Rudi was right on the other count, too. He pretended he wasn't searching, but when he found Antonia in the audience, his breath softened. He zeroed in on her. Although she was staff, like him, Antonia always got an invite to these functions, being the daughter of the Slovakian ambassador. Though "Princess" wasn't correct, it wasn't entirely inappropriate – she was regal, statuesque, with porcelain skin and dark coffee eyes. He watched her slink into her seat, and observed the fading holorium lights twinkle on her sequined dress.

"Naughty, naughty!" Rudi said. "Mustn't spy on staff."

Micah frowned, only in part due to the comment: she had a tall, suave escort. Switching the cameras to night-vision mode, he zoomed away from her, resisting temptation.

Rudi slapped his thighs and got up. "God, I'm sorry, man, I can't bear to watch another one. I'm going for a spin on the Optron. Catch you later."

The door hissed closed. Micah switched off four of the camera views to allow a central picture to emerge of the main holo-images the two-hundred-strong audience had gathered to experience. They were in for quite a ride, and he'd have to write a report later on their reactions, to fine-tune it for next time. He sat back, and waited.

* * *

Gabriel's wristcom located the surveillance weak spot at the rear of the holorium. He set it to emit a fold, allowing him to work within a three metre sensor void, rendering him invisible to normal security sweeps.

The lights dimmed. All eyes gazed forward.

He slipped on a black silk hood, donned his gloves, and switched his wristcom to nerve-stim mode. He curved his thinly-sheathed tongue inside his mouth to activate the hands-free control mechanism. Few could master it: a single cough, yawn, or inadvertent swallowing could be misinterpreted as commands. But to Gabriel it was the ultimate assassin's tool: internal, invisible to anyone looking for signs of subterfuge.

Turning away from the audience immersed in the holo-show net, he approached the vertical steel wall at the back of the holorium. He switched his genetically-coded boots and gloves to lizard mode, tough microscopic hooks and barbs crystallising within seconds. His breathing remained silent as he scaled the sheer face, taking care not to move too fast. He knew enough psycho-physiology and anatomy not only to kill efficiently, but also to use the strengths and weaknesses of human and animal perception: oblique, rapid movements were perceived by all mammals and reptiles faster than any other sensory signal, especially via peripheral vision, for self-evident survival reasons.

Six metres up, he positioned himself underneath a vacant balcony. He manoeuvred upside down, using his tongue control to activate gravitic contact pads on his feet, knees, waist and ribs. A millimetre at a time, he peeled his hands from the ceiling to test he was secure. His masked head fell backwards, upside down, like a gecko hanging from the ceiling, so he could see the audience. He had no interest in the holo. Tapping a short command into his wristcom to signal he was in position, he lifted an object the size of half an apple from his pocket and attached it to the ceiling. Last, he strapped the mono-pulse barrel with sighting lens to his forehead. He could see everyone in the audience – the backs of their heads at least. Everything was set.

He waited, immobile, an obsidian gargoyle ready to spit fire.

* * *

In the darkening holorium, the last murmurings of the audience died away as all attention fell on the iridescent holographic net descending around them – as if it was snowing diamonds. A fanfare of brass horns and an explosion of eye-wrenching white erupted throughout the room. The audience flinched and squinted, before the light condensed into stars racing away from a central glowing hub. Holophonic tricks whirled and sustained a spiralling crescendo of strained violins. People gasped as they fell through space, away from the centre of the galaxy, coasting along a spiral arm towards a yellow star and a small, blue-green ball. As the image slowed and the tones merged into a softer cadence, a deep, stone-calm voice spoke.

"Earth. A jewel. A gift from heaven. Our home for millions of years."

The audience broke through the atmosphere, surfing cirrus strands until Everest reared up beneath them. They dived through a sea of clouds, speared over verdant Himalayan valleys, picking up speed. Streaking over the Indian sub-continent, they dodged the outstretched arms of the Mumbai Tower, the tallest building in the world, in the shape of the goddess Kali. They swept across a sparkling aquamarine Indian Ocean, soared over the Serengeti plains of Africa, disturbing hordes of wildebeest, and looped Kilimanjaro. The audience accelerated, skimming across the steel-grey Atlantic. Breathless, they breached the shores of North America, zipped over a subliminal patchwork of maize and soybean, slalomed through the Grand Canyon, then slewed upwards, punching through the cloud layer back into space.

Micah watched dignitaries clutch the arms of their seats during this roller-coaster ride. *Good opening.* He sat back in the Media lab to listen to his script's perfectly synthesised voice, designed using the latest emo-ware.

"This amazing world, this incredible resource, here for all mankind." The evangelical tone made even the hard-nosed magnates listen. "And then…" The holorium contrast grew stark, then grainy, as the green-blue globe changed colour. Swirling amethyst clouds bubbled forth across the Earth's face, acid on flesh, leaving in their wake a rusty swathe raking across half the globe. Pock-marks appeared on the surfaces of North America, Europe and Asia, visible from space. Though this vision of what had happened to Earth was not new, the impact was palpable. Members of the audience bit their lips, nostrils flared, one or two of the women dabbed their eyes, and several men clenched fists. Micah tapped coded entries into the audience reaction slate, while many shook their heads with exasperation, and more than a few inspected their feet. *Some here aren't without guilt.*

The audience relived the relentless degradation of their planet, in fast-frame.

"How did we get here?" the voice asked, as the audience segued through pages of Pre-War history, images of humanity's progress and prowess leading up to the War.

Proud of this part, Micah zoomed in to see Antonia's reaction. Her eyes widened at the grand vistas of the exploration of Mars with its unexplained crystal caverns, and the underwater Arctic oilfield-cities of the first half of the century. Her lower lip trembled when the legendary

African Conglomerate doctors from the medical "Golden Age" stood before her, brandishing their Nobel Prizes in one hand, and the vaccines for malaria, AIDS and CoR16A in the other. Her eyes steeled as she witnessed the First Generation robot soldiers quelling the Turkmenistan rebel invasion, paving the way for robot peacekeepers across the world, ushering in short-lived hopes for an end to war. He zoomed out; it was about to get rough.

The vidcom buzzed, catching him unawares. He hastily took his feet off the table, then relaxed as he realised the message was audio-only.

"Sampson?" The voice was sharp and clipped, the caller's register blank.

"Sanderson. My name is –"

"Okay, okay, *Sanderson*. Security here, so pay attention. We need you to check something. Just before the show started, we did a head count. Should have been 208, but for a moment we had 209. With the show running it's hard for us to see anything on our monitors. You have bio measures, don't you? You can scan the number of people?"

"Er, well, maybe." He called up the biometric screen, tracking audience heart rates and pheromone levels.

"Well?"

"Um. The thing is, they're macro measures, designed to look at whole audiences, not individuals." The vidcom became muffled; he thought he heard the word *Jeez!*

The sound cleared. "Look, just see if you can filter them, okay? If you get a count, just hit call-back – think you can do that?"

"Sure." It cut off. Micah raised a third finger in silent protest, then turned to the bio-filter controls. He wished Rudi hadn't left, they could have done this quicker together. Glancing back at the Holo Control Screen, he saw he'd missed the collapse of the Chinese Dragon Hegemony, and the nano-plague. He caught the tail-end of the bungled US-led anti-terrorist nuclear bombing in Afghanistan, which finally triggered the three-year-long World War between the United Secular Nations and the "Big Five" Religious Front countries.

Micah knew that most saw the War as the inevitable blood-letting following two decades of increasingly polarised basic religious rights: fervent believers on the one hand, whose beliefs affected all aspects of their lives, and on the other, those who either did not believe, or believed in moderation. The War's outcome, with a price tag of a half-billion dead, was the Global Tolerance Pact, with the inter-meshed Fundie religions exercising power – and in some cases neo-Sharia law, depending on the country, at local but never national level – and the secularists running governments and international trade. Global freedom of movement meant people moved to where they felt they fit best, if they could afford to move.

Following the fragile truce borne more from mutual exhaustion than true reconciliation, Peacekeeper forces merged with anti-terrorist agencies to form the much nastier and hence more effective Chorazin Interpol, semi-autonomous agents accountable only to national governments and the fledgling New World Alliance Council. Despite a pessimistic post-war outlook, the peace had held for ten years.

But Micah scowled. The War's secondary ignition points, which had escalated a tragic but singular event into global carnage, had all occurred in the vicinity of places such as the Venezuelan deep-ocean oil fields, the Botswana uranium mines, the Amazon rainforest – what had been left of it – and the Asian e-stock market. The War had also been about money and resources, as usual, all of which had been depleted during the bitter fighting.

He picked up his cold coffee, downing it in one gulp to chase away morose thoughts, and focused on his new task, staring at the forest of green and red biofeedback signals shuffling across the monitor. He munched on a stale noni-muffin for inspiration.

He decided to go with heart rate rather than any of the other measures – the rest were too sensitive, too evanescent. If he could predict when certain reactions would happen, he should be able to obtain a number of correlated signals. The perfect event to elicit a visceral reaction was just about to happen. He set up a parameter file, hit "track", and turned to watch the audience.

Silent visions of nuclear detonations in Frankfurt, Dublin, London, Moscow and his own Los Angeles were unleashed in the holorium, amplified by the vibration devices in the audience seats, slowed down to show their devastating power. The audience felt the warm lick of holographic flame fronts spreading outward from incandescent mushrooms.

He drew his arms around him. He'd left out the bass, grinding sound, partly because this way allowed more artistic impact, but also because, like many survivors, he knew the sound of a nuclear detonation only too well, and would panic if he heard it again.

The image pulled back, showing the final stages of the "browning" of Earth. He noticed some audience members were distressed. He brushed aside a momentary pang of guilt – the Eden Mission needed the money, being fifty per cent funded by donations and advertising. Kane, with his political influence, somehow kept their financial head above water – not easy after two expedition failures. If it weren't for him, the Mission wouldn't survive another month.

He edged forward and zeroed in on Antonia again, then wished he hadn't. Her eyes were wet, but worse, the man next to her was squeezing her hand, offering comfort. Micah bit off another chunk of muffin.

A single beep rescued him. He swung over to the biometric monitor and froze mid-chew. The number of hearts beating in the holorium was neither 208 nor 209: there were two additional hearts beating.

That wasn't all. Two heart rates had remained completely stable during the nuclear detonation scenes. He'd never seen that before.

But now the data had merged again. He glanced sideways toward the vidcom, wondering what to do.

* * *

Gabriel's wristcom twitched. He manoeuvred his arm to see the text-space through the autofocus gun sight. A single name appeared – *Kane*. He'd hoped it would be someone else, given Kane's philanthropy, but he didn't question orders. Beneath his name was an hourglass symbol: *not yet*. He checked to see if anything else followed, then his head returned upside down to scan the audience. Locating Kane's front row seat, he zoomed in, and found the tell-tale mole on the left side of the man's neck, nestling below a well-groomed hairline. He locked his target.

* * *

Micah cleared his throat and tapped the vidcom.

The reply was instant. "How many?"

"Well, the only stable count I got was during the nuclear scene, that's when the filters have most chance –"

"Answer the question."

"Two-ten," Micah said, annoyed at himself. He heard a muffled silence.

"Okay, leave it to us now, no need to monitor any more."

The vidcom clicked off. Micah stared at it, then at the biometrics. He flicked the main viewer to a bird's eye view of the holorium. He filtered out the holoshow, switched to infrared, and began counting the blobs on the screen.

The effusive voice from the show continued: "… that mankind was on the brink of extinction. But we were not extinguished. As the politicians and the people realised that they were about to be destroyed, we pulled back, just in time."

Micah's teeth clamped down at these last words. He always left them in the speech, but for him they were laced with bitterness. He'd been a fifteen-year old draftee, his squad captured on their very first field training mission, three weeks before the end of the War. He took a deep breath, forcing himself to exhale slowly to the count of ten, suppressing the memories of his brief incarceration – nights littered with tortured screams; the naked silence when they abruptly stopped.

Ten years on, the episode still clung to him like a phantom limb.

Yet in many senses, he knew mankind had been "lucky": all the computer models of global nuclear theatre had proved wrong. Only a few countries had suffered blanket attacks, and most other nations had found their situation "recoverable", especially after scour-tech had been developed to dampen rad-levels. Life was still tough – he only had to look out a window to see the relentless heat haze rippling buildings in the distance or stars at night, and rationing of food, power, fuel and aircon would go on for decades. But it could have been so much worse – terminal.

He recalled a few pundits who'd argued that the results of the War were so counter-intuitive, the only rational explanation was that it had all been orchestrated by an unseen organisation, controlled to do limited damage. *Conspiracy whackos.* What possible motive could there be? He was just thankful it hadn't gone too far.

He resumed the head-count. From the corner of his eye he saw the main holo screen suffuse with green, showing more upbeat images. He'd been advised by the Mission psych, Carlson, that in Post-War culture, lifting people up after taking them down a guilt trip was the best way to wring out money. He knew the show by heart anyway – the audience were trundling their way through the genetically-modified Astrasa wheat fields of snow-less Antarctica, which still fed most of the world's population.

208. No question about it. He shook his head. Maybe the equipment was faulty. He'd have one more shot at it, but he'd have to wait. He slapped a control, restoring the full holo-show image. The prototype

dark-matter-powered propulsion system whisked the audience away from Earth, accelerated past Mars and then executed a sling-shot around Saturn to whiplash out of the solar system. He'd fused original vid-footage from both the ill-fated Prometheus and Heracles missions. Most people assumed it was sped-up for effect; in fact he'd had to do slow it down. What he was unable to show, because no one really knew what it looked like, was what happened next. Once well past Pluto's orbit, the long-researched Alcubierre drive kicked in, forming a warp shell around the Ulysses, its dark energy wave front slicing through normal space-time.

The audience catapulted forward to Eden, a purple-green world bathed in blood-orange sunlight from its star, Kantoka Minor, then screamed down through its outer atmosphere, piercing puffy, ivory clouds. They re-emerged and pulled up at the last moment, scraping so close to the mountains that most of the audience half-stood, then sat back down again, laughing, as the vista panned out, unveiling Eden's virgin lakes and forests.

It reminded Micah of pictures he'd seen of pre-War Switzerland, albeit with a mauve tint. He could almost feel Eden's sunlight, though it was over a hundred light years away. Still, just knowing it was there warmed him.

* * *

Gabriel didn't allow himself to tense, though the main lights would flick back on soon. When they did, his chances of being spotted would spike. He would wait until the signal. Perhaps his masters wanted him to terminate Kane and be discovered. He had the standard suicide unit. His wristcom pulsed again. *Secure.* He pressed his jaw together for one full second to release the target auto-lock from Kane. The message meant two things: first, Kane must be protected, not terminated. Second, another assassin was hidden somewhere in the chamber, with Kane in their sights. This time Gabriel tensed. He had to up his game; this was no simple hit anymore. He scanned the audience, checking to see if anyone was paying more attention to Kane than the show.

* * *

Micah reached the point in the show where he could do one last heart rate check linked to the final emotional event. He tapped *track*. Seconds later, each member of the audience saw the four Ulysses astronauts – Blake, Zack, Pierre and Katrina – standing right in front of them, as if they were with them aboard the space station Zeus I, hours before the Ulysses' departure for Eden, three months ago. He pumped up the volume.

"They will be arriving in Eden in less than a week's time, and when they breathe in Eden's atmosphere they'll be taking a breath of fresh air for all mankind. This whole venture has given humanity the solid hope we so desperately need. Of course, it will take decades to transfer a sizeable portion of the population. But Eden represents a second chance for us all, and that helps keep peace here on Earth. The hope – the dream – must continue."

The final, only completely fictitious scene in the show, pictured the Ulysses settled on Eden, its four astronauts walking atop a ridge above a Mediterranean-blue sea, to a background of stirring music, the New World Alliance anthem.

The holorium lighting returned to normal. Kane strode tall onto the stage to rapturous applause, the audience rising to their feet. Far away on the other side of the building, Micah stood up, took a mock bow, and sat down again. *Not bad.*

Kane held up a hand as he spoke into the microphone. "Hopefully, we'll all be seeing real pictures and accounts of Eden from our four heroes in just over a week. We wish them God's protection, and all religions pray for their safe return. Mankind is moving on to a better future."

The beep brought Micah back to the biometric analyser: 210. He trawled his fingers through his hair, unable to work it out. Then he remembered the man who moved like a dancer, and looked like he didn't belong there; Micah couldn't see him anywhere. He noticed several agitated security men enter the chamber, looking over the heads of the crowds, toward the back of the holorium. They were armed. Micah sat up, and instinctively searched for Antonia.

* * *

Gabriel activated the visual diffuser as soon as the lights went up. It would mask the area in front of him, though only temporarily. Once the security guards arrived, he knew he had to act quickly. He sent an electronic signal to a small explosive device eight floors down in another part of the complex. Within seconds the security guards each moved their left hands to their earpieces, then quit the chamber.

* * *

The final wave of applause sputtered to a close as people quit their seats. Micah watched Kane stride to the front exit to press the fatty palms of his wealthy guests, sending them on their way to visit the rest of Eden Mission Control; every handshake worth millions of credits.

Micah saw the security guards depart, and leant back in his chair, guessing it must have been some kind of false alarm. He flicked off all the monitors except one. Antonia's backless, low-cut silver dress clung to her as she stood up, hair held high with a gold clasp. He touched her image on the screen with the tip of his finger, then drew it back, trying to ignore her depressingly handsome escort, looking instead for any sign that she was unhappy, that something was missing from her life, but saw none. Who am I kidding? Rudi's right. She's class, and I'm –"

The comms screen flashed on. "Nice work, Sanderson," Vastra said. "Just spare me the fucking down-to-the-wire heart attack next time, okay?" He cut off without waiting for an answer.

"You're welcome." Micah watched everyone leaving, and gave up on the heart rate monitor – it was useless now, and Security was down there.

Facing the opposite wall, his gaze fell upon the solitary poster of the four Ulysses astronauts standing at the Zeus I airlock, helmets in hands. He tried to imagine himself there too, a fifth astronaut. Like thousands of others, he'd taken the entrance exams as soon as he was twenty-one. The psy-profile had screened him out: over-analytical. He'd thought about that evaluation a lot, not missing the irony. At least they'd given him a job. He remembered what Rudi had said one day.

"Micah, with you the glass isn't just half empty – you think the liquid is wrong – your life is a beer glass, but you want champagne."

Maybe he was right. Micah stood up and stretched. Now his mind was free of the holo-presentation, he returned to the problem he'd been wrestling with the past few weeks: the missing lighthouse markers in the recent Ulysses data streams. If the third one was no longer there, it could spell trouble for the astronauts. He quit the Media Lab, as if discarding an old shoe. Rudi's right, I don't know why I do this. Eager to immerse himself back in Dataland as they called it, he headed off to join Rudi in the Optron Lab.

* * *

Gabriel scanned the holorium using his sighter's fish-eye mode as the last of the delegates, attendants and security left, Kane shooing them onwards until he was alone. The hit was imminent, but Gabriel could see no one. Kane paced a little then made a call on his wristcom. Just in case it was relevant, Gabriel activated his eavesdropper. It only picked up Kane's side of the conversation.

"We need to meet... Yes, I have it... No, not on an open line... Very well... Tonight, late, let's say midnight... Don't worry, I'll be alone."

Kane flicked off his wristcom and spun around towards the exit, to catch up with his entourage.

The tiniest flicker of movement caught Gabriel's eye, in a darkened and disused glass-fronted control booth on the right side of the holorium; it had been his own back-up choice as sniper location. The woman – from what he could see of the side of her face – had waited till the last moment. He used his sighter to auto-zoom in. Her eye met the sighting-glass of her pulse rifle, forefinger curling around the trigger. Gabriel flexed his tongue against his lower gum, and a red spot appeared on her left temple. As he heard Kane grab the exit door handle, he clicked his teeth, fast. There was no recoil. The laser pulse passed straight through the glass booth window with minimal refraction. A black hole of charred flesh, the size of a small coin, burst open where the spot had been, accompanied by a wisp of grey smoke. The woman slumped on the table she'd rested her rifle on, then slid silently out of sight, the weapon toppling after her. He hadn't been sure if the booth had been soundproof, but was relieved to find that it was.

The holorium doors closed behind Kane and the lights dimmed. Gabriel de-activated the gravitics and fell, twisting like a cat to land on all fours. He sprang up and raced to the side wall of the sealed control booth. Forcing open a panel, he entered the tiny room to find her spread-eagled on the floor, eyes glassy green.

All assassins knew this fate awaited them sooner or later. He rested his right palm on her forehead, closing her eye-lids with a fluid stroke of his fingers. "Be at peace now, your part is over. Rejoin the river." He said it in Tibetan, incanting their shortest prayer for the dead.

He searched her matt black clothes and her body for any signs of her origin or who she worked for, not expecting to find anything; she was clearly a professional. On instinct, he pulled up her tunic and checked her waistline for a clan assassin's tattoo, but saw no mark. Gloves off, he ran his fingers around her lower waist. He encountered a rougher layer of flesh above one hip – a stencilled tattoo had been erased, though not without leaving a trace – the yoga mudra symbol. So, she was from Indistan, most likely ethnic but gene-altered to render her skin white and her hair blonde, though her eyes should have remained brown. He re-opened one eye-lid and placed a finger-tip on her eye-ball, dislodging the tinted contact lens.

Satisfied, he heaved her limp frame over his left shoulder, carrying her rifle in his other hand, and headed towards a nearby maintenance shaft leading to the furnaces, seven floors underground. As he opened the hatchway to the vertical shaft, a gust of hot air greeted him. He wondered if she had climbed up it to get into the booth, since the only other way in was through a heavily secured area. He inhaled deeply, but smelt no traces of sweat from her body. Not good. Unlike him, she'd had inside help, which meant Kane was still in danger. He tapped in a coded message: *target not safe*, and waited.

Gabriel's wristcom twitched three times – *return to base* – he would be instructed to kill again. He launched the corpse into the shaft, re-activated his boots and gloves, and descended, ignoring the searing heat. He recalled Kane's last words – a meeting tonight, at midnight. His instincts told him that whoever had arranged this hit would do all in their power to make sure the meeting never took place.

Chapter 2

Ulysses

Kat heard the footfalls pounding behind her, getting louder, closing. She sprinted towards the Lander, cropped black hair glistening with sweat, muscular arms punching through the gritty breeze. Her slate-grey eyes remained locked onto the desert terrain five metres ahead, like she'd learned in the Falklands. She dared not look back, partly because she might trip, but more because she would freeze if she saw it bearing down on her. Two hundred metres. The open hatch promised sanctuary. Zack – be there!

She ran full throttle, clutching her helmet in her right hand. She'd seen the scalpel-sharp claws: one slash and she was history. She flung the helmet over her right shoulder, and counted. One – Two … She winced at the crunching noise. As if it was egg-shell, not carbo-titanium, for God's sake! How far behind? She couldn't work it out. It didn't matter; the hatch was barely a hundred and fifty metres away. She raced, ignoring the muscle-lock cramping her lungs, the strain in her thighs begging her to slow down. Go to hell!

Pumping her arms harder, she drew in a breath, and vaulted a table-height rock, grazing her left knee and almost losing footing as she landed hard on the other side, arms flailing to maintain balance. As she got back into her stride, the ground shook as the creature hit the deck behind her without missing a beat. Her legs finally got the message – she increased her speed.

* * *

"Now would be good, Pierre," Zack bellowed. He watched Kat's mouth twitch, her thin lips pull back in fear, eyes darting wildly beneath pale eye-lids. His instinct was to place one of his stocky black hands on Kat's shoulder to comfort her, or else shake her to bring her out of it, but he stopped short – they'd agreed not to wake her. Pierre strode in as fast as the synth-grav would allow, deftly manoeuvring between the stasis cots in the cramped second compartment, pianist-length fingers meshed in a tangle of short black hair even a crew-cut couldn't subdue.

"About time," Zack said.

Pierre primed a contact syringe, and in one smooth movement flicked it switchblade-style towards the side of Kat's neck. There was a hiss, like a sharp intake of breath. A wash of deep red crawled across her face then vanished.

"Will it calm her down?" Zack frowned at her normally smooth, fine-featured face, now crumpled like a piece of paper, slick with sweat.

"No, but she'll realise she's in a dream. If she remembers, she can control it."

Zack looked down at their youngest crew member. Yeah, if she ain't too shit-scared. Her chest rose and fell with increasing speed. "Her vitals okay?"

Pierre tapped the holopad next to the cot – several red spikes radiated outward, but none pierced the edge of the surrounding green hexagon. "Tolerable. In the dream she's running, so her lungs work faster."

Zack chewed his lower lip. The nightmare was coming more regularly the closer they got to Eden, and Kat reckoned it wasn't a normal dream, always exactly the same. So they'd decided to try a lucid dreaming technique, injecting a stim during the nightmare, so she could maybe control it, and recall what was chasing her.

Pierre gazed into the mid-distance as he discarded the syringe. "Do we run because we're afraid, or are we afraid because we run?" He said it as if reciting, a hint of his Parisian accent lingering.

Zack sighed, wondering for the hundredth time why Pierre wasn't back in MIT, surrounded by his best friends – equations and a muon-scope. "Spare me the psy-crap, Pierre." He glared at him. They both knew why she was running.

"I have to go. I'm finishing some tests. There's a strange variance –"

"Whatever." Zack gave him a sideways look. "I thought you liked Kat?"

Pierre hung there for a moment, then spun on his heel, and retreated to the cockpit.

Zack re-focused his attention on Kat, planted himself on a mag-stool, and leant back against the graphite-grey inner hull. "Take it from me, kid, sometimes it's okay to run. You run as fast as you damned well can."

* * *

Kat felt a pricking on the side of her neck, like an insect bite. Her cheeks and scalp burned. It was the signal she'd rehearsed, so she knew she was in the nightmare again – the same one she'd had every night for the past week – injected with the stim as planned. But it didn't help – just because she knew she was in a nightmare didn't mean she wasn't terrified. Yet she needed to see the creature, to bring back details that would be flushed away as always, moments after waking. She knew what she had to do to control the dream: hold her hand up in front of her face and see her palm. That was all.

Even as she began to raise her right arm, a bone-shaking roar erupted from the creature. Her ears shrivelled in pain. The wake of the primal howl hit the back of her head. Though she didn't think it possible, she increased her pace one final time, as if her transition from mortal fear to pure panic allowed one last gear-shift. But it was right behind her. She wasn't going to make it. She tried to believe it was just a dream, telling herself: *Look around! See it before you wake up!* But she couldn't – she imagined its claws raising, ready to strike.

For the first time she noticed that although she was in a desert, the light was a ghostly green, like an old radar screen. Why? No time to figure it out. Zack was at the hatch, beckoning wildly with one hand, levelling the shoulder-mounted cannon with the other. She tried one last time to turn to see the creature, but her neck refused. "Get down!" she heard Zack shout, just as the creature swiped her feet from under her, and she fell, flying through the air like a high diver in slow motion, before sprawling downwards, crashing through the desert floor into blackness.

Kat sat up sharply and hit the rubber pad above her cot with her head. "Shit! Every – bloody – time!" She collapsed back, breathing hard. She drove her fingers through wet, matted hair, and laid her forearm over closed eyes, waiting for the tremors to subside. She was safe, back on the Ulysses. Not that she'd left it in the past three months since they'd departed Zeus Orbital. She breathed out slowly to bring her pulse under control, and tried to recall. What had been chasing her? What had been so important, aside from the obvious – to escape? She couldn't remember. Vague, receding thoughts uttered muffled cries through a thick fog in her mind – something about colour – something was green. But what?

And why did it matter? By the time the mist had dissipated there was nothing but the distant low grumble of Ulysses' engines, cushioned by the susurration of the aircon, with its attendant hospital-like smell. The nightmare, along with all its secrets, was gone, as usual. Her shoulder and neck muscles unwrapped, and she let out a long sigh. She wanted to sleep more, but not at the risk of nightmaring again. She heard the scrape of a mag-stool and left her forearm in place. "You babysitting me again, Zack?"

"Good thing we placed that rubber mat there, else you'd have head-butted a hole in the hull by now."

Kat nudged her forearm upwards just enough to reveal Zachariah Katain, his large, oval black face grinning downwards, framed by wire-mesh eyebrows and a gleaming bald pate. His jaw stuck out, as if permanently mocking life. His eye-lids were a different story – they always seemed to be a fraction closed – alert, as if targeting something. She'd met other vet attack-pilots who'd had that same perpetual hunter look, like they couldn't switch it off any more. It reminded her that although Zack appeared to be a regular, jovial wife-and-two-kids guy – because he was – he also had that killer instinct just underneath the surface.

He beamed. "Been dreaming about me again, babe?"

The banter was part of their routine. It helped. "Course. But you know it's not that kind of dream. Your weapon was bigger this time, though."

He belly-laughed, mock-punching her shoulder with his fist, then grew more serious. "Well?"

Kat replaced her forearm blindfold. The dream had gone again, sunk back through the crevices in her outer cortex to the inaccessible, squishy middle regions of the brain.

"Don't worry, kid. Next time."

She heard him pad back out to the cockpit. She decided to rest a while longer; still had an hour off duty, not that there was anywhere to go, or anything to do, as far as leisure was concerned. *A day in the life of an astronaut.* An image of her four-poster bed back in New Oxford flickered seductively, but she rinsed it from her mind. No point. She'd made her choice.

She closed her eyes, determined not to sleep.

* * *

Zack ducked his head as he entered the cockpit the Ulysses' chief designer had once explained to him was "compact". He squeezed past his Captain and their Science Officer – Blake and Pierre as they'd become after three months of sardine-can intimacy. Busy, as usual. Both working separately – *ditto*. Pierre was in Virtual again, immersed by his visor in data slipstream analysis, oblivious to his surroundings.

From the back of his pilot's chair Zack caught his reflection and sighed. He'd have traded his cobalt one-piece uniform for his old flying jacket any day of the week. The one consolation was the golden-winged image of Daedalus – the wiser father of Icarus, now employed as the Eden Mission logo adorning the crew's chests. The crests glinted in the cockpit spots, especially Blake's, since he polished his every morning.

Zack plumped himself into his servo-chair at the front of the cockpit, to the left of Blake and in front of Kat's empty comms station. *Three men and a girl in a tin can.* But then he'd seen the early Mercury and Apollo craft, the Endeavour, and even the Mars Intrepid – those guys would have wept over such luxurious real estate. He fingered the two multimode joysticks that made him one with the ship, and felt his mood lighten. He couldn't manoeuvre with the warp online, but once they decelerated... He could barely wait.

He stared out at the black velvet of deep space, punctuated by random pinpricks of ice-cold light sliding towards him with a glacial grace. Constellations that'd been his friends since childhood were gone. A girlfriend had said one night, a lifetime ago, that as long as you can see the stars and their patterns, the Big Dipper and Orion, you're never lost, you'll always find your way home. Zack's substantial bulk, maintained despite space rations, shuddered.

He glanced across to Blake, his Captain and vet War buddy for fifteen years, studying a small-scale hologram of ship integrity. It showed the cockpit near the front end of the fifty metre long Ulysses, resembling a hornet's body, its four sections and two back-up conical ion engines and dark waste exhausts at the rear. Zack frowned. The energy exchanges going on in the back of the fourth compartment were measured in yottawatts, off the imaginable scale. Only Pierre really understood it, but even he'd admitted that if the engineers had got it wrong, they'd be dead in a picosecond. Zack thought of the crew of the Heracles, lost with all hands. He'd known each of them personally.

The harsh red flicker from the Ulysses holo reflected off Blake's rusty hair and chiselled features, lighting up the bow-shaped scar above his right eye from hand-to-hand combat in Thailand, and the pockmarks on his left cheek from the gassing at Geronimo Station. Blake had lost a lot of men in the War, but always got the job done.

"Seventh nightmare in the past week," Blake said, in his Texan drawl. He didn't look up from his display.

"Yep," Zack replied. It was starting to affect morale, his own, at any rate; superstition and ill omens made lousy companions on long, confined trips. Seafarers had known it for millennia. Space was like the sea, just infinitely less forgiving.

Blake swivelled his chair to face him. "Anything new?"

Zack understood the implied question: was it like that screwed-up mission ten years ago, where one of their marines kept having nightmares for two full weeks beforehand? He shook his head. Blake resumed his work.

Zack toggled the forward screen control and with a flick of a finger, a single star changed to red – Kantoka Minor, Eden's star, dead ahead. One more week, he mused; one more week before setting foot on another planet.

Then they'd see if Kat's nightmares had any substance.

He kicked back in his pilot's chair and pondered: neither the robot-based Prometheus nor manned Heracles missions had returned. Prometheus had arrived three years ago on Eden, but stopped transmitting after an hour. A year later, the manned Heracles had exploded, just five days before arrival, the list of possible explanations long and wild. Still, as they approached the nebula where Heracles disappeared, he was getting edgy, spending more time in the cockpit than was good for his spine; they all were. He glanced at his holopic of Sonja and the kids, smiling and waving, tucked into his console. He tried to smile back.

Kat slipped into the cockpit, furtive as usual, as if she'd just stolen something.

"Anything exciting happening?" she ventured.

Pierre stowed his visor and responded. "I'm afraid so. I've been checking and re-checking for the past hour. There's no mistake. We're losing oxygen."

Blake collapsed the holo. Kat halted mid-step.

Zack reached base first. "You're kidding, right? I mean, you have no sense of humour, Pierre, but this time?"

Blake interrupted. "Data."

Pierre handed Blake a holopad. "There's a consistent one per cent oxygen depletion rate per hour. I don't know where it's going. Not outside, otherwise there'd be transient ice micro-crystal formation on the outer hull, inside the warp shell, even at this velocity. The air purifiers are working well, unless the sensors are malfunctioning. But I don't think so."

Zack joined in. "Why the hell not? This wouldn't be our first sensor glitch."

Pierre continued to stare at Blake, as if the Captain had asked the question. "I looked at the increased rate of carbon dioxide build-up in the recyclers, and also the growing power usage of all three independent gas exchange systems, and I used Kat's breathing rate while asleep – before the onset of her nightmare – as a baseline. The covariance is undisputable."

Smart, Zack had to agree. He and Blake hunched over the pad to check the calcs, but Zack had no doubt – Pierre was never wrong when it came to facts and figures. After the second check, he sat back. He'd wanted something to relieve the monotony, but not this. The data stated flatly they were losing oxygen, but there was nowhere for it to go. It didn't make sense, but unless they worked it out...

Kat piped up. "Well, if it's only one per cent... I mean there's a whole planet-full of oxygen on Eden, and we'll be there in a week." She looked to Blake.

Blake handed back the pad. "We'll be dead in two days." He turned to Pierre. "You sent this to EMC?"

"No, Sir – I wanted to be sure. I'd assumed it was an anomaly of some sort – calibration drift of the sensors, for example – but I confirmed it in the past hour. Then I ran some simulations to consider ways of conserving oxygen, but none of them will be sufficient."

Zack shook his head – Pierre ought to have informed Blake from the start. He just never did *get* military protocol, never understood the chain of command.

"Very well," Blake said, "this is how it's going to be. Kat, you check those purifiers by hand, just in case it's a local sensor problem. Zack, you work with Pierre to see how we can either increase oxygen output or cut down usage. Zack, I'm looking for some of your usual unorthodox suggestions." He stood. "Answers in two hours, people. I'll handle Comms and send the transmission – the turnaround time for messages sent back to Earth at this distance is currently two days, so I don't have to tell you we can't count on solutions from home. I'm hoping we can find the cause before then. So, let's –"

Pierre butted in. "Captain, there's one more…" he paused, the end of his sentence wilting under Blake's glare.

"Yes, Lieutenant?"

"Well, Sir. Whatever this is, I don't think it's a normal abnormality, if you understand me. What I mean is that we have seventh generation redundant and diverse systems here, and the engineers took account of all credible, and to be frank, some highly improbable independent and common mode failures. So… it's just… this could be sabotage, something done to the ship before we left."

Zack scowled. It had been the number one Heracles theory, and for good reason. Despite Earth being on the brink of environmental collapse, the terrorist group known as the Alicians – anti-tech and anti-Eden – argued the War had been a sign for mankind to work out its problems on Earth, and return to a simpler life-style. Not content with rhetoric, they'd assassinated the original Ulysses crew during a training flight.

Zack's security background extrapolated Pierre's proposition to the next level – *what if one of the crew was involved?* He buried the idea, knowing it was a shallow grave he'd have to return to later.

"That's why Zack's going to be working with you," Blake said. "You may be the best science officer there is, Pierre, but Zack can smell a rat at fifty parsecs. So let's get to it, our air's burning."

Zack stole another glance at the holopic of his smiling family, taken the day he'd left. He'd looked at it hundreds of times before, but now, for the first time, he sensed the look of worry behind his wife's sunny smile. He thought about the crew of the Heracles. Is this what happened to them? Sabotage? But this was different. No explosion this time, just a painful, slow asphyxiation.

He shifted over to share Pierre's console. There, the Frenchman opened up all his holo-data portals so they could inspect them together. Zack spotted a digital countdown of oxygen depletion rate in the corner of the screen: *Time till irrevocable loss of consciousness: 42 hours, fifteen minutes, thirty-six seconds*. He ran a sweaty finger around his collar.

And then the irony hit him – for the first time he hoped Kat's nightmares of being hunted by a creature on Eden were true. Not that he believed them for a moment, but at least that way they'd die on their feet and have an enemy to fight, rather than arriving on Eden as canned corpses.

Chapter 3

Lighthouse

Micah paced the Telemetry Analysis Room – the tar-pit as he and Rudi called it, since they tended to get stuck there. There wasn't much ground to pace over: the white-tiled lab was filled with dark, glass-fronted computer cupboards, almost no visible wall-space. Myriad beads of light twinkled silently as the computers sifted the Ulysses information streams from cosmic noise. Two beige metal desks with angled fluidic touch-screens flanked the lab centre-piece, the Optron: a gleaming chrome artifice marrying together a dentist's chair and what looked like a laser cannon on an articulated boom, aimed straight toward the head-rest where Rudi's head lay immobile. High tension cables around the Optron made the floor resemble a snake pit, reinforced by numerous skull-and-crossbones signs plastered on the main struts and solid parts of the device. This was no toy or cheap holo-sex device.

He glanced at his wristcom. *Seven minutes left.* Rudi was still hooked in, two titanium optrodes at his temples winking green every three seconds. His eyes were closed, but the facial muscles were taut, and the REMs behind his eyelids showed he was very much awake, simply … elsewhere.

Rudi was thirty minutes overdue. If Micah missed this slot, he'd have to wait another two weeks to check the third and final marker. He wanted to find an excuse to break into Rudi's session, but that would arouse suspicion, especially with Rudi. He'd been aware of a change in Rudi lately – seeming to be laid back, but always observing. Recently, when Micah came out of an Optron session, he'd find Rudi sitting watching him, or double-checking Micah's data searches, seeing where he'd been. Micah knew his father would have confronted Rudi about it. But he wasn't his father.

He paced some more and went over the problem again. One of the markers had disappeared two weeks ago. That could easily have been a system fault, especially with something as complex and covert as a lighthouse sleeper code. But then, yesterday, he'd searched for the second hidden marker from the Ulysses' third module. It should have flashed orange in the data landscape, but it never showed up, even though he'd waited an hour. He'd hardly slept. If the third marker was gone, the key one from the cockpit, well… A double-click announced Rudi disconnecting, accompanied by a slow descending whirr as the machine wound down. Micah pretended to read a print-out.

"Oh, Mikey, hi there. Sorry man, over-shot again."

He ignored the nickname and turned with fake nonchalance to see Rudi rubbing his eyes. All Optron Readers did that, even though the optrodes hooked straight into the visual cortex, bypassing the eyes completely. But after all, the eyes carried on moving even if they weren't actually seeing anything.

Micah cleared his throat. "No worries. But I should probably get started." He walked over to the recliner.

Rudi paused mid-yawn, and then gave him a sideways look. "In a hurry?" he said, with an easy smile Micah knew relaxed most people onto the treacherous slope of honesty.

"No," he lied, making sure to return the eye contact and not look away, remembering the tricks his Mom had taught him throughout the brief Occupation, during the daily random interrogations. "Just – you know – I promised Mom I'd watch an old vid with her later, and there's still a lot to finish up here."

Rudi nodded thoughtfully, but didn't budge. Micah waited, fighting an urge to check the time. He wondered if Rudi somehow knew about the lighthouse markers, but then dismissed it. They only showed up periodically, and Rudi hadn't been checking Micah's searches long enough.

Seconds drizzled away. He'd need three minutes to find the file, if he was quick.

"What's the vid? Your Mom's into the really old stuff, isn't she?"

Shit! This could be a ten minute conversation. What the hell was on tonight that he could use, because Rudi might just check? Then he remembered. Perfect! "There's one on the Asian Campaign. You know, that's where Dad…" He stared at the floor.

"Oh. Look, sorry, man, didn't mean to…" Rudi levered himself out of the recliner.

"Its okay," Micah said, and began climbing in.

"Wait, let me wipe it down, you know, we all sweat a little on this baby." He went over to his desk.

Micah saw the tell-tale imprint of Rudi's back on the fake leather upholstery.

"Don't want the Med girls getting upset, do we?" Rudi brought back a couple of strips of tissue paper and wiped the chair methodically.

Micah sneaked a glance at his wristcom when he was sure Rudi couldn't see, even from reflections in the Optron slave screens. Four minutes. He tried to appear blasé, forcing his hands to relax.

Rudi finished rubbing it down. "There, that's better, all yours. And say "hi" to your Mom for me, eh? And listen – sorry if I've been… well, you know, a bit of a jerk lately, work's kinda getting on top." He half-smiled.

"Yeah, sure, I'll tell her. And it's no problem, I'm a bit tense too," he added. He slotted into the seat, slapping his optrodes to his temples, and flicked three switches. Rudi seemed in no hurry to leave, even though he'd already passed his duty hours for the day, but Micah had no time left to wait. He closed his eyes. A silky female voice whispered the automated countdown: 3 – 2 – 1… His mind surged forward out of his body, surfing over a mutant sea of dimly fluorescent data streams: writhing, multi-coloured eels of digitised information swirling amongst frothy uncertainty riptides. The entry process was like being tossed into a moonlit stormy ocean – the untrained usually threw up in the first thirty seconds. He flew toward solid "land", soaring over a still, twilight desert, and began searching. In his visual field to the left he saw the transparent aquamarine rectangle upon which key parameters glowed red.

Although the Optron was immersive, he could still sense a little of what was going on outside, if he concentrated, if he peeled his mind back. He sensed Rudi was standing there, watching the slave screen, able to see a much simpler, digital version of what Micah saw, in particular the data streams he was about to access. Too bad, a risk I'm going to have to take.

He ran a few random files first, then selected file kappa-237. The hidden marker which should have been inside was gone. He waited a few more seconds then changed to a new file. It was hard to carry on doing random tests on parameter accuracy and system health, knowing what he had just found: the Ulysses' telemetry was being corrupted in some way, which meant the astronauts could be in trouble.

It meant he could be in trouble, too: the insertion of his own health markers hadn't been sanctioned. Ever since Prometheus and Heracles missions had failed, security at the Eden Mission had intensified. He'd have to face some tough questions, but hopefully any disciplinary action would be waived in the light of his evidence that someone was tampering with Ulysses data.

He hoped the Chorazin didn't get wind of it, though; they'd like nothing more than to take over Eden Mission's security, and wouldn't hesitate to interrogate him to see if he was an Alician spy. The thought of the Chorazin chilled him – a necessary evil, an Interpol with unlimited powers and jurisdiction, supposedly accountable to governments, but he had his doubts. They were the logical counterpoint to the Alician global terrorist threat which had sprung up a year after the War, apparently the dark heart of the Fundie movement, religious zealots who never accepted the armistice and its tolerance pact. It was a miracle Kane had kept the Chorazin at bay this long. The thought resonated: *Kane – he's the one I have to go to.*

He continued for another twenty minutes checking a further forty files, hoping it would throw Rudi off the scent. Then he turned to the rectangle on his left and focused sharply on the red square, the Exit symbol.

When he disconnected, Rudi was lounging at his desk, idly juggling a couple of data holo-cubes while staring at his desktop display. Rudi snapped his fingers and the cubes vanished. He gestured for Micah to come over, without looking in his direction. Micah took his time – he was still groggy. A light vertigo lingered, and he had no desire to keel over.

"Hey, buddy, what's the interest with that kappa-237 file? Third time you've accessed it in a month. We're supposed to do random but comprehensive searches, not go over the same files. There are thousands to check, you know."

Micah rubbed his eyes a little longer than usual, faking drowsiness. He had to think fast. "Kappa file?" He walked over and saw the dense, time-indexed matrix of digitised records, K237 highlighted in red. His eyes grew wide; Rudi had been surreptitiously checking his access of that file over the past two months. He recalled his Aunt, who'd been in the underground during the War. She'd lied successfully for most of the occupation, pretending to be a housewife, till someone finally betrayed her. "A complete lie can be undone by counter-evidence," she'd said. "Then you are caught, like a lobster into the pot. No way out. The best lie is half-true."

"Oh, the kappa file," he said, hands massaging his temples. "I know we're supposed to do random, but I sometimes do a re-run, in case of hysteresis-based faults, you know, ones that come and go. I just pick a file at random, check it again a few weeks later. I guess three times in a month is a bit excessive, though. Hadn't realised, to be honest." He tried to look gullible, goofy even. It came easier than he liked.

Rudi studied him. Then he flashed one of those smiles where the lips spread wide but the corners of his eyes didn't move. "Probably a good idea. Maybe I should try it." He tapped his nose with an index finger. "Don't worry, I won't tell," he whispered. He stood up, stretched his back, picked up his jacket and walked to the door. "Hey, wait a minute – Sphericon Five is on the net tonight – you'll miss it if you watch the vid with your Mom."

Micah pulled a face, but at least this was safer territory.

Rudi grinned. "Come on, Sphericon really kick alien butt!"

He'd wanted Rudi to leave, but couldn't let this one go. "I just don't buy it. You do *remember* Fermi's Paradox, don't you?"

Rudi rolled his eyes and waggled a finger at Micah. "Don't even go there."

"Okay, putting aside the fact we've never seen any aliens or sign of them, why is it, in all our Sci-fi vids, we're the smartest kids on the block? And it's always about aliens trying to plunder our resources, right?" Micah gestured to the window.

Rudi affected a yawn. "Yeah, yeah, Earth is pretty much toxic, I got it already. Well maybe their idea of resources is different from ours." He slung his jacket over his shoulder. "Whatever. The babes in S-5 are hot, Micah. Even your Mom would agree." He opened the door. "It's your life, such as it is. As for me, Debra from Tech-Support is coming over to my place to watch it on my new holoplayer." He winked. "So long, buddy, enjoy the War vid."

Micah let out a long breath and surrendered to his chair. He kicked aside the image of Rudi and Debra locked together in a passionate embrace, and stared at the Ulysses poster, wondering what was really happening onboard. He drummed his fingers and glanced at his wristcom. Five pm. He checked the intranet and found Kane's agenda – he was in a meeting for another twenty minutes.

Gazing through frosted windows to the milky light outside, he wondered if he should take his weekly ten minute sun-dose. Instead, he visited the washroom, splashed cool recycled water on his face, and changed into a new shirt.

* * *

He'd never been inside the Director's office suite before: real teak, late 20th century. It fit Kane, the Ulysses Project Manager, perfectly. The one man Micah knew he could trust. But he reckoned Sandy wasn't pleased to see anyone arrive at 5.29, one minute before the official workday ended.

He shifted his weight from one foot to the other in front of her desk, until she raised her head from her holopad, eyes kestrel-sharp. He read her mind by following her eye movements – she glanced at his temples just under the hairline where two tiny red dots marked him as an Optron Reader. She looked down his body – he'd only just tucked his shirt in, and had hastily put on a tie – from the way her nose pinched, he wished he hadn't bothered, though it hadn't been for her benefit. At least she couldn't see his sneakers from where she sat. She probably thought him some low level nerd, but it didn't matter. She glanced at his badge.

"Yes, Mr... Sanderson? May I help you?" she said, but to Micah's ears it sounded like a barbed wire fence had just been erected in front of him – any help she offered would require drawing his blood first.

"I need to see Mr. Kane, the Director."

"I know who Mr Kane is." She let the words dissipate, and it appeared she was going to say nothing more, least of all take his request seriously.

"It's urgent."

She sat back. "I see. And what is it about?"

Micah tried not to squirm. "I can't say. It's, uh, sensitive."

She propped a finger to the corner of her mouth and cocked her head to one side, raising her eyebrows. "And I don't suppose you would have something like an appointment?" She looked to her screen, beamed back at him, and said, "Ah – no, I would know that, wouldn't I?"

Micah frowned. He hadn't thought it through – why would Kane see him, an analyst way down in the hierarchy? But it *was* important; he had to break through this bureaucratic wall guarded by Kane's assistant. He switched into analysis mode. It took only a second, his mind flickering in saccades while his eyes remained fixed on hers: highlighted hair in a bob; expensive make-up making the best of an almost-pretty face, a blemish under her right eye; taut body; professional but slightly revealing suit accentuating her assets up top and drawing the eye away from her legs for some reason; hazel eyes, alluring and open, flints of bitterness in the background. He made his assessment.

"Look, Miss Mindel. I know you probably think I'm just a nerd, but this is very important. I need to see him – *please*." He gestured to the double doors at the other end of her office.

"Why don't you come back tomorrow? Better still, I'll talk to Mr. Kane and see if he can speak to your manager later in the week, okay?" She reached for the off-switch on her console. He swallowed, took a deep breath, and leaned forward over her desk.

"No. I need to see him now." He held his ground. The air temperature between them freefell. She stood up.

"Listen very carefully," she said. "In five seconds my foot is going to activate the security button, and you'll be in big trouble, little man, unless you're gone." They stood, locked onto each other's gaze, the only sound his breathing. He took a few steps back, towards the entrance. She sat down, and began shutting down her console.

Nothing to lose. He hoped to God the rumours were true. He tried his best to sound confident, worldly – like his father, dammit.

"Of course it would be in your interest for me to see him."

She didn't look up, but paused. "Excuse me?"

"I mean, if he hears me out, he'll need to work late. Very late."

Her face darkened. Her eyes flared, and what he'd sensed earlier came into the foreground. It wasn't pretty. She trod hard on something, picked up a silver-handled paper knife, and skirted round the desk towards him, much faster than he'd anticipated. She stopped very close, her breathing laboured. He tried to ignore the paper knife in her right hand, level with his groin.

"Look, you little piece of shit. I don't know who you think you are, or what you think you know, but you'd better cut this crap right now, or so help me –"

The double doors opened with a sharp click and a swish. Kane, elegantly tall with a shock of white hair, around fifty yet still exuding the strength of an ox, stood framed in the doorway, the shaded early evening sun behind him.

"What's going on, Sandy? What does this gentleman want?" His voice was as commanding as it was reassuring.

"He was just leaving, Sir," she said, facing off Micah.

Micah knew it was now or never. The next few words counted more than anything. He turned to Kane. "Sir – Ulysses is in trouble. There's been a security breach." He held back the rest. Nothing else could be said here.

Kane met his eyes head on. "Then why haven't you taken it to Mr. Vernt, our Head of Security?" he asked.

Micah had no choice but to confess. "Because… because I inserted my own security check into the Ulysses' telemetry systems. It's unofficial."

Sandy raised a disbelieving eyebrow, shook her head and walked back to her desk.

"A moment, Sandy," Kane said, holding up a hand.

She levelled the paper knife at Micah. "Sir, he said something to me, of a personal nature, so I de-activated the recorders. But now he's confessed to a misdemeanour, probably a sackable offence. We should record it. Even if he's right, Vernt will want to see it."

Micah looked from her to him. He was, as his aunt would have said, in the boiling pot, or at best dangling above it. At least the cameras and recorders were off. He remembered his aunt had also said that in times like these, words were just so much extra rope. He stayed quiet.

"All in good time, Sandy. First, I'd like to hear what this young man has to say. And if I have any trouble, clearly you are ready to defend me." He nodded to the paper knife, still in her right hand. She replaced the knife on the desk, and folded her arms.

"Now, please do come in, and sit down. You'd better tell me about it." He gestured to the open door into his executive suite.

"Oh, and Sandy, you'd better call my wife. I'll be home late tonight. She should understand – it has been a while since I had to work late. And I might need you here later on, would that be possible?"

"Of course, you know I'm always…" Her voice trailed off. "Yes Sir. And I'll switch the cameras back on in here."

Micah walked into Kane's office, feeling Sandy's eyes burrow into his back.

Kane closed the doors behind them, gesturing to an antique leather chair.

"Alright, Mr. Sanderson – Micah, isn't it? You'd better start from the beginning. And don't worry, there are no cameras or recorders in here."

Kane spread his hands flat across his varnished desk. "So, let me see if I've got it straight. Four months ago, you inserted your own covert security program into the telemetry software for Ulysses, because you'd been worried on account of the Heracles and Prometheus. I applaud your motive, even if I cannot condone your method." He cast Micah a stern look, then continued. "The program is called a lighthouse, because it only shows up periodically, meaning it's hard for our system's anti-virus security systems to detect and clean it. Essentially it says the telemetry hasn't been tampered with. If the signal disappears, it means that we're not receiving valid data. Is that a reasonable summary?"

He nodded. His faith in Kane had intensified in the past hour. In any case, he had to trust someone – he couldn't figure this out alone.

"So," Kane continued, "we're receiving telemetry that says everything is okay, and in fact it is not, or may not be."

"It could be used to mask something happening on the ship."

"But we don't actually know what the real telemetry should be?"

"No, just that we're receiving false telemetry, module four being the longest one having disguised readings."

"And the parameters affected are?"

"Environmental and visual."

Kane planted his hands on the desk to stand up. Micah followed suit.

"This is very serious. You did the right thing to bring it to my attention. Well, it will take us a couple of days to communicate this to the Ulysses crew. I'll need one of my people to check all this out of course. Tonight, before you and your colleague return to work tomorrow morning."

"But Sir, I could stay –"

"No, go home young man, we'll take it from here. We'll talk again, very soon. And say nothing, not a word, to anyone, understood?" He nodded to Micah and to the doors.

Micah hesitated at first – he'd imagined himself being involved in the investigation, playing a key part. But Kane's statesman-like smile continued to indicate the way out. Micah got up and walked to the double doors, Kane following him, as they swung open automatically. They shook hands in full view of Sandy. Micah nodded briefly to Kane, threw a sideways glance at Sandy, whose eyes were glued to her screen, and made a quick exit.

* * *

Kane waited until Micah was gone, then walked over and handed a piece of paper to his assistant.

"Please call these people for a conference at nine o'clock this evening in my office, and get Vernt on the vidphone right away." He headed back to his office and closed the doors.

She made the calls. When she saw the line between Kane and Vernt disconnect, she transferred all incoming lines to the answering system, switched off the surveillance cameras, and input her leaving time into the system as 19:00.

She opened her drawer and inspected her reflection in the small mirror inside. She sighed. She'd looked far better – and worse. She rose, adjusted her skirt, made sure the lace stocking top covered the fencing scar on her right thigh, undid another button on her blouse, went over to the entrance door and locked it. She walked to Kane's suite, knocked gently three times, and then entered, closing the doors behind her.

* * *

Micah took one of the tubes heading below ground to the Bubble station. He thought about his dead father and the psych assessment. *You see? I can act when required. My way – not yours.*

But as he sardined his way home amongst other commuters, his thoughts turned to the mechanics of telemetry manipulation. It had to be someone inside the Eden Mission. His first thought was Rudi, but he didn't fit the profile – he had everything he wanted, and was too laid-back to get involved in espionage. Drawing a blank, he switched to thinking about Ulysses. The false telemetry was environmental and visual. Something was happening to their environment. He wondered if they were aware of it. He shivered, despite the balmy temperature.

As he crossed one of the myriad pedestrian bridges in underground Sylmar, he felt his neck prickling. He spun around, sure someone was behind him in the shadows, watching him. It wasn't that late, and usually there were more people around, but not tonight. The lights were dim, and all he saw was a stray cat; but the cat was looking in the same direction as Micah, towards a closed street booth that sold coffee and snacks in the daytime. Micah waited half a minute to see if anyone emerged. No one did. He carried on, quickening his pace till he arrived at his door. Some distance behind him, a cat shrieked as if in pain. He had the prickling feeling again, but this time didn't turn around. He fumbled with the key, slipped inside his apartment, and double-locked the door.

Chapter 4

Ghoster

Pierre's wristcom twitched twice: twenty-four hours of breathable air left. He closed his eyes for a moment, squeezing the bridge of his nose between forefinger and thumb, the way grand-pere used to. Eighteen hours after discovering the oxygen depletion, the crew were still no nearer finding where it was going. This looked like the last day of their lives. As a scientist, dying without even knowing the cause was the worst end.

He and Kat re-checked environmental systems, while Blake and Zack worked in the cockpit on ways to put them all into stasis for the remaining five days before their arrival in Eden. But even if that plan succeeded, they would wake up on an airless ship. Both tasks reeked of futility.

Kat's incessant finger-drumming on the console made it difficult for Pierre to concentrate. They'd checked all components related to atmospheric control for three hours, manually and via main and back-up computers. The onboard diagnostic wizard had drawn a blank, its only output being "insufficient data; good luck". Neither he nor Kat had said a word – not even an expletive – during the last sixty minutes. He stared at a holo of a neural-wiring cluster, unable to focus on account of Kat's dashboard arpeggios. He strode through the holo-image and thrust his hand over her drumming fingers, flattening them.

She glared, but didn't start up again. He returned to his writhing spaghetti.

She kicked something he didn't see. "We're too stupid to work this out, and we're going to die."

He shook his head. "We're missing something. Either it's defying the known physical laws of gases, or else –"

"Somebody's screwing us over. Somebody's pissing themselves laughing ninety light years away. You're supposed to be the clever one, remember? Figure it out!"

He winced. As the principal scientist onboard, everyone expected him to find the answer. It reminded him of the bad old days at home, solving problems under pressure, battling sabre-toothed enigmas unleashed by his father into the supper-time coliseum of their dining room. But he liked Kat, though he hid it – buried it, to be precise. He'd never told her, and the way things were going, he wouldn't get the chance.

He was getting nowhere. Normally, whenever he worked on a problem, whether his father's conundrums or scientific puzzles he'd faced back at the Sorbonne, it was like a yacht's sails catching the wind, his mind billowing like a spinnaker, the boat surging ahead with a clear direction and land in sight. This time, however, he was adrift in a windless ocean.

He gathered himself, and picked up his air-pen. "Let's try one more time."

Kat adjusted her slouch.

He wrote in liquorice-black in the ether between them, reading out each premise. "One: oxygen is being depleted." He paused with the pen, filling in the narrative gap orally. "Normally the carbon dioxide we exhale can be re-cycled to recover the oxygen, but –" he flourished the pen again "– two: something is stripping it out; three: no condensation or ice outside; four: no sign of hull depressurisation; five, no airflow disturbance that would signify a leak." He stopped. The first line had already started to melt. He folded his arms, staring at the premises as they lost cohesion, dripping out of reality. "We've checked everything organic that uses oxygen, and anything inorganic that could, in theory, bond with it." He tossed the pen back onto the table, then smeared the last of the holo-words out of existence with his hand.

Kat's face softened. "I like it when you skywrite, Pierre – you should teach me sometime." Her voice snagged on the last word. She put her heels onto the chair's edge, bringing her knees up to her chest, muttering something he didn't quite hear. He tried not to stare at her, but her eyes caught his. He coughed.

"One of our assumptions is wrong," he said.

"Obviously – but which one? Nothing you wrote just now – something so basic we don't see it." She folded her arms. "Killed by our collective blindness; not a great epitaph."

He sat down. "How to see what you don't see…?" He pictured his father lecturing him, striking the dinner table with the blade of his right hand with each argument he made. Right now, Pierre would welcome the childhood ritual torture as long as his father could solve this particular riddle. If only he were here.

The wind caught the sails of Pierre's mind. *If only he were here…*

"Of course!" His hand chopped onto the table, bouncing the pen onto the floor. He shot to his feet. "It's been here all along, but it changed state!"

"What?"

He fished around in a sheaf of a dozen flimsies, found the one he was looking for.

"*What*, Pierre? Talk to me!"

He stared at the figures and charts on the transparent sheet. "Merde," he whispered. He lowered it and looked at Kat, his eyes unwavering.

"You're starting to scare me, Pierre, which is pretty good going, considering."

He took in every feature of her face. He'd been worrying about them dying – about her dying. But this… He walked towards her, wanting to take her hand. Instead, he touched her arm gently. "Come on."

Kat followed him.

"You're absolutely sure?" Blake said, just as Pierre and Kat entered the cockpit. Zack nodded once, heavily.

"Sir," Pierre said, almost standing to attention, "I have a new hypothesis." His pulse raced, sure he was on the right track.

"So have we," Blake said, as he and Zack turned to face Pierre and Kat. "Sabotage: we've found evidence of a Minotaur virus planted deep in the comms software."

Pierre dismissed it in a flash. "That's not it, Sir. The comms software has no primary or even secondary functional connection with life support. The neural clusters use immunity protocols to prevent cross-functional contamination. I've checked them three times."

Blake and Zack exchanged a quick glance, and then Blake stood up, facing Pierre. "I don't think you're hearing what I'm saying, so let me make it pulse-beam clear for you – we've found a level six labyrinthine virus in the software that links us to Earth. We haven't been able to disable it yet –"

"Is it active?"

"Excuse me?"

"The virus – has it been activated? Or is it still inert? Because if it's not activated, it isn't the cause."

46

Pierre felt Blake's eyes burn into him. Logic wasn't always appreciated in moments of crisis, and Zack would always back up his friend.

Blake spoke softly. "It would take someone very knowledgeable on software to hide such a virus – an expert scientist, perhaps."

Pierre didn't at first grasp what Blake meant – of course it would – but then he saw the sideways look from Zack, and stepped backwards as if slapped. "Sir – no – never…" His throat dried up. It felt like the time as a boy when his father had wrongly accused him of stealing money from his mother's purse. He almost turned to Kat, but maintained eye contact with Blake.

Zack intervened. "Maybe we should hear him out, Skip."

Blake's glare slackened off. "You're right. Sorry, Pierre – I know it's not you – it was most probably uploaded on Zeus, in any case. And you're right about the software, it hasn't activated – yet – I'm just damned annoyed about it. God alone knows what it'll do when it *is* triggered."

Pierre noticed how tired Blake looked.

"So, Pierre, why don't you tell us your theory."

He collected himself. "My father used to say that when you've ruled out everything and still have no solution, it's because you've dismissed something incorrectly, something unthinkable. We've been looking for either a leak, or something which could strip out oxygen from the air."

Blake leaned back. "You have our undivided."

"The most obvious thing to strip out oxygen is one of us. That is, not exactly one of us, but… someone else."

Zack slapped his thighs. "A stowaway! Brilliant! Why didn't I think of that? Now you mention it, I saw someone I didn't recognise just the other day in the kitchen making coffee –"

Blake held up his hand.

Pierre sped up. "The security screening for this mission has been incredibly intense, especially for any conceivable explosive, and anything which could interfere with our drive systems. Everything checked and scanned before entering the ship, and triple-checked afterwards: organics, chemicals, moving parts, everything."

He paused, to hammer it home. "Nothing, aside from us, was alive when we left Zeus. But something else *is* alive now."

Blake's eyes narrowed. Zack hauled himself upwards. "Now wait a goddam minute, Pierre, if you're going where I think you're going –"

"What?" Kat asked, "will *somebody* please tell me what he's getting at?"

Pierre watched Blake, who stayed perfectly still, tight-lipped. "I'm sorry, Sir. I know you have some personal experience –"

Zack grabbed Pierre's shoulder. "Where's your evidence?"

Pierre swallowed, trying to remain calm. He handed the flimsy to Blake. "I correlated the oxygen depletion rate with data from post-War studies. When one of them comes out of hibernation mode, the oxygen usage rate is significant. As you probably know, they process all of it; there's no carbon dioxide afterwards for stripping.'

"A Ghoster," Kat said. "That's what you're talking about, isn't it?"

Blake glanced at Zack. "The aft compartment, the reserve food stocks, in sealed vacuum-packed crates."

"Skipper –"

"Did you check them, Zack? Did you break them open?"

"I … they're scanned for bomb material and techware; what was in them was only organic material, cold meat… I mean nobody would have thought…" He bowed his head.

Pierre glanced from Blake to Zack. Having breached land, his sails began to collapse. "You two are amongst the few to have ever survived a ghoster attack. You must know how to take one down."

Blake got up and ripped the seal off the weapons locker at the back of the cockpit, grabbed a pulse pistol and checked its charge. He passed one to each of the others.

Pierre felt his own fear rising. "You killed one, in Kurana Bay, though the records are vague."

Kat cradled her pistol. "How many were you when you met the ghoster?"

"Twenty," Zack answered, priming his pistol. It emitted a low start-up hum. "A full platoon of experienced soldiers."

Pierre swallowed. He was a scientist, he'd never seen any actual combat. He thought the next question, even as Kat asked it.

"How many of you came out?"

"Let's go," Blake said, heading out, Zack right behind him.

Kat fumbled with her pistol, arming it. She glanced up at Pierre. "We're so screwed."

If he'd been someone else, he'd have held her, comforted her in some way. He glanced down at his own pistol – he wasn't much of a soldier, certainly no match for a ghoster. His brain – that was the only weapon he had that could be of any use right now. He hurried after Blake and Zack. *Think,* he heard his father say, smacking the dining room table, *think fast!*

Chapter 5

Chorazin

Micah lounged on the sofa, catching up on the news with his portly mother, her brightly-dyed chestnut hair making up for a lack-lustre floral dress. An overdose of facial powder gave her a striking appearance – "she who shall not be ignored" – as he'd joked to his school-friends when younger. He sipped the soy-beer she'd poured him after they'd had another disagreement. It had started as usual about his not having a girlfriend, at his age…

"There's that lovely girl, Antonia. You used to talk about her all the time."

"Don't start, Mom."

She humphed. "You'll find a nice girl on Eden one day."

He tried to change tack. "How do you feel about going there? You could maybe find…"

Her scowl choked off his words. "Don't you worry about me, I had quite enough of *that* for one lifetime, thank you very much." She kept her back to her husband's military portrait. "Besides, I'm not going."

He stared at her, as if he hadn't really looked at her in a long time. "But, I assumed –"

"You know what your father always said about that word."

He sighed. *Assume makes an ass out of you and me.*

"Besides, this Lucy Beer rocket –"

"Alcubierre Drive."

"– isn't for the likes of me. It's – what do they call it – payload limited? Why would they carry my old carcass that distance?"

She had a knack of getting the words wrong but understanding the essentials nonetheless. Much as he hated his life, he hadn't thought of leaving her behind. His gaze swept around their magnolia sitting room, cluttered with memorabilia of his father, the Great War hero, who'd been a complete bastard to his wife. And now she wouldn't leave his ashes behind. "Anyway," he said, "it'll be a long time before they start transporting people."

She wagged a finger. "Long after I'm dead and buried, that's for sure."

That was below the belt, on two counts – he didn't want to think about her dying, and she was right that it would take a very long time. The new drive couldn't break light speed unless its payload stayed below a narrow limit, so no mass transport until someone figured it out; or else stasis for a hundred years...

He clicked on the late hour news summary. Beef had hit 300 dollars a kilo, not that he could remember the last time he'd tasted real beef. There'd been a rumour of a sub gone missing near Guam, and another fire tornado in New Missouri, flattening the shanty town that had just been getting on its feet. Micah swigged a gulp of his beer, brooding.

"One step forwards, three back," he muttered.

"I don't know why they bother!" his mother piped. "These fringe towns get nowhere. They should have built underground like we did here, before the War. The desert lands are too hot now –"

He lip-synched the words as she uttered them for the umpteenth time.

"– baked like a cake. It'll be centuries before anyone can live there again."

He reckoned they didn't have centuries. His mind sieved through the statistics, lies, and propaganda: half a century at most, probably less. But he didn't say it. At least she wouldn't be around to see how much worse it was going to get.

"Things always look clearer with hindsight, Mom. We were lucky. The pre-War aerial attacks and the rising temperatures pushed the Cave Bill through. This place was almost ready to move into when War hit." He looked out the window of their subterranean two-bed flat across the cavernous Kaymar Precinct: forty other blocks thirty storeys deep, glistening bubble-bridges criss-crossing at every fifth level. Biofuel copters dodged in and out of the towers, the day-time sun-globes replaced by neon advertising strips.

He couldn't see into any of the other apartments. All windows became opaque whenever anyone wanted it that way, which was always. We were lucky, he reminded himself. Only twenty nukes hit the US during the War, low-yield thanks to the Pact of '36. Pretty awful, of course, maybe irrecoverable. But it could have – no, *should have* – been much, much worse, according to all the tit-for-tat predictions.

The vid they'd caught earlier had interviewed some of the surviving "fire-breakers", a handful of soldiers and generals of different nations who couldn't bring themselves to detonate the nukes when instructed to do so. Most had been executed for treason in the final days of the War, but the few who survived were later hailed as heroes. It was one of the few episodes of recent history which stopped his cynicism plummeting into freefall.

He tried to lift the mood. "If the fringers can survive a year, the grass might stick, and we can start to reclaim the land. God knows we need the space."

"No, no, *no!*" his mother countered "Rushing too soon, that's what drove us to *this* –" she waved a mottled hand at the window, "– in the first place. Life got too fast. No one had any time, everyone running around, losing touch with each other and nature."

He rolled his eyes.

"Yes, my boy, *nature*. Your forefathers didn't care about the environment. It was always about the quick buck, and the quick –"

"*Mom!*" He couldn't abide it when she feigned to be coarse. Or maybe it was the fact that she'd had more sex in her day than he was having now. But she was in full flood.

"Good, hard-working people rebelled. I don't side with them, of course," she glanced at the portrait of Micah's father in battle dress, "but they did have a point. Humanity had lost direction. It's not surprising these funnies –"

"Fundies."

"Yes, well, whatever, it's not surprising they took up arms. It was a wake-up call. And we damned well needed one!" She folded her arms in an unassailable conclusion.

He sagged. To say anything now would only invite another tirade. He focused on the vid, and with a jolt he realised the reporter was speaking about the Eden Mission. His mother's sour face suddenly beamed.

"Oh, Micah! Look! Do you think we'll see you this time? Why are you never on the vids, when you do such important work?"

And why do I still live with my mother if I do such important work? He tuned in to what the newscaster was saying.

"... A break-in at Eden Mission Control earlier tonight. We have little information but members of the Chorazin have been in and out of the building for the past two hours. No further news at this stage. The Gov-pod says that there is no impact on the Eden time-scale."

Break-in? He wondered if it could be connected in some way, but it seemed far-fetched. He switched off the vid.

"What did you do that for? What does it mean anyway, you were there only a few hours ago, weren't you? Did you see anything?"

He turned away so she couldn't see his face. She was a lot shrewder than she let on. He headed for the kitchenette and opened the fridge. He ignored the Molsen lites; he needed to clear his head – maybe an ultresso. He barely heard her come up behind him.

"What is it?" she said quietly. "You're not in any trouble, are you?" He turned to face her, saw the concern in her eyes. Truth was, he was tired, and the argument had worn him down even further.

"I honestly don't know, Mom." He was about to say he'd done nothing wrong, quite the opposite, when the door buzzer made him start. They both froze. She gazed up at him, and he saw how frail she was, like worn china. He knew she was wishing his father was there. He sure as hell wasn't.

"Don't answer." she whispered.

He shushed her, and headed for the door. Before he reached it, it opened. Two figures entered: a man and a woman, wearing the instantly recognisable grey Chorazin uniforms, the regulation jackets cut off at the waist, lightweight and bullet-proof, a small red eagle insignia on the left breast. The man, late thirties, athletic and bald, carried a small brown sack in his hand. They didn't appear armed, but Micah knew better.

The man strode to the centre of the lounge, immediately taking control of the apartment, and its occupants. He looked Micah over, then held out his hand. Micah shook it warily. It felt like rock.

"My name is Vincent. You can call me Vince. This is my associate Louise."

Micah glanced in her direction. His eyes lingered: a hawkish blonde, hair lashed back in a tight bun. She moved around the room with the grace of a gymnast. She held a small scanning device, though he guessed she relied on her senses far more. She met his gaze briefly. His eyes dodged back to Vince.

"You are Micah Sanderson, employee of the Eden Mission, working in Telemetry?"

He found Vince's ice-blue eyes disconcerting, like staring into the vertiginous blues of an ice-field.

"Er, yes." Then as an afterthought, "And this is my mother." He turned to see his mother standing in the kitchenette doorway. Her face was stone. He'd not seen that expression since his father's funeral, when an old admiral had made a muffled, snide remark about her dead husband. With alarm he noted she was clutching the bread knife.

"May I sit, please? It's been a long day," Vince said.

Micah appreciated that he didn't sit down straightaway, but actually waited for permission, so he nodded. Micah and his mother perched on the sofa, Vince on a hard-backed chair facing them, placing the small sack carefully on the floor between his feet. Louise walked over to the window, apparently uninterested in their conversation. Micah's vision was drawn to her perfect ass in stretch pants. She glanced over her shoulder, alert, elfin eyes catching his look. Her gaze struck him like ice on his neck, but there was openness, too, daring him. The sort of woman his mother would tell him to avoid. Louise raised an eyebrow. He cleared his throat and turned back to Vince.

"Er, Mom?" he said, prying the bread knife from her fingers, laying it to rest on the coffee table.

Vince seemed about to say something then paused. "Is that a battle commander top you're wearing? Looks like the original nannite-protective model."

Micah had forgotten he often wore it now in the evenings when the windows were open, the massive turbo-fans blasting a chill breeze around the stalagmite-like tower blocks. It pleased his Mom, and he had to admit it was comfortable. It had been his father's in the War. He never quite knew why he liked to wear it – somehow it was to spite his father, who when alive had never as much as let Micah touch it.

"You know what it's worth, I suppose? Probably more than this apartment."

Micah nodded and caught his Mom's approving eye. He glanced at his father's stern face in his military portrait on the wall.

"Family heirloom. Non-functional of course. Otherwise I'd have it registered with the Nannite Oversight Commission." And you'd know about it already.

Vince nodded. "Have you seen the vids tonight Micah? May I call you Micah?"

Did anyone ever say "No" to such a question, Micah wondered? Vince seemed like someone you could talk to, but shouldn't. He didn't like being on familiar terms with the Chorazin. "Yes, we just switched off. What happened? The reporters didn't seem to know anything."

Vince rested his finger-tips on the table as he leaned forward. "We were rather hoping you might be able to help us there."

"Well, no idea really," he answered hesitantly. "I left several hours ago."

Vince nodded." At 18:45, to be precise. Working late? You are, of course, aware of the anti-overtime laws? I believe the Eden Mission isn't exempt."

The beer had definitely been a bad idea. He wished he'd had time to fix an ultresso. But Kane had wanted to keep "it" quiet. He took a breath. "Things are pretty busy now, with less than a week till Ulysses reaches Eden. I'll take time off later. That's allowed." He sat back, trying to remember how to look relaxed.

"Nothing out of the ordinary?" Vince said.

There had been no cameras in Kane's office. "No, nothing really." He caught his mother's curious eyes on him. Shit, even she can see I'm lying!

Louise's voice cut in, deeper than he'd been expecting. "So you normally have after-hours meetings with Mr. Kane, the Eden Mission Project Manager?" She looked him up and down. "Seems unlikely."

Micah bridled. "I did drop in to give a status report. Nothing unusual."

She cocked her head and considered him for a few seconds, then returned to the other side of the room. With some difficulty he stopped eye-tracking her.

"And then?" Vince said.

Micah felt like he was a ball in a tennis match – with hard hitters. "Then I came home. That's all."

"And he's been here with me ever since!"

Thanks Mom, that's all I need to make me look guilty. "What's this all about anyway? Why are you here? What do you want from me?"

Vince said calmly, "We want to know who killed Mr. Kane at seven-thirty pm this evening, and why."

Micah's mouth dropped open. "What?" He tried to replay in his head what Vince had just said. He heard his mother gasp. She began wringing her hands, looking to the portrait. He tried to regain control. "Killed? But how? I was there earlier, and he was…"

"Alive?" Louise offered.

"What? Yes." Then it really hit him. Kane was dead. He'd just been talking with him a few hours ago. He walked unsteadily to the window, turning to face them all.

"Wait a minute! You don't think I…" He flushed. "I – I've been back here for ages. I mean, how did he die anyway?"

Vince placed the tip of an index finger on his sternum. "Stiletto. Professional. And, lucky for you, we know you didn't do it, for two very good reasons. First, the crime scene investigator pinned the death down at 7:32, and yes, you were here by then. The tram and bubble-cams show that. Difficult to fool so many of them."

Micah needed time to think. But his head fuzzed up, and these Chorazin kept throwing him off-beam. "Second reason?"

Vince opened the sack he had brought in with him and pulled out an object the size of a grapefruit, made of gleaming metal. There were a few wires visible and some kind of timing device. One of the wires had been cut.

"Oh my!" his Mom exclaimed. Micah stared at it, his mouth reluctant to verbalise what his eyes recognised.

"Exactly, Mrs Sanderson," Vince said. "You're lucky we found it. We always inspect premises before entering for an interro –" he paused, "– before an interview. Happily, my associate is very thorough. She found it in the heating duct outside your apartment. It was set to go off –" he held up his wristcom "– around about now." He tossed it back into the bag. "It would have taken out three whole floors. Alicians are also known for being thorough, though excessive is a more appropriate word."

Micah felt dizzy. He leant against the window frame. "Is it true, Vince, what they say about the Chorazin? Shoot first, question later, take no prisoners, takes a criminal to catch a terrorist. Etcetera."

Louise answered. "That's what the recruitment brochure says. That's why *I* joined."

Vince rapped the table twice with a finger-knuckle. "Micah, assuming you did not kill Mr Kane, we nevertheless have an interest in what you were discussing with him."

Micah suddenly remembered. "Sandy!"

"Excuse me?" Vince said.

"Sandy, his personal assistant. What about her?"

"Files show she left shortly after you did. Why?"

"She was still there when I left, didn't look like she was leaving. In fact Kane asked her to stay late." His breathing was rapid. He was trying to think. Could she have killed him? Surely not, but then... He remembered how defensive she'd been, not allowing him to disturb Kane. Was that to get him out of the way? But she didn't seem capable of killing, and the rumours were that they were lovers.

"You're sure about this?" Vince asked.

Micah nodded. Louise walked to the kitchenette, activated a sub-dermal earpiece, and began talking in coded Chorazin language. The only intelligible word Micah heard was "Sandy". Vince got up in one fluid motion. "We need to know what happened between you and Kane. What did you discuss?"

Micah's mind felt like an out-of-synch vid channel. He ran through the data he had: Kane had been killed two hours after their meeting. Kane's office was well-known for its anti-surveillance technology. No one else knew what they had discussed. That meant only one thing. Someone Kane had contacted – and trusted – had killed him.

Vince's voice took on a harsher tone. "Talk to me, Micah!"

Micah needed air. He turned and opened the window, trying to decide what to say, trying to think faster than the speed at which Vince's patience was failing. The cacophony of urban nightlife flooded in, but it actually helped. He focused. Once I tell, then it's out, it'll be on their internal net. Kane would have called people he trusted, Eden security. Some of those had to be Chorazin; the Eden Mission was too big to escape Chorazin surveillance from the inside. And if a Chorazin had killed him, then that person by now would have had me killed, and would have stalled Vince. Vince doesn't seem to know anything yet. So – I should be able to trust him.

Vince raised his voice. "Micah, close the window and sit down. Trust me, you've nowhere else to go, and I'd rather not send you to interrogation. But if you don't talk right now, I will arrest you as a suspected accomplice."

Micah turned to see his mother get to her feet.

"No, you mustn't – he's a good boy!" Her face was white marble, ready to crack.

In that instant Micah decided to tell Vince everything. But as he took a breath, he heard the shrill whine of a copter. Everything slowed down. Louise sprang towards him, arms outstretched, aiming to push him out of the way, but not in time. He felt the projectile hit him sledgehammer-hard in the back, knocking him off his feet, sending him crashing through the glass coffee table. As he sank into blackness, the last sound he heard was his mother screaming.

Chapter 6

Code Red

Blake stopped two metres from the darkened hatchway, fingers flexing near his holstered pulse pistol. He couldn't believe it was happening again. He'd lost eighteen men last time, all about Pierre's age. Nineteen men, he corrected himself. At the end it had come down to him and the ghoster, and his intuition told him history wanted a re-run. The tremors re-surfaced in his right hand, shakes he'd not had since Kurana Bay. He squeezed his fist hard to stop them.

"The lights are off inside," Pierre said, inspecting a small panel adjacent to the airlock connecting them to the fourth compartment. "Since zero-two-hundred, though the cockpit systems said they were on – I checked an hour ago."

Zack sighed. "And the night goggles would be – let me guess…" He gesticulated towards the pitch-black porthole in the airlock hatchway.

Pierre confirmed with a nod.

"Figures," Zack said.

Pierre closed the panel. "As we suspected, whoever planned this did a good job. The air circulation sensors were looped so we wouldn't detect where the oxygen loss was coming from, and the emergency vents to the fourth compartment were wired open. I've sealed them now."

"Good. Both of you, suit up," Blake ordered. "Arm yourselves as you think fit."

Pierre hesitated. "Sir, reports state that it can take four days for a ghoster to regenerate after extended hibernation, and the oxygen depletion started just two days ago. Maybe it's still comatose, buried inside one of the food crates?"

"Pierre, forget theory right now," Blake said, "or you'll die in there."

Pierre held his ground for a moment then gave in, following Zack to the weapons locker.

Blake peered through the airlock porthole, but only saw his reflection. His breathing slowed of its own accord, the way it always did just before battle.

When they returned, he saw that Zack had retrieved an item from his personal area. He ignored it. But minutes later, as Zack and Pierre were donning their standard space-suits and oxygen backpacks, Pierre spotted it.

"Zack, you can't be serious, taking a commando knife in there? We'll be in spacesuits and in a vacuum if we have to go to Plan B."

Zack grinned, and slipped it into its sheath under his backpack, hilt pointing downwards. "You never dress commando style?" He leered at Pierre. "This knife has saved me more times than I care to remember. Think of it as a good luck charm. You asked how we killed it last time; well, my knife played its part."

But Blake knew how they had taken out the ghoster in Kurana Bay – the slow gun. They didn't have one aboard; why would they? He switched on Zack's backpack, three telltale green lights and a single beep indicating it was fully functional. "Each man takes in what he feels appropriate."

Pierre bristled. "But plasma pulse rifles, right – according to procedure?"

Blake finished with Zack's suit, and moved to check Pierre's.

"Actually, Pierre," Zack said, as he picked up his helmet, "I'm taking a pulse pistol. It's not that big a compartment, and if there's a need to use something, it'll be close quarters."

"But the rifle charge is more powerful."

Blake snapped on the switch to activate Pierre's backpack – three greens and a single beep. "Pierre, how many of the people who wrote those standard procedures actually went into space, or dealt with ghoster combat situations?"

Pierre frowned. "You haven't told us what you're taking in there, Sir, if it comes to that."

Zack laughed, wiry eyebrows stretching into grey mesh. "Man's got a point, boss. Care to share?"

He eyed them both. "No."

Pierre hefted his rifle, and shook it in pump action mode to arm it. It hummed softly. "Sir," he said, swallowing, "this is my first real combat situation."

Zack spoke as he donned his helmet, muffling his words. "You're shitting me, right?" Zack shook his head, settling his "fishbowl", as he called it. His voice came through clear on the speakers. "Just try not to shoot me in there, okay? Boss, maybe I should go in alone – seriously."

Blake picked up Pierre's helmet. "Keep your head, Pierre, or you'll lose it." Pierre donned it, and with a click and a sound like a gulp, it sealed.

Blake noticed how stiffly Pierre stood, how he held the rifle like… like so many men he'd sent into battle who'd never returned. He wanted to go in there first with Zack, but this was about strategy. Most likely scenario was that the first two who entered died. The third one had to be able to react fast, see what they were up against, and finish the job. Best credible scenario was that Kat alone survived, and they stopped the ghoster before it sabotaged the engines – if they lost the FTL drive, they'd all die in any case, drifting in space until everything ran out.

He picked up two lanyards and handed them to Zack and Pierre.

"For Plan B, if it's mobile. Remember, this ship wasn't built for a man overboard scenario. Either of you go out the window, you're history, so stay clamped at all times."

Kat cut in from the cockpit; Blake had almost forgotten she'd been monitoring them via intra-vid, listening to everything.

"Captain, telemetry's set up, just get some light going in there as soon as possible, I can't see much from up here."

"We'll do what we can. Kat – I want an open four-way com-line during the entire operation. No unnecessary comms."

There was a pause. "Understood. Open four-way comms as of now."

He pressurised the inner airlock, then spun the wheel to open the hatch. "Good luck."

Only Zack nodded acknowledgement. Pierre stepped first into the airlock chamber. As Zack followed, Blake patted him once on the shoulder, and sealed the door behind them. There was a sucking sound, a clunk, then silence. His hand hung onto the airlock wheel. He tried not to think about last time. He didn't have to. The pit of his stomach felt like it was in a vice. Instead he started thinking about Plan C.

* * *

Shoulder-to-shoulder inside the airlock chamber, Zack heard Pierre's ragged breathing across the intercom.

Pierre checked the dials. "Fully pressurised inside the compartment."

Zack chewed his lip, peering through the small porthole into the darkness beyond. "Time to check on our guest." He opened the inner door to the fourth compartment. As it swung open, the light spilled in from behind them, revealing the outlines of a room ten metres deep crammed with cylinders, boxes, and crates, all strapped down. It looked just like it had done twelve hours ago when he'd checked it over. The lattice of harnesses resembled a giant spider web laid over the contents of the compartment. He stared towards the far wall, behind which the dark matter engines lay, adding to his unease.

They each took one pace into the compartment and clipped their lanyard karabiners onto hull eyeholes. Zack's gaze swept the room, but he didn't use the flashlight attached to his left wrist. If there was anything in here, he didn't feel like lighting himself up. Pierre's rifle sighting beam flashed upward to the escape hatch which was their Plan B – the ghoster-overboard plan, as Kat had christened it.

"Zack, I don't see anything." Pierre took a step forward.

"Wait." Zack squinted through the semi-darkness towards the crate at the far end of the chamber housing the neutralino detonator. It was one of two, the other used to start the dark matter ignition after Saturn, enabling them to get up enough speed to engage the warp shell. This one was for the return journey. Something was behind the crate. His eyes tracked to the left, knowing from theory and experience that unaided night vision worked best if you looked slightly off target. He saw it. His head recoiled inside his helmet.

"Kat," he said, voice taut. "Tell me what you see through the internal cameras" He still hadn't aimed his flashlight, instead straining his eyes towards the location of the detonator. Her reply came through, rendered grainier than usual by the voice-com transmitter.

"Not much. I need more light."

When Pierre went to shine his flashlight on the crate, Zack gripped his forearm.

"Don't." He was sure now, though he had a hard time accepting it.

Blake's voice cut in from outside. "Report."

Zack let Pierre reply, while he began to think of tactics to outmanoeuvre what he believed was crouching just behind the detonator. He still had his hand on Pierre's arm, and felt Pierre's body jerk.

"Sir, it… *mon dieu.*" Pierre's breathing accelerated, bordering on hyper-ventilation. Then he exhaled deeply.

Zack removed his arm. Good – remember your training, because if you don't we'll be dead a lot faster.

Pierre's voice was edgy. "I can see a human head, but… it has no eyes."

Blake didn't respond. Zack could only imagine how he was reacting; it was Kurana Bay all over again. Zack couldn't remember unholstering his pulse pistol, but it was in his hand. He ramped it up to maximum, then spoke in a steady tone. "Don't move, Pierre. Get ready to fire." He took a deep breath, as he did before any close-quarter battle. His palms sweated inside his gloves. He gripped the pistol harder.

"Skipper," he said, "it's a ghoster alright, fully awake. Lock us down, seal us in. We're going to Plan B."

* * *

Kat couldn't see Blake on her screens. "Captain? Where are you?"

Blake re-appeared, suiting up. "Kat, get on the comms. Issue Code Red to Earth – at least this time they'll know it was sabotage and not an accident. Fast as you can, then confirm."

Kat cursed as she realised her own rifle was two compartments away. Not that it would help. She took one last look at the silhouetted figures of Zack and Pierre, then shifted position and began typing fast.

<Code Red> She paused, looking at the letters on the screen. Then she hit the button. <Transmit>

<Unable to transmit> flashed up on the screen. Her brow furrowed. Now what? She typed it again, and got the same message.

"Captain, the message; it won't transmit."

"Slow down, try again."

Pierre cut in. "Kat, wait – don't try more than twice. Do you hear me?"

But she'd just hit "Transmit" a third time. Large bright red letters on the screen said <Goodbye>. The screen blanked.

She stared at the lifeless screen. She leant back in her chair, allowing her foot to rise up and then stomp down hard on the dead console. "Alician mother-fuckers!"

"Kat, what's happening?" Blake shouted.

She suddenly felt how small and defenceless they were, hurtling through a pitiless vacuum, light years from help. She bit her lip hard.

"It's dead. It said 'Goodbye,' then shut down. It's the virus." *Please God, tell me this is just another nightmare.*

"Kat, listen to me – Zack hotwired an emergency protocol to disengage navigation, propulsion and life support to a secondary sub-processor – press the red plunger on Zack's console – do it now!"

She sprang out of her chair, spotted the plunger, and slammed her hand down on it. "Done!" She knew without that switch, the virus would spread to propulsion and navigation within minutes, and they would disintegrate under obscene torsional forces as soon as they slipped out of their flight envelope.

"Kat," Blake said. "Salvage as many secondary systems as you can, but keep an eye on the screens, in case the ghoster moves."

At first, she didn't understand – Zack and Pierre would see it if it did anything – but then she remembered the tales of how quickly ghosters could move – and kill. "Understood."

* * *

Blake sealed his helmet, the familiar muffling sound lending him confidence, shutting out extraneous noises, allowing him to concentrate. He peered through the porthole. "Zack. Do you have line of sight?"

Zack's voice was low but steady. "It's right behind the detonator, in front of the reserve oxygen cylinders. One miss and we're all dead."

"The detonator – activated?"

Zack sighed. "Was afraid you'd ask that. I see two red lights, one green. Pierre?"

"There's only one safeguard left. A final control command to arm it, then a one-minute countdown. The arming control is in front of us. If it goes for it we'll get a clear shot. We caught it just in time."

Blake leant his gloved hands against the door. He took three measured breaths. He'd trade their remaining oxygen for the slow gun. "Options?"

Zack replied with a snort. "Not many. Plan A, we circle the perimeter. It'll come out screaming, moving like a bat, and we'll probably shoot each other in the crossfire, but maybe we'll hit it enough to stop it. Plan B…" he paused. "Pierre?"

"We blow the hatch. The problem is, ghosters can function for several minutes in a vacuum. If it manages to anchor itself inside the compartment, it will arm the detonator before we can react, and defend it until it blows. We need a Plan C, Sir."

"Skipper, he's right. All we'll do is slow this thing down a few seconds. You know they're practically unkillable without explosives or industrial lasers. We're in serious danger of becoming another fucking Eden Mission mystery."

Blake was only half-listening. Abruptly he went back to the weapons locker to pick up his Plan C. He secured the bagel-sized explosive charge with pushbutton actuator – a hand-made land-mine – to his chest.

* * *

Inside the compartment, Pierre spoke, his voice unsteady. "Zack, why doesn't it have eyes?"

Zack lodged his flashlight on the floor, not taking his eyes off the grey-skinned scaly head and neck. He grimaced as he met the dark sockets where its eyes should have been. His mouth felt dry as sandpaper, but he tried to reassure Pierre. "It has eyes; they're permanently open underneath a protective membrane. They have no weak spots. Makes people hesitate, too, because it looks blind – got many a soldier killed in the War – not to mention the scream when they attack. If – when it moves, just aim for its trunk – don't look at the face."

"What's it waiting for?"

He felt sorry for Pierre – his first real battle experience, and encountering a ghoster was a supernova of a baptism. He knew Pierre's instincts would be playing push-me-pull-you between fight and flight; waiting wasn't instinctive at all. But if they moved now, they'd have little chance. He tried to appeal to Pierre's intellectual side, to help him keep his nerve.

"Its higher cortical functions are suppressed; you can't negotiate with it, and it'll never question its instructions. A ghoster's reptile-brain fighting instincts have been heightened. But it still has basic tactical abilities. It has a mission, a goal, and is fucking adaptable. Its goal is to destroy the Ulysses, probably by activating the ND. But it knows if it tries now, it might fail, because we'll have clear line of fire. But if we move first, it'll strike in fast random attacks. We've got weapons trained on it, so it's waiting for an advantage."

"Waiting for us to blink?"

"Yeah, you could say that." But a chill ran down his spine as he recalled what he'd said earlier – a ghoster's eyes were always open behind the membrane – they never blinked.

* * *

Blake primed the mine. Him and the ghoster. That's how it was always going to be. Now he'd accepted it he felt calmer. The tremors vanished.

Kat defied protocol. "Not exactly regulation issue."

He glanced toward the camera and offered a bare smile. He picked up two pulse rifles and shook them into readiness. "You're in charge of the ship now, Kat. Auto-lock the hatch when I've gone through. If I fail…"

"Don't you worry about me, I have my pistol." She tried to laugh.

For a moment he wished he'd gotten to know his crew better. Like all captains, he'd been trained to keep a distance.

"Okay, Zack, Pierre, get ready. I'm coming in. When the inner hatch opens on your side, the ghoster will see it as an advantage or a threat. Either way it will attack. Each of you break to your respective sides and open fire. Leave a pathway open between it and me. No discussion. I have a little surprise for our guest."

He spun the wheel.

* * *

Through the comms system, Kat heard the hiss of air as the outer hatch opened. Sitting alone in the cockpit, she pulled up her knees and locked her wrists around them, the pistol resting on her console. They'd all probably be dead in the next few minutes, and no one would even know what happened to them. Silently, she saluted Blake. But even as she did so, the Minotaur virus reached environmental system control. Lights all over the ship started to fade.

Chapter 7

Star Council

Gabriel knelt in the gothic church, hands clasped in prayer he didn't believe in. He tried again to still his mind – he'd gotten further than any Sentinel before him, close to finding the leader of the Alician Order. A slim chance to overturn their endgame was at hand. But the bitterness of remorse threatened to overwhelm him: he'd just killed his best friend.

Samuel, like him, had been in deep cover working inside the Alician cell-structure, living, breathing, and sleeping in the enemy's ranks. His mission had been to uncover the facts about the loss of the Prometheus and the Heracles. In doing so he'd unearthed the ghoster plot on the Ulysses. Samuel had been about to release it on the nets: the Alicians made a pretence of being anti-tech for their Fundie supporters, whereas ghosters were tech-weapons, reviled by every soldier who had survived the War.

An Alician section led by Brother Marcus had surprised Samuel and Gabriel during a meeting. Samuel had immediately acted as if Gabriel had found him first, and had reached for his pistol, knowing Gabriel would have to react. There had been a brief glimmer of forgiveness in Samuel's eyes just before Gabriel shot him. The worst part was that Gabriel had not been able to close Samuel's eyes, with Marcus and his men present, and had to leave his corpse in the rotting apartment for the rats to plunder.

For four hours Gabriel had incanted the Tellurathonicat, the long-lost song for the dead. Although he didn't believe in God, he believed in his best friend. He closed with "Amen".

The emotional gale that had threatened to undo him from his own mission died down, and a hollow semblance of calm finally arrived. He would need it to honour Samuel's sacrifice. He scanned the rows of wooden benches around him. Since the War, churches were rarely empty – there were so many lost loved ones that people used the churches to commune with the dead. Cemeteries had become a thing of the past, every last scrap of decent soil used for crops. Funerals culminated in cremation and vitrification of the deceased's ashes into a dusky glass teardrop that fitted into the palm of a hand. Four people knelt, heads bowed down on the bench's ledge, arms outstretched, holding the "pearls" as they were called, as if offering them to God, or perhaps, in the silence and impunity of prayer, asking "why?"

In order to concentrate, he parked everything about Samuel. He pressed his left palm to his right, his right palm to his left, with equal force. He was about to penetrate an Alician Inner cell. He needed to get into the role again, immerse himself in the thinking patterns of the enemy: believe like one of them, react like one of them. He recalled the scripture: structure, discipline, equanimity – the three principles of Neo-Fundamentalism. Even the posture for praying was critical. If the base was strong, all else would flow correctly, and all action emanating from such a structure would be right.

He checked his wristcom. Two small green lights on its side, linked to micro-sensors on his jacket collar, told him there was no one behind him. Reaching into his pocket he snapped open a mini-phial with his thumb, bowed as if in prayer, and smeared a trace of clear liquid onto his lips. It evaporated in moments. He rose silently, and trod softly as if still in prayer towards an alcove and a bolted iron door. He didn't touch the handle. Placing his eye to the peep-hole, he circled his eyeball once to let the ret-scan do its job. The door, bolt and all, heaved upwards like a mute portcullis. It descended behind him as soon as his rear foot had passed the threshold, encasing him in total darkness. He remained perfectly still.

"A boy kills his sister with a gun. Who is guilty?" The tone invited feelings of unworthiness, the voice of a man who commanded people to serve in a Holy war. Gabriel answered immediately – *reflex not reflection* – as he'd been taught.

"The father, for letting it fall into the hands of the son." He spoke louder than intended; he instructed his body to relax.

"Who else?" The voice was aggressive.

"The mother, for not admonishing the father." Gabriel heard the speaker pace. Still not enough. "The government, for allowing weapons in the population." Continued silence and pacing. *Was the speaker carrying something?* Gabriel detected unevenness in his step, favouring one side. As an assassin, he'd been trained to hear the nuances in every movement. He would not be allowed too many more attempts. "The manufacturer, for not equipping the gun with a child-sensor-block." As soon as he'd said it he knew it was wrong – too tech. The pacing stopped, a sleeve rustled, something being lifted. He didn't panic. Then he realised what was expected.

"Scientists, for making the weapon possible." Gabriel relaxed. He knew it was right. He felt balanced again. A whisper somewhere in the chamber; something metallic put down, a drawer closed. He heard another speaker, female.

"Welcome, Brother Matthias," she said, an accent he couldn't place, her voice guttural yet fluid. "Change and join us in the Inner Chamber." She left, followed by the other man, the coldness from her voice lingering in her wake.

Bright light deluged the room, stinging his eyes. He found a simple grey robe neatly folded on a stool. He didn't look for the weapon the first man must have been carrying: he knew he was being watched, one always was. He undressed, removing the wristcom that otherwise never left him, and put on the robe, naked underneath, as the Structure required.

In the nearby mirror he performed the mental self-examination ritual: *regard truthfully that which the Creator has fashioned*. A gaunt face, fringed with black hair, jet-black eyes. Know thyself, the Structure taught. Killer's eyes, he said to himself, the last things my victims see, eyes of a Cleanser, one who releases souls to God. The ritual satisfied, he opened the door, and walked through the ultraviolet-tinged archway that scanned for any hidden devices or bio-implants. Anti-tech when it suits them. He flushed away the thought – he had to play the role, be the zealous assassin they believed him to be.

The inner chamber was cave-like; myriad candles scattered shadows onto whitewashed brick walls. Five figures awaited him, draped in white robes, hoods covering all but their chins and mouths, hands concealed inside billowing sleeves. Each stood on the point of the blue chalk pentagram drawn on the smooth granite floor. The points were connected with gold lines, creating a star inside the pentagram. Gabriel stood in the star's centre, hands open by his side where the others could see them. He bowed deeply.

"Welcome, Brother Matthias. You may report." It was the voice of the man who had questioned him in the Outer Chamber; the leader of this Alician Star Council, the *Cultivator*. He stood at the pentagram's vertex, facing Gabriel.

Gabriel was concise, in accordance with what he knew about Star Council etiquette. "From the Devil's craft, all contact has been lost. An analyst in the Project suspected something, told the Project Manager. Both have been cleansed."

There was no reaction from any of the five until the Cultivator spoke.

"All is not as you say."

Gabriel's breath closed in, his sinewy muscles tensed. To lie in the Star Council meant death. He waited. In theory he could kill all of them in less than two seconds, but he'd heard that lasers targeted the centre of the star, primed to activate in case of sudden moves – he was fast, but not *that* fast.

"The Eden Manager is indeed cleansed. The analyst, Micah Sanderson, lives on."

Gabriel didn't see how that was possible, he had made the hit himself, as ordered – but the Cultivator would not lie.

"In addition," the female voice cut in, "a woman is missing –"

Gabriel preferred the man's voice: his was like bracing seawater; hers was like a wave of rotting seaweed, concealing broken glass.

"– we do not know where. The Project Manager's assistant, Sandy Mindel."

Gabriel had seen her file.

The Cultivator cut in. "She must be brought to God, Brother Matthias, as quickly as possible, by whatever means."

Gabriel knew the "by whatever means" included doing it in public, in which case he would be discovered. Before he could voice his question, the woman spoke again.

"You must find her, Brother Matthias, and eliminate her. She may have seen our brother in the Eden Mission. He cannot be unmasked; his work is not yet done."

He raised his left hand in front of his shoulder, palm facing the leader.

"You may speak, Brother Matthias," the Cultivator said.

"I will do this. But if I am caught?"

The woman lashed out, "Then you will kill yourself as you have been trained, and go to meet your maker!"

Gabriel's tongue involuntarily flicked back to his false left molar. Painless, so they said, but he didn't believe it – he'd seen a comrade's contorted face after one had been accidentally broken during a training bout. Besides, he'd seen too much death to believe it was ever painless. He bowed his head in silence. Inside the Star, respect for the Council was paramount, even if the interviewee had been misunderstood. The Cultivator rescued him.

"I believe, Sister Esma that Brother Matthias is referring to the ramifications after his body is found."

Gabriel knew now why this man was the leader of this Council. Sister Esma was the most righteous, but sending people on suicide missions was not just about orders from God, it required careful handling. However, the fact that the Cultivator had used her name was not good news for Gabriel.

"If you die while executing your mission, the Chorazin will realise they had an Alician within their midst. Even though you left them ten years ago, this will be damaging to them. A Chorazin agent becoming an Alician Cleanser is unheard of. If you are caught performing this act, it will focus attention on you, drawing it away from another Alician agent."

So, an Alician was inside the Chorazin.

The Cultivator continued, "Such a finding will cause fear and increased self-monitoring in the Chorazin; it will slow them down at a time when we are moving forward at a greater pace."

Gabriel knew they were telling him far more than they should. They firmly believed – presumed – he would be dead in the next twenty-four hours.

"Then my sacrifice will be all the more beneficial," he replied, and bowed deeply. Although the disciplined group remained motionless, he nonetheless heard their collective breathing ease, reflecting their satisfaction with his answer, with the exception of Sister Esma, whose outbreath was a derisive snort. He also perceived that the session was over, that he was about to be dismissed. He pressed his luck, raising his left hand again. Sister Esma inhaled sharply, but the Cultivator got there first.

"Brother Matthias, you have a *further* question?" His tone was a potent cocktail of surprise and menace.

"I have a question, but am not sure I am permitted to ask it."

This time Sister Esma did not wait. It had been what he had hoped for. He knew the leader would be annoyed by the question, but would be even more vexed by Sister Esma's abrogation of his authority.

"You know very well the Dictates of Structure, Matthias!" she shouted.

He noted she had dropped his earned title of "Brother".

The Cultivator broke in. "To ask any question is your right, Brother Matthias, but you must take responsibility for what the answer brings."

He foresaw a power struggle between these two – it would be ended by the assassination of one or the other, as was the usual course of Alician internal politics.

"Brother Matthias, what is your question?"

He thought of Samuel: *this is for you.* "I understand, Your Eminence, that a ghoster may have been installed on the Devil's craft." There, he had said it. He heard the two behind him gasp. Sister Esma said nothing, but her hooded head moved momentarily towards the direction of the leader, before she checked herself. *She hadn't known.* The Cultivator drew himself up to his full height. Clearly, he had.

"Where did you hear this?" His voice was a drawn blade, seeking blood.

Gabriel knew he had to answer this question, or forfeit his own life here and now.

"In the Fourth Chapel."

"WHO?"

Gabriel bowed his head lower. "Brother Marcus," he said quietly. He saw the Cultivator make a quick hand movement, and the one behind Gabriel's left side immediately left the Chamber.

The leader's voice softened. "You have done well to bring this to our attention, Brother Matthias."

In Gabriel's mind he closed Samuel's eyes.

"And why does this concern you, Brother Matthias?" Sister Esma was no doubt enraged that she had not known, another reminder that she was not the leader; not yet, at least. Gabriel did not hesitate this time, but answered directly.

"Ghosters are an abomination. They are derived from science, and…" he paused, "even though they start as humans, they have no souls."

He waited for the answer. This time the Cultivator placed his hand on Sister Esma's robed arm, and spoke as if delivering a sermon.

"Brother Matthias, ghosters are a tool. In this war – and we are in a war – we must use whatever weapons we have to secure victory. If we must use the devil's own tricks against him, then that is what we will do. The ghosters these days, few as they are, volunteer for the procedure."

Gabriel found the idea of anyone volunteering to be changed into a ghoster an unlikely prospect. Alicians outwardly eschewed technology, to lure a blind following from gullible and angry masses, but he knew they were more advanced in some ways than most military governments.

"Go now," the Cultivator said, "release this woman Sandy's soul. Do not fail."

Gabriel dropped to one knee, lowering his head. The Cultivator proffered his hand so that Gabriel could kiss it. With head still bowed, Gabriel stood and backed away to the entrance. It was done. As soon as he was back in the chamber he picked up his wristcom and wiped his lips on it, downloading the Cultivator's pheromone signature.

Gabriel stood on the barely-lit street outside the Church, dressed in his original clothes. A light drizzle fell undisturbed by any breeze except the steam rising from hot-ground level. He walked over to the sleeping tramp on the otherwise deserted sidewalk – the rad-level was high even up here – and bent over to pick up what looked like a discarded plastic food carton. He snatched it up and glided over to a nearby disposal chute, retrieving something before discarding the box, and placed both his hands in his pockets. It was an antique silver locket, a four leaf clover carved on its front, his only connection with the past. He was relieved it was still there, where he had left it five hours ago. Luckily nobody picked up rubbish anymore, least of all that which lay next to a stinking, radioactive tramp. Gabriel had drugged the man just in case – Cleansers who left things to chance did not survive long.

He stared up into the rain, not bothering to shade his eyes from its acidic sting. Somewhere up there the dart-drone waited, primed with the Cultivator's pheromone signature. As soon as the man left the building, the drone's sensor would pick up the scent. Then it was just a matter of time. Samuel's sacrifice had not been in vain, though he wished he could have taken out Sister Esma as well.

He took an elevator to the mid-levels and walked towards his squalid apartment in the ruins above the orange level rad-zone, passing the Virtual Sex boutiques. He lingered outside one. A flabby sleazeball with waxed moustache called out to him, vaunting lurid promises Gabriel did not even hear, but he approached the man. Gabriel knew he was being captured on some vid system. They'll think I know I am about to die, and wish one last carnal act before the end. He held his wristcom to the man's reader, confirmed the credit transaction, and stepped inside.

No real women there, of course; that made the charade easier. He found an empty booth smelling of cheap deodorant, entered, and sealed the door. Inside were the usual plastic-sheeted padded table, an immerser headpiece, and a data crystal port.

He ignored the table and sat cross-legged on the floor. Pulling out the locket, he flicked it open and gazed at the holopic of the young girl inside, noting the family resemblance. He touched the picture, pulled out a sliver of quartz the width and depth of a fingernail, then snapped the locket shut with a click.

He got up, removed the sex menu crystal and jacked his own data shard into the port, donned the headpiece, and lay back on the table. It took only a few seconds to adjust. He was in a white room, so uniformly bright it was hard to see where walls, floor and ceilings began and ended. He heard stiletto heels, and turned around.

"Good evening, nice to see you are still alive," she said, a stunning redhead with green, feral eyes. She wore a vermillion tycra mini-dress. Gabriel and his Master always played along like this, just in case anyone hacked in. Of course in reality she could be fat and forty, or, in this case, a seventy year old pony-tailed male. *What you see is all you get*, he remembered, echoing the ambivalent ad of the Virtual Sex industry. But he wasn't here for games. He switched to an undocumented Tibetan dialect, just in case any porn-hackers bypassed the audio jamming code built into his crystal.

"The Cultivator is taken care of. Samuel is gone, as I'm sure you know, but he is avenged: Brother Marcus tonight. Sandy Mindel, Kane's assistant tomorrow."

"We have paid a high price for this. Nonetheless, Samuel would be proud of you," she replied, her dialect more polished than Gabriel's. "There is a slim chance this Miss Mindel may know the password – if not, it died with Kane. We've already searched the city for her, but there is no trace. Not an easy trick with all the micro-surveillance these days." She smiled coyly, all part of the show.

Gabriel knew her words were a challenge to him to find Sandy, but he said nothing. She seemed about to turn, and then cocked her head at him. "You know where she is, don't you?"

Gabriel nodded.

Her smile vanished. "The battle we have anticipated for a millennium is almost upon us."

"How close?"

"Maybe a week. We must find the password to open the ships. Then we can destroy them." Her face was grave, the charade suspended. She nodded once and turned, just as another woman entered. For the sake of the show, the two women embraced, languorously. Gabriel, embarrassed, wanted to look away, but that wasn't possible inside a V-Sex scene. A low shanga beat started up as the platinum blonde let the redhead depart, and slinked over to Gabriel, stripping before him. His crystal had tactile sensory effects disabled – just as well, as she promptly sat on his lap and began to grind to the music, breasts brushing his chest, lascivious lips pouting centimetres from his own. He mentally disconnected from the scene, though it had been a very long time. He voided the thought and decided to end this – it was an illusion after all, like life. Letting his breathing rate increase, he began to moan, and within a minute faked an orgasm. It wasn't so hard to counterfeit a climax – virtual sex booths enabled mental orgasm without its usual physical messiness – allowing the sex industry to escape certain laws, and sidestep health regulations. The too-perfect blonde stood up and sauntered off into the background. The entire scene faded to black static.

Gabriel slipped off the headpiece, removed the crystal, and put the locket back in his pocket. A week till they arrived; till the end of the world. So his own days, maybe his hours, were numbered. But he would play it out. Hundreds before him had died in the silent war that had endured nine centuries. In the fifteenth century Sentinels had gained the upper hand, but not for long. And now, trained Sentinels were few and far between, living on the run.

Outside, he smoked a cheroot he bought from a street trader in a darkened alleyway, watching the few people who dared the mildly acid shower scurry past. He leaned over a railing, his eyes following the cascade of rain plunging to ground level two hundred metres below. He remembered his real, non-Alician Master teaching him that life was like a drop of water in a waterfall. Each drop felt alone, confused, tumbling in chaos. But when it hit the water below, it rejoined the river and was at peace again. Gabriel let go of the cheroot, and watched its red ember blaze as it fell amongst the drops of rain.

Back in his apartment, he waited until midnight, then opened a psy-locked suitcase – letting the locking mechanism scan his EID signature. He thought of his dead sister, his emotional password. The carbo-titanium composite lock buzzed, then cracked open. He fished out his favoured S&W plasma-bullet pistol, night lenses, navcon, and a pulse grenade. He fixed the locket around his neck, tucking it under a tight-fitting Chorazin vest.

Descending from his apartment, he took a service elevator down to ground level, entered a disused building, and forced open the rusted door. Broken glass crunched under his boots, sending several dinner-sized rodents scampering away. He continued down a metal spiral staircase until he reached a lead-lined storm door in the basement. Prying it open, he entered the stinking sewer that ran between the still-radioactive ruins of old Los Angeles, and the rad-free cave cities deeper below ground. He headed for the Eden Mission complex in New LA, five kilometres away. He knew why they couldn't find Sandy anywhere in the city – she'd never left the Eden Mission building.

Chapter 8

Snow

Micah lay half-awake, half-dreaming that he was on Eden, with something alien crouching over him. He didn't want to open his eyes. He heard a rustling sound, like sand-paper being crumpled. Inside this grating noise he could hear his name.

"Micah. *Micah!*"

It shouted his name, shaking him, screaming at him, growing to an ear-splitting roar.

He jerked awake with a gasp, clasping linen sheets. Hospital room, he assessed straight away, from the white everywhere and the sharp smell of disinfectant. A twang of nausea gripped his stomach. A blonde woman leaned over him, emerald green irises reefed with sharp brown borders. The way she studied him reminded him of a bird of prey. After a second he placed her as Louise, the Chorazin agent in his apartment. In the room's cruel brightness he noticed several lines around the eyes – she was older than he'd first thought. He tried to smile but was overwhelmed by a throbbing that hammered outward from the centre of his brain. His face contorted into an ugly grimace. He rolled to his side, groaning, sure he was going to throw up.

"He's awake," Louise said. "I'm out of here."

Despite the churning in his stomach he rolled back so he could see her. She reached over his head to do something he couldn't see. However, he got a ring-side seat, observing the honed contours of her torso as it stretched within the narrow confines of her black tunic; all sinews and taut flesh. He heard something mechanical twist, and a flood of cooling rain burst in his head, drowning the pounding that had been there moments before.

"Trimorph, Micah," she said. "Pleasure and pain, never that far apart, really."

She left his field of vision, stiletto heels clacking her way out of the room. She paused at the doorway. "Later?" she asked, clearly not talking to him. Micah didn't hear a reply, but the door swished behind her a little harsher than necessary. He listened to the dull susurration of the aircon, and the distant gurgling of assorted liquids invading his body via catheters in his wrists and neck. His eyes glazed toward the tiled ceiling, but despite the gentle warmth flushing through his body, as if he'd slipped into a foaming bath, he didn't relax. He'd already guessed who else was in the room.

"Welcome back from the dead, Micah."

The crisp, word-perfect enunciated speech-pattern was still fresh in his mind, from just before whatever had happened to him. He scrunched his face, trying to remember. He'd been at home, in the lounge with two Chorazin agents, Vince and Louise, questioning him; Mom with the bread-knife; and he'd just decided to tell Vince why he'd gone to see the Project Manager… who was *dead!* Then that sound – a micro-lite. And then – here.

His speech came out like little black slugs. "Er…Vinz? S'at you?" He coughed, trying to get his larynx to work properly. Some spittle dislodged, and he swallowed, which took some effort, making him gag into the bargain. He was glad Louise had already left. "What happened? Where's my Mom? Is she okay?" He tried to sit up but nothing happened. His heart accelerated – was he paralysed? Whatever it was had hit him in the back, he recalled. He saw a black sleeved arm reach above him, and he felt the upper part of the bed inclining slowly, accompanied by a low motorised hum. As his viewpoint shifted, he recognised that he was indeed in a small private hospital room, one bed, a single window to his left, a couple of metres away, and an opaque sliding door directly ahead of him. Two uncomfortable-looking chrome chairs, one on each side of the bed, were the only other furniture. But it was suspiciously quiet for a hospital – at least any he'd been in before. No muffled sounds or cries of infants, or even creaking trolleys. He guessed he was in a Chorazin medical facility.

"That's better," Vince said, in such a clipped fashion that Micah wasn't sure who it was meant to be better for. His uncertainty didn't last long.

"Now we can see each other. We have a few important issues to discuss."

He cast an eye over Vince: gun metal grey uniform, the vermillion Chorazin crest on the left breast, showing an eagle, one claw clasped around the blade of a dagger. Micah had read somewhere that no one outside the Chorazin knew what it signified. He watched Vince stalk over to the window. Every step measured. Micah presumed it was a holo-window, since it had a pre-War view – nowhere in this State had that kind of sunshine and blue sky anymore. And birdsong, that was too much. No birds lived in the cities anymore, or anywhere near them, especially as there was no longer any grass to give rise to the insects they'd eat.

The holo-window meant they could be anywhere, even underground. Vince turned to face him, hands behind his back, still standing bolt upright, not bothering to lean on the window ledge. This guy is all about control, tightly wrapped.

"You were shot with a voltage compression charge – a bullet big enough to cause massive organ damage and death, and an electrical charge high enough to fry your heart and engrams at the same time." He smiled thinly. "Best of both worlds. They wanted you dead – twice – first the bomb under your apartment, and then very quickly afterwards with a reliably terminal weapon. Some consolation for you is that the assassin is probably experiencing difficulties for failing twice to claim his or her target."

Micah stared at Vince, mouth open. Why kill me? He didn't say it out loud, it seemed so ludicrous. He was just a systems analyst, a telemetry expert for heaven's sake. But then why was he still alive? That question seemed less preposterous, somehow.

"Then, how come…?" he tried to gesture with his right arm, but a thunderbolt of pain stopped him dead within a centimetre. "Fuck!" Panting, he experimented, very slowly, and some movement returned. He placed his arm back on the bed. He closed his eyes momentarily, the pillow supporting the back of his head. Not paralysed, then.

"The jacket you were wearing, Micah. You told me the nannites were inactive, as per the law."

Micah raised his eyelids to see Vince walk towards one of two metallic chairs, laying a hand on one, but remained standing, looking down on him.

He concentrated, with difficulty. He knew about the nannite-embedded jackets, worn by high-ranking military commanders in the last war. The nannites could react unbelievably fast, in picoseconds, changing the composition of the jacket to become a momentary barrier, protecting the wearer from harm, or at least usually from death. He couldn't recall his mother ever saying it was *inactive* – he'd just assumed it was. Nor had she ever explained how his father had come to own one, since he wasn't high-ranking, although he'd died with honours. Micah had never studied the medals that closely. They were gaudy reminders to Micah of where his father's priorities had always lain, away from his family.

He knew, as everyone did, of the infamous Nannite catastrophe which in only a month morphed fifty million people into muddy mush, and came close to infecting the whole planet. Since then it was highly illegal to own active nannites, in any form. Even in the War they were only brought out in limited supply after too many generals were assassinated by DNA-homing darts.

The risks of nannites mutating were deemed so high that possession alone carried the death penalty. Ignorance might commute the death sentence to life, but was difficult to prove in a court of law. He had to tread very carefully.

"So, it was active? I guess that means I'm in big trouble with the NRC?"

Vince walked over to Micah, very close, so that his head filled Micah's whole field of vision. He had the type of streamlined baldness that zeroed you in on its owners' eyes. Micah felt cornered by a cobra.

"Micah, it means three things. First, your mother has confessed to knowledge of the nannites and stated that you knew nothing. You should be proud, particularly in an era when most parents these days take out indemnity covenants in case their offspring decide to sue them later on in life. Second, it means that if we go to the public authorities, she will be executed, or with leniency, serve her remaining days in the state penitentiary." He strode to the window, turning his back.

Micah made to clench his fists, but his hands failed pathetically. His instinct was to find something spiked to throw at Vince's back. But he was in no condition to attempt any such thing, and suspected in any case that Vince would dodge it, or worse, catch it in mid air. *This is what Chorazin do. Keep you off-balance. I must play this out at his level. Remain calm.* He spoke, his voice not as steady as he'd hoped.

"That jacket saved my life. From some terrorist murderer, most likely. She saved my life. How could you let her be prosecuted? What possible good would that serve?" He tried to think *Chorazin*. He knew that compassion wasn't in the Chorazin lexicon.

Vince stared outwards, as if he hadn't heard Micah's outburst. Micah tried to think. What did Vince want? And then it struck home. Micah had to acknowledge he was caught, to submit, to surrender. He thought of his mother, and his father, the big hero to others, no longer round to protect her. *So be it.* He decided to try and gain some kind of concession, though. He'd seen enough vids…

"Alright, you said three things. What's the third?"

Vince spun around, fixing his eyes on Micah's; no emotion.

"Third – you go back to the Eden Mission, but you work for me. We root out, then neutralise, the Alician threat. Afterwards, the jacket ends up an anonymous donation to the Memorial Military Museum, you never see me again, your mother is released, and she bakes you apple pies." He flashed a pencil-line smile.

Micah scowled. He felt like a rodent half-inside the mouth of a snake. He needed to find an edge, some act of defiance, no matter how small.

"And if you die, Vince, before it's over? Do my Mom and I go down with you?" On instinct, he added, "Would you leave me in the hands of Louise?"

There was a subtle shift in those eyes, something small. The analyst part of Micah's mind jumped to a conclusion that there was tension between Vince and Louise. He clung to it, some small reaction at least. Reluctantly, he considered what his father would have said. *Why not try it?*

"I want my mother released unconditionally. I'll work for you, you have my word."

Vince nodded. Micah calmed down a little, though it had seemed too easy. Vince touched a panel and the door swished open, revealing an empty white corridor. Micah thought he heard a distant cry, or was it an adult scream?

"Wait," Micah said. "What happens next? I can hardly move for the pain. What am I supposed to do like this? And where's my Mom now – is she okay?"

"Your mother was released two hours ago."

Micah's relief at this news barely compensated for the instant humiliation he felt.

"You can call her before you leave. The doctor will give you something for the pain. We call it a booster. They were used in the War to keep people going when they should have really been in hospital in a coma. The pain will disappear. You'll actually feel very good, for at least seventy-two hours. In an hour you go back to work. However, you've lost thirty-six hours, so we called in sick for you – you had a random rad-check at your local clinic, according to the records." Vince's smile radiated ice. "You do your job for now, Micah, and your job is to re-establish the real link to the Ulysses."

Micah couldn't disguise his surprise.

"We found out why you went to see the Project Manager. While you've been out cold, we've been busy. Mr. Kane got a message out before he was killed, but our man didn't arrive in time."

Vince's brow furrowed for a moment, as he appeared to weigh something up in his mind. His face smoothed again, as he touched the panel, sealing the door closed again.

"Micah – I'm going to give you some information, because it's important you understand the gravity of the situation. You also appear to put things together pretty fast – that's your training as an analyst, I assume." He interlaced his fingers and then pushed them outwards, cracking the knuckles.

"Bad for the joints," Micah offered.

"Unfortunately, the Alicians have also been busy. Fifteen key Chorazin operatives worldwide were assassinated early this morning in various cities around the world. My own network – aside from Louise – was eradicated. We don't yet know why, or whether it's connected with the Eden Mission. But we believe the Alicians are accelerating their operations. Again, we don't know why."

Micah still found it all surreal. How could he be mixed up in this? He'd often fantasised about being involved in some grand plot, but – fifteen people dead! His new-found tough self-image that he'd been basing on vid characters had to hit the slope sprinting. And it wasn't a vid – real people's lives had just… stopped. And he'd nearly been one of them.

"But am I meant to do things, you know, covertly? My colleagues, especially Rudi, will know if I start checking into the transmission source."

Vince cocked an eyebrow.

Micah tried to sit up, to think straighter, but couldn't. Then he understood. "Bait! You're using me as bait!"

"Your analytic training wasn't a complete waste of money. Yes, the Alicians will try again. They never leave loose ends. You might as well be performing a useful function. And we'll be watching your back."

"The jacket saved me last time, not you." He felt a welling-up of anger – at being shot, at suddenly being thrust into all of this; anger about his job, his life, Antonia, his father; at being coerced into a probably fatal role in some game he neither understood nor cared about. He began to fear he'd be overcome by this sudden torrent of emotion, even though he realised it must be at least partly related to the drugs coursing through him.

Vince gave a small shrug. "Fair point," he said. "This is a war, Micah. You and I aren't each other's enemies. The enemy is out there. They want you dead. They also want Sandy dead."

He'd forgotten about Sandy, and although his last encounter with her had been abrasive, she was like him now, a pawn caught up in something neither of them had volunteered for.

Vince added, "She's still missing. Louise is trying to find her before they do."

He knew Vince was right, but despite himself, he launched a fresh attack.

"But why *are* we at war, Vince, eh? Why are the Alicians here? Does it ever occur to you that they only exist, only thrive, because of the Chorazin and its excessive measures?"

Vince laughed, shaking his head. He walked over to the window, touched a small panel on the wall. 'Outside', it began to snow. "Well, I can see you're feeling much better. Anger is a more useful emotion than people realise, and you're going to need your strength. I'm neither philosopher nor historian, Micah – I'm a pragmatist, so I'm not going to get into socio-political rhetoric with you. I never, *ever* sympathise with the enemy. But let me leave you with something to ponder." He reached over to the drip feeding trimorph into Micah's veins and shut it off. For Micah it felt like being thrown out of a warm bed into a bath full of ice and glass. He gasped, but gritted his teeth, determined to say nothing.

"Our most recent intelligence suggests that the Alicians are a much older organisation than we ever suspected. I know what you're going to say – their very name, *Alicians*, a nickname taken from one of the early, vitriolic verbal assaults on them by our late President before they took up arms, comparing their political naivety to Alice in Wonderland – is too recent. But did you ever wonder *why* they accepted this name so quickly?"

Micah decided to store these points for later analysis. He simmered. He glanced upward at the trimorph control, out of his reach.

Vince carried on. "You're right, of course, at least partly – the situation surrounding the creation and rise of the Chorazin may have actually increased their support and given them a substantial legitimate political base via the Fundies. But I assure you Micah, that even without the Chorazin, they'd be here. And maybe they want people to think just the way you do. The greatest weapon in earth's history has always been ideology. With ideology you can persuade millions to fight, to revolt, to resist, or to give up and never fight. So, Micah, the question is, what do the Alicians really want?"

Micah had no immediate answer. He'd always considered them as counter-point to the Chorazin. It was his turn to shrug, painful though that was.

"Exactly," Vince said. "One of our intelligence agents recently uncovered something, a deeper scheme. He was terminated before he could give any information over a secure network. But he was one of our top operatives, and he was pretty scared. Well, we found a few pieces of him yesterday morning." Vince faced Micah again. "So, Micah, you decide who your enemy is. And if you're ever unsure, take a look at the bruises on your back. Or ask your mother. And one more thing. You should freshen up before you go to work. Trust me, you look infinitely worse than you feel."

Vince walked to the door, palmed it open, and stepped outside into a bland corridor, the door swishing closed behind him.

Micah watched the snow falling for some time, cooling his anger. He'd read about the Chorazin, how they were trained in advanced psychological manipulation techniques. Perhaps Vince was telling the truth, but probably only as he saw it. The Chorazin used ideology themselves, and precise, constrained information flow. Disinformation as well, to keep Chorazin members aligned and on track. Fear – always a deeper, more sinister plot – the favourite myth of the despotic hierarchy. He decided then and there that he didn't believe a word of it. But now that the anger had subsided, the full extent of the pain from his back returned with a vengeance. He hoped the doctor would turn up soon with this miracle booster injection. Reluctantly, he also wished his mother was there to comfort him. The tough hero image he was experimenting with could re-emerge later.

But as he lay there, thoughts of his father intruded. He'd died in a decisive battle for Indonesia, near the end of the War. Died a war hero. Micah had had heroism rammed down his throat since he'd been a child. Yet he'd seen the other side of it, how it tore up families, how heroes usually had sharp edges with their spouses, how they couldn't tolerate weakness from their own offspring – they could save people they didn't know, but fail to protect and nurture their own.

He'd not shed a single tear at the full military honours funeral. Nor had he ever really considered how his father had actually died. For the first time, he imagined his father lying prone on that blood-soaked battle-ground in Jakarta, the life draining out of him while all hell was breaking loose, the din of combat all around. He wondered what his father would have been thinking in those last moments, whether the heroism, the honour, even the war itself would have been finally irrelevant as he'd felt life slipping away. Instead, maybe, just maybe, he'd have focused on the smaller people in his life, his family.

Micah shut out the hospital room, the world. He imagined himself on the bloodied battlefield, sitting by his dying father. He wouldn't reach out his own hand unless his father did first, which was unlikely. Still, Micah remained, not speaking, not looking at his father, just staying there with him at the end, as the snowflakes slowly settled on both of them. It was the best he could offer.

Chapter 9

Decompression

The outer airlock door hissed closed and clunked into its locked position. Blake peered through the porthole into the fourth compartment. In the dimming light he could just make out the helmeted silhouettes of Zack and Pierre. Even in the near darkness, he could tell both men were stressed, shoulders tensed inside their suits. They were immobile, like statues from the New Smithsonian. He secured his lanyard to the airlock eyebolt, and strained to see the ghoster.

"Pierre, very slowly, lower your flashlight to the floor, point it to the ceiling like an uplighter – it has good night vision, we don't."

As Pierre obeyed, Blake caught his first glimpse of the creature – still basically human in shape. It crouched behind the neutralino detonator. The last time he had seen one… he skipped over the memory. He glanced down through his visor to check the self-rigged short-range land-mine lashed onto his chest. The push-button actuator protruded two centimetres. It would kill him and the ghoster, but the others should survive.

He circled his tongue inside his mouth a few times to generate some saliva, and then swallowed, angling his two pulse rifles forwards at rib height. "Okay, everyone listen up. This is what'll happen. I'll count down in one second intervals from five to one. On 'Two', Zack go short to the left, Pierre, go three metres to the right, so you don't shoot each other in crossfire. On 'One' I'll open the door, and that creature will do one of two things – it'll either come straight at me, or go for you, Pierre. I know you have the pulse rifle, but at close quarters Zack is a better shot. Reel out your lanyards so they don't auto-stop when you jump. Kat – stay sharp and speak only if urgent. Any questions?"

"Just one, Skip," Zack said. "What's the surprise you have in store?"

"Then it wouldn't be a surprise, would it?" He couldn't tell Zack, or else he'd try to save him, and they'd all end up dead.

Blake took the silence that followed as assent. He drew in a breath. "Five."

Pierre reeled out several metres of lanyard, not taking his eyes off the ghoster, nor lowering his weapon. He couldn't help but wonder if he was being used as bait because of the friendship between Blake and Zack. But there was logic in the plan. Even though he had the rifle, he'd never been in a real battle, and might freeze up. Zack wouldn't.

"Four."

A trickle of cold sweat rolled down Zack's spine. He'd been in too many battles to worry anymore about whether he would survive. He just wanted to get as many shots into the ghoster as possible. He wasn't too sure of the "surprise" – especially after Blake's once-only hesitation to kill the last one in Kurana Bay. He flexed his knees, shifting his weight onto his thighs, ready to spring.

"Three."

Thirty metres away, Kat sat in the cockpit, wondering how long it would take after the others were dead for the ghoster to make it to her, if it bothered at all. The landmine was a noble gesture, but she'd heard how indestructible these genetically re-engineered soldiers were, having been morphed with reptile genomes to make them fast and very, very tough. She chewed on a knuckle as she watched the screens, oblivious of how hard she bit down.

"Two."

Blake watched Zack and Pierre dive to left and right, and open fire. The ghoster leapt faster and higher than seemed possible, ricocheting off the ceiling, heading straight towards Pierre. Its head bobbed lizard-like to left and right, making it a tempting but elusive target.

"One!" He rammed the "open" button with the rifle muzzle. The airlock door stayed closed. *Christ! Not now!* "Kat! Power!" He smashed a glass panel with the butt of his rifle to gain access to the manual lever, knowing it could take thirty seconds to open the hatch by hand. He cursed again, as he had to put both weapons down to try and get the door open.

He watched helplessly as Pierre got five rounds off into its chest before the creature smashed the firearm out of his arms, almost dislocating Pierre's shoulder, and lunged forward with a claw-like hand to break his neck. Zack fired successive shots into the creature's knee, causing it to lose its balance. Pierre kicked hard at its left side, trying to knock it over, as he dived out of range. A swipe from the ghoster's claw-like hand hammered onto the floor where Pierre's head had been a split second earlier, denting the metal deck.

The ghoster sprang backward off its good leg and spun in mid-air, hit the front of the neutralino detonator, and then rebounded off, colliding with Zack, knocking his pistol out of his gloved hand. Zack dodged the ghoster's gnarled fist just in time as it pistoned into the hull, sending a deafening echo around the room.

"Got it!" shouted Kat, re-energizing the relays. "Captain, it's armed the detonator! Fifty-seven seconds!"

The hatch slid open. Blake snatched up both rifles in one fluid motion and began firing, just as it stamped its good leg down on Zack's knee. Zack yelled with pain, while Pierre got to his feet and loosened his lanyard, his shattered pulse rifle lying next to him. Six shots from Blake pounded into the ghoster's right side, enough to make it turn. Zack, his faceplate close to the ghoster's eyeless head, rammed his knife into its stomach, between ribs that criss-crossed its torso, twisting the serrated blade between the scales. The ghoster's scream intensified as it leapt off Zack towards Blake.

He fired both weapons at the ghoster in synchrony. Each double-pulse shot shoved it back, but still it closed on him. The ghoster's mottled scales glowed red where the pulse charges hit. It leapt forward and swept Blake's arms aside, spinning his pulse rifles against the walls. Then it saw the landmine on his chest and recoiled. For a fraction of a second, Blake could discern the features of the human face that had once been there, and almost faltered, but then he seized the ghoster's wrists and tugged it towards him, pushing his own chest outward.

With a strangled shriek, the ghoster was yanked backwards, breaking Blake's grip. Pierre's lanyard was taut around the ghoster's neck, like a lasso. After a moment of disbelief that he wasn't dead, Blake dived for one of his rifles, rolled and came up firing again, this time aiming at its head. It was losing strength, but it yanked Zack's knife out from its ribs. With its double-jointed shoulders it slashed the lanyard behind its neck and once again went for Blake, raising the knife high.

Zack, his voice choked in agony, shouted. "Pierre, hang on to something fast!" Zack fired his pistol at the escape hatch panel. Pierre threw himself towards two large crate straps and locked his arms around them. The ghoster saw where Zack was aiming and moved to grab a harness. At that moment, a shrill ghoster-like wailing erupted from the comms system, causing the ghoster to spin around to see where it was coming from. Blake fired twice hitting it straight in the face, knocking it off-balance. At Zack's third shot, the hatch flew open.

The room depressurised with a thunderclap and a howling wind. Zack had already anchored himself. Pierre clung on for his life as his legs lifted off the ground.

Blake was whisked off his feet, suspended in mid-air by the decompression, tethered by his waist lanyard, but he kept firing at the creature. The ghoster hit the man-sized hole and almost passed through it, but clung on to the edges with its claws digging into the metal, trying to pull its body back inside the ship.

Blake knew that if it hung on for a few seconds longer, the room would fully depressurise, and then it would enter the room and once again attack.

Kat shouted "No!" as he retrieved his own knife and in one smooth cut slashed through his lanyard. The suction propelled him head-first into the ghoster. He spread his arms wide and smashed into the ghoster full-on, head-butting its chest like a human cannonball. With one last gurgling scream, the creature lost its grip and reeled into space. Blake's shoulders tore at him as he fought to prevent himself being dragged out too. With his head poking through the hull, he watched the ghoster flail wildly, spinning away from the ship. When it reached the invisible warp shell, it blazed bright as a meteorite for a second, then was gone. The depressurization ceased, and the artificial gravity pulled Blake back inside.

Kat came on-line, desperate. "Pierre, the detonator!"

Pierre sprang over to the ND console. For a moment he stared at it. He hit several keys, his left hand steadying his right wrist. The counter stopped at two seconds. He slumped down with his back to the ND, raised his knees, and rested his helmeted head on them.

Blake had landed hard on the floor, where he crouched, panting, sweat streaming past his ears inside his helmet. He lifted his wrist console and checked the heart rate indicator: 192, descending.

Zack spoke first. "Sweet Jesus! I just aged… ten years. Nothin' to do… with relativity. Kat. Trimorph. Please… Leg …" The rest was mumbled expletives.

Blake helped Pierre upright while he flicked a few more ND switches. The counter reset to zero and three green lights glowed.

"It'll take 30 minutes to shutdown fully, Sir, but it's safe now. I'll come back later. I can seal the escape hole, but to save on air, I suggest we transfer the three remaining oxygen cylinders out of here and leave this room depressurised."

Blake was still catching his own breath. "Agreed. And thanks Pierre, that was a pretty unorthodox move back there."

Pierre was visibly shaken, but a smile cracked across his face. "Just came to me. My mother once sent me to a ranch in the Pyrenees, to get me away from equations. I spent the summer working with wild horses. They usually broke me rather than the other way round, but I learned a few rope tricks."

Blake nodded, and then looked to one of the internal cameras. "I assume that was you, Kat, distracting the ghoster."

She laughed nervously. "Felt pretty helpless up here – had to do something. I figured the one thing it wouldn't expect to hear was another ghoster. I recorded one of its screams and played it back over the speaker."

"Good work, Kat."

Blake moved over to Zack, squatting next to him. "How are you, buddy?" He stared down at his mutilated leg. The word "ugly" didn't cover it.

"Shattered. Cracked rib, too. You gonna... take off... your surprise?"

Blake tilted his head downward. The actuator had been pushed half-way in. Gingerly, he eased it back out, then twisted it clockwise, locking it into safe mode. He unhooked it and set it down on the floor.

Zack tried to laugh, grimacing. "That was... your whole... fucking plan?"

He shrugged. "Kat, meet us outside the hatch with the trimorph. He watched Zack's face contort with pain. "Double-dose."

Blake re-entered the cockpit where Zack, leg plastered in an ivory gelcast, tried unsuccessfully to find a comfortable position. Pierre and Kat slept. They were all exhausted, but someone had to stay awake – he was Captain, and Zack was in too much pain to sleep, despite the trimorph.

"That was pretty close," Zack said. "A little too much like the old days."

"Unless Eden becomes a real possibility, those days will be back soon enough." He brooded, while the silence congealed around them. He hadn't noticed how noisy the cockpit had been, until the virus wiped out most of their systems.

"What's up, Skip? Is it Robert?"

He hadn't been thinking about his dead son, though he knew why Zack might assume he was. He stored it for later. "Something else. You won't like it."

"I didn't sign up with you for happy endings."

Blake got up and walked around the small cockpit, testing various pieces of equipment; most of it didn't respond in any way. "The Alicians hold three as a holy number."

Zack's brow furrowed. "Oh, I get it. The ghoster and the computer failure: that makes two." He looked around. "You thinking another piece of equipment?"

"No. They call it a trinity attack. The three attempts must be of a different nature."

"Boss, I'm just a simple astronaut from Queens."

"You see, a computer – something electronic; a ghoster – something bio-engineered."

Zack leaned forward. "You know I'm crap at this. What comes next?"

"I'm not sure. There's no textbook, but it would be something more subtle."

Zack nudged him on the arm. "You have a hunch. What the hell is it?"

Blake frowned. "Trouble is, once I say it, it's out, there's no going back, and if I'm wrong…"

"Goddammit, Blake. Tell me what you think it is. What if you're right? At least let me know, just in case, you know…"

"Something happens to me?"

Zack shrugged, then winced with pain.

"Okay. Here it is: one of us. Unconscious implant, so we'd get through the screening, unaware until a pre-set trigger event or signal."

Zack sat back and let out a whistle. "You're right. I don't like it at all. We'll be watching each other like hawks, knowing that once the implant is triggered, that person will turn into a homicidal maniac." Zack pounded the upper part of his cast with a fist.

Blake raised an eyebrow. "Does that help?"

"Sometimes one pain can dull another." He scratched his cast where he'd just been hitting it. "Makes you wonder though, don't it, why they've gone through all this trouble to stop us getting there?"

Blake pursed his lips. "They feed on people's desperation. Eden is hope; spoils their rhetoric, not to mention their balance sheet." He wanted to spit.

Zack shifted position, grimaced, and shifted back. "I guess." He heaved himself up, and began limping out of the cockpit, then paused. "Hey, hang on a minute – the oxygen situation. How's that fit with your implant theory?"

Blake spoke quietly. "Pierre said the oxygen left will just do if two of us go into stasis until we get within half a light year of Eden."

"So, which two? If one of us has an implant…?"

"Good question, my friend, good question."

Chapter 10

Stakes

Four months earlier…

Blake stood on the threshold of the antique wood-panelled office. The smell of leather upholstery, mingled with the residue of a Havana cigar, drifted out into the corridor. The mid-afternoon blinds created a lattice of orange shafts of light which sliced diagonally across the office. The rays framed the slim, seated figure surrounded by a nebula of drifting dust motes. It gave Blake the overall impression of a miniature galaxy, this one man as its epicentre.

From his silhouette, Blake recognised someone who used to be a fit soldier. But age and battle had exacted their toll, lending a hollowed-out leanness to the body. Still, the alertness, obvious in the angle of the neck and head, spoke of someone who was no stranger to command. The seated man with five polished stars on his shirt collar looked up from a holo-pad and punched a desk control, snapping the blinds shut, restoring the lighting to a more tolerable sunset level. Blake had seen what was on the holo-pad before it had cleared – photos of the four assassinated astronauts who were to have led the Ulysses mission to Eden. Blake had wanted this mission like hell, but not at this price.

"Come in, Blake," he said, his voice raspish but firm. "And don't salute me. I sit behind a desk too much these days to respect myself, so I don't want it from you of all people."

Blake saluted anyway, and waited, standing to attention.

"At ease, soldier," General Kilaney sighed.

Blake nodded and sat down in the chair indicated. He remained straight-backed, refusing to surrender to the inviting black leather. He noticed how much weight his old mentor had lost.

"I see you haven't lost the tricks of the trade." The General passed Blake a glass of iced water. Blake took it and clinked glasses with him. A single splash of bourbon escaped from the General's tumbler, as he met Blake with defiant eyes. "To absent friends."

Blake held his glass high. "To absent friends." He savoured the cool water. It was thirty-five Celsius outside, even in the depth of winter high in the Rockies. Somewhere he could hear soldiers marching, being drilled. Some things never changed.

He sipped gingerly and watched the General – his erstwhile mentor – wondering whether he would indeed end up like him, stuck behind a desk these past ten years, shuffling papers instead of soldiers, riding a holo-rig instead of a real fighter, wasting away in endless meetings. Still, he respected the General. The NWA, the shaky Post-War coalition of some fifty-three aligned nations, needed people like him near the top. He waited while the General scrutinised him over the rim of his glass. His eyes hadn't lost their edge.

"How's Glenda doing?" the General asked.

Blake's grip on the glass became iron. "Fine, Sir. She's doing fine," he replied. "Thanks for asking."

The General slammed his glass down on the edge of his desk, grabbed the sides of the chair and hauled himself up. "Stay put, Captain! And don't give me any more bull. This is me you're talking to. I said how the hell is she?"

He took another sip, not meeting the General's gaze. He felt the soothing water travel down his throat, but a moment later it felt as dry as the Potomac river bed.

"First cancer successfully treated.' He took another sip. "With the ambient rad-levels, it's almost certain to return within a year." He paused, feeling the pressure rise in his chest, pushing up against his throat. He didn't want to say it. He hadn't said it to Glenda, though she knew well enough. He took a breath. "Then she'll have a few months at most – second timers don't usually…" He willed his fingers to ease off the glass.

The General perched on the desk. "Damned sorry. You tell her that, Blake."

He wanted to change the subject. "Sir, why – "

"You pretty much have command of the mission, there's just the final psy check tomorrow, then it's yours."

He nodded once. He'd worked so hard for this, even if others would assume he only got it because of his so-called "hero" status.

"Thank you, Sir."

"Well, I don't mind telling you and no one else – I always had you as first choice. Kacheng was a good man, sure, but his assassination put you back in front."

He flinched at the memory of Alpha Team's shuttle exploding in a shroud of white-hot flame seconds after take-off to Zeus. He stared down at his glass. The last shards of misty ice surrendered to the afternoon heat. "Who's my team, Sir?"

The General slumped back down into his chair. "Zack will be your first officer and Chief Pilot."

Blake allowed himself a sigh of relief.

"The other two – well, one thing about the Forces is I don't have to argue with you about it. You'll have Pierre Bertrand as Science Officer and our Katrina Beornwulf, on Comms."

He stiffened. "Bertrand – you can't mean Professor Bertrand's son? After his father blocked all our gen-defence research during the War? And Beornwulf – you want me to baby-sit?" He stood up and walked around to the back of the chair. "Permission to speak freely, Sir?"

The General's eyes glinted as he raised his glass in a mock toast. "Denied. I know neither one is your choice, but Pierre's a genius, and smart too, and you and I understand both the difference and the rarity of the combination. Don't blame him for the sins of his father. Beornwulf – well, she passed all the exams. Practically a comms wizard, and the last thing we need is a third loss of communications. Anyway, her uncle and all that… You can't always avoid politics. God knows we owe both France and England enough."

He noticed how weary the General seemed, the hollowing around the eyes, that haunted look. He instinctively glanced to the General"s right wrist, under the shirt-sleeve cuff. He could just make out the tell-tale small triangular holes of a micro-transfusion implant. He met the General"s gaze again – the look on his face confirmed it, but the General continued unabated.

"Blake, there's more. And it's Black level. You don't tell anyone – not Zack, not Glenda, not even your mistress if you damned well had one. Nobody outside this room."

Blake leaned forward.

"Why do we need Eden?"

He sharpened his eyes on the General. He couldn't be joking. "We need its resources. In the longer term, a sister planet for Earth – we can colonize it, though it will take around –"

"Fifty years." The General finished the sentence for him. "We have ten, that's all."

Blake's mouth opened involuntarily. He thought of all the things he could say, but there would be no point. He studied the deep lines on the

General's face that spoke of heavy responsibilities and things nobody would want to know, but somebody had to.

"Sir?"

"The biosphere isn't going to recover. Not for around fifty *thousand* years. We have maybe ten years like this, hiding from the sun, waking and sleeping in our sweat unless we're fortunate enough to live underground. You know the only remaining productive food farms lie in the Polar grain-belts, but a couple of years after the last sub sea permafrost is gone, the *average* temperature outside will shoot up from forty-five to sixty-five degrees Celsius. In one year. Unsustainable."

Blake needed to be sure. "But the research – I'm no scientist, but I took a good look. The re-forestation; the Arctic re-freeze project…"

The General waved a hand. "Statistics and lies – garnished with some truth, of course, but the climate cascade we instigated with our little nuclear catharsis is locked in. We'll actually have a drop in temperature of a couple of degrees in the next five years, but then it will rise and keep on rising, linear at first, and then after a decade, a step change."

"What about the lunar projects? Mars reclamation?"

"Won't work on the moon without Earth's resources. And Mars – well, Mars is probably what we're going to look like a million years from now; after we've cooled down again."

He trusted this man's judgement – he was high enough in the machinery to have quality information. He sank back into the chair, draining his glass.

"Now you see, Blake. You see why we *need* Eden. Survival. Plain and simple. We have a decade to start colonizing it, and start building as many ships as possible."

"We'll only move a fraction of the population, even if things go well. The Alcubierre Drive won't handle transport-sized ships."

"I know, it'll be tough. But we've had some luck recently with this new dark matter tech. Maybe with another research break… If we can get Earth organised… But only if there's the dream – if Eden fails, all humanity will see is the abyss – we'll tear ourselves apart before the end. So, Eden's the only game plan, our last chance. Someone needs to set foot on it, come back, talk about it, shout about it."

Blake nodded slowly, but in so doing, he knew he was transferring the tremendous weight from the Old Man's shoulders onto his own.

"You can handle it, Blake. Frankly, I don't know another who could – except maybe me, fifteen years ago." He heaved himself up out of his chair. "Two more things," he said, as he picked up the bourbon bottle and held it out. This time Blake nodded, and watched the cedar-coloured alcohol sluice into his empty tumbler.

"You have to return with good news. Eden is like propaganda during a war, but this time everyone needs it – they need the dream, or God help us all. Whatever it takes – that's why I wanted you in the first place. You get the mission done, even if you have to leave people behind."

Blake winced inside.

"Oh, I know you lost a lot of men in Kurana Bay. But you completed your orders. You understood what I taught you all those years ago. Mission first, men second. It sucks. Most soldiers can't handle it. You can. It'll be rule number one on this mission."

Blake gazed into the bourbon. He'd been having the old nightmares again, seeing faces of the dead, their unseeing eyes wide, as if they still had something to say. "Second thing, Sir?"

"Heracles didn't suffer an accident. It was sabotage – we don't know how yet, but there's no question about it. Explosion. Tore the ship apart. They never stood a chance."

Blake felt the hairs on the back of his neck prickle, but he wasn't surprised. He'd known that crew well, too. "Alicians?"

"Seems crazy, but the more society unravels and despair sets in, the more people turn to those bastard Fundies, and the more support bleeds into their terrorist wing. They're a virus, and they're making us weak just when it's our last chance to be strong and survive. It almost makes me long for the days of the Chinese Dragon Hegemony before WWIII tore that abomination apart – at least they thought long term."

Blake narrowed his eyes as he remembered something. "You know what Professor Bertrand said? He said that the rise of a global religion, with easy-to-follow rules and a multi-cultural God was inevitable after a global war." But then Blake remembered more – he'd said the rise of fundamentalism had been *engineered*. No one had paid much attention to him by then – he'd moved too far beyond his comfortable scientific domain to the treacherous landscape of politics. He'd also developed a habit of ranting in public. And after he'd been assassinated, gigaquads of his data disappeared in the infamous web-net crash. "I never quite grasp why they fear Eden, Sir."

The General swirled the remaining bourbon in his glass. "Well, my father told me a long time ago the last thing a priest wants to see is a genuine miracle – it reminds ordinary people that priests are servants – representatives – not the real thing. Alicians don't like it. But Eden's a miracle alright, and we damn well need it. And we'll fight for it all the way." He raised his glass.

Blake remembered how different the General had been at his and Glenda's wedding twenty-three years ago, bursting with life and energy. Everyone had told Blake he was marrying too young, but this man, a captain then, had told Blake to listen to everyone, then do what his heart commanded, and never second-guess himself afterwards. It had been his way of life ever since. He owed this man a great deal. "You can count on me, Sir."

The General eased backwards and closed his eyes, a hint of a smile emerging.

Blake stared again at the General's wrist, wrapped in frail skin like waxed paper. Glenda had the same microporous chemo transfer system. He sensed the formalities were over, and cleared his throat. "What stage are you, Bill?"

The General's smile faltered, but his eyes stayed shut. For the first time in Blake's presence, he spoke softly, his voice no longer in uniform. "I should be around to hear you arrived on Eden, but I'll miss your homecoming. Now, go home to Glenda, leave an old man in peace."

Blake knew better than to push the issue – dignity, the last vestige of this man's identity, was all that was keeping him going. He got up quietly, and parked his half-full glass on the desk. At the doorway he took one last look, saluted and held it for a long moment, then closed the door behind him with a soft click, as if closing the coffin lid on a dear friend.

Chapter 11

Kurana Bay

Ten years earlier…

Zack heard the shouting voices, including his own, screaming at Blake.

"Pull the trigger; take him out for Christ's sake!" Zack saw the ghoster leaping from man to man, ripping out their throats like they were paper soldiers on a daisy chain. Only Blake had a clear shot. But he wouldn't take it. The screeching of the ghoster was mind-numbing, but Zack fought against it. Ted and Abe fell as the ghoster smashed their skulls together, ignoring the two commando knives they had both buried half-way into its thorax.

"Blake! Shoot! For fuck's sake shoot!" Zack knew why he didn't. *Sons of bitches!* He limped, blood pissing from a gaping wound in his left leg, his left arm already broken, a machete in his right hand. Shots rang out but only Blake had the Slow Gun, the ghoster killer that embedded a delayed pulse charge inside the body, exploding it from the inside. Archie and Kalim were grappling with it but it was triple jointed and soon it had them, snapping both their necks with a dual, sickening crunch. Only three of them remained. Charlie pinned himself against the wall, terrified.

"Charlie, high and low, you high!" Charlie glared, knowing it meant his death, but he bit his lip and screamed like a madman, flinging himself high in the air, two razor sharp machetes raised to strike it, while a fraction of a second later, Zack dropped onto his back, pushed off from the wall with his good leg, and slid in the blood-soaked floor. The ghoster caught both Charlie's wrists and was about to bite through his jugular when beneath him Zack slashed six inches through the ghoster's groin. It couldn't raise a foot to crush Zack's skull because Charlie's weight was still on him. It spun Charlie's left wrist, breaking it, and drove one of the machetes through Charlie's neck, decapitating him. Blood sprayed the walls. Zack chopped the left leg of the ghoster clean off at the calf. It somehow kept its balance, threw Charlie's slack body away, and hopped to face Zack, Charlie's machete in its claw. Zack gazed into those hooded eyes he had once known so well. There was a dull popping sound and a flash of light.

The ghoster looked down at the hole in its stomach, then it exploded, flinging parcels of flesh and clay-coloured blood over the entire room. Blake had fired the weapon.

Zack crawled over towards Blake, past the open-mouthed head of the ghoster, finally silent. Blake sagged against a wall, bleeding from a chest wound caused in the first seconds when they'd encountered the ghoster, only a minute ago, after having destroyed most of the ghoster complex and set free a dozen captives, and killed four more ghosters already transformed but not activated. Once transformed, there was no way back.

Zack leaned against the wall too, next to Blake, surveying the carnage. They both looked inevitably towards the ghoster's head: the trace of curly black hair still apparent if you knew where to look; a scar on the cheek from a farming accident two years ago; the mottled Caucasian skin. Zack noticed Blake's right hand trembling. It had never done so before, not in nearly three years of battle. But Zack knew why it did now. It was the hand that had pulled the trigger.

They'd come to Kurana Bay, deep behind enemy lines, because they'd captured and interrogated a ghoster scientist to find out the location of the processing centre. They'd heard a rumour they were using POWs as ghosters. After the questioning, they were going to send the man back to base for further interrogation. The scientist had known he would be tortured by Chorazin there, so he'd taunted Blake with terrible information, and it had worked. Blake had slit the man's throat from ear to ear and watched him bleed to death, convulsing for a full minute. It seemed too lenient now, as Zack gazed at the head of the boy he'd been godfather to.

Zack studied Blake's ashen face, as he stared at the ghoster's – the boy's – head. And when he spoke, it was not the voice of his captain Zack heard, but of a man distraught, chopped up inside, who would never be whole again. He turned to Zack, tears streaming down his face, mixing with the bloodstains of his offspring.

"They took my son, Zack! They took Robert and they stole his soul!"

There was nothing Zack could say. He gathered up the dog tags of their dead platoon members, got the released captives – young boys Robert's age – and Blake, outside, then torched everything. A heli-jet picked them up minutes before the enemy's reinforcements arrived. They had to leave the burning bodies of their men behind, to give room for the half-drugged captives they'd saved. Zack gave Blake a heavy dose trimorph shot. It seemed the best thing to do. Robert was listed as Missing in Action. No one ever found out he'd been at Kurana Bay. Blake and Zack made sure no one ever would.

Chapter 12

Mariana Trench

Jennifer knew a prize worth fighting for when she saw it. Professor Dimitri Kostakis was a burly, brusque Greek – not the statuesque version. His goatee beard and large mahogany eyes danced in accompaniment whenever he laughed, which was often. His hands seemed far too big to manipulate the cramped submersible controls, let alone work the students he seduced.

Jennifer was the current young researcher willingly under his spell. She'd ignored the warnings, even the sad evidence of his damaged cast-offs. He was a true genius, and when they were together, they skated along the rim of scientific discovery, peering over the edge. She was along for the ride, and had no illusions about how long it would last. Besides, many of the women left in his wake were themselves now highly sought-after researchers, so great was the influence of working with this man, his mind, and his legendary resources.

Jennifer didn't consider herself pretty, being short, and a little stockier than she would have preferred. But she possessed shoulder-length auburn hair and dark bottle-green eyes, a combination she knew how to use to effect. She'd snared him when he was going through an awkward break-up with another student. She had arrived to console him when he was working late in his University office. At one point, while they were both studying a large oceanographic map of the Solomon Trench, she'd leaned across it to reach a far-flung pencil, and stayed there. She turned her head and gazed at him. He'd been surprised, but hadn't disappointed her.

A year later, given that she was now alone with him ten thousand metres underneath Pacific rollers, in the most advanced research submersible in the world, she guessed he wasn't disappointed with her either. It wasn't exactly a honeymoon, though, in the middle of nowhere in the Pacific, mid-way between Japan and New Zealand, with no decent toilet facilities since departing Guam.

She stared into the darkness outside the bathysphere's single porthole. She imagined a giant milky eye being lowered into the depths on a fishing line. But they hadn't seen anything interesting for two hours, except the ubiquitous suspended sediment, shining like lazy white worms in the bright halogen lights. Sometimes it was there, a hypnotic snowstorm, but at other times it was as if someone had painted the portholes black.

The pressure outside gave her a chill. She imagined a continent of solid, ice-cold water sinking them ever deeper, burying them so they would never return. There was no plan B, no rescue plan if anything went wrong: no standby sub, and they couldn't exactly swim ten kilometres upwards holding their breath. She switched tracks; this line of thought was on its own downward vector.

They hadn't spoken for at least thirty minutes, and she longed to hear his musical voice, to dispel the silence that hung like damp fog in the air.

"How are you?" she asked, though she hadn't been oblivious to his constant tampering with the controls for the last half hour. He'd exhausted all his funding reserves on this trip. Six months earlier a deep-probe robot sub had been lost in this God-forsaken place, but not before it had transmitted a single picture. Analyzed a thousand ways, all it revealed was a blurred angular silver shape in the vertiginous depths of the trench, with a massive metallic structure in the background. After initial media hype, it was dismissed as a camera refraction error, or at best a new species of deep-water shark, and promptly forgotten. Deep sonic probes from the surface picked up nothing, but Dimitri had argued that the very symmetry of those sonic results was suspicious. She'd been one of the few non-sycophants who also found it sinister. He had tried to link this incident with ancient stories from aboriginal tribes in the Caroline Islands, tall tales of a giant comet crashing into the seas a thousand years earlier. But whenever he'd gotten close to current sources of those oral myths, people had disappeared, unable to be traced.

She asked a second time. "I said, 'How are you?' "

He stopped fussing with the controls, and returned her gaze, his face lighting up. "I'm fine so long as you are here with me."

She loved his clichés, because she knew he really meant them, even if they all had a makeover date, when some new girl would catch his eye and become his mistress. Most Greek men, she'd heard, were like this – boys who never really grew up. She didn't care. These days, it was refreshing to know someone with so few emotional scars or hang-ups.

"You're worried," she said, hoping to spur him into conversation. If it hadn't been such a small space, she'd have expected him to stomp up and down as he did in his office, or when he was giving a lecture, exasperated at his students' inability to see beyond the equations to the larger principles, to the meaning, to the very passion of life he saw in everything. But instead she saw his ox-like shoulders sag, as he leant back in the pilot's seat that struggled to embrace his girth. He savoured all good things in life. *Gourmand*, she knew the French would call him, which English-speaking people would incorrectly translate as "greedy".

"I had hoped to find something by now. We're at least as deep as the probe was."

She'd observed him many times in action, crossing verbal swords with other academics in treacherous public scientific debates resembling gladiatorial matches. He'd left ego stains and ruined careers scraped across auditorium walls. She countered his uncharacteristic glum mood in the only way she knew would work with him. She shifted gear into scientist-mode.

"Remote probes have significant variance in calibration integrity at extreme depths. We don't know what actual depth the incident took place, or exactly where it was, to more than a precision of five hundred metres. And its black box was crushed when it imploded." She smiled, as if she'd just answered an oral exam question – with honours.

He nodded, but the frame of his smile faltered.

She knew why: it had been a major part of the mystery. The remote probe, needing no human crew, had been very tough, rated to twelve thousand metres, far deeper than where implosion occurred. As for the black box, they were all but indestructible these days, and the probe's umbilicals, once wound back up to the surface, had looked as if they'd been bitten through by very sharp teeth.

She remembered her father saying this region was one most submarine captains – *Perishers* as they were called inside the navy – avoided if at all possible. They called it *Lucifer's triangle*, a reference to its surface cousin off Bermuda. There had been strange sightings at depths, he'd told her, and the unexplained loss of at least four nuclear submarines in the last seventy years, though only two of those were ever made public. She touched the silver locket around her neck, her father's picture in full dress uniform on one side, her brother at age sixteen on the other. She rarely looked at the pictures. She didn't need to.

Dimitri's hand reached across to take hers.

"You miss them, don't you?" he said. "Is there really no one left for you back home?"

Images fast-framed across her mind: the aerial nuclear detonations, the return to her incinerated village, the news of her father's submarine lost with all hands, her brother killed in action somewhere in Tibet, and two years of Irish urban guerrilla warfare – when she'd done as many unspeakable things as had been done to her. She'd even had to change her identity for five years afterwards until the general amnesty came into force. She bolted a smile in place.

"No one," she said, and added, before her smile caved in like quicksand. "What about you? Your family in Greece?"

"Ah," he said, eyes downcast, "My beloved Santorini is still there, sheltering my mother underneath that hideous sunroof across the whole island – but from the cliffs she gazes down over the hazy sea, not up to the scorched sky. She is still sturdy, and manages to bear the forty-five degrees. Of course, she stays in during the summer. My brother Kostas lives in the Achilles dome just outside Athens; it is more for climate control and water reclamation than staving off radiation." He gazed through the hull into a remembered distance. "Greece was lucky in the War – unlike your unfortunate emerald isle – but it is now being rent in two by the Fundie movement – those for, those against. I even had mother, an Orthodox Christian all her eighty years, suddenly quoting the Alician Structure to me last time I was home. Still, maybe it is preferable to the previous seven years of bitterness after she lost two sons in the War. The happy Greece of my childhood and adolescence, of laughter, sea, sun and – "

He skipped over a word, and she appreciated the afterthought.

"– friends, is now relegated to antique postcards. Whenever I return to my University, both sides plead with me to speak for them, so I ..." His voice cracked. He stopped.

"What?" she asked quietly, leaning forward. She rarely heard him talk about home. In fact, she realised she'd never heard him speak like this about anything – he usually concentrated on his work, where he was so upbeat, so positive.

When he looked at her, she realised it was as if he was naked before her, nothing to hide behind. With something between shock and elation, she realised he *trusted* her. His cast-offs would kill her if they knew.

"I *hide* underwater." He uttered a solitary, mirthless laugh. "That's what my brother said, last time we spoke – shouted – at each other."

She reached out her hand. "Dimitri –"

A single harsh beep intruded, shattering the intimacy. His eyes widened more than usual. He twirled his chair back around to the multron panel. Her hand hung in mid-air for a moment, before she too returned to her displays.

His voice regained its exuberance. "Something is there! And it's big!"

His excitement caught her. "Two hundred metres to port," she read from her display. As the image updated with the next sonar sweep, she saw it more clearly. "It's huge," she whispered, as the sonar revealed the outer edge of a colossal structure.

"We have to go in closer," he said, almost shouting. "Prepare to release the umbilicals!" He stood up, rocking the submersible as he did so, moving to the release panel overhead.

"Wait!" she said. "Give me thirty seconds, I want to send a data-stream up before we release."

"We can send data pods up when we get closer." He began punching in the release code.

Her fingers worked fast; she had her own suspicions about what had happened to the probe. "Please, darling, just twenty more seconds." She hit a key and the upload began.

He waited only ten. "There, my love, you've had your twenty seconds!" He tapped in the final digit.

She glanced at the screen. She'd done it, the data-squirt had left one second earlier, racing up the umbilical comms line.

The sphere wobbled back and forth like a skittle not quite knocked over, as the submersible unshackled from the ship ten kilometres above, a puppet severed from its strings. The auto-thrusters switched on to compensate. Dimitri threw himself back into his pilot's seat.

"Now, let's have a closer look!" He planed the sphere forward and down as fast as it would go, 25 kph. The pulses from the sonar increased in frequency as they approached the source. It was so large Jennifer had to reset the range parameters on the sonar screen. When they were fifty metres away, he brought the sphere to a halt, and switched the forward beams to maximum. They both crouched at the porthole, peering outward to see it with their own eyes. Neither of them could speak.

Jennifer was reminded of the time her father had taken her at age seven to a Navy dry-dock, to walk beneath the new Tsunami class nuclear submarine. She'd felt her senses almost sucked in; the vessel had so much *gravity*. Words had failed her then. Yet what she saw now was more majestic. She switched on the microphone and started recording, one of her tasks on this mission.

"This is DSV Cousteau 12, Mariana Trench, July 19, time index 17:34:02, piloted by Professor Dimitri Kostakis, assisted by Dr. Jennifer O'Donnell. We are seeing a massive structure – estimated nine hundred metres in diameter, approximately round – no, more like, er, a cooling fan, each section blade-like, stretching out from a central core structure resembling a tower. "Take us over to the tower, please," she whispered, her hand over the mike, then continued. "The structure –" what was it, she wondered: a machine? A city? A ship? "– is… about seven levels high, then on top is the tower, another four floors. The whole object is slate grey in colour, evidently metallic – no rust, abrasions or markings." She clicked off the microphone for a moment, and glanced down at the laser spectrograph display. It read << Unknown>>. The only time she'd seen something similar was when her father had shown her secret radar images from a prototype stealth submarine just before the War. She gazed at it through the wide porthole. Who could have built this, on such a scale? Her mental search of all the dockyards, even the covert ones from the days of the Chinese Hegemony, came up negative.

"Composition unknown. Perhaps stealth technology."

Dimitri tore his eyes from the porthole a moment to cast a question mark in her direction, but she continued. "Age indeterminate, spectral dating process unable to interrogate. Sensors unable to penetrate its exterior."

She felt knots tying themselves in her stomach. The ship looked like it had been dropped into the ocean yesterday – as if nature wouldn't touch it. Some of the more paranoid-sounding hypotheses about the lost probe gathered force in her mind.

She clicked on again. "Approaching the central tower – one or two windows of some description." She felt her pulse racing, her scientific curiosity competing with her preservation instincts. "Cannot see inside, but I can now confirm six outward radial sections. And –" *what was that?*

"Did you see that?" Dimitri shouted.

She'd seen a glint of silver at the edge of the porthole, something moving very fast out in the open water. She put the microphone down and began typing rapidly. She downloaded compressed files to a pod and let it go, hearing the thud on the hull as a burst of air sent it wobbling up to the surface.

Dimitri turned to her, surprised. "So soon? We only have three."

Her instincts had kicked in with a vengeance, but her scientific mind wasn't sure yet. "Sorry, guess I'm a little trigger-happy."

A higher-pitch sonar beep – faster, rising steadily with each pulse – made her start. It signalled something getting closer. She felt an icy shiver abseil down her spine. They both focused on her sonar scan, because they could see nothing in front of them – whatever it was, it was coming from part of the ship that was now behind them. With each sonar sweep, it was changing heading, erratically.

"You know what this means?" he said, as he worked the controls to turn them around.

She prayed it was his path to the Nobel Prize, but her intuition was screaming that they were in big trouble, and should leave now, though she wasn't sure it would matter anyway. They both glimpsed something pass the porthole, a hundred metres to port. A flash of grey-silver. At first it reminded her of a hammerhead shark she'd seen off the Shannon coast on a diving expedition – it had that same demonic feel to it. It was at least four metres in length, she reckoned. They stared out the porthole, waiting, counting. After five seconds it passed again, heading in the opposite direction. It was zigzagging, but getting closer with each pass.

She did the mental calculation, and kept it to herself.

"It's going amazingly fast for an underwater creature – maybe seventy kph!"

She nodded. It appeared to have legs, and moved in short spurts. Was it riding something, or did it have some kind of sleek harness and propellant system? She was thinking quickly, the way she used to back on the cinder-streets of Dublin when she and her gang were hunted by kill-drones. It was on an attack vector, closing with each pass. They had no weapons, and their manoeuvrability was pitiful. She kissed a fore-finger and touched her silver locket, closing her eyes briefly, and then spun into action.

She checked to see that the optic scanners had properly recorded it. They had. *The next crew will be better prepared.* She started downloading the file. As she turned back, she saw her lover still staring, enthralled, now projecting a ghostly green head-up display onto the porthole plazglass showing its speed, size, and proximity, so he could watch its progress, homing in on them, moving inexorably closer. It made its fourth pass. It was bigger than she had first thought, yet able to move with terrifying speed through the water. She predicted that the fifth pass would collide with them. She terminated the download and jettisoned the data pod toward the surface, sending it off on an oblique sideways angle behind them before it would head straight up to the surface.

He turned to her, his face a question mark. "Jen, why –?"

She bit her lip. "I love you." She hoped the non-sequitur might get through to him. She watched the recognition dawn on his face – he grasped what she'd already intuited was happening.

He looked from her, to the silver creature, then back to her. His face became stern, as he gripped the controls tightly. "No, Jen, I won't allow it. We will not perish here! Look," he pointed through the porthole.

She followed his gaze and made out an oblong black hole within the structure, at the base of what seemed to be the conning tower on top of the leviathan ship – some kind of hatch, and it was open. Dimitri slewed the submersible forward, engines whining as he gunned the thrusters to steer them toward the entrance.

We won't make it! Still the creature didn't hit them, and they got closer. She dared to hope, her eyes falling on her lover's determined face. But as sanctuary lay within just a few metres' grasp, the soot-black gaping mouth of the hatch about to swallow them whole, the submersible was struck and knocked sideways as if it had been hit by an underwater train. She flew like a toy to the opposite wall of the sub, her head banging with a nasty thud. The lights failed, except for electric blue flashes punctuating the black, their own personal lightning storm. Power relays shorted all around her, releasing the acrid smell of burning cables. A precious few dashboard lights held their ground, preventing her from being plunged into abyssal darkness.

The submersible clanked onto the external metal surface, and settled. She held her breath a moment, waiting. At first there was no sound, but then a laboured creaking ushered a series of stabbing hisses as stress fractures surrendered to the pressure, and pungent seawater punctured the hull with ice-cold needle sprays. Bruised, broken and bleeding, the shock deadening the pain, she crawled blindly forward and found Dimitri's unresponsive hand. With relief, she heard his unconscious breathing. However, the water, stinging only for a few seconds before it numbed flesh completely, lapped around her feet, like Death's embalming fluid.

She coughed, tasted blood, and then spat it out. *No, not like this!* Her mind tried to outrace her two immediate enemies: the rising water and the onset of the temporarily shock-deadened pain. They were only a metre from the opening. She tried to think. What still had power? She plunged her fractured elbow into the freezing water to give her a few more vital seconds to concentrate. But the pain burst through, like red hot scalpels stabbing into her, and she allowed herself one stark cry of anguish through clenched teeth, her good hand reaching out again for Dimitri's bulk, squeezing his arm hard. She caught her breath after the first smarting flood of hurt eased off, then grimaced again, as she realised there was only one system that had any power remaining – the emergency escape hatch. She was sure she'd been in worse situations during the War, but nothing came to mind. The water rose. She shook violently. She clamped her teeth together to avoid breaking them.

Her father had taught her that in real emergencies underwater you had five seconds to decide what to do and act on it. The freezing water clawed at her waist, Dimitri's bulk floating off the floor. She pulled him towards her, cradling her elbow around his neck. She took three deep breaths, sealed his mouth and nose closed with her left hand, and kicked at the hatch release.

SSV Ganesh, Mariana Trench

Four men skulked around a broad oak table in the conference room two floors beneath the ship's bridge. The horizon rocked back and forth every eight seconds, and every third pitch downwards was accompanied by a yaw to the left, then the right, which was in turn succeeded by a rolling action that meant any object slid off the table unless it was held fast.

One man chain-smoked, one looked sea-sick, and another held a closed vidcom. The fourth man was Captain of the vessel, his wiry beard long ago bleached white by unremitting sun and sea-spray. They hunched around the sturdy table that had seen many years at sea, and many discussions, but few as sombre as this one. They all wore Indus Valley Systems weatherproof parkas.

"So, he was right after all," the smoker said, blowing a ring of pale grey smoke.

"Dead right," Jason said, beginning to turn green.

"Didn't know you had a sense of humour, Jason," replied the smoker.

He chafed at that, loosening his collar, trying to keep his eyes fixed on the rolling horizon.

The man with the switched off vidcom played with it idly. "What about Calder?" he said. "He's the reason we funded this in the first place."

The smoker stubbed out his cigarette with his left hand, while his right flourished another. "Disappeared. No trace. Either Chorazin or Alicians have him. Probably dead either way. We need the special sub, the new armed one the Indonesians have."

Jason got up and began pacing. "Jesus! Let's just head back to shore and work this out. We're obviously way out of our depth here – literally. Two people just died, or will be dead soon enough, and we lost a fifty-million dollar sub." He staggered to the window, grabbing the rail just in time. "And for what? We don't even know what's down there, only that something lethal is protecting it."

"We have to try again," the smoker said. "Word will leak out soon, and if we leave, another ship will take our place, our stake. Do I have to remind you all? The Corporation needs this find." He lit the new cigarette, and threw a sideways glance at Jason. Maybe he shouldn't have brought him along after all. He was too new to the company.

Jason turned back towards the table. "Maybe we should go public – I mean, this is bigger than a corporate find – Christ, whatever it is down there, it's not from here, is it?" He stared at the faces around the room, failing to find purchase. He walked back to the table and slammed both palms down, hard. "Hell, guys, am I the only one who recognises we're no longer in fucking Kansas?"

The smoker made his decision. He raised his hand and fixed Jason straight in the eye.

"You're right. We should abort. You go on ahead. Take the V-jet back to Guam. And the pictures from the pod we recovered. Encrypted of course. Meet with our man there, brief him and wait for instructions. I'll call Head Office."

Jason nodded. "Hallelujah! I'm out of here!" He raced out, ushering in a blast of strong salty air, and headed below to pack his things, interrupting himself to lean over the side as a vicious roll of the ship caught him unprepared. The door swung closed, the sound of the wind and the sea muted again. A blast of spray lashed against the windows.

The man with the Vidcom stopped tapping. "Never seen Jason get seasick like this before. Must be those pictures. Scare the hell out of me, too."

The smoker drew in a long breath, exhaling slowly through pursed lips. "The V-jet will be intercepted of course, assuming it even gets as far as Guam. Satellite's too risky – it'll be hacked for sure."

A scratchy voice from the Vidcom, not switched off after all, came on-line.

"Indonesian Government just agreed to dispatch their newest IP Attack sub. It can be with you in forty-eight hours."

The man with the vidcom eyed the smoker, waiting.

The smoker nodded. "Get the sub here, and give Jason false data, suitably encoded. Make the V-jet ditching look like an accident, but ensure the files are found." He exhaled slowly. "No survivors."

The Captain glared at both men, and stood up, hammering two balled fists onto the table as he faced the smoker. "Then I'll pick a pilot who isn't married."

He didn't look back as he launched himself through the door into the sea spray outside, his footing firm despite a brutal wave breaking over the side. The storm was getting worse.

The man with the vidcom spoke as soon as the sound of the sea receded.

"Kostakis and the girl – I'll notify their next of kin tomorrow morning. I served once with her father in the War, though she didn't know me." He paused and looked out to the sea. "He was a good man."

The smoker nodded ruefully, stubbing out his barely begun cigarette. He gazed forwards towards the heli-deck where the Captain was already talking to someone. "They usually are."

Chapter 13

Booster

The beetle-shaped aero-taxi powered straight upwards like a glass bullet emerging from the barrel of a gun, as it exited the underground shaft towards ground level. Micah held on to the steel handrail as he was spat out into the granite sky, skyscrapers looming around him on all sides. The pilotless vehicle slowed its ascent, pitched forward as if gathering breath, then sped off through the towers, a small buzzing insect hurtling through giant redwoods.

He'd only travelled in one once before – they were so expensive – on the occasion of his father's funeral, and he'd shared it with his mother and only sister, who had followed their father three years later courtesy of radiation-induced multiple cancers. She'd been that much closer to LA zero, the largest detonation.

The sun never quite managed to chip its way through the rice-coloured haze above New LA, though occasional splashes of orange dribbled around the hills near sunset, like melting wax. Just as well, he thought, with so little ozone left. The aero-taxi crossed an invisible boundary into NLA Central, sailing between the most recent and fanciest buildings, all at least two hundred floors high, the first thirty or so window-less, shielding against the background radiation, most concentrated at ground-level. *And the dust.* Millions of people had been instantly cremated in the initial shock attack on LA – city of angels – and once somebody had pointed out that the fallout contained the ashes of millions, it became impossible to forget. People wanted to live and work high up, or else underground. Almost no one walked the city streets, even though the ashes had long ago been washed away, scoured clean by acid rain. At ground level, ten hours a week was maybe safe, but after that you had a dose that would start looking for cells and genes to mess with.

The aero-taxi, slightly bigger than an old-style car, was mainly made of the ubiquitous transparent and tough plazglass, so Micah had impressive views in any direction, including down. Most skyscrapers were traditional block-shapes, but some of the latest ones were triangular, like sharply rising stepped pyramids. Off to the left the Global Fundamentalist Headquarters came into view – a vertiginous, twisting tetrahedron, a three-sided building that swept up from the mucky city floor on three massive graphite-coloured spokes. There were no floors until mid-level, but entrail-like lift tubes stretched down to ground and subway entrances. Its gold-tinted windows reflected the sky in sepia. Micah had to admit it was impressive, majestic even. They certainly had money, and knew how to make a statement. 'Better to inspire than coerce' was one of their mottos. He suspected they did both.

He stared forwards, past the automated control console – automatics steered all public transport these days – to the distant edge of the city, and beyond to the old LA centre levelled a decade ago by three separate nuclear detonations on the very first day of the War. He shuddered. He remembered the sirens, him and his two school-buddies laughing and joking that some idiot had let them off a day early before their regular weekly test. He stumbled backwards shielding his retinas when the first flashes lit up the sky above LA Central ten kilometres away. They'd played this game often enough, but now it was for real.

They ran full pelt ahead of the shock wave – a broiling tsunami of rubble and flaming cars and trucks consuming buildings in its wave front – radiating outward toward them. Micah had always been the fastest, and tore ahead of Timmy and Jonah, running in the relative silence, in and out of cars and machinery stopped dead in their tracks by the EM pulse, dodging people not realising what was happening, until they saw a burning cloud rushing their way. Micah knew that if he *heard* the blasts, then the wave would be upon him, and it would be too late.

He remembered diving for cover through the closing shield doors seconds before the scorching wind caught up. Timmy and Jonah, and other people had been behind Micah, running for their lives too. They were never found. No one knocked on the glowing shield door for a long time afterwards.

The ground kept warping, the seismic after-shocks rippling outward for two whole days, making even the reinforced nuclear shelters hazardous. Micah had been lucky. He'd been granted a day off school since his father was home after a long mission. Micah had wanted to be anywhere but home, so had cycled to a suburb, near the hills. His friends, his teachers, all of them had died. Ashed.

He recalled lying in a shelter with imperfect strangers: quiet, confused people, all in deep shock, terrified. Only the babies made any noise, the rest sat, arms around knees, some rocking, listening to the rumbling and occasional crashing down of buildings merely crippled by the first batch of incinerating shock waves. He lost track of time, since it was dark even during the daytime, with the smoke above, and the thick dust that tasted like metal, everywhere. They had a pump to keep positive atmospheric pressure, so the dust stayed out, mostly. But he saw and tasted it whenever they opened the entrance to let someone in, always watching, waiting for his family to arrive.

At these moments he glimpsed the sky, ravaged by curling talons of fire and black smoke – the only reference he could think of was an image of William Blake's painting of Dante's Inferno he'd seen in the art gallery on a school trip. But the three flashes left his vision blotchy for days, and he couldn't stop his body's violent tremors – his own internal earthquakes.

Everyone had known it might come to war, the government had been so gung-ho. The satellite-based anti-missile lasers, as well as the aerial patriot robots were thought to be impenetrable – God knew they'd cost enough. LA wasn't alone in the first wave – the White House and the Pentagon, along with New York Central, had been obliterated in the same moment as part of a tightly co-ordinated attack; the government finally held accountable for their arrogance, their hubris.

His parents had survived; they'd taken a day-trip to Santa Barbara. One day his mother arrived in the shelter, then his father initially joined them, but had to leave them as he was an army major, and felt he had more chance of finding Micah's sister from inside what was left of the military machine. So he said goodbye to Micah and his mother, telling Micah to pull himself together – a tough order for any thirteen-year old – to look after them both while he was gone. But Micah cried, held onto his father's sleeve, begging him not to go. His father threw him a cold contemptuous stare, unpeeling Micah's fingers from his jacket, one by one, until Micah grasped air, hot tears tumbling down reddened cheeks. Micah's mother immediately grabbed Micah and held him close. From that moment on, Micah knew he was no hero, not like his father, and from then onwards, he never wanted to be. His father returned, two years later, with the hero's rank of military colonel – at least that was what it said on the coffin.

Micah realised he was gripping the aero-taxi seat arm tight with clammy palms. He let go, averting his gaze to look eastwards, towards the Eden Mission complex. It was a purely functional affair: three brown, closely inter-connected blocks, the tallest reaching two hundred floors. It had been hastily constructed, then extended numerous times as it became more ambitious, and as The Heracles failed to deliver. Its blandness was intentional – it sent a message that no money would be wasted on extravagance – only the pursuit of colonising Eden.

Like many others, when space colonisation had become a realistic possibility, Micah jumped at the chance to work there. His father's credentials got him through the tough security checks, and though he'd never be an astronaut, probably would never even make it to the planet, he wanted to work on that dream. But as he looked at the Eden complex, seeing the chaotic pattern of construction, the lack of forethought, he couldn't help but wonder if humans would just drag all their baggage with them and trash Eden as well.

Then, as if on cue, he felt different, more positive. The doctor had said it would happen, that the booster had psychoactive properties that would make him feel more confident, more in control – he would see opportunities where before he'd seen insurmountable challenges. But there had been a warning, too.

"You'll feel better, and with it, cockier, more powerful. You'll take more risks, maybe say things you always felt you should say; things that have been bottled up will get released. You can get yourself into a lot of trouble on boosters. That's why they're illegal, not to mention psychologically addictive. Just watch yourself, think before you speak or act, and try to go through things habitually. And when it wears off, be prepared for an equivalent scale of depression – best to take a few days off when that happens. Oh, and just so you know, and you will soon enough, you'll feel a lot more libido. Be careful of that, too, there are enough diseases out there… Well, I don't have to tell you."

Micah had asked whether he would get another one after 72 hours if his mission was not finished by that time.

"No, on two counts. First, Vincent said you'll be finished by then, one way or another." The doctor had cleared his throat at that point. "Second, three boosters in a row tend to cause sterility and impotence; five in a row and that becomes permanent. And since you're one of the thirty percent safe-sterile men left on the planet, because you got to the shelters fast enough, you should hang onto that."

The booster had arrived in a syringe that looked like it was destined for a horse, and had left a lump in his upper arm, which the doctor had said would go down in an hour or two. Micah had taken a shower and changed into some new clothes, and seen how beat-up he looked, especially his back. The doctor said the booster would help with the bruising. Micah tried to see his image in the aero-taxi plazglass, but it was too bright outside.

He was, however, really feeling a lot better, no matter how he knew he must look. His mind turned to Antonia. He wondered if his temporary confidence would enable him to get noticed by her. But his mind jumped of its own accord to Louise, and an array of images paraded through his mind. He shook himself. *This stuff's pretty strong.* He faced the exit door as the aero-taxi docked at mid-level on one of the Eden complex towers. He saw from his wristcom it was 08:35.

His retinal scan passed security, and he joined the queue for the express elevator to the upper working levels. He was the only one in the aluminium-walled lift smiling.

Rudi arrived at 10:30 am. They went straight for coffee in one of the lounges scattered through the complex, some four hundred metres above ground level. This one was an octagonal affair, furnished with several coffee and stim machines. The room contained a variety of red leather seats, holographic notice boards, and a vid-screen running a news channel continuously without sound. The place was decked out with bland oval tables at standing height, which was what people used most of the time, since they spent enough time sitting when they were doing their jobs. Half a dozen people were already there, but Micah knew none of them by name; over nine hundred people worked at the Complex.

"You're in pretty late today, Rudi." He tried to say it innocently. Rudi's short black curly hair and dark-ringed Hispanic eyes made it impossible for Micah to ever tell if Rudi had had much sleep – he always looked like he had been out till the small hours of the morning. With his features, Micah always assumed he had a string of women.

"Well, actually, I've been in a meeting all morning with security. And you can talk; you didn't even show up yesterday."

Micah coughed on his coffee, which didn't go unnoticed, but rather than play it down he decided to play it up. "Random rad-check, you know how it is. No big deal. Security, eh? What have you been up to, something naughty?"

Rudi looked pissed off.

Micah smiled, but it erupted into a grin. "Hey, just messing with you!"

Rudi didn't smile back. "Well, cut it out, man. The Project Manager's dead and there are –" he looked around, lowering his voice. "– there are *Chorazin* in the building, man. Fucking Chorazin! Here! What's gotten into you, anyway?"

He'd almost forgotten about Kane. He felt disoriented. He had to take the doctor's advice, think before talking. Act naturally…

"Listen, sorry Rudi, you're right, I – er – took something this morning, left me kind of heady. Anyway, what did security want?"

Rudi took a sip of black, steaming Alaskan mocha. "Actually they were asking me about you."

Micah froze. Then Rudi slapped him on the back, laughing, "Just messing with you man! Hey, your face was a picture." He laughed some more. "And on that subject, what the hell did happen to your face?"

Micah made up a story about falling asleep on the sofa and smacking his head on the coffee table when he woke up in the morning; it had enough grains of truth to carry it off.

Rudi mentioned a hot Chorazin agent called Louise. Micah managed not to react, so Rudi gave it up. They chatted about nothing for a while, and just as Micah realised Rudi hadn't actually told him why security had interviewed him, Antonia strolled in, impeccable as always: two-tone blonde-brown short hair, no make-up that Micah could detect, a stylish white blouse, open deep at the neck, revealing a platinum-coloured necklace with a single fire jewel, blouse tucked into a navy, knee-length pencil skirt. Micah was mesmerised.

"… and he said, no man, *you* keep the money! Hey, Micah, are you even listening to me? Oh, I get it." Rudi nodded in Antonia's direction.

"Sorry Rudi, I, er, got distracted."

"Yeah man, join the line!"

He was encouraged that Antonia wasn't part of Rudi's harem.

"Anyway," Rudi said, "I need to head back. You coming?"

"Er, I'll be up in a minute."

Rudi left, muttering something like *in your dreams, buddy,* while Micah gazed openly at Antonia from behind as she selected her drink. He needed to say something – anything. She was actually on her own, without her usual entourage of equally attractive girls, or worse, male model look-alikes. Downing his coffee too fast, so he swallowed the bitter granules at the bottom, he squeezed the nearly-disappeared lump on his arm for one last spurt of confidence. He strode towards her purposefully, just as she turned without looking, towards him. Her arm hit his, causing a fountain of coffee to rise up between them, her zappucino showering over both of them.

"Oh my god, oh my god, I'm so sorry!" she said quickly, in an Eastern European accent.

"No, no, it was my fault. Really." He stood there, arms opened wide, not moving lest he spread it more. He hardly noticed the hot, stinging coffee. He'd never been this close to her. Before he knew what he was doing, he said "There's some on you." In slow motion he watched his own right hand as he brushed a splash of coffee from her left breast. But his fingers lingered on the slope, and stroked her nipple. In an instant her eyes transformed from doe-like and apologetic, to razor-blade angry. He retracted his hand and froze, staring at it like it wasn't his. He couldn't believe what he'd just done. He looked at her and was about to say he was really sorry when the slap hit him, hard. She whirled around and disappeared out of the room. One or two stifled giggles from the others in the coffee lounge cut through Micah's frozen moment, as he stood there, a large brown stain down his shirt, and a red handprint smarting across his cheek. He heard a crisp, female voice.

"Mr Sanderson, if you're not too busy, I'd like a word, please."

Louise. She had obviously seen the last few moments, and was wearing a school-teacher expression.

'Please put your arms down and follow me." Without another look she pirouetted and headed off.

He did as asked, wondering if things could get any worse.

He followed her into the lift, where neither of them said a word. They alighted on one of the uppermost floors, and Micah figured where they were headed. They left the elevator, and she walked ahead of him. He tried not to notice the way her pert buttocks salsa'd before him inside her tight black skirt, pony tail swinging from side to side. When they arrived, Louise told the two security men guarding the crime scene to leave for an hour. They departed without a word, sealing the door behind them.

She sat in Kane's leather executive chair, Micah opposite across the antique desk, where he'd been sitting less than ten conscious hours ago, though it had now been nearly two days. She lit up a cigarette, one of those long filter-less ones. So few people smoked these days, it surprised him. She didn't speak for a while, just watched him through the coils of smoke. Booster or not, he couldn't return her stare. His eyes roved around the room instead. There was a chalk outline between the desk and another door that was ajar. From Micah's vantage point, it seemed to be a bathroom. He could see some kind of cubicle, and part of a large mirror behind the bath.

"Booster trouble, Micah?" Louise said, high heels on the desk. She puffed a smoke ring.

He was jolted back to the situation, and also began to wonder whether she operated outside of normal Chorazin dress code regulations. "Er, no! Well, yes, maybe a little. My hand just –"

"Well, don't let it, or any other part of your anatomy, *just* do anything. Or else, if you are going to do something, don't apologise for it afterwards. Life is unbelievably short."

There was that cold but open gaze again, daring. He tried to ignore it. "Right. Sor –" He was in foreign territory. His track record with women was laughable. She got up and glided around to his side of the desk, perching on its edge. He tried not to look at her, especially her legs. He didn't trust her, but he was definitely having booster-related issues with her this close. Is she doing this on purpose?

"We interviewed Rudi this morning to give you time to search unimpeded. Did you get anywhere?"

Of course. He kept acting as if he was on his own, but he wasn't. There were others working to help him: Louise and Vince. Like it or not, he was on their team. He tried to look straight into her emerald eyes, gave up, glanced down to her hips, then away.

"No. I mean I used the time to make some overt searches, but nothing yet. This is going to take time, maybe days rather than hours. If Rudi wasn't around…"

"You mean you want him out of the way?" She raised an eyebrow.

He recalled he was dealing with Chorazin. "No! No, I mean, well, not like that. But if there was a work reason, maybe he could be reassigned for a day or so?"

She leant very close toward him, almost whispering, "Don't worry, Micah, we're not the cold-blooded killers you think we are." She remained close to him. Her eyes had that same look he'd seen in the Chorazin med facility – no warmth at all – someone, or something – had done a real number on her, screwed her up, he was sure of it. The bitterness had cemented-in a long time ago.

His hormones, however, had an agenda of their own, circumnavigating his rational mind. Despite himself, he began to move towards her mouth. She was wearing velvet crush lipstick – he'd read about it in an e-zine – some crap story about a femme fatale actress. Yet its darkness teased him, enticing him to explore her mouth. She straightened up before he arrived, and strode toward a closet. Shit – what's going on with me? He felt dizzy. He needed a glass of water. Cold water. His heart pounded a deep bass rhythm. "I think I should head back to the Optron."

She opened the closet and pulled out a pressed shirt. "Here. This should fit you more or less. Let's clean you up first." She turned toward the bathroom. He couldn't help but trace her curves as she moved away from him. Then he caught her checking that he was watching her via a mirror next to the closet. He flushed, his pulse racing. She opened the bathroom door wide.

"I need you focused on the task, Micah, not distracted by young girls."

He swallowed. Antonia flashed into his mind. He considered bolting for the other door, the exit to Kane's office, but it seemed ludicrous.

"Micah, we don't have all day. Take off your shirt and clean yourself up."

It sounded so reasonable, but so *not* innocent. *Seduction is the lie that allows us to do what we really want to do,* he'd heard on some vid somewhere. Still he hesitated. He remembered something a professor at school had once asked his class. Does a moth know what a flame is? Micah wondered, and extended the aphorism: would it fly there anyway, even if it did? He made up his mind. He reached for the shirt, snatched it from her and stepped into the bathroom and tried to close the door. But she was too fast and strong for him, slipping inside too, locking the door behind her. Her skirt fell to the floor, and she removed her top in one deft movement. He backed away as she approached him in stockings and heels. He looked away only to see her reflection in the mirror.

"As I said, Micah, I need you focused on the task." She pushed him against the bathroom wall. "Don't worry, I won't hurt you." She smiled, for the first time, cleaving in two his resolve not to sleep with her. His mouth collided with hers with a vengeance.

He sat cross-legged, propped against the bathroom wall, naked except for a hand towel draped over his groin, and watched her dress. His eyes were drawn to the tattoo of a red dragon that climbed her sinewy back, its ruby eyes level with her shoulder blades. He detected fine diagonal lines scratched underneath the tattoo. With a shock he recognised the scar pattern from some old vid about the darker hours of the War, something to do with rape camps in demobbed China. Female soldiers caught by the gangs were tortured with a neural whip until they submitted and performed. Micah counted a lot of scars.

She caught his eye in the mirror, her lips a thin line. "They'll be back in about twenty minutes. I'll see to it that Rudi is busy elsewhere this afternoon and all day tomorrow."

The way she talked was so matter-of-fact. Like they were in a meeting – a fucking meeting. It sounded funny, but it wasn't. It had all happened so fast. He felt blown away by it all. It was either the best sex he'd ever had, or the emptiest, or both at the same time.

"Leave everything just as it was before, Micah. Take a shower elsewhere. They'll notice otherwise." She smoothed down her skirt.

He wondered if it was part of her job, some pre-planned event to bond him to her, or just to regulate the booster. He had to admit he had no idea what motivated her.

"I'll come by and see you at 6pm, to see if you've found anything." She checked herself in the mirror. "Are you okay?" she asked, tying her hair back into the pony tail. He'd been surprised by her hair – when it was down, it transformed her – softening her. But now she was Chorazin again. Again? Who am I kidding!

"Yep, fine. 6pm. No problem." Like this happens all the time. Like never.

There was a question he felt he had to ask. "Louise… you and Vince… Is there anything –"

Her head turned on him quickly. "Don't go there," she said. She came over to him, bent down close, as if she was going to kiss him, but her eyes blazed. "Ever." She waited till he nodded.

And she walked out. No kiss. He saw his reflection. Is that me? He heard her close Kane's office door and then the outer door, behind her. He was alone again. He remembered Antonia, wondering where she was now. The coffee event had only been forty minutes ago; the very idea staggered him. If she saw him now…

He stared out into Kane's office at the chalk line on the pile carpet. "This is one truly weird day," he said out loud. He heard a click. It seemed to come from the next room. Another click, closer this time, coming from the horizontal mirror next to the bath. He backed away. With a gentle swish, the mirror slid aside, revealing a darkened recess behind. Out stepped a bedraggled, half-naked Sandy, straight into the dry bath, her clothes crumpled, a furious expression clouding her face.

"Tell me about it," she seethed, "please tell me how much fucking weirder it can get!"

Chapter 14

Nebula

Pierre faced Blake in the cockpit. Blake aimed the pulse pistol at Pierre's chest, his arm as steady as his gaze. Physically Pierre knew he was no match for Blake, so everything would depend on what he said in the next few moments. His mind flashed through the last fifteen minutes which had led them both to this point…

Pierre sat in a semi-lotus position in his narrow tube-bed, his back to the hull. He glanced at the cots occupied by Kat and Zack, the rotating glass entrances misted up as always with stasis, though their hearts only beat twice a minute.

He'd been running a series of complex calculations. Most of the computer systems were still down or couldn't be trusted since the virus, but after working on it for twelve hours straight, he had come to the cot to rest. But that wasn't happening. He could have turned on the delta-band sleep inducer, but there was something else on his mind.

He unfolded his legs and lay down, sealing himself inside the cot. The routine sounds of the ship, the humming, the little clicks and knocks, evaporated. They were replaced by the type of hush that arrives with its own reverberation, an echo of former unheard, unlistened-to sounds, when all external noise is switched off, and the ears anxiously search for the slightest tinkle. That too faded, and he was in total silence. The lighting automatically dimmed to a twilight setting inside, but his eyes remained open. The holopic he'd stuck on the ceiling of the cot showed a smiling middle-aged couple, him as a late teenager, standing almost to attention between them. It had been taken nine years earlier, the summer before his father died – was killed, he reminded himself. His mother had followed a year later, one of the so-called first-wavers of a virulent form of skin cancer.

"Well, maman, papa, not quite the trip I was expecting." He'd thought he would never need a photo to remember them, but he'd been surprised to find that after all, it helped to see their picture. He couldn't recall all the lines of their faces.

"Dad, I need some advice. The calcs, the technical aspects of the job, well, you know they're not a problem. Challenging, sure, but I'm comfortable with that part of the mission. Even the ghoster. I found I could function, somehow, even if I was pretty shook up. But it's the team. That's it. The team. We're no longer a team, if we ever truly were one. Kat... well, she's not the issue." Not this one, anyway. "And Zack, well, he pokes fun at me, but it's not serious. But the Captain – Blake – he never gives me a millimetre; always on my case. And if I do a really good job, then it's just about adequate. Papa, you taught me not to be emotive about these things, because that leads to bias, but... Well, truth is..." He drew in a breath; he needed to say this out loud. "I think he dislikes me, and I have no idea why."

Pierre knew what he had to do. For three days since Zack and Kat went into stasis, he and Blake had been avoiding each other. *There is no right time,* he heard the echo of his father's voice inside his head, *there is only now.* Pierre abruptly opened the cot and clambered out, heading for the cockpit. As he left the second compartment, he caught sight of his reflection in a mirror and noticed his face looked thinner, more angular, more set than in that holopic. His parents, even during the War, had aged gracefully over their years, always looking younger than their true age. He wasn't sure he would have that luxury.

"How are their vitals?" Blake barked the question as soon as Pierre entered, without turning his command chair around to face him. Pierre noticed Blake change the screen image just as he entered – something he didn't want Pierre to see. And he thought Blake quickly slipped something into his right hand pocket.

"They're fine, Sir. I compensated for the stasis effects on Zack's leg. It will continue to heal, albeit at a slower rate than normal." He paused. Blake continued staring at the one remaining cockpit console that worked, occasionally tapping at a key. Pierre automatically half-turned, ready to leave, then stopped himself.

It had been four days since the ghoster event and loss of communications with Earth. Three days since Kat and Zack went into stasis, after a heated debate. Kat was the junior officer and saw herself as the least contentious candidate. But Zack had been furious. Pierre had laid out the logical arguments: Zack's broken leg, the need for a scientist to try and retrieve the comms and other computer functions. Eventually, after some thirty minutes of discussion, during which time Blake hadn't said a word, he had suddenly turned to Zack and said simply, "Pierre's right." Zack had flared, but said nothing. He'd just turned and stormed off, limp and all, to prepare for stasis.

In the three days since, there had been minimal communication. Of course there was some logic to it given the oxygen situation, but it was pretence rather than sense, and they both knew it. Somebody had to make the first move.

"Sir, I was wondering if we could talk."

Blake's index finger paused above the touchpad. He cocked his head, though not enough to see Pierre. He sighed as he turned back to the screen, and carried on tapping at several more keys. "What's on your mind, Pierre?"

This was the farthest Pierre had got in three days. He didn't want to blow it. He needed something of mutual interest. In a moment he had it.

"Sir, your implant theory that it's a likely third Alician option; I'd like to know more about it."

Blake swivelled his seat around to face Pierre, looking haggard, blackness ringing his eyes; he'd hardly slept since the others went into stasis. No, Pierre corrected himself: since Zack went into stasis.

"Take a seat; you'll use less oxygen sitting down."

Pierre sat at his post, leaned forward, and waited.

"Well, Pierre, you're our mission scientist, you know about implants. You studied terrorist psychogenic methods. What is it exactly you think I know more about?"

"I know the theory. Implants were originally piloted in the last century in the so-called cold war – they called it brainwashing – and for sure also in the Korean and Vietnam wars, and the Sumatra episode in 2028. But in the last war they got more technical. More advanced psychological techniques, particularly acute traumatisation to prevent the memories from surfacing, even under deep counter-intelligence probing. The implant must be triggered by a very specific event, usually visual, best if a composite or superimposed image with depth, one that would only be encountered in the desired circumstances. Once triggered, the trauma overwhelms more recent memory since the implanting process happened, so the subject doesn't second guess the original programming based on more recent experience."

"Victim, Pierre, not subject – victim."

He nodded, knowing such academic insensitivity fuelled people's distrust of science. But this wasn't going right. He been speaking like he was in an exam, or worse, lecturing. Blake looked disinterested, as if he was about to turn back to the screen.

"So, Sir, what I'm wondering, specifically, is why you think there is an implant that wouldn't have already been triggered?"

Blake gave him a sideways glance. "That is the question, isn't it?"

Blake's eyes sharpened. Pierre realised he'd been missing – needing – the Captain back in control.

"Let's review the facts, Pierre. The ghoster was meant to activate the detonator without us ever detecting it. The Minotaur virus was there as a back-up in case we did. So, whatever happened, the Alicians wanted it to be another mystery, another unexplained failure. That way a fourth mission would never get funded.

Pierre nodded. So far it made sense, and they were communicating, at least. He began to wonder if the whole "team problem" was in his own head. "The Heracles didn't have a comms position. I always wondered about that. Is that why we have one, to have more redundancy onboard?"

Blake leant back in the chair. "Heracles sent a distress message just before it went dead."

Pierre wanted to say *No, you're mistaken, I've seen the logs.* But he knew Blake wouldn't make such an obvious error. "But, Sir –"

"I know what you're thinking. But the Code Red operates on two wavelengths, one on a much lower register – fractally encoded – appears to be stellar radiation noise, unless you have the right sequence decoder. Doesn't show up on the logs. Almost no one knows about it, but it's there." Blake's eyes roamed the largely dark console, where the central panel fluttered many red indications and a few Spartan greens, and then he continued. "Except the Alicians obviously found out about it, and made sure that it couldn't be transmitted this time. If indeed the logs themselves haven't been altered for the entire mission."

Pierre sat up. "You mean they're inside the Eden Mission itself? That's pretty hard to believe."

Blake laughed, "You mean pretty hard to accept! I'm surprised at you, Pierre, aren't you scientists meant to have open minds?"

Pierre reddened. "Do you have any evidence? Scientists try not to indulge in wanton paranoia."

Blake almost grinned. "A little defensive today? You're beginning to sound like your father."

Had Blake known my father?

"Well, unfortunately," Blake continued, "I do have some evidence, albeit circumstantial. You see, Kat's quite a wizard at carrier signals."

Pierre glanced briefly over to her empty chair.

"And she has a 'friend', a member of staff in the Eden Mission. They were sending each other coded messages disguised as background radiation. Harmless messages. Of course Eden security knew about it. But guess what?"

Pierre parked the info about Kat having a "friend" for later; he wasn't going to miss the opportunity to redeem himself with Blake. "They let it happen because it was another way of knowing that things were working properly."

Blake raised an appreciative eyebrow. "Exactly. Only, a week ago, something happened."

"It stopped?"

Blake shook his head.

Pierre's brow furrowed, and then smoothed. "It started repeating!"

Blake nodded, "Kat realised something was odd a couple of days before the ghoster attack, as she hadn't heard from her friend for some time, and had been running some tests to check the telemetry output. She told me afterwards, a bit sheepishly mind you, as far as Kat can be sheepish, that is."

Pierre analysed it. So Eden Mission personnel should have spotted it. "Did security try and warn you?" he asked.

Blake shook his head. The mood shifted, the game part of this little exchange was over, Pierre realised. "So you believe they've infiltrated security?"

"Probably just as well we're not in communication. I'm not sure I'd trust any orders right now."

Pierre frowned; the implications were enormous. But in particular, it meant they were truly on their own.

Blake stood. "So, the ghoster was initiated, we defeated it, but lost our comms. That left a third approach."

"Have you figured out the trigger?"

"Maybe. Something very unique. Only seen once in a lifetime."

Pierre started to look around the cockpit. But that would make no sense – nothing much ever changed in the cockpit, especially after the virus struck.

"Eden?" he said.

"Alicians don't want any human footprints on the planet. In any case, too few distinctive landmarks we know of, nothing to act as an implant trigger."

Pierre had known it was wrong as soon as he'd said it. And then it hit him.

"The nebula! Of course. It's the last unique phenomenon between here and Eden. But it would have to have been seen from an unusual perspective. We could have seen a holo of it before. I mean, I have, for example."

"Me too," Blake said. "But not like this," he said, leaning outward and tapping the viewscreen. Pierre stared without comprehension. And then he understood. They could have seen pictures of the nebula. But here they saw something else as well – their own reflection. And it fit perfectly with the psychogenic implant theory.

"There. You have your father's genes after all." Blake said.

Pierre side-stepped the barb, and followed the logic to where they were today.

"But now two crew members are in stasis. So, you had to gamble which two, including yourself."

Blake stretched his back, and looked through the plazglass to the nebula. "It doesn't do anything for me." He moved aside.

Pierre hesitated. He hadn't yet inspected the nebula, hadn't had time since they arrived in its vicinity several hours ago. He crossed over to Zack's seat, and took a good look. After all, if anything was to happen, he had better make sure it was now, while Blake was prepared. He took in not just the nebula, but his own reflection superimposed over the image.

"Well?" Blake said.

Pierre's vision embraced the violent clash of silky blues and reds, frozen waves of colour expanding outwards to solid gas edges. In his mind he mapped the equations defining the sheer brutal energy behind this phenomenon. He registered his own awe-struck face superimposed on it. He waited for what should come next if he had an implant, within seconds. But he was simply swept away by this fantastic vista, gliding past them like a giant, hallucinogenic butterfly.

"It's more impressive than any of the pictures. It's... I could study it for years!" He turned smiling to Blake, but froze as he saw Blake aiming a pulse pistol at his chest.

"Pierre. What's Kat's nightmare?"

He tried to swallow. "Captain, Sir, it's okay, it's me, there's been no reaction."

"Answer the damned question, Pierre. Recent memories!"

His heart pounded. For an instant, he was tongue-tied, unused to having a gun aimed at him point-blank.

"Now, Pierre!"

"S-she's running, running from something on Eden. We don't know what, but it scares her to death." He caught his breath. "We fought the ghoster four days ago. You had quorn rashers for breakfast today, and you skipped most of it. You decided to put Zack, and not me, in stasis. And two minutes ago you accused me of sounding like my father." As if you had actually known him.

Blake lowered the weapon, placed it on the console, sat down in his own chair, and dragged his palms over his face and head.

"Sorry, had to be sure."

"Right," Pierre replied, his immobility masking the raw emotions cascading helter-skelter through him. He tried to focus on the implant threat. At least he could see now why Blake had been so tense, so distant – he'd been concerned Pierre had the implant. But then why had he put Zack in stasis?

"Sir, if you thought it was me, then why –"

Blake looked at Pierre square. "Now you're not being scientific."

He glanced from Blake, to the console in front of him. He hadn't until this moment seen what Blake was studying at his console. Blake tapped *refresh*. It was a personnel file, but it wasn't Pierre's.

"You think it's Zack?" Pierre's eyebrows rose.

Blake stared at the file.

Pierre tried to reason it out. "It's logical; he would have been the pilot, the first to see the nebula. The one most likely to survive, if anyone did, if the ghoster attack had not quite gone to plan." He saw Blake's lips were tightly pressed together. He clearly didn't like this. Of course, it feels like betrayal, especially having this conversation with me – of all people.

Blake spoke up. "Initially I assumed it wasn't him. Nor Kat – too young and inexperienced, and always under surveillance, being Beornwulf's daughter. But as Captain I had to consider all the possibilities. The more I thought about it as an Alician strategy, the more I thought it could be Zack. He was missing in action for ten days in Thailand during the War – the only survivor from his platoon that time – long enough to carry out the trauma conditioning phase of the implant procedure. And shortly after we were selected for this flight, he went missing one night – said he got drunk and ended up with another – well, it doesn't matter, but he could have been kidnapped, and the final trigger implanted then, a holo-image of the nebula as sent back from the Prometheus. And Zack of course none the wiser, and feeling guilty over something he didn't do."

"But what if it triggered?"

Blake's eyes flared. "Mission before men, Pierre. I'd do what I'd have to do. Zack knows that and would expect nothing less."

Pierre thought about it. The pieces slotted together. "You haven't talked to him about it, have you, Sir?"

Blake shut the pistol back in the weapons locker. "I'll be honest, Pierre, I was hoping I wouldn't have to." He shrugged and smiled. "But I will, when he wakes up."

"There's no treatment for implants, Sir. You know that. And if we come back, we'll have to put him in stasis for the return, just to be sure."

"Maybe I'm wrong about the trigger. Maybe there is no third plot, and I'm just being – what was that phrase – wantonly paranoid?"

Pierre, for the first time, detected a morsel of trust. He still wanted to say so much, to ask if Blake had known his father. But he decided to quit while he was ahead. "You look tired, Sir. Really."

"You have no idea. I'm going to hit the sack. You have the Con, Dr. Bertrand." He left the cockpit.

Pierre sat down. He looked over to Blake's chair. When he'd said "You have the con", it meant he, Pierre, was in command. He could sit in that chair. He could try it for size. He'd never once sat in it, not even for a moment, in the past three months onboard.

He stayed where he was.

He remained in the cockpit another three hours, trying to salvage more from the computer systems, peeking occasionally at the nebula, then gave up. With Blake sound asleep, he went aft and dug deep under his cot mattress to pull out a small phial and old-style syringe. He injected it into his left elbow crease carefully, and then discarded both phial and syringe in the usual manner. He waited. After a few minutes, an ugly grey-black bruise like spilt ink flushed around the needle entry point for thirty seconds, accompanied by a razor-like slash of pain, and then vanished beneath his skin. He regained his breath. Satisfied, he headed for the shower.

As he passed Kat's cot, he thought he noticed movement inside. He tried to see through the condensation. Kat was fast asleep, but was clearly dreaming – he could see her eyes darting about beneath her eyelids. He was surprised. You weren't supposed to dream in stasis. He laid his hand, with a tenderness he could never show if she'd been awake, on top of the glass covering of the stasis tube. "I hope for your sake, Kat, it's not the nightmare – because you're not going to wake up for another two days."

Chapter 15

Rudi's World

With one last shove the naked body tumbled down inside the furnace chute, seven floors underneath the Eden Mission. Gabriel heard no sound, no crashing or explosion, no cry or scream. He knew his job. Closing the vent, he wiped his hands on the dead janitor's greasy faded brown overalls he now wore. There had been no blood: a snapped vertebra at the base of the neck, a hand clamped over the mouth and nose.

He listened, hearing nothing but the dull whirr of air circ pumps. Satisfied, he picked up his rucksack and pulled out a syringe, inserting the auto-anaesthetising needle into his neck. With a measured motion of his right thumb, he coerced the algae-coloured contents inside him. He began consuming water from the six litre-size bottles he'd taken from the supply cupboard. He barely had time to lift the vent, toss in the two first empty bottles and syringe, and throw the rucksack on top of the furnace housing, before he started to convulse. But he made no noise, not even clenching his jaw. *It will pass.* In his head he recited the Ashkram Elat. Its rhythm helped him control his breathing, taking his mind off the tearing pain.

Shaking on the floor, he drank another litre at the end of each stanza. By the time he reached the last one, the burning sensation ebbed. He opened his eyes, and got to his feet, leaning against the hot metal of the furnace shield. Standing unaided, he uttered the final two lines aloud, to see how his voice had changed.

Gabriel looked down at his body: heavier, like the man he had just released from life's strains. The water content around his waist took on a less fluid quality and behaved like fat. He tested the puffiness of his face with podgy hands, and inserted the contact lenses rendering his black irises a dull blue. The sim-skin mask, which minutes earlier had been placed over the janitor's limp face, took a while before it moved synchronously over Gabriel's own features. He checked his reflection in one of the panels: no line visible between skin and mask; the chameleon pigment-blend worked.

Stooping, he attached his janitor's name-badge, and shuffled towards the service elevator. As he entered it, his tongue flicked to the false wisdom tooth at the back of his mouth. He flexed his forearms to confirm the retractable blades were in place. He didn't glance at his watch – he knew the exact time. He pressed level one-eighty-five.

***

Micah hunched over his console computer data, some flat on flimsies, some in 3D holos: digital cylinders rotated and twinkled, mathematical contours of rainbow hues like the hallucinogenic ski-slopes you could surf on the vidnet. The air tasted of high-end fluidic computers hard at work – a metallic taste like coins. He'd been nagged by his mother to try plants to add some relief, but even the cactus had wilted.

Rudi had been called away fifteen minutes ago, none too happy about it. Micah had shrugged, offering insults about the jerks upstairs.

"You know what they're like, assholes one and all, and as for the Chorazin…" He'd ranted for a while and Rudi seemed to swallow it. Micah didn't need to put up much of an act in any case. He didn't trust the Chorazin a micron.

With Rudi gone, he focused on his Optron session; he needed to find out what had happened to the missing lighthouse markers he'd installed in the Ulysses' matrix. But he was plagued by a menagerie of images: Antonia slapping him, Louise writhing on top of him, and Sandy coming out from behind the mirror. Sandy had gone into the main office to retrieve some spare underwear from a drawer in her desk, used the toilet, and had stolen back inside the hideaway, squirreling water and snacks from Kane's drinks cabinet. There was nowhere else for her to go.

Micah couldn't believe she'd been there for two nights, though she'd emerged once or twice in the small hours. There was no way out past the internal cameras. Clearly she knew who had killed Kane, and it scared the hell out of her. She wasn't about to tell Micah, though he'd guessed Security were involved. She'd made Micah swear not to tell anybody she was there – reminding him of what she'd just witnessed between him and Louise – she would pick the right time to emerge.

He'd tried to persuade her to talk to Louise, and then suggested Vince. She said the Chorazin weren't safe – Kane had called them, too. Micah had promised to come back later to help her leave the building.

To calm down his mind, he used an old Japanese breathing technique from Optron School – breathe in five seconds, hold twenty, breathe out ten, then hold "empty" for a further ten, then repeat twice more. His mind settled, and he climbed into the Optron chair. This moment always reminded him of boarding a roller-coaster sled with his sister when he was a kid. He hooked in. As it powered up, there was a brief sensation of falling, as if the chair had dropped through the floor, then he was weightless, floating above a kaleidoscopic topography of metallic-hued geometric shapes and symbols. This was the Foundation, the rudimentary building blocks for Optronic landscaping. He fast-forwarded past it.

Skimming over multi-coloured data landscapes, he sent mental commands to organise the flow, using shape imagery. Ninety-seven basic types of data were slip-streamed back from the Ulysses, and he and Rudi and others had long ago developed complex patterning techniques to enable all but a few data parameters to stay in the background, and then focus on a select few to look for irregularities. The program adapted to each individual, so even though they used the same technique, he and Rudi would see different landscapes. Micah soared over rolling fields, islands of dense trees, grazing animals, flocks of birds, rye and barley, rivers and streams, nostalgic structures such as farm houses, tractors, roads, and a steam railroad. An archaic and long-gone English landscape his mother used to show him in vids and even some actual printed books from her childhood in rural England.

He had no idea what Rudi saw in his own landscape. They never discussed it, because to do so could subconsciously interfere with the program, and in any case the whole point of having two analysts was to look for the same things in different ways.

He experimented with the two main constructs: data packets represented by different animals or birds, and data channels, symbolised by the landscape architecture such as grass, trees, rivers and "man-made" structures. He picked clusters of data and brought them out of the background. In one case, the grass glowed red, and in another certain birds fell to the ground, frozen stiff, but they recovered quickly. He knew which Ulysses lighthouse markers had disappeared, but not what had happened to them. Deleted markers should leave a trace, such as grass burned to ash, or something rotten, like a carcass. He reversed time so that the landscape unripened from summer to spring, and then winter. But still he couldn't figure out what had gone down. He ran through every tactic in the book, and then switched to the unorthodox ones which could induce psychotic feedback inside the analyst's mind. Nothing. He was getting nowhere. The answers weren't there.

With an inward curse, he exited, shut it off, and pulled the Optron headpiece boom away from him, rubbing his eyes. The fluorescent lights smarted after his benign virtual environment. He got off the reclining chair too fast, stumbled, and then regained his balance. He looked at his watch. An hour! He usually did thirty minutes, tops. He headed for the closest coffee machine in the corridor outside, almost colliding with Ben, the janitor, who looked pretty rough. Micah keyed in for an ultresso, just as Antonia turned the corner. They both froze. Micah made to speak, but she whirled and disappeared around the corner. He hadn't even gotten the word "sorry" out. He turned back to Ben, but he had also gone. He shrugged, grabbed his cup with its steaming black liquid, and returned to the telemetry room, ignoring the *Strictly no food or drinks* sign. He blew across the top of the coffee, savouring the synthetic cannabis aroma. Time dripped away. If only they'd given him a mental, rather than a physical booster.

He knew what he had to do – he had to enter Rudi's world, see if any clues were there. But it was a violation of sorts, and could get him into serious trouble with the Optron committee if they ever found out. His eyes fell on the poster of the Ulysses crew. God alone knew what was going on up there; the people they were relying on had proven untrustworthy. He wondered if the astronauts were aware of it, what comms they were receiving from Earth, if anything. The key to re-connect with them was here, somewhere, he could sense it.

He downed the ultresso in one gulp and glanced at his wristcom. Four-thirty. Enough time for one more session. Micah went over to Rudi's console, and searched around the desk, inside the drawer that Rudi avoided whenever Micah was watching. There was a picture of a scantily-clad girl, and on the back a nine-digit code, his Optronic frequency! He raced back into the chair, leapt onto it and reached for the 'trodes, setting the Optron to Rudi's frequency. If Rudi caught him, it'd be ugly. He took a breath.

He was immediately hit by the most basic of problems. It asked him for a password. Micah didn't use a password, and assumed Rudi didn't either, though of course it was allowed. It made him think he was on the right path, at least. But what could the password be?

Rudi loved women most of all – Micah had given up keeping score, and Rudi had thankfully long ago stopped recounting his sexploits – that game was only sustainable when there was at least occasional reciprocation. Micah suppressed the notion that he finally now had something worthy of grabbing Rudi's attention – Louise – and tried to remember the names of Rudi's lovers. It wasn't that there were so many – just that none of them meant anything to Rudi. He swept aside the preposterous idea that Rudi would use his mother's name.

Then he remembered Rudi's reaction earlier that morning. He glanced at the keypad. He tapped in A-N-T-O-N-I-A and held his breath. The console light stayed red. Dumb idea. But it stayed in his mind. Maybe not. He recalled what Rudi called her. He keyed in P-R-I-N-C-E-S-S, and green lights illuminated Micah's smile.

"Rudi! I always said your sex drive would be your undoing." He took one last look at the poster of the Eden crew, and activated the Optron.

He tensed as soon as he entered, completely unprepared for what he saw. He didn't know if his physical body recoiled or not, but as soon as he arrived in Rudi's world, as usual from a medium height above the landscape, he shot back upwards, away from the scene. The sky was a swirling mess of fierce blue and purple, streaks of scarlet zipping from one horizon to another. But that was not the worst. Beneath him was a charred city, bodies strewn amongst the ruins. Mutated human figures staggered amongst the carnage. Micah had difficulty controlling his breathing, and then realised why: a stench of burnt flesh. His own landscape was visual, but some analysts also used taste and smell.

Micah had never seen anything so apocalyptic – or had he? He remembered in training, once, the professor had briefly shown his students a landscape that had been used to develop a highly resilient and aggressive computer virus.

He thought about it: a virus, but not a normal one that just destroys. What had been done had been subtle, an "Emperor's Cloak" virus. It prevented real data getting through and supplanted it with fake data, what you wanted to be seen. But this was also a virus in the more conventional sense, eviscerating a vast data-stream. Micah pulled back and gazed towards the horizon. Flames billowed in the distant sky; voluminous clouds of grey-black smoke drifted across the land. He flew, increasingly fast, to see how far it extended, whether the whole landscape was the same, and whether the virus had affected everything.

He covered a dozen kilometres surveying the devastation below, everything dying or dead. Raven-like creatures tore strips of flesh from corpses; it meant non-recoverable data deletion. Although it was sickening to watch, he was impressed – data streams were highly protected by security protocols – to do this inside the Optron environment must have taken immense skill on Rudi's part. He saw a green flash down below, the colour catching his eye. He dropped down. It seemed to be a figure, hiding behind the large stump of a tree. He was stunned when he got close enough. It was Katrina, the astronaut. Micah had never met her, but ten minutes ago he had been looking at her on the poster, even if she now had a jade green body. The simulacrum beckoned to him. He drew closer, at first reluctantly, and then he chided himself – nothing physical could happen to him here.

"Take me to the South river," she said. Her voice was scratchy, synthetic, she clearly had problems speaking. Micah knew that it meant her program was degrading. Yet there was desperation in her voice. He had no real plan in any case, so he nodded, and moved behind Katrina. Then he realised he did not know where South was, so he asked. She pointed to the right.

Weight wasn't a problem in the Optron landscape, so he picked her up, holding her by her waist as they flew. There was little sensation of touch, Micah noted – presumably Rudi had toned down that particular sense – not surprising given the violence all around.

Carrion birds flocked in the distance. "Higher. Go higher," she gurgled.

Micah complied and whooshed above the birds. They were now so high it grew dark, though there were no stars. Katrina coughed. He knew the simulated air rarity affected her programming, and he made to descend, but she shook her head vehemently.

"Not yet."

After five minutes that included gut-wrenching coughing on her part, she pointed down to the right, and Micah swooped below. He saw green in the distance. He accelerated. With a sense of exhilaration he realised that it was his own landscape: beyond a boundary of red-soaked earth, lay green hills and trees, and a river winding toward the horizon.

"Stop!" she screamed, coughing in spasms that juddered Micah. He slowed down, intending to land on his own territory.

"NO! Stop NOW!" Lime green blood sprayed from her mouth.

Micah stopped dead, and they hung for a moment. Her body relaxed, though the coughing continued. Slowly he descended to the ground. She was a mess. She curled up in a foetal position on the damp red heather, and pointed to the other side, a few metres away.

"Walk," she croaked, and then resumed coughing.

Micah looked from her to the green lawn, and walked towards it. As he made to step onto cool grass, he collided with an invisible wall; it

133

connected with his foot, knee and head, and he bounced off, falling back onto the turf. It hadn't hurt him, just been a surprise. He got up again and tested the barrier. He could barely see it, but it was impenetrable. No wonder she'd screamed at him to stop. He glanced back to her to check Katrina wasn't going anywhere, then shot straight upwards at high velocity to find the top edge of the wall. About a kilometre above the ground, the glass curved backward behind him. *A dome. No way through or out.*

He traced his way back to the simulacrum. She'd crawled to the barrier. He realised there was another figure, on his own side. That worried him. Had Rudi inserted a virus in Micah's landscape? But as he got closer, he froze. Katrina knelt with her two hands against the wall. On the other side was another green figure, her palms placed against the wall too, so that their hands appeared to be touching. Tears streamed down her face, and her body shook.

It was Antonia.

Micah dropped to his knees. He felt like he'd just been hit by a hover-car. As he watched them, his hands tore some of the grass up by its roots, and he dug his fingers into the soil. Abruptly, he pushed himself back up. They were oblivious to him. He felt a sucking vertigo, dangerous in an Optron landscape, so he shut down his emotions and switched into analyst mode.

They don't belong here, he thought, in either landscape. Someone had inserted them – a very smart programmer. They'd been hidden from him and Rudi for a long time. Autonomous programs. Secret contact channels, he guessed, and because the emotional representations in the programs were intense and well-scripted, they were encoded by the two personalities themselves, or at least one of them with the others' consent. It was ironic. Love had been programmed in because it meant that these programs could hide, could adapt, and wouldn't give up. As a systems analyst himself, he had to admire it, but in terms of what it told him about Antonia, it added iodine to the wound. *She has a relationship with Katrina.* The sting of that thought made the desolation of the landscape seem fitting. He looked away, toward the butchery in Rudi's world, and then through the barrier to his own landscape, green and naïve, completely missing what was really going on. He hung his head.

After a while, he cleared his throat to gain their attention. He was burning Optron time. Katrina kept one hand on the glass wall, and turned to face him. Antonia seemed to be trying to see what was going on but couldn't make out Micah, perhaps because it was too dark on his side, and too light in hers. He was glad for it.

"You should go now," Katrina said, her voice a thin scratch across his ears.

"What about you?"

"You can only help me from the outside. Or maybe from in there." She pointed to Micah's world. He stared through the glass to note certain landmarks in his landscape to find the border again. He wondered if the Antonia simulacrum would remain there. He doubted it. These two would hide again quickly. The carrion birds would erase Katrina if they spotted her.

He gave the mental command to exit, and changed the setting on the Optron to his own landscape. In that brief instant he thought maybe he heard a small noise in the real world, but he didn't have time to check it out; and there was no sign of Rudi.

It was refreshing to be back in his world. Rudi's had been so stressful, in more ways than one. He headed to the far North of his landscape. After some minutes, he saw the landmarks: a telegraph line, a deserted stone farm building, and the river. But he could see nothing of Rudi's world. He slowed down. In the distance, a similar telegraph line and a deserted stone farm building. He stopped and looked back, then forward. *Idiot!* He glided down and stood at the bank of the river. He saw two depressions in the grass where Antonia's simulacrum had been, and in front of him, his reflection; a mirror, the perfect metaphor for reflecting a data-stream back on itself, and one difficult to spot given his chosen landscape format.

He tried to reason it out: Rudi's landscape was chewing up the real incoming data from Ulysses, and feeding his with false data. But where do the false data come from? Rudi couldn't create that, and it couldn't be a copy of the Prometheus or Heracles data as they wouldn't match. *Later.* He needed to get out before Rudi returned.

Micah imaged the exit symbol, kneading tired eye-balls with the heels of his hands, and peeled off the 'trodes. As he opened his eyes, about to get out of the chair, he stopped dead. Rudi stood before him, aiming a pulse pistol at his face.

"Hello, Mikey, been anywhere interesting?"

Chapter 16

Eden Approach

Kat sprinted at breakneck speed but it was closing fast. She saw the hatch door open. Someone was shouting, egging her on. With a shock she realised it was her elder sister. In an instant she knew that was wrong – her sister had been dead for years – she must be in the dream again. Abruptly, her viewpoint shifted and she saw herself from above, running across Eden's landscape towards the Lander. Eden was no longer green as she'd seen from the Prometheus vids – instead it was a sickly rust colour. For the first time she saw the creature chasing her. It was hard to make out. It ran in a strange way, in spurts, like it was jumping, or hopping. It was long, longer than a horse. She tried to count the legs, when it jerked suddenly, left the ground, and flew upwards towards her. Its head had small mandibles, but it also had a human-like face. She recognised it, wild with anger, the features screaming at her. She shrank back as it seized her shoulders and opened its blood-red gaping maw wide.

"Wake up! Kat, wake up, dammit!" Zack shook her hard.

Kat woke, drenched in sweat. Pierre stood behind Zack, looking at small holo-readouts emanating from her monitor. "She's not supposed to dream in stasis," he said.

Zack huffed. "Well, she sure as hell was. Seemed like a real shitter, too. You okay, girl?"

She could see and hear them but she felt drugged, as if a transparent pillow was over her head. She didn't know how to respond, her mouth not yet connected to her brain.

"She's still pretty groggy," Zack said.

Although she couldn't feel her tongue, she decided to try to speak anyway. She lifted her head.

"Kreechhhur; froo..." she rolled her eyes and flopped her head back down to the cushion.

Zack squinted at her, while talking to Pierre. "You sure she ain't brain damaged?" He winked at her.

"Well, she just made a lot more sense than you did in the first five minutes of your revival phase yesterday." Pierre collapsed the holodata and turned to leave. "Give her a few minutes. I'll be in the cockpit. The captain wants to give us all a briefing as soon as Kat's capable."

Zack grinned at Kat, ran a stubby finger down the right side of her face, and made to go, holding the end of a makeshift walking stick. "See you soon, kid."

Kat managed to find the muscle co-ordination to grip his wrist. She needed to tell him. She tried to speak, but just gurgled.

"Hey, okay, take it easy. I'll stay a while. Must've been some nightmare, eh? Deep breaths now. Try to move your tongue and jaw – loosen them up."

Kat tried. Her throat felt baked. She was desperate to tell someone what she'd seen – the creature, the desert. It was already slipping from her mind, like sand falling through floorboards. Finally she found some words.

"Saw it – big – fasht – aily-in... alien." Kat caught her own reflection in the stasis lid: hair matted with sweat, and the four days of stasis had brought out freckles on her cheeks.

"Wait – you mean after all these nightmares you finally saw the thing chasing you?"

"Yessh." Her tongue was swollen. She coughed. Zack reached somewhere out of her line of sight, and produced a chrome mug of warm liquid, and brought it to her lips. Half of it didn't stay in her mouth, but it was strawberry sweet, a hint of menthol, and soothed her throat. She gulped it down, then gasped for breath.

Zack's features sharpened, the fuzz lifting from her brain. White noise she hadn't even noticed phased out. Her shoulders relaxed.

"Thanks, Zack," she sputtered, coughing.

"S'nothing. Took me fifteen minutes to come round properly." He leaned closer, a heavy hand on her shoulder. She'd never minded before that he was physical with her – he never meant anything by it, and she could tell the difference – but this time... He must have seen a small reaction, because he shifted his hand to the edge of the cot.

"So, tell me. What'd it look like?

She'd been struggling to remember what it reminded her of most. Her first thought was of an insect – a praying mantis – but that wasn't quite right. A grasshopper wasn't right either. It didn't look like anything she'd ever seen. She imagined how Pierre might describe it – objectively, matter of fact. She closed her eyes, placing her mind in free-recall mode.

"Three metre long insect; can bend in the middle; six legs, trapezoidal head like a hammerhead; black body; six wet-looking slit-eyes, dripping red, no iris or pupil; no wings… muscular, armoured like… like a rhino." She opened her eye-lids wide and stared at Zack. She shuddered. She was relieved she'd been able to remember it, but now the terror of it was more real. It was fixed in her mind, and from now on it would haunt her when awake.

Zack pursed his lips and blew out a long breath. "No wonder you were running, kid." He frowned. "And Eden? Did you see Eden this time?"

She squeezed her eyes shut again to help remember, then opened them.

"Yes! But it was reddish-brown, dry. Not green anymore. Withered trees scattered around. It was a desert."

Zack snorted triumphantly. "Well, there it is then, Eden's greener than Earth – than Earth used to be, that is. So, just a nightmare, kid. Case closed." He made a mock salute. "I'll inform the skipper we can land there after all! That'll teach you to eat too much cheese before going into stasis."

Kat offered one of her crooked smiles.

"Now, you get up in a few minutes, and take a shower, because, I'll let you in on a little secret of my own – after stasis, you stink! Then join us up front, okay?" He turned, grinning, and shuffled off, his metal cane clunking on the floor.

She knew he must be right. This past month she'd been having premonitions of Eden – that some terrible alien was there, waiting to kill them all. And the fact that it was in a desert, and her dead sister – what was that all about anyway? And of course the face. She hadn't told Zack that part, it would have upset him. In the last few seconds before the monster reached him, its face had changed into a human face: Zack's.

Shaking her head, she attempted to sit up, but her arms were jelly, and she collapsed back down. She tried again, slower this time, and realised how sweaty she was. *Definitely time for a shower*. She crawled out of the cot. Her legs quivered, weakened from stasis. *All that running*, she thought, and laughed.

Setting the shower-head to "Rain", she let the hot water cascade over her head and body. As she relaxed, she remembered a detail she'd forgotten – it hadn't seemed important at the time. But she'd studied dream psych at college, and you almost never saw yourself from above – except in near-death experiences – not in dreams or even nightmares. And that top-down viewpoint – whose view was it? The creature had attacked *it*, no longer chasing the Kat figure on the ground. She didn't know what that meant, but somehow the thought chilled her. She shivered. But she didn't believe in anything metaphysical. Zack was right. Just a dream, nothing more. Dreams don't have to make sense, don't have to mean anything. She set the water to *very hot*, adjusted the nozzle to "Needle", and turned around, leaning her head against the misted cubicle door, hoping the pinpricks of steaming water would melt the shivers from her spine.

The cockpit was more cramped than usual: they'd had to adapt Zack's pilot chair due to his leg being in a cast. Kat's area, directly behind Zack's, was now squeezed. She envied Blake's position, and Pierre's science station looked positively spacious. Real estate was a prime commodity on a space-ship; she laughed inwardly – space ship – now there was an oxymoron!

She watched Zack rig up for decel. He operated a compound joystick and neural interface connected to an oculometer, a small device that fit like glasses, which shone an infrared beam onto his right eye. It allowed him to make rapid course changes if necessary, simply by looking in a direction he wanted to go and uttering a sub-vocal command through his throat-mike.

Kat envied his pilot skills – not many people could use this kit at all, let alone with his precision and response speed. She knew it came from his battle experience: dodging heat-seekers and blister-mines that took out half of all aircraft in the War.

They were nearing visual sighting of Eden. Zack, his leg propped up on a non-functioning part of the console, had been making minor course adjustments for the past two hours to get them there in the fastest possible time. All the calculations and contingency plans had been prepared and triple-checked manually. She noticed more instrument lights were on than when the virus had first hit. Blake and Pierre had been busy while she'd been in stasis. They'd managed to restore thirty per cent of the software, so they'd have good sensors, and alarms would sound if they were too steep or shallow on orbit intercept. But for the rest, they were in Zack's hands.

It was quiet, the only sounds occasional thruster burns, Zack's wincing noises, and the "beep" that occurred very two minutes confirming they were still on target and lined up for Eden.

Kat felt a subdued excitement. After all they'd been through, they were finally about to reach Eden, the salvation of humanity. And they had oxygen to breathe, at least enough to get them down to the planet's surface, where they could replenish supplies for the trip home.

As astronauts, it was the ultimate dream: to reach a new, habitable planet. The first major step had been that of Neil Armstrong, onto the moon's surface. Then there had been Yanni Sorensen, the first man to set foot on Mars, and Carlita Fernandes, the first woman to place a foot, or a fin as it had turned out to be, into the icy quagmire of Europa, floating around the awesome spectacle of Jupiter. But none of these worlds had been remotely habitable. They could build stations there, but the resource requirements meant they were unsustainable, and all such stations except a couple of so-called strategic bases on the Moon had long since been abandoned Post-War, due to the sheer cost, with almost nothing in return except abstract scientific data.

Their mission was different. Everything had fed forward to this point. Over a century of space exploration had been building to this moment. The whole crew sensed it, and despite being cut off from Earth, those back home would be aware that they were nearing Eden. Better still, they were out of harm's way, the Alicians couldn't touch them. Despite ghosters and viruses, they were going to make it.

She studied Blake, his eyes fixed outside the spaceship hunting for Eden, seeking it out in amongst the millions of points of light, a look of resolve welded onto his face. *He's willing us to Eden.* They picked the right man for the job.

Zack interrupted the silence and her train of thought. "Okay, folks, this is it. Time for decel. Buckle up!"

They all fixed their harnesses including forehead straps. Kat didn't have to be told to do it properly. The first experiments on deceleration from dark matter drives had been wildly successful and simultaneously catastrophic for the crew, who had ended up splattered all over the cockpit, their internal organs shredded by the decelerative forces before they had escaped the body's fickle confines. The harnesses in fact were a minor part of their survival kit. Most of the work was done by the Schultz-Piccione inertial dampening system inside the ship. She was relieved when its tell-tale *thrum* kicked in. Her body started to tingle, then vibrate, as its pitch rose. Pierre had told them once, over dinner, that if the sound rose to roughly high C, it meant that it was failing, and they were about to explode, but that they would probably lose consciousness. Pierre wasn't one to take along to dinner parties.

Kat shook so much she finally realized how a cocktail must feel: she felt her abdominal organs moving around, though she couldn't tell which. Speech, and even yelling were impossible. It was advisable to keep her mouth clamped shut – the nearest dentist was a long way away. But soon enough it began to die down. Her relief was blanketed by nausea. She hit the harness release buckle, eager to see out of the cockpit, and stood up, leaning on Zack's burly shoulders, staring forwards.

"Welcome to Eden," Blake said, as they all gaped at the main viewscreen. It was still some way off, a medium-sized disk, a silhouette in front of its own sun, some hundred and forty million kilometres away on the other side. They were still travelling relatively fast, but decelerating at a speed that could now be handled by the inertial field. She felt a thrill run through her, even though they couldn't see much yet.

It had been so long just seeing stars, dots of white light, that she'd forgotten what it was like to see a whole planet again. The last one they had seen had been Saturn, before the slingshot out of the Solar System. She felt a lump in her throat, and apparently Pierre also was moved, because he placed a hand briefly on her shoulder – at least she hoped that was the reason.

Zack chimed in. "She sure is a sight for sore eyes! Hang on to something, this'll be worth it!" He moved the joystick forward, and the ship gave a spurt of acceleration – catching Kat off-balance, so that Pierre caught her. The ship veered outward in an arc, placing the sun initially behind Eden, creating an eclipse, and then showing the sun burst out from behind, forcing them all to shade their eyes until the screen polarized. Kat regained her balance.

For the first time they could see colour on Eden. The lush forest green and Mediterranean blue, after so much black, silver and white made Kat gasp. The continents were very different to Earth's, and two small polar caps blazed like icing on a spherical cake.

"My God, it really is Eden!" She wanted to whoop.

Blake nodded to Zack. "Well, my friend, you've got us this far, take us into orbit. Kat, Pierre, take your stations."

She felt a cautious happiness, like a small animal daring to come out of its hole into the sunshine. So much of her personal life had gone badly wrong.

Pierre jarred the mood. "That's unusual."

She turned back round to catch what the other three were now staring at. At first she didn't see it. But as they headed further to the sunward side of Eden, it was unmistakable. A circular orange-brown patch decorated one of Eden's continents.

"Looks like a desert," Pierre said, "but it wasn't there when the Prometheus came two years ago."

Kat glanced at Zack's face reflected in the screen, but he didn't return the look. She gazed again towards Eden. It was a desert alright. No question.

Blake broke the silence. "Okay, we'll figure it out later. First things first. We get into orbit and then prepare for descent. Stations, please."

They all sat down and busied themselves. It proved trickier than they had thought, but they achieved a stable orbit on the first attempt. Kat glued her eyes to the console, not wanting to face Eden right now, nor Zack. She wondered if she should tell the Captain or Pierre. But it would seem ridiculous, and wouldn't help anything. For the first time in a while, she thought of her faraway lover back in Eden Mission Control.

A red light on her console flashed, her earpiece automatically activating. Pierre swung out of his chair and leant over her shoulder – he had obviously picked it up on the science console, too. Blake turned around. Zack was using the neural interface and oculometer, so couldn't even deviate his eyes to see what was going on.

"Report," Blake said.

Kat's stomach turned to ice when she heard the com-message.

Pierre waited for her to answer, but when she didn't, he offered what he knew. "It's a com signal, Sir."

She turned her right palm towards her and stared at it, in case she was in the nightmare again.

"From Earth?" Blake asked.

Her breath sounded raspish in her ears. She listened again, praying she'd misheard. She regained control. "It's... from Eden."

The ship veered slightly, then recovered. Blake stood up, faced Kat, and placed a steadying hand on Zack's shoulder, leaving it there.

"What does it say?" His voice was quiet.

Kat removed the earpiece and handed it to Pierre.

Pierre cleared his throat. "It says, Captain, that is, it keeps repeating..." He looked out toward the planet below, which was now occupying most of the screen, then back at the Captain. Blake didn't say anything, just waited for him to compose himself. None of them had ever known Pierre hesitate before. He cleared his throat again.

"It says, 'Do not land here. Eden is not safe. Eden is a trap.' Then it repeats."

Everyone held their breath. Kat gazed up at Blake. His face locked itself down. "Where is it coming from exactly, on the planet's surface?"

Pierre returned to his station and ran a triangulation algorithm to fix it. Kat slumped in her chair. Pierre was getting an answer from his console. But Kat already knew, and spoke, her voice uneven. "It's from the desert, isn't it?"

Pierre gave her a sideways look. "How did you know?"

She didn't answer, just stared at her console, wanting to punch it. She remembered her dream, the running, running to save her life, running to save everything. It was all going to come true, somewhere down on the planet's surface. And when it did, she knew this time she wasn't going to wake up.

PART TWO

EDEN

Chapter 17

Furnace

Micah's heart pounded up into his throat as he stared into Rudi's dark-ringed eyes, peering at him over the barrel of a pulse pistol – what sort he couldn't tell, but at this range it hardly mattered. Rudi's hand wasn't steady. Micah didn't know if that was a good or a bad sign.

He was strapped into the Optron chair with safety harnesses. His arms were free, but he couldn't reach the release buckles which Rudi had moved to the back of the chair.

"Rudi, what is this? I was just –"

"Save it, Micah, I know you've been inside my world. So you're a smart guy, you know at least part of what's going on, enough to put me in prison."

Micah saw a movement behind Rudi, in the corridor, someone bending down. Maybe he could attract their attention. Or stall until Louise arrived.

Rudi's usual smooth tones took on a ragged edge. "Did you like what you saw? Not what you were expecting, eh?" He appeared to be gloating.

Micah thought fast. He'd always been seen as the clever one, the higher ranking of the two of them; that must have irked Rudi over the years. Low-level flattery might buy some time.

"To tell you the truth, I was impressed. And the mirror? Real smart. I would have hit it except for…" He stopped. Did Rudi know about the simulacra?

Rudi tilted his head to one side. "Except for what? And how *did* you find out about the mirror – you should have slammed right into it and exited the programme immediately. There was a bio-feedback loop installed to create an energy build-up in the Optron if you hit it. Would have knocked you out, at the least."

Micah tried to work out the ramifications of telling Rudi about the Kat simulacrum. In any case, would Rudi really kill him? Here in the lab? Somewhere else? He noticed the Optron was still on, fully powered.

"Rudi, listen, can I get down from here, I've been here for –"

"Stay put buddy, you're not done yet."

So that was it: Optron overload, rigged to kill or mind-wipe. His time was running out. Could he overpower Rudi? Not a chance, tied to the chair. He took another tack. "Where's the third program, Rudi, the third interface? You get the real data, mine sends back spurious shit – but what feeds my program?"

Rudi lowered the pistol, but gestured to Micah to stay put. He strutted around in front of Micah, never taking his eyes off him.

"You were always the intellectual. The natural pattern recogniser, manipulator of equations. The geek, Micah, you fit the part perfectly. But I was smarter, I had any woman I wanted, pretty much. Life was good, but I didn't fit the profile. I had this idea, years ago, but couldn't express it in math. They wouldn't listen. Thought I was a good guy to have a beer with, but not the real deal. I was going nowhere, fucking nowhere. And then someone did listen, someone who understood my talents. One thing led to another." He shrugged.

Micah had never thought of Rudi as a friend, had never been out with him for drinks, but never thought of him as a spy. Now it all seemed to fit. Rudi had enough character traits to fit the role. But still, he never thought Rudi had it in him to be a traitor.

"Alicians?"

Rudi laughed. "Do I look that dumb? Bunch of fanatics! No, I'm working for another corporation. They helped me with the mirror simulation. It's a beaut!"

There was a gleam in his eyes. Micah recognised the old Rudi he'd met four years ago, cocky but full of ideas. But it crumbled, like all of Rudi's ideas over the years. Rudi had finally gotten his dream to come true, but Micah knew that without recognition it wouldn't soothe the pain. The old Rudi was gone, which meant Micah's situation was grim.

"What does the other corporation want?" He guessed the mirror was the third interface, even if he had no clue how it worked. Still, it would need an access portal out of the Eden Mission, through the firewalls. "Which corporation, and why?"

Rudi glanced at his watch, then at Micah and the Optron. "Sorry, Mikey, out of time." He raised the remote control and pressed a button that moved the boom to connect to Micah's head, pinning him to the chair.

Micah started to panic, reaching for the Optron headset, but there were no wires to pull, only cold, implacable carb-steel. The auto-electrodes clamped onto his temples.

"Rudi, for God's sake, you don't have to do this!" he yelled, the loudness of his own voice sending him further into panic. He kicked aimlessly.

Rudi's previously confident voice now sounded strained, but laced with bitterness. He glanced towards the door.

"You're right, Micah. I don't have to do it. But I will. I'd say sweet dreams, but we both know that would be a lie. I've switched you back to my world. Before brain death, the carrion birds will eat you alive. It won't be real of course, but you'll feel it just the same. So long, little big shot."

Rudi flicked a switch and the Optron emitted a low hum, climbing in pitch.

Micah fought helplessly, squirmed, kicked, and screamed "No!", and then he heard a small gasp, and something heavy slump to the floor. He was unable to turn his head. The Optron gleamed in front of him, and he felt himself being sucked in. He didn't want to die, not like this. And for the first time in his life, in his mind he called out not for his mother, but for his father to help him. Then he felt something touch his neck, and a tingling coldness spread like a freezing cobweb across his face and down his arms; an icy chill that squeezed him out of consciousness.

He awoke on a dusty floor in a dark room, little bigger than a broom closet. He'd been roused by a clanging, but he couldn't make out where he was. He couldn't move. He tried to get up, but nothing happened. He opened his eyes with a massive effort. Then he heard movement – someone else was there, manoeuvring around him. He felt a sharp pricking sensation in his neck. Nausea surged through him; tremors wracked his body, then vanished. He fell forward and vomited, remaining on all fours, trying to recover his breath in between spasms of retching. A graveyard voice came from behind him.

"Your colleague is dying. What awoke you was the sound of the furnace chute door closing. He is burning to death below. He will be gone in a few moments. In such a predicament fear and pain usually trigger a heart attack before the burning boils the brain. I am a Cleanser. We believe that death, and in particular the pain of death, is a necessary cleansing process before meeting the Maker of all things. I drugged him, so he will neither move nor scream, but he will still feel everything."

Micah retched again, his eyes watering. What looked like a towel, in the semi-darkness, dropped next to him.

"Clean yourself and stand up."

Micah pulled himself up, his legs trembling. Everyone knew about Cleansers, though most hoped they were only legend, something to scare children into behaving well; perfect assassins who knew no mercy. His only option for now was to obey.

"Turn around."

Micah did so, reluctantly, guessing that once he saw this man's face he would not be left to live. He stared in disbelief at Ben the janitor, except that even in this half-light, something was wrong with the way he held himself – like a panther ready to lash out at a moment's notice. Micah also noticed the hands – podgy, yet expressive, fluid in motion. Not Ben, for sure.

"I will ask you a question. I will only ask you once. You will only give one answer. I will know if you are lying. If you lie to me, you go into the furnace. Alive. Nod if you understand me."

The words were flat, but had the same effect on Micah as a saw cutting into exposed bone. His legs shook, though he tried to hide it. He sweated as he looked at the "janitor", who stood statue-like. His mind was racing, but there were only two logical outcomes – either he refused to answer and would die now, or else he told the truth and would probably also die, though not immediately. Trying to lie to this Cleanser was not an option. He thought again of his dad, a war hero – what would he have said or done?

"Do you understand your options?"

Micah nodded. He had already guessed the question.

"Where is Sandy?"

He didn't want to answer. He envisioned Rudi's skeleton disintegrating to ash down below. A hand shot out and closed around his throat, lifting him off the floor and pinning him against the wall. The Cleanser's other hand threw open the furnace lid. A blast of hot air and a blood-red glow flooded into the small dark space.

"I will allow you to scream." He moved Micah's body with pathetic ease towards the opening.

"Wait!" Micah cried, despite knowing that whatever he said his fate might be the same. But he had to cling on. The Cleanser did not let him down, but brought Micah's face closer to his own. Micah looked into those eyes and knew there was no way to lie to them.

"Kane's office." The words came of their own accord, before Micah could stop them.

The Cleanser stared a little longer, then released him so that he fell to the floor. Micah felt disgusted, as if he'd just signed Sandy's death warrant, and his own. In what he realised was probably a futile act, he kicked hard at the Cleanser's leg behind the knee, thinking maybe he could escape and summon help. But the target blurred out of reach, and Micah's groin exploded with pain. As he lay on the floor, trying to breathe in, the cold voice spoke close to his ear.

"Don't."

Micah managed to take in a few straggling breaths.

"Get up. Make yourself presentable."

Micah did his best to compose himself. As he rose he sneaked a glance at his wristcom: 6:05. He prayed Louise was on time and had found he was missing.

"Listen carefully," the Cleanser said. "We take the service elevator on the left. It is twenty metres. We come out on level 200 and turn left. You approach the security guards at the office and tell them Louise sent you."

Micah's wide eyes betrayed his surprise – this man knew his stuff.

"Then what?"

"Once inside the office you show me where she is."

Micah forced himself to look into the Cleanser's eyes. "What if they don't let me in?"

The unwavering black pupils answered the question for Micah.

"And me?" Micah said.

"If I have to kill you, I'll make it quick."

Micah didn't know whether the "if" was honest or just to gain his compliance. This assassin exuded professionalism, or fanaticism, he didn't know which. But there was integrity about him – he appeared to take no sadistic joy from killing. At least the vids had that part wrong. But Micah had made up his own mind. He wouldn't stand by while Sandy was killed, even if it only meant delaying the inevitable. He brushed himself down.

"I'm ready."

Moments later they emerged, Micah first, followed a few feet behind by the innocuous figure of a hunched over janitor pushing his trolley stuffed with brooms, cloths and bottles of detergent. He told Micah that if he did anything out of the ordinary or tried to run, he'd be dead in a second. Micah didn't doubt it.

As they waited for the service elevator, Antonia came around the corner. She stopped when she saw Micah, but the anger that had suddenly drawn like a curtain across her face melted as she saw Micah's taut, resolute expression. She glanced at the janitor fiddling with his trolley, then walked towards them. Micah turned back to the elevator lamp – the lift was descending, but was still five floors above them. He didn't want her caught up in this, and wouldn't look at her. *Don't stop now. Walk on past!* To his relief, just as she sauntered past, the lift arrived. He wondered if she would ask him why he was taking the service elevator, but instead she addressed the janitor.

"Hi there Pops, how you doing today?"

Without missing a beat, he answered, in a reasonable impression of Ben's voice. "Why, fine, sweetheart, mighty nice of you to ask, but must be going now, one more floor to clean."

As Micah stepped inside the elevator, the Cleanser pushed the trolley in too, blocking Micah in, all the time watching his eyes. But she had already passed. The Cleanser closed the door and hit the button for floor 200.

Micah usually had a strong urge to speak in lifts, but he could find nothing to say as they swept upwards. The lift pinged and the door slid open.

"Remember my instructions. You go on ahead; I'll be right behind you. But first, put this on. Lift your arms."

It was a black waist band that fit under Micah's jacket. Micah had no idea what it was, but complied.

"If you want to live, don't touch it."

Micah looked down briefly and then back to the Cleanser.

"Go. Now."

Micah walked slowly at first, then at a brisker pace. The creaking of the trolley wheels tracked behind him. He came around the corner to Sandy's office, which acted as antechamber to Kane's suite. Two Eden Security guards, not Chorazin, stood outside, fully armed. As he started to say he'd been asked to come here at six o'clock to meet with Agent Louise, one of the guards deftly pushed him face to the wall, a pistol against the nape of his neck. A firm nudge behind his legs knocked Micah to his knees. His hands went to the wall to maintain balance. While one guard held a gun on him, the other patted him down. When he got to the waistband, he patted it once and then stopped. He tried to say something, and then keeled over backwards. Micah heard a whoosh and as he turned he saw the second man, the one with the gun, crumpled on top of the first, a knife handle sticking out of his throat. Yellow gelatinous fluid bubbled around the blade – Micah guessed it stopped the blood spraying. The man's eyes were wide open. The Cleanser was already there, next to Micah.

"Don't move," he said. He removed the waistband. "Get up."

Micah tried, but the first man had fallen across his legs. Before he knew what was happening the Cleanser pulled the man off him, and was searching for a key card in his pocket. He held it out, but Micah was transfixed by the first man, not yet dead, eyes blinking fast, his body convulsing. The guard's jaw moved as if he were trying to say something. Micah looked to the Cleanser.

"Contact poison," said the Cleanser. "Colombian kokai frog. Instant paralysis – his lungs cannot work anymore. He'll be dead shortly. Open the door."

Micah took the key card but still couldn't move his feet. He gaped at the dying man whose face was turning blue, his eyes screaming in silence for help.

With a muted crunch, the Cleanser's right hand whipped out and snapped the man's neck.

"Open the door," he repeated.

Micah obeyed, fumbling to get the key card in. At the third attempt he heard the soft magnetic click and the door slid open. The room was empty. Micah was followed by the Cleanser carrying one man across his shoulder. He had pushed the other one on top of the trolley and wheeled him in. He closed the door behind them and locked it, backed the trolley up against it, shoving the second corpse in front of the trolley. Micah drew away from the doors, and leant unsteadily against Sandy's desk. He saw the letter opener lying there, and wondered if he could slip it inside his jacket.

"Don't even think about it, Micah." The Cleanser stood up, and with a tearing motion, removed the sim-skin mask, so that he no longer looked like the janitor. For the first time Micah saw the lean, tan face underneath.

"Where?" The Cleanser ripped off the overalls revealing a black, one-piece jumpsuit underneath. He appeared unarmed. Micah was puzzled because he still appeared to be carrying body fat, but moved like a gymnast. The Cleanser raised an eyebrow. Micah nodded to the two doors that led to Kane's suite. The Cleanser gestured to him to go first.

151

Micah pressed the gold door handles and opened the doors wide and walked in. At first he thought the Cleanser had stayed outside, but then he heard the soft click of the doors being closed, and saw him checking around the suite. After a moment, including a brief bathroom inspection, he came back to face Micah. Micah suddenly felt cold steel being pressed against his neck.

"Last chance."

Micah tried hard not to glance toward the bathroom. "I lied. She's gone. You'll never find her."

Micah had expected to feel the blade slice into his throat, to see those eyes flash in anger, but the Cleanser lowered the knife, and stood between Micah and the bathroom.

"Listen to me, Micah. I'm not here to –"

The Cleanser spun away from him as the bathroom mirror shattered outwards. A pulse bullet ricocheted off the Cleanser into Micah's shoulder, sending him reeling backwards. Another shot fired but the Cleanser had vaulted out of the line of sight from the bathroom. Micah saw Sandy kneeling behind stalactites of glass, gun aimed outwards, her hand unsteady. Instinctively Micah crouched down on the carpet.

At the other end of the suite, the double doors burst open. A black-helmeted, body-armoured female Chorazin agent hurtled through the air, rolled across the floor, slammed a round object onto the floor then sprung up, levelling a rifle at the Cleanser.

Two bullets from the Cleanser knocked the rifle out of her hands. He stood, legs splayed, rapid-firing his weapon, both arms locked out in front. Micah saw the agent driven back by repeated gunfire hitting exactly the same place on her helmet's visor. A loud keening shriek erupted from the object on the floor, making Micah clasp his hands around his ears. He knew what it was – an audio grenade to make them all black out. He tried to hang on.

The Cleanser fired again and again. No matter where the agent ducked and dived, he always hit the same spot, denting the shaded visor. Micah glanced to Sandy, but like him, she was incapacitated by pain that felt like a needle piercing his eardrums. He turned back to the agent and saw a crack appear on the visor as she tried to regain her balance. She dived sideways and flung something in the Cleanser's direction, but he launched himself upwards, still firing even in mid air as he twisted out of the way of a stream of darts spitting across the room, impaling the wall behind him. The rising crescendo shattered the windows, as Micah rolled onto his back in agony, but still he watched through pain-slitted eyes.

The agent tried to protect her visor – now a spiderweb of fractures – with her forearm, but a bullet slammed into her elbow, flinging her arm to the side, as another punched into her visor. She somersaulted backwards, a bullet pounding into her back, sending her sprawling onto the floor. Micah's eyesight began to blur. Sandy was already slumped in her hiding place. The Cleanser stepped toward the woman's prone form, and aimed the weapon down towards her head. Micah lost consciousness.

* * *

Louise waited, panting, but the kill-shot never came. One of the drill-darts had gotten through; it had just taken longer than normal to paralyse him. She stared up into the assassin's eyes, knowing that he was using every ounce of will to pull the trigger, but it was too late. She yanked off the helmet, removed the protective earphones, and manoeuvred into a seated position. She kicked out hard at Gabriel's stomach, and he toppled over backwards like a broken statue. Getting to her feet, she checked that Micah and Sandy were out cold, then knelt over the Cleanser, lifting his face towards hers.

"I know you can hear me, Brother Matthias, although you shouldn't hear anything after that sonic grenade. Nice shooting by the way," she said, showing him the helmet visor. "One more and I'd be dead." She tossed it to the floor.

His lips twitched. She grabbed his jaw.

"No, no. Shhh. Don't try to speak," she whispered. "I know what you want to say. That you came here to find Sandy, to protect her from the Alicians, not to kill her, and that there's a double-agent in the Chorazin." She unpeeled her right hand glove. "Did you really think you could fool Sister Esma?" She smiled, forcing his mouth open with her forefinger and thumb. "Don't worry, Sandy's safe with me now. Relax, your part in this is over. Time to die." She found the false tooth at the back of his throat. She squeezed and snapped it open. His eyes widened a fraction. "Good to be awake when you die, that's what you Cleansers say, isn't it?" She let his head slip to the floor.

Four other Chorazin agents charged into the room. She stood up, facing them. "Medic, get a goddammed medic, fast," she screamed at them. "He's taken poison!"

Micah felt his face being slapped gently. He heard a female voice.

"Come on, Micah, wake up, there you go, only a flesh wound this time. Not bad for your first day. Found the girl, found the assassin – maybe we should hire you." She smiled, but Micah was in too much pain to return the favour. His ears rang.

He stared up into Louise's face. "Sandy... alive?"

"In custody. We'll protect her."

Micah was still trying to come round. "The Cleanser?"

Louise helped him sit up so he could see. The Cleanser lay prone, eyes and mouth open with a look of surprise – not pain or fear. His body was much thinner now, surrounded by a pool of pinkish water.

"Pretty good disguise, don't you think?" she said. "Temporary extreme water retention. Intensely uncomfortable, but these Alicians, well, you know what fanatics will go through. At least now you do."

"You killed him?"

"We wanted to interrogate him, but he had a failsafe device. Died instantly. He couldn't penetrate my armour, although the sonofabitch hit my visor, the weakest point, nine times before I dropped him."

"How did you know we were here?" Micah asked, wincing from the shoulder wound. Every movement felt like a knife cutting him open.

Louise smiled, and moved aside so he could see. "Your little friend told me, you know, the one you like to share coffee with."

Standing at the doorway was a white-faced Antonia.

"When she saw you with Ben, or whatever his real name was, she noticed something was wrong. So she called him *Pops*. Apparently the real Ben hated that word. When he didn't react, well, things just fell into place."

Micah nodded towards Antonia. "Thanks." But as he said it, he remembered her simulacrum crying, reaching out for Katrina. He didn't know how she read his face.

She spoke to Louise, her voice quiet. "May I leave?"

"I'm afraid you're involved now, Miss Laschtiva, you'll need to be processed. Agent Montaigue will handle you; we have several rooms set up for de-briefing."

Before she left, Antonia gave Micah a long, measuring look.

"Come on Micah," Louise said, helping him up. "You need debriefing too, I'm afraid. Vince will want to question you."

He struggled to his feet. He knew he should feel relieved, but something didn't seem right. He was glad to be alive, but it was all a little too neat. He remembered the Cleanser had been about to say something to him before Louise had burst in, something important. Louise was acting as if everything had all been wrapped up nicely, but his intuition told him it was far from over.

His analytical mind kicked in as he was escorted groggily down the corridor, and he came to an irrevocable conclusion: Sandy was the key. She knew something, maybe didn't even know she knew it, probably something Kane had known. Kane, Rudi, and the Cleanser – they'd all died to protect a piece of knowledge – he had no idea what. But it meant she was still in mortal danger. He wanted to tell Louise, but something held him back. He wasn't even sure he could trust Vince. Still, he had to do something. Rudi's landscape – he had to go back in. Somewhere in there was the answer. Rudi was smart enough to have left a clue, an insurance policy in case he was betrayed. Micah had to find it.

Chapter 18

Quarantine

Zack lowered his voice. "Don't let the Skipper hear you talking like that."

"What seems to be the problem?" Blake strode in and stood behind them.

Zack winced, and sat back in his chair. "Too late," he muttered.

Kat turned to face Blake directly, her back to Eden vista'd by the external 3D cameras. "It's perfect, Sir. Mountains, lakes, grass. No animals. Like renting an unfurnished apartment. We can move in tomorrow."

Blake looked beyond her, and uncorked a smile. Perfect indeed! At last mankind had the second chance it needed. Eden had been the right name after all. He itched to get out there, recalling running around his grandpa's fields as a young boy, not a care in the world. He wanted that back so badly, not for him, but for everyone, so humanity could heal itself.

"Sir, don't you think it's just *too* perfect?" She peered around him. "Pierre, back me up here, what are the probabilities?"

Blake tore his eyes from the panoramic vista, towards Pierre. "Well, Pierre, what does science have to say?"

Pierre touched a control and the data encircling his head collapsed like a waterfall that had just run out of juice. "Sir, there's been a lot of debate on that since Prometheus first sent back images. Basically, we only have our solar system to go on; this is the first planet we've visited outside it. The Bayesians and the Frequentists have been arguing –"

"*Pierre!*" Kat pleaded.

He cleared his throat. "There's… a lot of fundamental disagreement." He hit the control and retreated inside the chimney of data rising around him.

"Which is why we're here," Blake said, turning back. "Sometimes you need a little faith, Kat."

"And the desert? The one that didn't exist two years ago? And the message?"

His smile shortened. "We'll find out soon enough." He stretched his gaze to the horizon east of the mountain range, and found a rust coloured fringe. He hadn't intended landing this close, but a thruster failure had careened them a thousand kilometres off course to this place, with the desert's heat haze glistening a mere twenty kilometres away. He'd also seen one puzzling screen shot during the approach: a fuzzy picture of a broken-up structure, perhaps the remnants of a crashed spacecraft. Since Prometheus was on another continent, they'd all immediately thought it could be the missing ship, the Heracles. But it didn't look right, and the Heracles' telemetry had indicated it exploded near the nebula, five light years out from Eden. As for the message... None of them had any idea what it meant nor who could have sent it, but he refused to take it at face value. He pushed all of this to the back of his mind, unwilling to sour the moment.

He ached to explore the hazy mountains, rendered purplish by the afternoon rays of Eden's blood orange sun. Yellow clouds the shape of cigars drifted across the sky. He could almost smell the coarse grass, feel it under his ship, beckoning.

Pierre stood up. "Sir, I've checked rad levels, atmosphere, temperature, meteo, and a host of other parameters. We're good to go."

Blake and Pierre suited up and depressurised the outer airlock. The final hiss came, and he twisted the wheel-lock handle and shoved open the heavy outer door that had been sealed for more than three months. Gravity was five per cent less than on Earth, and he used the short auto-ladder to descend to Eden's surface, two metres below.

He paused at the last rung, and then placed his right foot firmly on the scorched grass beneath. As he put his weight on his foot, the ground sank a little, and he was reminded of the good planting soil on his ancestral farm. He remembered rolling in it while mock-fighting his younger brother, snatched away from him later on by the enemy. He recalled watching his son Robert, just fourteen, grinning and freckled, sitting atop a huge combine harvester.

"Sir? It's a momentous moment, I know."

Blake jogged his mind back into gear, brought down his other foot, and then took a few steps. Each pace away from the Lander etched its way into history – mankind's new adventure, its new lease of life. Instantly he thought of his wife Glenda, imagining her waving him on. This planet will save her.

His visor shielded him from the glare of the mid-afternoon sun, a little more distant than Earth's. He gazed across the plain, and was reminded of Africa's Serengeti – without the animals or birds. No decent theory had been provided yet as to why Eden was devoid of animal life. Truth told nobody important back on Earth cared. Kat was right, it was always better moving into an empty new home than having someone else's furniture to contend with.

"Well, Skipper, what's it look like from out there?" Zack's voice boomed across the intercom.

Blake stared at the trees a few hundred metres away. "Pierre, are our visors working okay?"

Pierre looked up from the tripod of equipment he was setting up. "More or less. The onboard computer probably adjusted the colours to fit what it was expecting. There might be some auto-compensation in the helmets, too."

"Huh?" Zack said.

"What he means, Zack, is that the colours out here are stronger – the grass has a blue tinge, and the trees are a very dark shade of green. The sky itself is definitely purple, the clouds a striking yellow." Blake tried to ignore it. It was subtle, in any case, like a normal view through a tinted lens. Probably meant nothing. We'll just have to get used to it, and even if we don't our children will. He wanted to lift his visor, to see it with his own eyes.

He felt a slight giddiness, as if he'd just stood up suddenly after lying down. He glanced at his wristcom to verify that the oxygen pressure in his suit was normal. It was. He steadied his feet, feeling nausea wash over him, accompanied by a cold sweat on his palms. He recognised the symptoms right away: *Deep Space Affective Disorder*, the psychs called it. *Pressure cooker syndrome* was Zack's label. The psychologist had warned them during training that arrival could be a powerful emotional event, and could affect their judgement after such a long space trip. Blake hadn't taken it too seriously; or rather he thought he'd be watching for signs in others, not himself. He usually had his emotions tightly wrapped and under control, but right now he felt as if he was on a cliff edge.

"You okay, Boss?"

"Fine, Zack. Send Kat our here, too. Everything's fine."

"Sir, I'm still testing," Pierre said.

"Carry on. Kat can join us."

Focus: that was the key, and action. Doing something decisive would chase it away. He knelt down on one knee, dug his gloved hand into the soil, scooped up a handful of Eden's dirt, and let it run through his fingers, watching it fall, framed by the maroon sky. It seemed too soft, more like ash than hard peat that would yield crops. His middle finger grazed something hard. So, topsoil only. Nothing substantive would grow in this field.

The thought that he had never been able to bury his own son, crackled uninvited into his mind. He knew this should be a moment of exhilaration, an epiphany. But the old farm decimated by a firestorm, what was left of his brother coming back in a body bag, his son in Kurana Bay, all flooded back to him, a dark whirlpool in his mind.

He took some deep breaths, and turned around to stare at the Lander, instead of the landscape that was affecting his mood. He stood up. "We should get started, Pierre."

Pierre busied himself with his scanners and samplers. "I'll just need a moment to get it calibrated, Sir."

Blake felt his heart beating strong in his carotid artery. Not fast, but like a distant hammer. He tried to calm himself by checking the grey hull of the Lander. It was a trick he'd learned long ago as a scuba diver: to counter the effects of nitrogen narcosis, concentrate on something, engage the brain in analysing something concrete.

The Lander was in as good a shape as could be expected. He traced his hands along the atmospheric entry scorch marks near the base of the hull, like coal-black scars; bubbled in places, but no cuts in its metallic sheath. Kat joined them outside, jumping down most of the steps, vidding Eden's landscape.

Zack cut in, the envy in his voice coming across the com system. "Hey, how is it out there, really?"

"Awesome. You're missing out, big fella." she replied.

Blake was relieved to hear her humour had returned – Zack had quietly informed him of the desert in her dream. *If she can be upbeat, then so the hell can I.* He felt he should add something. "It's mighty fine out here, Zack, mighty fine." But the words rang hollow.

Zack came back on-line. "Watch out for any snakes, or for that matter, naked babes bearing fruit. See any of the latter, just send them on in!"

Kat gave a dismissive wave back towards the Lander's external vidcorder.

Blake smiled, but his creeping unease wouldn't go away. All the instruments had shown it should be safe to take off their helmets. And God knew they needed to replenish their air supplies very soon. Pierre was still fiddling with the equipment. This was taking too long. They'd checked everything before coming out. The test should be just a final routine confirmation. His breathing sounded loud in his ears, reverberating in his helmet. "What do you say, Pierre?"

"Not yet, Sir," he answered without looking up. "I need another minute."

A minute passed. Five more dripped away. Blake circled the Lander three times. Still Pierre took more readings. Kat and Blake inspected the external transmitter recessed in the hull.

"Not good, Sir. The Trojan triggered an overload in the slipstream crystal diode. No comms with Earth unless we find a new one."

He nodded, and headed back over to Pierre, slight tremors in his right hand. *Damn, not now.*

"Well Pierre? And don't ask me to wait another minute."

Pierre stopped hunching over his machine and stood up, visor-to-visor with him.

"Sir, there's a small variance in the atmosphere I can't account for. It didn't show up from inside, but now we're out here, the equipment is more accurate. There's something in the biosphere I can't interpret."

The words hung in the air inside Blake's helmet and in the cockpit. Blake waited, knowing Zack would double-check Pierre's readings relayed back to the cockpit.

"Skipper – he's right. Don't know what it is. It's a trace element, less than a millionth, unknown on Earth. Inorganic, the computer reckons, possibly a metal, dense crystalline structure."

Blake's jaw clenched. "Toxic? Chemically reactive? Inert?"

"Sir," Pierre said, "I don't know. It seems inert, but the element, or material, doesn't exist on Earth, so we'll have to gather it in sufficient amount to study. But with half the computers still off-line, I'm not sure we can be precise about its effects. I'm sorry, Sir, we just don't have the kit to do this properly. I'd need a mass spectrometer and a cache of software that's been garbled by the virus. It needs genetic-impact testing."

Blake held up his hand. "What do you propose?"

"I can set up a nano-mesh filtration system after some basic testing here. In a few hours we can replenish our air supplies in safety. But we need to stay suited for the rest of the mission, Sir."

It was like being shot in the back. He stared at Pierre in disbelief, replaying the words, at the same time knowing it was the correct course of action. But he understood the deeper meaning: another mission in two years time to come back and determine what they were here to find out now – whether man could survive on Eden. Lab tests would be carried out back on Earth by scientists, but ever since the nannite virus, public trust of science wasn't worth a cent. And the politics were desperate, funding for a fourth mission would never happen, the Alicians and Fundies would see to that. He knew all the protocols and procedures by heart, and they worked fine in a rational world, but back on Earth, things were unravelling. He remembered what the General had said. *Bring back good news.*

"Tests would ultimately need a human subject, right Pierre?"

"Skipper –" interjected Zack, before Pierre could reply.

"What we need right now, is a little experiment," Blake said, raising his hands to the seals on his helmet.

"Blake! No!" Zack shouted.

He released the hermetic band on his helmet, and slowly eased it off.

Kat and Pierre stared, transfixed.

Blake waited for something to happen. He was struck by the colours, now the visor's auto-compensation was gone – the purple sky, the orange desert, small yellowish clouds, blue-green grass – definitely odd, reminding him of a Van Gogh. But he immediately felt calm. The tremors vanished. The theory was correct – decisive action cleared it like smelling salts.

"Might as well breathe in, Sir," Pierre said.

Blake realised he'd been holding his breath, and laughed, a little shakily, then took a cautious breath.

"Pierre, maybe you do have a sense of humour after all, buried under those equations." He inhaled and exhaled deeply several times. After three months in a tin can, as Zack called the Ulysses, the air tasted fresh. The tension trickled out of him, down into Eden's soil. He turned to the cockpit vidcorder and gave Zack the thumbs up.

"Well Pierre, care to join me? It actually smells like fresh mown grass, a little sautéed by our engines. I can feel a small breeze on my face, and the warmth of Eden's sun." He lifted his face toward Kantoka

Minor, feeling another star's rays warm his forehead. A smile flourished across his face. We could live here. This could really become home.

Pierre stepped back behind the testing machinery tripod. "Actually, Sir, I don't think that's a good idea."

Blake's sunny smile clouded over. He knew what was coming. Bold actions always had a price tag.

"I'm sorry, Sir. We'll need to quarantine you outside the ship and see if there's any reaction."

Blake took another breath. He felt fine, absolutely fine. But he nodded to Pierre. "You're right. Still, we need to replenish our air supply for the trip home. You work on the nano-filter. You can co-ordinate with Zack." He saw Pierre nod, but look away. "What is it?"

Pierre studied his boots momentarily, and then spat it out. "Sir, it's the trip home. There's only one quarantine option. That's stasis, Sir. The entire trip, barring emergencies."

Blake narrowed his gaze. His science officer was right again. But there was no way he would submit to stasis for the whole trip back.

"We'll decide that later," he said. "We clearly have a new priority to analyse this element, and develop a filtration system."

He then addressed them all, re-asserting command before any doubt about his judgement could take seed.

"Okay, listen up everyone; this changes things. We now have several priorities. The original task of taking samples and determining the suitability of the biosphere, remains. We now have an important additional problem with this rogue element we've never seen before. It needs to be collected and analysed. We also need to replenish the air stocks and clean out the oxygen strippers. This links to the first problem, because either we filter out this new element, or else we all become guinea pigs. We'll never be allowed back on earth. They'll probably divert us to Lunar Station Beta."

He stared beyond Kat and Pierre, to the desert. "The other priority is to identify the source of the message, find out who sent it and why, and use whatever material we find from that crash site to repair our comms system. Last, we need to find out more about this desert, where it's come from, and whether it's growing. That's a challenging set of priorities, and we have four days to achieve them all. Pierre, you're the best analyst – you stay here, around the ship; keep in line of sight with Zack, open comms at all times."

Pierre nodded to Blake, and then to Zack in the cockpit.

Blake turned to his comms officer. "Kat, I want you to forget all those dreams you've had about the desert."

"Zack told...?" She glanced accusingly towards the Lander.

"You and I are taking the skimmer direct to that crash site. The best way to get rid of your demons is to confront them."

Kat straightened, nodding.

"Now, even if I think that Kat's nightmares are just that, given what has happened to us so far on this trip," he glanced at her, "I want each of us outside the ship armed at all times. Questions?"

He heard the breeze rustling the bushes nearby. It was a welcome relief from the silence. No birds, no animals, and he hadn't seen any insects so far. He brushed it aside for later.

"Zack, you're in command. Kat and I are leaving in the twenty minutes it'll take to rig up the skimmer. We have about five hours of daylight left, and a round trip of three to four hours to the crash site. We'll be out of comms range, so if we get stuck, or need to stay there for any reason, I'll launch a green sonic flare at 8pm Ulysses time. Either team has a serious problem, they launch a red flare."

As Blake and Kat unloaded the land skimmer, a jet-powered hover-bike for two, Zack spoke to Blake on single channel.

"Skipper, you okay?"

Blake sighed. "I am now – wasn't back then. You probably didn't notice."

"Yeah, right."

Blake really wished Zack was mobile.

"Blake – remember she's just a kid, okay? Go easy."

"Don't worry, Zack – out here, we're all rookies." After a few seconds he heard the line click back to open channel.

* * *

Kat kept uncharacteristically quiet as Blake, in front of her, threaded the skimmer around the orange dunes at 150 kph. She was no stranger to speed: she'd been an astro-surfer before the War, falling to Earth from twenty kilometres up atop a hover-board. But she kept thinking she saw flecks of silver in the distance, hiding in the seamless orange carpet all around them. The plume of sand behind them would be visible from ten kilometres away, maybe more. She guessed the glints were tricks of her mind. She was reminded of a story her older sister, Angelica, had told her about surfing in Cape Town's White Shark Alley, famed for its Great Whites, before oceanic poisoning wiped them out. She'd asked Angel, as she called her sister, what she would do if she saw a Great White coming toward her.

"That's just it," she'd replied, "in the blue you won't see one until after it's taken a bite out of you, a leg usually. They detect you long before you see them, and then they come at you from behind or below, or from the side."

Kat stared around and held on. She knew the silver flashes she thought she saw were tricks of the mind because, like the Great White, the creature in her dreams would only be seen when it wanted to be seen. After a while, she closed her eyes, embracing the Skimmer's vibration and rolling engine-whine. As the Captain leaned slightly to the left or the right to avoid an upcoming boulder, she leaned with him, eyes closed, putting all her trust in the driver.

She remembered being ten years old, riding Pacific breakers on the back of Angel's long board, as her elder sister pulled them through a tube, Kat's first time inside the thunderous roll of a crashing wave, stealing a half-second ahead of it to emerge free. Remembering that experience, her fears subsided. *Let the sharks come. We'll stay one step ahead of you.* But just as she relaxed, she heard a voice inside her head. It made her tremble, sending a shiver down her spine. It sounded like Angel's voice, uttering three words, and then it was gone.

"Kat, come quickly."

She held her breath for a moment. Had she really heard it or just imagined it? Angel was long dead, and she had no truck with any metaphysical life-after-death bullshit. But she was convinced that something had just communicated with her. Instinctively she knew it must be the sender of the message they'd received in orbit, warning them not to come. She spoke into the helmet microphone.

"Captain?"

Blake's voice clicked on through the intercom. "Yes, Kat?"

"Can we go any faster?"

There was a pause, and then Kat felt a surge as they accelerated toward the top speed of 200kph.

With the helmet mike off, Kat said in a low voice. "I'm coming, whoever you are." As she watched the endless dunes and scattered, solitary boulders flash past against a deepening purple sky, she realised that right now she would have no way of knowing if she was dreaming or not.

Chapter 19

Debrief

Micah checked his wristcom: he'd been waiting two hours in the Optron Lab to be de-briefed by Vince, and to make matters worse, his computer privileges had been withdrawn. His computer and the gleaming Optron lay dormant. He knew the answers – and maybe the right questions, lay hidden inside the landscape somewhere. The Eden astronauts were in trouble, he could feel it in his stomach, but here he was killing time waiting for Vince, who was probably going to try and send him home now the assassin had been killed. Micah needed something to bargain with, but had no idea what. His foot swung underneath the chair, idly nudging a table leg.

He cast a glance over to Rudi's desk. They hadn't exactly been close, but he remembered when they'd joined the Eden Mission Project four years ago – the champagne, the speeches, the feeling of being part of something. Rudi's empty desk resembled a marble grave.

He imagined the furnace, how close he'd come to ending up there, mingled with Rudi's ashes. *No one deserves that*. Rudi's chair was pulled out from his desk, as if he might return any minute. He walked over and pushed it underneath the desktop. It felt like sliding closed the lid of a coffin. He sat back down at his own desk.

The lab doors burst open. Vince marched in, yanked out Rudi's chair unceremoniously, skidding it across the floor close to Micah, and sat with the back of the chair in front of him. Like the first cut of a surgeon, his voice sliced through the air. "When did you first suspect Rudi was a traitor?"

"Traitor? I never thought of him as –"

"Then catch up fast."

"I… I began to notice small things over the past few weeks, maybe a couple of months."

Vince rested his elbows atop the back of the chair, fingers interlaced. He stared, eyes burning across the silence between them.

Micah shifted position. "Well, he was a bit secretive, would stay late, said he had to work on something, but was pretty evasive. Sometimes I'd come in early and he'd been there two hours already."

Vince did a good impression of a waxwork statue.

Micah coughed. "About four weeks ago, I came in real early. Couldn't sleep. Rudi was around, but not in the lab, I guess he'd gone for a coffee or something." He wished Vince would make a wisecrack, or shout, or something. "So, anyway, there was some print-out on his desk. Only it wasn't ours."

"How so?"

"It just looked... different. It had a logo on it which wasn't ours."

"Indus Valley Systems," Vince said. It didn't sound like a question.

Micah coughed again. Vince strode over to the recycled water-cooler in the corner of the lab, and brought back a half-filled plastic cup.

"Thanks." Micah took several swigs.

"Who did you report it to?"

He shifted in his seat again. "I opened it. I supposed he'd borrowed it from another analyst, looking for new methods. It happens – there are only a hundred analysts like Rudi and me around, and sometimes we communicate, looking for new ideas.

"But this concerned Ulysses."

"Yes, at least our methods. I was a bit shocked, since it potentially compromised security. I noticed the Optron was set to my frequency, not his. I went looking for him, but didn't find him till I got back. Rudi had logged into his own landscape and the document was gone." He gulped down the last sip of water.

"So you didn't tell anyone."

He shook his head, and studied the bottom of his empty cup. "I figured he was fed up, had been talking out of line to an IVS analyst, that's all. I mean we have all sorts of firewalls, there's nothing serious he could have done alone..." *You were way ahead of me, Rudi, let me believe I was the smarter analyst, got my guard down.*

Vince stood. "We checked the furnace, but ash is ash. We assume two corpses were dumped in there in the last six hours."

"Ben... the janitor?"

"Cleansers don't leave loose ends. You were lucky, Micah. If Louise hadn't bumped into that girl, you and Sandy would be dead."

"And the other jan... I mean the Cleanser?"

"Cyanide pill. Dead, unfortunately."

It didn't sound unfortunate.

"Louise is trying to find out his real identity, and which Alician Chapel he was operating from."

Micah glanced sideways.

Vince cocked his head. "Are you and Louise getting along okay?"

"Sure."

Vince sighed. "A word of warning, Micah. She's dangerous. Very. Rough ride in the War, left her pretty jagged. You're smart enough to have worked that out. Just remember what black widow spiders do with their mates."

Micah nodded, faking a worldly nonchalance.

Vince paused to let it sink in, then continued. "As of 09.00 today, a new link has been set up, using back-up optronics, two new boys, mil-tech. Probably don't have your flair, certainly not Rudi's, –"

Micah winced.

"– but they'll get the basics done and keep out the hackers. They're trying to establish contact now."

He was amazed how quickly a back-up crew had been brought in. But there was still no contact with the ship. "Ulysses – it's past the nebula, where the Heracles disappeared."

"Correct. Hubble IV picked up a tracer two hours ago, two days old. That's all we have for now. They should be on Eden." He brushed down his tunic, ready to leave.

Micah felt cast aside. Despite the danger of the past couple of days, he'd been more alive than since he could remember; since the War. He didn't want to be dropped from the picture.

"What about me? What do I do now?"

Vince looked surprised. "Do? You go home, and you stay there. Haven't you had enough adventure for a while? You're not an agent, Micah – you'd just get in the way."

He sat up. *Now or never.* "There were simulacra in our landscapes."

Vince gave him a sideways look, and deposited a foot on the chair. "I'm listening."

He told Vince of the two figures, explained what they meant, or might mean. He didn't mention the other one looked like Antonia: "just a girl, couldn't see her too clearly". Vince wanted to hand it over to the mil guys, but Micah said it wouldn't work, each setting was tailored to a human reader – Micah and Rudi were two of the few who'd worked together enough to be able to read each others' environments, but to newcomers it would be a jumble of colours and shapes – they'd never find the simulacra."

Vince chewed his lip. "Alright, forty-eight hours, Micah, I'll reinstate your privileges. Find anything, you call me first, understood?" He handed Micah a slip with a number on it.

Micah recalled a question that had been in the back of his mind. "What about IVS? Are they being investigated?"

Vince turned to him. "You haven't seen the news?"

"Er... no."

"Biggest archaeological find since the pyramids?" Vince flexed his eyebrows. "Check the nets when you get home. We're trying to investigate IVS, but this ship they've found in the Mariana Trench is over-shadowing everything, even Ulysses. IVS security's closed up sphincter-tight. As for here, a new Eden Mission Management team came in at lunchtime, they've all passed screening, and we have thirty agents permanently in the building, which is pretty much in lockdown status, so Rudi's route out to IVS or whoever it was is closed off." Vince glanced at his wristcom. "Go home, Micah." He turned to leave.

Micah shot to his feet. "If you find something – the missing data – Rudi will have encoded it – I could decode it for you."

Vince was half-way to the door. He sighed, turning around. "Look, I know you're trying, and you mean well, so I'm going to give you some advice you're probably not going to listen to. I ran the profile on you, so I'm going to tell you who you are, so that maybe, just maybe you can help yourself, though I doubt it."

Micah leaned backwards against the desk.

"You got fucked up by your father, Micah. You're in his shadow. Daddy hero syndrome. We know all about him, what a prick he was to you and your family – heroes, always a black side, eh?"

Micah had thought it a million times, but never heard it from someone else.

"So you want to be a hero, too, maybe a different kind. Am I right?"

His throat locked tight.

"Well, let me save you the bother. He's dead. You need him to recognise you, accept you, whatever, and it won't happen, Micah, because... the sonofabitch is dead. So, step out of the shadow. He screwed up your life while he was alive, now you're doing it for him." Vince spun around and headed out. "Get a life, Micah, your own."

Micah breathed hard. Dozens of buried memories resurrected themselves. All were between him and his father, all were unpleasant: the put-downs, the patronising lectures, and the ever-present disappointment in his father's tone. Micah's fists squeezed hard. Uncorked anger rose inside him like bile.

Nobody, in all these years, even his sister, had ever validated him – not once – about his father. All the press, the vids, had nothing else to say but that he was the Great War hero who sacrificed everything for God and country, Colonel Victor Sanderson, the Gray Colonel... Micah remembered the storm shelter, his father labelling him a coward after the nuclear attack. He realised he was still trapped in that one, terrified, fifteen year old boy's humiliating moment.

Without thinking, he grabbed the arms of his chair, raised it above his head, and with an anguished cry brought it crashing down on his computer. He raised it again, slamming it down even harder, denting the metal. He swept everything off the desk, sending tortured fragments clattering across the floor. Two guards rushed in, then grounded to a halt.

"Calm down, son," one of them said.

Micah didn't know what his face looked like, but they didn't approach any closer. He cast aside the twisted chair and glared at them. "I'm nobody's fucking son."

Vince re-entered, glaring at the mess around Micah's feet. "Christ, do I have to get you escorted off the premises, or call a shrink? Forget the privileges, I'm bringing the mil in now."

"Wait." It had the ring of an order.

Vince threw him a sideways look. "Excuse me?"

"Just you and me, Vince."

Vince stood, legs splayed, folded his arms. "You're shitting me, right?" He shook his head then gave a crisp command in Chorazin. The guards left.

Micah glared, not caring that his hands were shaking or that his chest heaved. "This isn't about you, me or my father, right?" He didn't wait for an answer. "It's about them, right?" He pointed without looking at the astronaut poster.

Vince sighed. "Yes, Micah. But my patience is running low."

"We don't have a clue what's going on, do we?"

Vince stayed immobile.

"Well, I can maybe solve that, but you have to tell me what you know."

Vince frowned. "I don't know what that doctor put in your booster, but I need to have a word with him. Look, Micah, if you have information, just give it to me."

Micah grabbed a handle on his desk and in one smooth movement dragged the top drawer out, placed it upside down on the table-top. He detached the small syringe filled with a gelatinous brown fluid taped at the back of the drawer. "I don't have information, but I have a talent. You"re the one with the information.'

Vince glared at the syringe. "What is that?"

"How do you think we set up those landscapes in the first place? Lucidium; given to every certified analyst, but in short supply. We keep a spare for emergencies: inadvertent landscape erasure, accidents like that. Hallucinogenic, but mainly a mind enhancer. Our equivalent of a booster." He tore off the protective cap, pressed it to the side of his neck. It hissed. "Auto-sterilising. Won't take long."

His eyes rolled closed. He emptied his mind, the way he did before an Optronic landscape creation, imagining space, empty, dark, silent. He'd had to study with a Zen master in Palo Alto for six months to learn this trick of returning to what was called "Beginner's Mind", necessary for optimisation of the pattern-building talent he'd possessed since a child. As he captured the fleeting essence of silence, he pushed it out in all directions, like the wave front of a bubble, accelerating, leaving nothing at its centre as it travelled out into sheer black void. The anger dissipated. He wasn't sorry to see it go.

An image of Ulysses arose, first in orbit, then settled on the fertile planet. Immense silver ships on Earth floated up from the depths after centuries, breaking the surface of the oceans. Crystal threads entwined: the Alicians, the Chorazin, IVS, the last War, the discoveries since the war, all converged towards a distant blacker-than-black sun; whereas other strands – nuclear and nano-tech, solar system colonisation efforts, and sub-sea habitation – hung in empty space like shredded wraiths. He tried to focus on the distant black sun, but as he approached, it moved away.

Something was missing. There weren't enough pieces to this puzzle. Micah half-opened drug-heavy eyes. He spoke quietly, so as not to disturb his altered state.

"Something else… tell me."

Vince sounded far away, as if they both stood on two separate cliff-tops, a deep gorge between them. "Alright," Vince said, "I'll humour you, Micah, as you seem to be over the edge anyway. But you repeat it to anyone, even Louise, and I'll have you locked up for good. There was something else down there with the ship, protecting it. An unknown sea-creature. Nasty piece of work. It was recorded briefly before it destroyed the sub that first found the ship. It hasn't been seen since. One of the scans of the creature included a flash spectrograph – showed a new element in its hide, metallic, not of Earth origin. If the graph isn't fake, it means it could be alien."

"More…"

Vince sighed. "Shit. Okay. The ship is hard to date. But some bio-matter, probably decayed algae, must have gotten trapped inside when the ship arrived – a thousand years ago. And if this last piece gets repeated, Micah, I'll finish the Cleanser's job for him." He lowered his voice. "We may have found an identical ship in Qahuru, Central Australia, buried in the desert."

Micah sealed his eyes again, bringing down the shutters on the external world, and absorbed the new information. Images unfolded inside the bubble, and he watched, dispassionately. It wasn't a sun after all. It was a writhing sphere of black larval insects, squirming, hungry, glinting in the backlight of Earth's reflection, getting closer. A shining darkness.

He creaked open bloodshot eyes. His hands were puffy and stung – he assumed due to an interaction effect between the booster and the Lucidium. He felt weak in his legs. He realised he was shivering. But the Chorazin booster was making him come round much faster than last time he'd taken the drug.

Vince fetched him more water, which Micah downed in short, furtive sips.

"Your trip report, Micah?"

"First, you have to understand, it's conjecture – a projection. The drug-induced state helps to identify patterns, inter-relationships, increasingly implausible but limited by improbability mathematics. It's… complicated."

"Indulge me."

"The human mind tends to think in single threads – and usually not in a straight line, at that. But we can also think laterally and, more important for understanding complex phenomena, in networks, in multiple dimensions. However, it's hard for the unenhanced human brain. Some people have a natural ability for it. Good detectives have it, for example," he glanced at Vince. "But the drug can push us way beyond normal abilities. If used more than about once every six months it can fragment reality – you end up schizophrenic."

"What did you see?"

"It's not just visual, not with me at least. I mean I see things, but the connections are felt more than seen. Like reading tarot cards – it's the interpretation that matters. It doesn't always make sense at the time. Like déjà vu, you know, you finally realise what some dream meant just after the real thing has happened. Not always helpful." Micah knew he was rambling, but he was avoiding what he was slowly becoming convinced of, that humanity was in terrible danger. The drug-induced intuitions in his mind began to take on the solidity of truth. *God, I hope I'm wrong.*

"Give me something, Micah."

Micah stood. "First, if we do make contact, and if there's still time, we should tell them not to land on Eden; more of those creatures will be there."

As Micah continued to talk, he noticed Vince's blue eyes take on a grey, leaden quality. Micah talked only for a couple of minutes; it was fading rapidly.

Vince rose. "But if you think there are a lot more of these ships and they come from Eden, and these creatures own the ships, what do they want, and why did they leave them here a millennium ago? Need I remind you the Alicians seem intent on us not going to Eden, most likely sabotaging our ships en route. So if the ships are to take people to Eden, and if the Alicians are somehow connected to them, why have the Alicians been blowing up our own ships trying to get there."

Micah's head throbbed, his eyesight a grainy black and white, a short-term after-effect. It was getting hard to think. "Don't know. You're right, it doesn't hang together yet, but... we should act, somehow, warn the Ulysses crew, and maybe tell IVS and the Australians to be very careful."

"On what evidence? A drugged analyst's speculation?" Vince shook his head. "Okay, wait here, I'll make some calls."

While Vince was gone, Micah tried to regain the clarity he'd had when "under", but it was gone; the fragments didn't connect. He picked up a holopad out of the debris of his desk and sketched a mind map, connecting the ships and the creatures to the Alicians and Eden. He joined the ships and the Alicians to Earth. He tried to figure it out: aliens bring ships to Earth a thousand years ago, meet Alicians, make some kind of deal, leave ships, go to Eden, wait there. Alicians help us discover Eden, but try to stop us getting there. Ship found by IVS... He stared at it for five minutes, pen poised, then pushed the pad away.

He rubbed his eyes. He wanted to crack this one, and he knew why, aside from the obvious reasons. Lucidium was a difficult drug because it increased self-perception. But reluctantly, he admitted who he was trying to prove himself to. Maybe if he solved this one, helped humanity on the same scale as his father had done… Vince had been spot on.

Vince strode back into the room. "Didn't go down too well. We need hard evidence." He glanced at his wristcom. "It's late."

Micah stood, a little shaky. "Listen, Vince, I think I owe you –"

"Nothing. You've done your job; given me some leads even if they go nowhere right now."

Micah glanced toward the Optron. "Am I coming back?"

Vince nudged some of the fragments of the shattered terminal with his boot. "New computer will be here in the morning, Micah. Go home and get some rest, or else I'll begin to think you look like shit all the time."

Chapter 20

Desert

Eden's late afternoon sun strafed Blake and Kat, casting long shadows behind them as their skimmer wound through the dunes. After two hours of riding, Blake banked the skimmer in a tight arc, circling a bluff, conjuring up a swirl of fine sand. He skidded the vehicle to a halt on the summit's bedrock. Kat was surprised – this flourish was like a surfer's move. As soon as they touched ground, enveloped in a vortex of red sand, Blake leapt off, yanking a strip of clear plastic-looking material from a side compartment, and dashed toward the edge of the ridge. Kat stayed put, but armed her rifle, losing Blake for a moment in the temporary sirocco. Sand particles whipped against her visor. Blake returned, perched on the skimmer and waited till it settled.

Kat had no idea what was going on, but maintained her silence. She'd figure it out. The visibility returned, and she saw over the ridge to a huge bowl, more than a kilometre across. In the middle, some thirty metres below them, was the wreckage of a ship torn in half, definitely from Earth. She let out a sigh of relief. She surveyed the rest of the area, but detected nothing; no glints of silver.

"Okay, Kat," Blake said through the helmet intercom, "this is how it works. I get off and set up over there, where the plastic runner is lying crossways. You see it?"

She barely made out the cord laid out on the edge of the ridge. It was about as long as a grown man lying down, and finger-thick.

"Yes."

"Good. When I'm set up there, bring your viewer over and walk directly between here and the line, and lie down next to me so we can scout the ship. You got that, directly between the skimmer and the line. Stay within the line. Don't touch it."

"Yes, Sir." She still didn't understand, but it was a simple enough order to follow. Blake headed over and then lay down on the sand, propped up on his elbows, using a digi-viewer. Kat dismounted, retrieved her viewer from one of the skimmer pockets, and strode over next to him, her legs creaky after the long ride. Once down on the ground, she zoomed in on the wrecked ship.

Metallic objects and fragments, mainly silver and charcoal in colour, lay scattered around the crash zone. The ship, like Ulysses, had been compartment-based; only one section had survived impact. The cockpit, or what was left of it, lay split in two as if a machete had cleaved open a coconut shell. The whole area reminded her of a junkyard.

The silence, after two hours of the skimmer's constant humming, forced Kat to break the tension. She didn't know why they'd stopped. She reckoned Blake was testing her; she hadn't even worked out the test yet.

"Looks like they attempted a parachute landing," she ventured.

"Correct."

Okay; not on the wrong track yet. "Broke the cockpit clean in two. Not sure anyone would have survived. Must have come down pretty hard. Parachutes are usually only deployed for a sea-landing." She knew she was saying things Blake had already surmised, but the eeriness was getting to her. She stopped scanning for a while, and regarded Blake instead. Occasionally he focused on the other side of the ridge. Kat decided to check it out.

"Keep looking at the wreckage, Kat."

She tilted her viewer down. "Sir, what's going on?"

"Why don't you tell me?"

She had no clue. "Sir, I –"

"Tell me about your nightmares, particularly the recent one. All of it."

She bit her lip, clicking off the electronic imaging device, though she rested her head on her elbows as if still scanning. "They began about a month ago." She glanced sideways at Blake. He gave every appearance of still scanning and recording, and not paying attention. That made it easier.

"I was here, on Eden, being chased by something. Always the same, running back to the ship. Something terrifying was chasing me, and I had to get back. I had this feeling... like everything depended on it, not just me or the ship, but, well, everything." She glanced down at the glimmering sand. "Earth's survival."

"Continue."

She sucked in a breath. "Sometimes Zack was there, sometimes... it was someone else, I mean not from the crew, someone... who couldn't be there."

"Someone back on Earth?"

With a pang that made her close her eyes, Kat recalled her dead sister.

"Yeah, you could say that."

"Go on."

"Then, when I was in stasis, for the first time ever, I actually saw it. I mean the thing that had been chasing me. Silver and black, looked like a giant locust. Scared the crap out of me, and... we were in a desert."

Blake remained silent.

"That's it." Her mouth was dry.

Blake switched off the viewer, and put it down. "On your feet."

She got up, slower than Blake. They faced each other.

"Now tell me the rest, the part you haven't told anyone else."

She fumbled with the viewer, glanced over to the skimmer, but Blake's eyes fixed on her like meat hooks.

"I... It was nothing more a fleeting feeling, Sir, I'm really not sure I saw anything else."

"Listen, Kat. I believe there's more to your nightmare than we know. I'm responsible for this mission, our safety, and whatever it means for Earth. You have to tell me all of it. It's your duty, it's that simple. Anyone in this crew would agree with me."

And there it was, she realised: he was right. Zack would agree. Zack probably would have already told Blake if he'd known. She took a breath.

"Right at the end just when it was upon me... it had Zack's face." She stared straight into Blake's scrutinising eyes. Blake pursed his lips, then gave a solitary nod and bent down to pick up the cord, and headed back to the skimmer.

Kat remained where she was. "Sir, what's going on?" With a sigh she trailed after him.

Blake talked as he packed things away. "First, we've been scanning the ship and its wreckage. Someone did survive, because equipment was moved around after the crash, and the signal not to land is coming from the single surviving structure."

She turned back towards the ridge, then faced Blake. "Where's it from, though? It's not the Heracles, that's for sure."

"No, it isn't. It never made it here, was blown up en route, or ghoster-attacked. But it never arrived." Blake finished stowing the gear. Although the sun shone directly into his eyes, it didn't seem to faze him.

"This was an IVS ship. I saw the logo on a hull fragment, rusted like hell but there anyway. God knows how they did it, but they got a ship here without us knowing anything about it. That's one discussion I'd like to have with the survivor."

"But how do you know anyone's alive? The wreckage is at least a year old."

"Eleven months, to be precise, from the readings I took. And I know he or she is alive because whoever it is has been watching us from the other side of the ridge. Don't turn your head."

She managed to stop just in time. "One survivor?"

"There's a small burial mound west of the wreckage, and that's a two-person craft."

Kat shoved her viewer back into its compartment. She wanted to kick the skimmer. She'd looked hard, but had seen so little of what mattered. She hated to ask, but decided to get it over with.

"And the cord?"

"Diffraction generator. Skimmer's sensors picked up something moving – walking to be precise – a quarter of an hour ago. Whoever it is, is armed, most probably a pulse rifle, though the emissions are too weak to tell – their energy packs usually only last a year. Probably aimed at us as we speak. The cord creates a visual distortion. Anti-sniper device. Off-sets the perpendicular line of sight by a small angle, so that a good sniper will miss you by about a metre."

"So we were bait, seeing if he would fire?" Kat felt a shiver down her spine.

"He, or she, didn't. We'll meet this person, sooner or later. I doubt there are many callers. Might be hostile, but whoever is on the other side of the ridge is at least curious enough not to shoot us on sight." Blake mounted the skimmer.

Kat twisted to see the wreckage one more time, and then gazed across the ridge. Blake didn't stop her this time. *Whoever you are, we're here. Come on down, let's meet.* Inside, she was relieved. If a human could survive here for eleven months, then maybe the monster wasn't here. No monster, and Zack is just Zack. She straightened up, and in one smooth movement threw her leg over the skimmer, behind the Captain.

"Ready, Kat?"

"Yes, Sir,"

She wished she'd known Blake a long time ago. Her sister Angel and Blake would have got along just fine. Blake gunned the skimmer engine, and they catapulted off, skirting along the ridge, before veering down toward the IVS crash-site. Kat was reminded of sitting behind Angel in Bells' Bay near Melbourne, when a giant wave would catch their board and thrust them forwards. No more than a kid, she'd shriek with excitement, never fear, as long as Angel was in front of her. She closed her eyes, recalling the taste and smell of biting sea-spray, imagining for the first time in a very long while that Angel was with her.

Chapter 21

Interrogation

Sandy perched with one heel on the lip of the chrome chair in the Spartan room. Its chalk-white walls and ceiling were almost low enough to make her stoop. Operating-theatre clean, and about as relaxing. It smelled like a hospital, but she was there for interrogation, an operation she knew the Chorazin carried out with surgical precision.

She'd been blindfolded on the way in – not that she wanted to know where this place was. She stared at the over-polished floor. Maybe things get bloody in here, she thought, so they keep it sterile. The only door was currently shut, no handle on the inside. She hadn't heard such lack of sound since her temporary deafness after the first detonation. Strange to watch everyone running, screaming, and catching fire, with the sound turned down. She brought her knee closer to her chest.

She wondered why there was no one-way mirror. She'd seen the vids like everyone else. Chorazin didn't stop at extracting confessions, or even at the truth, which was, sooner or later, whatever they wanted to hear. Instead they always extorted additional information – intimate details, inside the dark recesses of the mind, fears they could use in the future. Mental finger-printing one Vid had called it. Mind-rape was her label.

The idea was simple and ruthless. Since the 104th Amendment, all suspects could undergo – at Chorazin discretion – DPP: "Deep Psychological Profiling". It meant intense probing, uncovering traumatic detail, and scenario-immersion to see how likely you were to commit a crime. By the end, the Chorazin had two things – a pretty good idea of whether you would ever commit a crime, and the level of crime you were capable of, on a neat ten-point scale running from shoplifting to terrorism. They saw criminal behaviour as a relative, rather than absolute, character trait.

It meant they ended up with some dirt on you, which acted as a deterrent. The 104th had been one of the most hotly-contested amendments this century. And yet within three years crime had dropped eighty per cent. Anyway, Sandy thought, I've got nothing to hide. Well, almost nothing.

She looked at her wrist again and cursed; they'd confiscated her wristcom, and there was no clock in the room. She was positive there were micro-monitors recording her every move. Her first two fingers rubbed together, longing for a cigarette between them. *Manipulative bastards.* At least when there's a mirror you know where not to look, or where to scowl when you don't care anymore. She wouldn't have minded the opportunity to tidy up. But this was no time for one of her fleeting moments of femininity – she needed to play tough.

The door slid open – barely an audible swish – revealing a slim, bald-headed man who entered as the door sealed behind him. He occupied the steel-framed chair opposite her; no table between them. She guessed it was supposed to make her feel more vulnerable, naked, more inclined to talk. But she didn't give a shit; especially after all she'd been through. She resisted the urge to put her knee down, and stared into his eyes; ocean blue, no flecks, just blue. She wondered how he got such clear irises; if they were indeed natural.

"May I call you Sandy?"

A crisp voice, she thought, well-spoken, honest-looking face – it all summed up bad news. This man's whole demeanour purred *"Trust me"* from every pore. She tried to recall the name of the evil character from a book she'd read in her childhood, about a snake and a boy in a jungle.

"Call me what you like. What do I call you?"

"You can call me Vince. Just Vince."

She raised an eyebrow. "Are you just?" The instant riposte, as usual, wanting to see his reaction, his reflex. A smile evaporated just as it was arriving. Of course she knew he must have heard that before. In fact, she wondered if he'd set her up to see if she would rise to the bait. She matched his stare for a few moments. He held up two fingers about shoulder level, and then put them down again in his lap. She didn't know what it meant, and had zero intention of asking. At least he had no holopad.

A knock on the door ushered in a brunette in a black pencil skirt and blouse with a cigarette pack. She gave one to Sandy, lit it for her, and left. All the time Sandy felt Vince's eyes on her. She noted that he hadn't answered her question. But she wasn't the type to ask anything twice. People always heard, she had determined long ago. Always.

"Are you going to ask me all the shit again about Keiji's murder? About what I saw, which was pretty much nothing. Why I hid?" She inhaled deeply, blowing out a long plume of smoke sideways, not at him. "That's the way it always goes in the vids, isn't it? Ask everything four times, story cohesion, all that bullshit?"

She watched him as he uncrossed one leg and crossed the other. Muscular thighs. *Shit*, she thought, as she flushed, *I don't believe this. What's this crap I suddenly have for bald-headed, athletic, blue-eyed men?* She wondered if he'd noticed; of course he had.

"No," Vince said. He spoke with an unexpected nonchalance. "As you say, that's what they do in vids. In any case the Sensex cleared you three hours ago of being Mr. Kane's murderer or an accomplice. According to your deposition you saw little, given your relative position to the killer."

Yeah, right, I was giving Keiji a blowjob under the desk when the killer walked right in.

"…And you yourself were potentially a target, depending on what the killer thought you knew. But staying there all that time was a little extreme, don't you think? The killer had made his getaway. You could have left."

Sandy crossed her legs, then changed the cross. His gaze didn't falter. She looked around for an ashtray. She flicked a small head of ash onto the floor, and took another long drag.

"You know that blondie Chorazin is screwing Micah? I had a ringside seat. She's kinky, you know. A bit out of his league." She watched for a reaction, a movement, a flicker of the eyes. Something; anything. Nothing. She pressed harder. "They must train you people pretty good not to react to shit like that. Must take stuff out of you, huh? You must lose something, you know, a piece of yourself."

Vince's eyes intensified then broke her gaze. He stood up and walked around to the back of his chair. "Actually, it's more like they put 'stuff' in."

She gave a short, hollow laugh. "Good grief, a piece of Chorazin philosophy! I'm honoured." She took a last drag and dropped the cigarette on the floor, stubbing it out with her shoe. She ground it longer than necessary with her heel, not looking at the messy stain.

"Okay. Here goes," she said. "As I'm sure you've been informed, we were having an – er – intimate moment, when the killer arrived. Keiji had always wanted that particular little fantasy – anyway he got it, just in time, you might say. And in case you're judging me, don't. We had a relationship once, but it burned out years ago and he went back to his loving wife." She smiled, all sweetness. "So, anyway, lately he'd been asking me for one more fling for old time's sake." She raked a hand through her hair, flashed her eyes. No reaction.

She continued. "And why not? He's – he was – a model citizen. Just that age-old sad and pathetic story of lots of love for wife and kids, but a bit short on passion between the sheets. So, where was I?" She wanted to see if he would make some low remark, like "with your head between his thighs", but he said nothing. The lack of repartee made her decide he was professional at least. She cut to the chase.

"So anyway, the killer arrives, and Keiji says his name, and starts to get up, zipping up first, signalling me to stay there – as if I was going to jump up like some girl out of a cake –"

Vince raised an open hand. "Stop. You've changed your story. You said you didn't know who it was. You lied to the Sensex?" He paused, and then smiled, and this time it hung around. "Ah – you knew the fellatio aspect could cover up an omission, because the Sensex would write off the electro-dermal variance as being due to embarrassment."

"Whatever. I know what I said. You want me to continue or not? Because this is important."

"It had better be, Sandy, because you've just earned some deep psy profiling, so you can never pull a stunt like that again."

She scowled at him, and held up two fingers, like he'd done earlier. Vince nodded once, to nobody in particular. The woman entered the room, and lit Sandy another cigarette. Sandy held out an empty palm, and gazed up at the woman. After a moment's hesitation the woman placed the packet in Sandy's hand, and left.

Sandy took another drag. "After all, I might not see these again for a while if I'm going for profiling?" She flashed a mock scared look at him, then leaned back on the hard chair.

"So the guy's name is Archie. As Keiji went around the desk to greet and talk to him, Archie must've pulled a knife on him, because suddenly Keiji shouted 'No!' and then I heard this ugly sound, knife puncturing flesh – I'm sure you know it – then slurping back out again. Keiji gasped, grunted, then hit the floor." She took the cigarette out and bit at one of her cuticles, not looking at Vince. For a moment she was afraid she was going to well up. She'd already cried behind the mirror, when they zipped Keiji up in the body bag. She bit her finger hard. It worked. She noticed that Vince didn't push her, even though she'd just announced the name of the killer.

"The rest is as I told it. I froze, held my breath. He walked back outside to my desk, and checked the vid-phone records to see who else Kane had phoned. Thank God he didn't check the bathroom, where all my stuff was. Then he strolled out. I came out from under the desk and went to Keiji, but he was already dead. I waited a couple of minutes, grabbed my gear and hid. Now you now know why, of course."

Vince nodded.

"So, thirty minutes later all hell breaks loose. Ten minutes later your friends arrived along with Eden Mission's Head of Security."

Vince looked at her. "Archibald Vernt. The killer, apparently."

She looked at him quizzically. "Aren't you supposed to jump up and say something like '*Let's go get him!*'?"

"Don't worry. As you would imagine, this conversation is being monitored. My colleagues are already tracking him down. He gave us his deposition this morning, but was called away on business this afternoon."

She fidgeted. "So, that's why I stayed hidden. Archie, our very own darling Head of Security and hobbyist killer, was still in the building, monitoring all entries and exits. And then, while he was there in the office, with you really smart guys, incidentally, the news came in that I'd never left the building. Only he and I knew what that meant. So I stayed. I had no plan actually, the vids don't usually get me this far. I didn't want to speak his name until I knew I was seeing someone higher up the Chorazin food chain."

Vince stood and pressed a finger to his right ear

"It appears you may be right, Sandy. Mr. Vernt's vidcom and wristcom have disappeared off the net, and his office doesn't know where he is. Naturally it would have been more helpful if you had come forward earlier, but given the circumstances, I understand perfectly."

She wondered if she should tell him the rest. She didn't even know what it meant. She felt those eyes probing her.

"Is there anything else?"

She shifted, knowing she was giving herself away. Vince sat down agan.

"Yes. Well, maybe. When Keiji was stabbed, he fell facing where I was under the desk. I saw him die, and saw the murderer's legs, behind him. I've never seen anyone die, not like that anyway." *I'm sure you've seen many, though.* "Thing is, he mouthed a word to me, just one word. At first I wasn't sure, but I've thought it over and over, and I'm convinced of it. I thought it must be a joke, but that wasn't his style, and – well, you'd know better than me – but I'm guessing most people's last words aren't very humorous."

"Tell me, Sandy."

"Not for the microphones. Just you."

He dragged his chair closer to hers. She leaned forward as he inclined the side of his head towards her mouth. She inhaled his scent, felt his body heat. Her lips moved close to his ear. She whispered the word.

Vince told those outside to let her sleep, and to place her in a higher security wing. No one else was to talk to her till he was back. No one. Vince went to his office and logged onto the nets. He carried out various Rosetta searches relating to the word and then found what he was looking for. He left orders for Louise and others, and booked one of the Chorazin fast jets to Mumbai, the site of IVS HQ.

***

Gabriel awoke to the sound of high-pitched buzzing. He instinctively cracked open the second false upper molar, and felt awareness and life course back into his system, courtesy of the synthetic adrenaline. He'd long ago replaced the standard Alician suicide pill with a neural and heart suppressant he'd acquired five years earlier from his Master in Tibet. It had slowed his heartbeat to once every two minutes, giving the semblance of death, simulating rigor mortis, leaving him in deep coma. During that time his body had reverted to what the ancients called tortoise breathing, exchanging air in his lungs at a very slow rate, just enough to prevent brain necrosis. Of course, Louise hadn't known that when she'd cracked the tooth open.

He lay naked on a robotic autopsy table, cutting tools hovering above him on gleaming multi-jointed arms. The sound that had awoken him belonged to a circular skull-saw. His muscles were still stiff from the drug, but the counter-stim worked fast. As he tensed his muscles he realized he was restrained, presumably because the body had to be held in position against the motion of the autopsy blades. But the bonds weren't strong – they weren't meant for live patients.

The saw was so close it was out of focus. Ignoring cramps in his legs, he broke free from the lower restraints and pulled himself down the table just in time, slipping his torso and head underneath the chest harness. He rolled off the operating table, snapping off a robo-scalpel. The door

184

to the oblong room burst open and a man rushed in. Gabriel launched the scalpel across the room straight into the man's throat, spattering his white lab-coat with blood. The lab-assistant staggered forwards, two more sprays issuing in fast succession, his gurgling gasps failing as he toppled head-first into a growing pool of his blood.

A second man in a grey Chorazin uniform flew through the same door, pulse pistol blazing at where Gabriel had just been. The agent ducked down to see where Gabriel was, when the wheeled operating table suddenly shot towards him, scattering various razor sharp instruments in its wake, making him fall over backwards. Gabriel rammed the table into the agent's neck just as he was trying to aim his pistol. Gabriel threw all his weight onto the table, sending the other end upwards beneath the agent's chin, resulting in a crunching noise as the agent's spine snapped. The agent slumped, eyes vacant.

Gabriel vaulted over the table and ran outside to the supervisory work station – the alarm was already sounding. From the console he saw it was 3am, so he had a few more seconds than usual due to lower night-time staffing. He guessed he was inside a Chorazin med facility, which would be underground. He switched off the cameras in the two rooms, locked the door to the corridor, and grabbed a fire extinguisher and a chair. Still naked, he stood on the chair and pushed open an air conditioning grill above the workstation. Placing the Halon gas fire extinguisher in the conduit, he tied the firing pin to the grill, re-sealed it, got down, and then knocked the chair over.

Retreating back inside the autopsy room, he stepped over the two bodies, ignoring the growing lake of blood, and picked up the pulse gun. He heard shouts. But they would be cautious – they could afford to be; where could he go? There were no windows, and no other exit beside the corridor now filling with agents. He noticed a square grill in the floor, about forty centimetres in diameter, evidently to collect blood and other bodily fluids. Gabriel knew it would go to an acid treatment bath somewhere below. He could distinguish the voices as they drew closer: short, clipped-speech commands: Chorazin, rather than normal security.

There was no way out – only the corridor or the grill. He looked around, controlling his breathing. *Three. Three is always the key. Where is the third way out?* He inspected the grill in the floor again.

Four Chorazin agents in battle gear, wearing gas-protective face masks, broke through into the lab. They saw the two bodies in the autopsy room, faces drenched with blood. The operating table was upside down in the middle of the room, which was otherwise clear. One agent detected the broken seal on the air conditioning grill above the supervisor's workstation, and the knocked-over chair. While the other three covered for him, the agent pried the hatch open. White gas jetted towards him, knocking him to the floor, engulfing all four of them in a cloud of Halon.

As Gabriel hoped would happen, another agent fired defensively into the shaft, rupturing the extinguisher and causing a shock wave of decompressing Halon gas, enough to knock the other three agents off their feet. In the fog of the gas, they didn't see the dead security guard leap to his feet. Gabriel, clad in the dead Chorazin guard's uniform, seized one of the prone agents' rifles from him whilst crushing the man's windpipe with his knee. He fired point blank at the heads of the three others, then ripped off the first agent's gas mask and took several deep breaths.

Smearing more blood down his right leg and face he limped unarmed down the corridor, still dressed in the Chorazin uniform, gesticulating and shouting for more guards, using perfect Chorazin-coded speech. "He's still in there – five down already!"

Several Chorazin ran past him, but seconds later there was an explosion that shook the whole corridor – Gabriel had turned on the oxygen taps in the autopsy room and had left the pulse pistol on overload.

He staggered along the corridor, then darted into a laundry room, put on some dirty but serviceable clothes, and found a service lift going to the surface. Opening the hatch in its roof, he climbed the greasy wires, eight floors up to ground level.

It took an hour and a roundabout journey to arrive at one of his safe havens: a "cube" that some of the poorest lived in – a cell two-and-a-half metres long, wide and high, comprising a cot, sink and toilet, vid-player and stove. There were stacks of them a hundred high in various parts of the city; a good place to pick up fresh diseases, and an equally useful location to lie low for a while.

In his hideout he injected a Chorazin booster into his thigh, and sat back for a moment. The booster kicked in, and he let his head fall back to the pillow, feeling its soft embrace as he stared upwards to the Himalaya holo-vista. He had failed to recover Sandy and secure the password if she had it, but at least had identified the Chorazin double-agent. He hoped Louise hadn't been able to debrief Sandy.

There was only one remaining option: the Alician chapter. He had to locate the true leader – the one that mattered, the one who belonged to the ancient sect of the Alician Protectors. *Sister Esma.* She must be cleansed.

Gabriel knew the chapter would have dispersed by now. But one thing would bring her out of the shadows – himself. At their last meeting she had wanted him dead. If he appeared again, she would want to be present to make sure the job was finished. But he probably wasn't the first assassin to try to cleanse her. He went back to his basic training: *never, ever underestimate your opponent.* He wondered if the legends were true, and if so, how old she really was.

Chapter 22

Phoenix

Kat peeled herself off the skimmer, and surveyed the football-field size crash zone where the craft had landed hard and rent apart, disgorging equipment like a broken toy. Much of it was recognizable – a stasis pod, metallic boxes and cables, a flight seat, and a metre high cube which had to be an early prototype of the neutralino detonator. Definitely from Earth.

The dark matter engines had disintegrated, leaving only a vitrified double-cone imprint in sand turned to shadow glass. She stood on the edge of one of the circles, peering down into a frozen blackness, only guessing how many kilometres deep it went. It finally proved the theory about what would ever happen in a dark matter high energy crash. She shivered.

Blake took off his helmet and pointed toward the detonator. Kat envied him. She was tired of wearing her fishbowl, listening to her breathing.

Only the occasional rustling of a sheet of gauze-like material in the sporadic breeze told Kat that her external sound system was working; the desert was so quiet. She knelt down in front of the detonator and inspected it.

"Seems to be intact, Sir." It was disarmed, but several lights glowed dimly. An unusual box-like device was attached to the arming controls. Blake tapped it with his finger a few times.

"A remote triggering device?" Kat ventured.

He nodded.

She wondered why; it couldn't launch anything from a planet's surface, only from orbit. Unless it had been rigged as a weapon. She remembered the early trials in the Sahara desert. A quarter of that great desert was now glass. But whoever had set it up knew their stuff – it looked pretty tamper-proof.

She followed Blake over to the cockpit, the second largest surviving structure, lying on its side like a giant clam cracked in two. She bit her lip; no one should have survived. Rust encrusted the interior, the console areas were smashed. A faded brown stain marked one of the seats: dried blood – a lot of it. She moved aside to let Blake climb in; he was careful not to snag his suit on ragged edges of torn metal. He stood on the edge of one of the two chairs in the cockpit, and checked the two weapons lockers. Kat could see them too, both empty. He lowered himself into the comms console. She tried to see what was there, but there was only room for one person, so she had to wait.

Blake hauled himself back out from the wreckage, jumped back down to ground level, and dusted off his gloves. "Not much left, comms ripped out, the rest fried. Two pulse rifles missing, a pistol or two." He stepped back from the shattered cockpit.

"Sir – why'd they tried to land this way? And why is the ND here rather than in orbit. It can't be used from here, except as a rather messy weapon."

Blake marched back to the skimmer, and retrieved his pulse pistol.

"Only questions here. Let's check the main structure."

Kat noticed something else before she left. One of the braking harnesses for the pilot's chair had been sliced through with a knife. Blake saw it too.

"Like I said, only questions here."

The remaining intact cylindrical module, the size of a bubble-train compartment, had a single airlock hatch at one end. Fragments of metal had been wedged underneath its sides to prevent it from rolling, though it would have taken a gale-force wind to upset it. Two oval plazglass portholes stared out from the giant carbon-wire can, too high for either Blake or Kat to see inside. The antenna on top of the module, undoubtedly the source of the "*Do not land here*" signal, was bent in a few places, but otherwise looked pretty serviceable.

At one end, the airlock had makeshift steps outside it, assembled out of old plastic food crates. Smiling at the thought of it, she wondered if they should knock. Blake fished around in the debris, and picked up a piece of shining metal the size of a hand, and a short stretch of piping split at one end. He pushed the two together, and gave Kat a half-smile.

"Old habits die hard," he said. He checked the direction of the sun – Kat presumed so his makeshift mirror wouldn't reflect sunlight into the compartment – then lifted it up to one of the portholes and tilted it a few times.

"Nobody home." He walked around to the foot of the steps and ascended to the hand wheel on the airlock hatch. Kat flicked her pulse rifle on, the short low buzz it made not lost on Blake. The hand wheel twisted easily. He opened the door a fraction and paused. Nothing happened, so he opened it wide, having to step back to ground level to do so. There was another inner airlock door. He tried to see if it would open, though one door should always be sealed in an airlock system. Surprisingly, it did.

"Interesting," Kat said. "Whoever's here doesn't fear the biosphere as Pierre does, or has decided it's harmless."

"Or else had no choice. But it does mean that what Pierre detected isn't fatal to humans in the long term."

She ventured up a step.

"Wait outside till I check it first."

She complied, but her instinct told her the threat was not from whoever might still be around. The threat, if there were one, wasn't human. Her dreams had rammed that home to her.

Blake disappeared inside for a minute then reappeared. "Okay, come in, and put something in the outer door to stop it from closing."

Kat found a small metal bar and propped it in the airlock entrance at the bottom and stepped inside.

She paused mid-step as she entered the main compartment. It was gloomy inside, but – she almost had to shake herself – someone had decorated it. The walls had been painted, and not bad a job. A vista of a russet-coloured fortress on a hill against a twilight sky spread along one complete side of the rounded hull. Stars decorated the ceiling, which was the colour of night, and on the other side the sun rose on an ornate pearl-white structure with four minarets, that looked oddly familiar. Dark-skinned figures knelt at the water's edge in the sunrise part of the fresco. The two portholes each had an orange curtain, drawn back at the moment, but within the frescoes these would represent the sun, one setting, and one rising. Kat was impressed by the clever artistry, especially since the portholes faced the right way to catch morning and evening sun. She cocked her head at Blake, but he was already hunched over the lone computer terminal, oblivious to the artwork.

Kat spotted the comms device in a corner next to the single stasis pod serving as a cot. She stepped over several taped-over fissures in the hull of the pod, trying to ignore the frescoes. Who had done this? What type of astronaut would ornament his spacecraft? The answer came to her – he thinks of this as home. He's not going anywhere, or has given up on a rescue attempt, and so he has adapted to this world, embellished his small shelter. Or his sarcophagus, she thought ruefully, were he to die here alone.

She inspected the comms unit, and her lips stretched into a smile. "Sir, this is in pretty good shape. If we could…" – she sought the right word, feeling like they were burglars – "… borrow some of this and hook it up to our system, we could contact Earth again."

Blake nodded, and then his eyes flashed to the doorway as a flood of sunlight rushed in, accompanied by the creaking of hinges on the rusted hatch. She'd heard no footsteps, and spun around awkwardly in the cramped cabin to see a silhouette: human at least, no suit either. Blake's pistol was already drawn, but she left hers where it was as the man pulled the door closed behind him and she got a good look at him: a tanned, lean figure in khaki shorts and threadbare tee shirt, unshaven for a few days. He was shorter than both of them and had open sandals on his feet. He put his palms together in front of his chest like he was praying, and gave a short bow.

Before either of them could speak, the newcomer greeted them in a lilting, almost musical, voice. "Welcome to my home."

Indistani! She'd had several good Indian friends at the academy, before the reunification with Pakistan and Bangladesh after the War, so she recognised the accent well enough. She smiled at the man, and without thinking, being closer to the door than Blake, held out her gloved hand. After a heartbeat's hesitation, the man stepped forward and took it, at first gingerly, then he shook it firmly, with both hands. Kat saw the man up close now, probably early thirties, with deep brown eyes, seemingly back-lit whites surrounding the irises. Kat turned to introduce Blake.

"My name is Katrina Beornwulf, and this is…"

Blake holstered his weapon, but left the securing clip undone – she didn't doubt he could draw it fast if required.

"Captain Blake Alexander, Eden Mission, New World Alliance, Sir. And you are?"

The man considered Blake, then turned to Kat.

"Why are you wearing your helmet?"

Kat cast an ignored glance at Blake. The man continued in his Indistani-English accent. "The harm from this planet will not come from its atmosphere. Please, both of you sit down." He gestured to the makeshift bed. Kat again looked questioningly to Blake who, clearly having never encountered a protocol for this particular scenario, indicated to Kat to sit, but gave a firm shake of his head when Kat gestured with a finger to her helmet. Not surprised, she sat, as did Blake, though he remained at the edge of the cot, on his guard. The man opposite pulled up the cushion in front of the computer terminal.

"You know, after a hundred years of computers, even us Indians have nearly forgotten how to sit cross-legged on the floor." He beamed at them.

Kat smiled back, hoping to compensate for Blake's iron regard. She guessed what he was thinking. It looked as if there had been a struggle in the cockpit, and one crew member was alive, the other dead, possibly killed before the crash. But she couldn't believe this man a murderer, or even capable of killing; his whole demeanour was so gentle. No, she thought – genteel, that archaic word almost lost by its near irrelevance to modern Earth's post-War manners, though she'd grown up in such a household in Oxford. She hadn't missed either that he referred to himself as Indian and not Indistani, but then he didn't fit the bill of a separatist either.

The man's brow creased as he focused on Blake. "Please forgive me. I am somewhat unaccustomed to speaking. My name is Rashid. Rashid Vishnaru, from Trivandrum, Indistan. Or India, as I'm afraid I cannot help but think of it. I have been here for eleven months, after a one year voyage to get here."

Kat's eyebrows lifted. A whole year! Three months had been bad enough.

"We alternated our time in stasis. You see it was a covert mission, and we did not have the best technology. Not the best at all, I'm afraid."

Kat wondered what he meant by that, but deemed it better not to speak unless the Captain spoke first. Blake, however, said nothing. Of course, she thought, this guy hasn't seen anyone for a long time; he won't need too much incentive to talk. But as if Rashid could hear her thoughts, he fell into a silence, and stared down.

After a long, awkward pause, Blake spoke. "What happened to your crewmate? Why did you crash-land here? And, in fact, what are you doing here at all?"

Rashid nodded three times, once for each question, still eyeing the floor. Then he took in a deep breath, and looked up to Blake, eyes steady.

"I have thought of this a lot – how to tell it. And I will, but first I must make some tea. You see I had been gone for two days already before I saw the trace of your craft amongst the stars. I made it back here just in time only by running for hours on end, like my old quadrathlon days." He smiled, flashing white teeth, jiggling his head sideways in that way Kat remembered her male Indian friends would do at the academy, confusing the hell out of their female admirers, as a "yes" was easily mistaken for a "no". Rashid got up and went to the third corner of the module, the first two occupied by the computer terminal and the comms set, to a compact sink unit and micro-fusion boiler. It instantly fired up and within thirty seconds he had poured boiling water into an authentic china teapot. Kat was amazed he'd been able to bring such a homely artefact on a deep-space mission.

Rashid paid diligent attention to everything he did, Kat noticed, wondering how she would have fared under such circumstances. She realized there must be an underlying discipline to this man, a strictness of routine to maintain some semblance of structure, to avoid one day simply waking up screaming and barking mad.

"You can take your helmet off, you know," he said, gesturing to Kat, and then looked to the Captain. "The complete biospheric analysis is there, filed under Eden Environment Analysis 12. It is a metal. One we do not have on Earth. Very hard, very tough, but inert – no, not inert - implacable, but no harm to you."

Kat stared at Blake, but his gaze was implacable, too.

"Thanks," Blake said, "but we'll have to get it checked out by our science officer, all the same."

Rashid set down the pot and picked up two cups. "A shame, I bet it is a long time since you had real tea, Katrina Beornwulf. You must miss it."

Against her own will, Kat's memory called up the taste of steaming fresh brewed tea, her mouth salivating uselessly. She sighed. As an English girl in the USA she'd always been stupefied by the fact that no one in America really knew how to make a decent cup of tea: she'd decided years ago it must be due to some deeply ingrained post-colonial resentment. But Rashid clearly did.

"And you, Sir, you are the Captain. If I am not very mistaken, a man of action more than a man of words, a military man. So, not trusting me yet, you will also miss out on my wonderful Earl Grey chai." He put the second cup back. He made a decision, then set the teapot and one cup on the makeshift chair, and sat down, cross-legged on a home-made cushion on the floor.

"There," he said. "I have to wait a few minutes. As my father used to say, you can hurry neither good tea nor a good woman." His eyes gleamed.

Blake leant forward. "Your crewmate was killed before you crashed, wasn't he, Rashid? Which can only mean –"

"Yes. I... killed him."

Kat drew back.

"But I am not a murderer." He clasped his hands together, took a breath. "We were only a month away from Eden. We were both to be awake for the final leg of the journey. A day after I came out of my stasis, I was working in the aft compartment, checking the medical kit, when Azil –" he glanced through the hull in the direction of the small burial mound outside "– he called to me and said: 'Hey! Will you come and look –'". He did not finish. Stopped, just like that, you see, in mid-sentence." He glanced from Blake to Kat. She sensed what was coming.

"So, this was very unusual," Rashid continued. "I was still carrying the medical kit as I walked through to find him standing in the middle of the cockpit, staring at a most beautiful vision. Azil turned to me, and a chill swept through my bones. I knew in an instant something was very wrong. Azil was no longer Azil. His face was feral, his muscles flexed. He looked first at me, then past me, to the weapons locker." Rashid, his eyes still far away, picked up the spoon, lifted the lid off the pot, gave the tea a single stir, shook the water off the spoon with a whip-like flourish, and replaced the lid. Blake remained mountain-still throughout, never taking his eyes off Rashid.

"During the War, I was a commando in the Indistani Special Services."

Blake's head shifted, ever so slightly, and even though Rashid seemed to be staring into the past, not even looking in the direction of Blake, he appeared to detect it too. Peripheral vision. She'd heard that some commandos were trained in it so much they could never switch it off.

"Yes," continued Rashid, "I do not look like one now, nor act like one, nor do I care to kill anymore, but for my Mother country – well, I was younger then. And the enemy was so terrible." He picked up the pot and poured a small amount into the cracked blue and white cup. He swilled it around, warming the china. Kat wished she could smell the aroma.

"During that time, one of our men suddenly turned on us during a mission. At first we thought he was a traitor, but he became wild, like the stories we'd heard of ghosters, though we never saw any of those." Kat's eyes flicked to Blake, but this time found no reaction in his captain's tightly-wrapped stare.

"Later, after that man had been disabled, having killed half my platoon, we took him back. He'd been implanted, you see." He looked to Blake for a sign of recognition of this term, and Blake nodded. Kat had a fleeting vision of Zack going berserk in the cockpit, no doubt inspired by her last nightmare. She crushed the image. Rashid filled his cup with steaming tea, the noise of the water sloshing into the cup.

"So, you see, this time I knew straight away what had happened to Azil. The contorted face, the hollow eyes. He recognised he had lost the element of surprise, as I was between him and the weapons locker. I had to act immediately, and turned to grab a pistol. But he was standing at the pilot's console, and he flicked the control into manual and fired the starboard thrusters. The effect was devastating. The cockpit – in fact the whole ship – lurched and began to spin. I was thrown to the other side of the cockpit, pressed against the hull. He was reaching for the controls to start separating the ship. Of course at that speed, spinning like that, we would have disintegrated. He saw that I had no weapon and so for a few seconds ignored me, his obvious encoded goal being mission termination. I was still holding the medical kit when I remembered what was in it. I managed to grab the back of his seat and kicked the lock at its base. As the centripetal force swung his chair around to face me, my left hand struck out with the scalpel from the kit, slicing straight through his harness, puncturing his heart."

Rashid lifted the cup to his mouth, closed his eyes, savoured its scent, and then took a respectful sip.

After an audible, unassuming gulp, his eyes rejuvenated by the tea, Rashid pressed on. "But in those few seconds he had done a lot of damage. It took me two hours just to stabilize the ship, and we were way off course. He had activated some kind of communications system virus, which sent a destruction message back to IVS, so they would think we had been lost."

"I thought of leaving Azil in space, but it was not his fault, and he deserved a proper burial, so I kept him in stasis. When I reached Eden, the angle of approach was too steep, but I had no back-up systems. I was down to manual control."

Blake spoke up. "You did a hell of a job landing in as few pieces as you did."

The creases in Rashid's forehead vanished. "You are too kind, Sir. I had been aiming at a sea area, but hit turbulence that deflected me by one degree. Four of the eight chutes tore up on entry, and in the last minutes, as I saw this pristine world about to become my grave, my astro-engineering training saved me."

Kat and Blake's eyes met while Rashid took another sip of tea; she had no idea how he had survived, and wondered if Pierre would have guessed.

"The stasis pod," Rashid said. "I remembered an old professor setting us an exam question to do with stasis and the so-called inertial dampening effect. It concerned the theoretical possibility of using a stasis field to counter the effects of severe acceleration, or in my case, deceleration. Well, I failed the question in the exam, but I had nothing else to lose, so I threw myself into a stasis pod having maximized its field strength. It did not completely work, but, well, you saw the cockpit and can imagine the impact stress."

Rashid leant back against the hull.

Blake stood up, and went over to the micro-kitchen, and picked up the second cup. He squatted down in front of Rashid and held it out. Rashid straightaway sat back up and filled it, eyes sparkling.

Blake clinked cups with Rashid.

Kat watched as Rashid's eyes brimmed, and she found herself staring at Blake, this man who, just when she thought he'd understood him, completely surprised her.

"So," Blake said, "you aimed for the sea, and landed in a desert."

"Ah, well," Rashid said, re-filling his cup. "Not exactly. You see, when I landed, there was no desert here. There were trees, grass and a pristine lake a kilometre away. I used to swim in it, and the water kept me alive for months." He sipped again from his cup. "The desert came later."

She thought of their Lander. They had touched down close to the edge of the desert, but still in the bluish-green, bushy grassland. She pictured her nightmare – in it, the ship was definitely in the desert, surrounded by barren rocks. She could see and feel her feet pounding into the sandy ground in front of her, racing for Zack and the ship's sanctuary, knowing that whatever was behind her, chasing her, would reach her first. How long, she wondered. How long have we got?

Chapter 23

Mumbai Tower

Vince stepped into the glass cylinder, a weapons detector at the foot of the IVS building, wondering if it would detect his DNA-masked subcutaneous knife. The glass door rotated closed behind him as he placed his feet on the footprints marked on the floor. He felt a tingling as waves of technology he wasn't familiar with swept up and down his body. Outside, four Indistani guards watched him closely. He noticed the safety switches on their pulse rifles were in the "off" position, and their forefingers lazed above the triggers. He forced his breathing to appear normal, trusting in the principle that there were as many geniuses of subterfuge as there were of detection.

He faced the two buttons in front of him – one red, one green – ignoring the camera pointed at his face. After ten seconds, the green button lit up, and the glass door in front of him opened. He'd heard grim accounts of what happened if the red light came on. The tube wasn't bullet-proof.

He stepped outside, poker-faced, knowing the security guards would misread it as Western arrogance, and so think him too stupid to be a serious threat. One of them frisked him and directed him to an elevator set apart from the others. Only inside the lift did he physically relax. Without looking down, he flexed his right forearm inside his black business suit – his Chorazin uniform would have invited more intrusive searches – to check the silicate stiletto glazed with sim-skin was still in place, hugging the contours of his arm, and still pliant. If he fully clenched his forearm for three seconds, the soft knife would detach, and the side currently touching his arm would solidify upon contact with the air, creating a sharp throwing weapon that would drop into his ready hand. He'd only had to use it in action once; it had taken two seconds for him to prime it and kill his surprised captor. He hoped it wouldn't be necessary this time; one stiletto would not be nearly enough if things went wrong. Although not officially at war, he was deep inside hostile territory.

As the executive elevator rocketed upwards, he retraced his steps. He'd arrived an hour earlier, feeling relaxed, not like he'd just travelled inter-continentally in a sub-orbital jet. Using his secure vid-phone, he'd called a sleepy Louise to keep an eye on Micah. He'd watched for a reaction from her but got none. *As long as she gets her job done.*

Vince had entered the IVS structure at ground level – Mumbai had a relatively low rad-score, never successfully targeted by a nuclear weapon during the three years of the War. IVS HQ had used sophisticated guidance-corruption devices to send any inbound missiles into the sea, the mountains or, in a few ingenious cases, back to their point of origin. IVS had powerful friends and could call upon one of the largest surviving armed forces if needed; after all, IVS had offered refuge to the Indian government during the War.

The immense IVS building, a towering monument in grey steel and Prussian blue diamond-glass, was built in the crude shape of the deity Kali, the first two hundred floors layered like a pyramid and so resembling a skirt, a hundred and fifty more storeys forming the torso, and thirty more spreading out like an expanded thorax, leading to the buttresses that jutted out like breasts, and finally a cylindrical top fifty floors high serving as the head. Most extraordinary, however, were the eight arm-like structures that stretched outwards and curved upwards to palms serving as take-off and landing pads, one and a half kilometres above ground level. It was the first time he'd seen it outside of the holos, and despite himself, it took his breath away.

The Kali Tower had caused a storm for many years before the war, in part because of its blatant Hindu origins in a Hindu-Muslim co-aligned country, but also because of its audacity. But after the War, especially with the destruction of the Taj Mahal and other sacred sites, it had become a symbol of Indistani resilience. To Vince, the building spoke of a force not to be trifled with – IVS were deadly serious about business.

The lift decelerated smoothly as it arrived at floor three hundred and eighty. He brushed aside a moment of nausea caused by the rapid ascent and drop in air pressure, and faced a frosted-glass corridor. As he walked along it, he could see offices on the other sides of the mottled glass, but he couldn't make out anything detailed. No one was in the corridor, so he walked towards the end, where a single door was ajar.

Once inside the voluminous empty office at the end of the "arm", he stared downwards. The view of old Bombay seethed below. He couldn't make out individual people but could just discern buses, and ant-like columns of what must be the tundra-fuelled tuk-tuks. There were also sky-taxis buzzing around Kali's skirt level. The rest of the buildings around the Tower were indiscriminate brown shapes stretching into the distance, all serving to emphasise by contrast the power of this place.

It was intended to be humbling. Not necessarily before IVS, but simply before whatever gods one believed in, or failing that, a stark reminder of one's mortality and the fragility of existence. Nevertheless, he wondered at the civil engineering of the arm he stood in, defying gravity. He was also impressed that such a building had survived fifteen years without a single successful terrorist attack, when it was such an obvious target. He surmised it was because IVS was not a dictator but a protector to this city and its people, indeed the nation – IVS had achieved what the former Chinese work-focussed hegemony had never managed – the people here actually worshipped this place, after a fashion. How could a terrorist or foreign army even get close?

Some ten metres behind him a door opened with a small sucking sound. Vince didn't turn, but used his ears and the warped reflections in the curved windows to discern a slim man entering the room, deferentially, as if entering a chapel. *He's not the one I need to talk to.*

"Sir, I am afraid that the Board cannot see you at this time. As you will appreciate, recent events have become very demanding. I am certain you understand."

Vince stared outwards. They were being monitored for sure. It was all a show, to see how he would react. He suspected the man was holding his hands together in supplication, but the humility was a sham. Vince remained quiet. He heard the small man shuffle, and then issue a polite cough.

"Sir – did you hear me?"

"I hear only the truth." There, let them chew on that. He heard a sleeve rustling, indicating a small arm movement – no doubt the man was raising his hand to his ear to listen to an instruction relayed by a sub-dermal earpiece. Vince remained steadfast. The man coughed again.

"Sir, the IVS and the Chorazin have not had... an easy relationship in recent years."

Ah, thought Vince, through to the next level. Time to take command of this little charade.

"Not surprising, since very recently you had a man inside the Eden Mission, now dead incidentally, feeding you telemetry whilst giving us bogus information. An illegal act of immense proportions – at the least transgressing our national security, at most possibly an act of war."

As Vince anticipated, the man exited without another word, his departure punctuated by the dull click of the door's magnetic seal. Vince closed his eyes and listened intently, hearing silence. When he opened his eyes, he was taken aback. A wiry man with a forehead that had seen too many frowns sat in an immaculate business suit at a desk in front of him, where there had been none before. He wasn't looking in Vince's direction, rather, out the window over Mumbai. Vince realised the glass had shifted back some four or five metres. The swarthy, none too healthy looking man smoked a cigarette, occasionally taking a long, deep inhalation. Now the glass wall separating them was gone, Vince smelled the menthol-scented nicotine. The ashtray was already half-full with stubs.

The man blew a trail of smoke coolly from lips that looked parched. Vince wondered how high up in IVS this man was. It was rumoured that the Indistani President always consulted IVS before making key decisions. Could this be the man the President talked to? But looking at his casual, disregarding manner, the suit and his invisible office, Vince sensed that the President talked to someone further down the IVS food-chain.

When he spoke, still not looking at Vince, the man's voice rasped the past lives of tens of thousands of cigarettes.

"It's quite a cute trick, I know." He flicked his head backwards to the glass wall behind him. "Being invisible, able to disappear. Smoke and mirrors, you know." He didn't smile at his own pun, Vince noticed.

"Holo-projectors and diamond-glass distortion effects," Vince said. "Impressive nonetheless."

"So, Vince, if I may call you that. What do you want exactly?" He took a deep, concentrated drag from his cigarette, its red embers flaring. Vince watched as the man focused on the exhausted stump, then stubbed it out firmly in the ashtray; the way a man might shoot a beloved but broken animal.

"Are you representing the Chorazin, the Government, the Eden Mission, or yourself here today?"

Vince couldn't help but admire the casual address partnered with penetrating directness. Someone worthy to spar with.

"The telemetry and all of the above except the last."

The man took out a fresh cigarette from a gold recess in the desk.

"I don't have the telemetry, and – no offence – you're not high enough in the Chorazin to represent those three parties. Senator Josefsson was quite astonished to learn of your visit." He rolled the cigarette between thin, dextrous fingers, assessing it in some way Vince couldn't fathom.

Vince knew that Josefsson was in IVS' pocket – it was level ten knowledge in the Chorazin, and he was level twelve. He had to admit that he had not yet gone through any of the proper channels. But after what Sandy had told him, he had to risk it. Once the ship was open, he and his government would have no bargaining chips left. The Eden Mission needed the telemetry – if what Micah had said was true, the Ulysses was in danger, and here he was playing verbal poker with this oligarch. Vince couldn't help but wonder if, for once, he was out of his class. Still, he had to play it through, raise the stakes, and get this man's attention.

"You need the password to open the ship. You don't have it, neither does Josefsson."

For the first time, Vince felt himself being surveyed by the smoker. He knew what he was thinking – that Vince had little to go on, nothing to bargain with.

"My dear man, we will simply go through all the words until we find the right one. It may take a few extra days, but we can wait."

Vince almost laughed at the tactics, those he himself might have used in such a situation, to force the other's hand. He let a wan smile spread across his face, but said nothing.

"Well, there it is," said the man, "so nice of you to drop by." Vince heard the door behind him swish open and the sound of two heavies enter. The smoker flipped open a lighter, pressed a button, and a flame appeared.

It was now or never. Vince prayed the last intel from his dead former partner three days ago was right, and had been worth dying for. Instinctively Vince's right hand formed into a loose fist. He felt the tightening of his skin against the hidden stiletto.

"There is, of course, the matter of the covert IVS mission to Eden. You know, the Phoenix." Vince had joined up the dots – Micah had been perplexed as to how IVS could have fed false data to the Eden Mission, since data from Heracles or Prometheus would have been easily recognisable. Vince's former partner, Ralph, had transmitted two coded words before being terminated: *Phoenix* and *Eden*. Ralph used to say that Indistan was like a phoenix rising unstoppable from the ashes of the War, IVS its head.

The smoker's nascent flame wavered, just out of reach of his cigarette. Releasing the button, the flame flickered and went out. He put the lighter on the table in front of him, let the unlit cigarette rest in the ashtray, and sat back. With a single finger raised, he stopped the advance of the two men. He peered at Vince through eyes outlined by crow's feet, framed by well-groomed but greasy and lank brown hair. He let out a small chuckle. He stood up and walked over to the plazglass window looking down on Mumbai. He touched the glass with nicotine-stained fingertips.

Vince walked over and stood next to him. He imagined he could hear the guards' muscles tensing behind him, but the smoker didn't seem perturbed. They both gazed outwards.

"It's a long way down, Chorazin-man." He turned to face Vince, who awaited the outcome, knowing that if the rest of the world found out IVS had sent a ship to Eden, it could trigger deep suspicion, enough to send their stock price into a tailspin. The mere hint of it would be damaging.

Vince had a reluctant admiration for this man – prepared to take huge decisions on his own, and wondered if he would be like him if things had been a little different. But he decided no, he was a field operative. A strategist yes, but when he killed, it was with his own hands. Not from a distance.

The man spoke to the window. "A trade. The password for the telemetry."

"And the rest?"

"There is no 'rest'". If any material on a supposed IVS mission to Eden should surface, you will find yourself, and your compatriots in a very difficult, painful, and most likely irretrievable situation." He turned and fixed his gaze on Vince.

"This building is in the shape of Kali for a reason." He looked away again. "That's the deal."

Vince nodded. "I accept. Where's the telemetry?"

The smoker tapped open a drawer in the desk and handed Vince a crystal data-cube. Vince leaned forward and whispered the password.

The man perched on the edge of the desk, and raised an eyebrow. "You know if it doesn't work you'll be dead very soon?"

Vince grinned, nodded goodbye, and headed out. Just as he was leaving, he heard the man whisper, "Well I'll be damned."

I'm sure you are already, Vince thought. But when you arrive in hell, they'll probably put you in charge.

Thirty minutes later Vince was onboard the fast-jet, taking off. There was of course a risk that his jet would experience an accident, but he doubted it. The smoker would assume Vince had a dead-man switch somewhere who would release the information if he didn't return in one piece. Besides, if IVS wanted him dead, it would take only seconds – which meant that the password had already worked.

As the jet soared above the Mumbai haze, he watched the Kali Tower glistening in the pre-sunset, rising above the evening clouds. He downloaded the crystal's contents. Although he now allowed himself to feel his fatigue, he found the contents so interesting that he only slept the last hour of the flight. The final transmission from the Ulysses suggested a ghoster attack, but the later, non-interactive telemetry showed they had made it to Eden's solar system. So, there was some hope, after all. He decided to give a copy to Micah, to see what he could make of it.

* * *

Sanjay Shakirvasta waited until Vince was gone, then picked up his cigarette and lit it, flicking open the vidcom. "Happy now?"

A voice from the vidcom replied. "Hell, no. How'd they find out about the Phoenix?"

"No idea. I suspect it was a lucky guess, but if we get some silence for that telemetry, it's a good deal. It won't help them in any case."

"And the password. *Sesame*. I don't fucking believe it!"

"Makes sense. This ship has been down there a long time, centuries at least. Entire cultures can rise and fall in that time. You need to use a word or phrase that gets into folk-lore, so it won't be forgotten. It's also the oldest trick in the conman's book – hide something in plain sight. Does it work?"

There was a pause. He took another drag, listening to the crackling of the tobacco igniting and twisting in the frenzy of its own fire. He half-closed his eyes, and inhaled deeply, feeling the warm grey haze fill his expanding lungs.

"Not yet. They're using a speech synthesiser to run through all manner of pronunciations, forty-three so far. Wait a minute... Holy shit! The hatch is opening."

"Do you see anything?"

There was no reply. He took one more drag. "Bill?" It was then he noticed that the vidcom was flashing purple, indicating a holo message.

"You'd better take a look yourself."

He snapped his finger and thumb, and the holo-vid flickered into view. It was not what he'd been expecting; possibly the last thing.

"Well, it seems I'm damned twice in one day." He leant back in his chair, and pressed another button. "Take the bomb off the Chorazin jet."

* * *

Three thousand miles east, a previously un-openable hatch slid open.

The pewter-grey ship had the breadth of five football fields, and was seven storeys deep. The lifting had been effected by the latest Indonesian attack submarine, taking a full day to breach the surface.

The ship appeared to be circular, with triangular sections cut out of it. The only notable structure was something akin to a conning tower, but much larger, like a cylindrical four storey office block. There was a hatch at the tower's base. The password had finally allowed fresh air to enter the dormant vessel.

Several IVS choppers had landed close to the conning tower, and Bill Torreanos with a handful of scientists, engineers, and demolition experts had been involved in trying to open the doors for two days. They'd tried everything from electronics to explosives and acid – but nothing dented, scratched or even warmed the metallic hull. After the IVS vid call, they tried the word "Sesame". The pronunciation which worked had been whispered, snake-like, with an emphasis on the "S's", keeping the final "e" silent. Then the door issued a loud clunk and hiss before unlocking.

Out stepped Professor Kostakis and his assistant Jennifer, both looking rough as hell, and a little thinner than last time Bill had seen them, but otherwise unharmed. Kostakis, as usual, was beaming. He rushed to the camera relaying the vid-footage and began gesticulating and shouting.

"We can fly to Eden in this! We can fly to Eden! It's a space-ship!"

* * *

Shakirvasta collapsed the holo with his hand. He let his eyes drift out toward the sun's tangerine rays streaming across the city. The windows automatically shifted their refraction to subdue the glare. He took a last drag and stubbed out the cigarette. He pressed a small button in the top of the smooth polished desk.

"Get me Josefsson."

"Yes, Sir... Sir, it's five in the morning there."

He said nothing.

"Certainly, Sir, right away, Sir."

He stood up and paced while he waited for the call. They'd believed Kostakis dead. How had they gotten inside the ship? How had they survived? Of course these were secondary questions – Bill could deal with those. But Kostakis had said it was a space ship and could go to Eden. It was huge, capable of carrying the population of a small town. Word on the IVS defence net was that there were now estimated to be at least two similar ships found in other parts of the world. From the IVS perspective, this set the stage for complete share dominance, possibly leading to what they had dreamt of for a decade – a structural change that would leave IVS as supreme economic power for centuries to come.

It also meant they could cancel the construction of Phoenix 2 and the futile research on the mass transit Alcubierre drive which confounded IVS' best astrophysicists and engineers. They also no longer needed to intercept Ulysses' telemetry, which had been cut off in any case. Ulysses might well have made it. But if IVS could get to Eden and come back first using these ships... It was being first to *return* from Eden that really mattered.

But he never, ever, believed in a free lunch. Where had these ships come from, why were they here, and why appear now – the timing, the synchronicity, were too coincidental. And yet he knew his reservations would be overruled by others' hope, optimism, and greed. He could see the media hype sweeping across a planet boiling with desperate people. IVS should surf on that tsunami of optimism. He reminded himself of an epithet he used when he had lectured at Harvard all those years ago: "He who hesitates is crushed underfoot by those who do not."

The call came in, a grating voice on the other end. "What in God's name is worth waking me at five am on a Sunday for?"

Shakirvasta knew how to hook people and reel them in.

"Senator, when you told me once you wanted to be President of the United States one day, how serious were you?"

Chapter 24

Bubble

It had been a long day. Micah was bone tired, and broody as hell; the booster was wearing off early, aggravated by Lucidium withdrawal symptoms. His mind swirled with dark thoughts, like sharks circling, hunting bait-fish. He headed toward one of the high speed bubbles that wormed out of his building, to start the trek home, then slowed; the back of his neck tingled. He turned around, sure someone was following him. But all his eyes met was a flood of flushed, rush hour faces, irritated he had blocked the flow, delaying them a few precious seconds. Unable to pick anyone out from the crowd, he carried on and squeezed into the lozenge-shaped bubble that would flush him and his fellow commuters down to Kaymar Nexus. Just as the doors were closing, someone slipped in behind him.

It was so packed he couldn't turn around. Hardly anyone ever spoke on the bubbles. Dismal music played, mercifully drowned out by the whooshing and rattling of the mass transit system kids aptly called the pea-shooter. Several teenage commuters wore I-vids – opaque sunglasses cradling their eye sockets, evanescent light patterns occasionally leaking out – seeking refuge outside of the present.

He felt eyes burning into the back of his head. A synthetic, incomprehensible female voice blurted out the name of the next station. Micah decided he was getting off, no matter what. The noise whined down and they jolted to a stop, the doors opening a little too early so that the person behind him stepped out. Micah twisted to see a bedraggled Antonia standing on the platform, eyes edgy, in amongst passengers trying to board. With an effort he carved through them and disembarked from the bubble, whose doors zipped shut, as it catapulted down the tunnel to its next destination. The bubble's wake blew her skirt around her legs. He tried not to look.

There she stood, the girl of his dreams, right in front of him on the platform with its ebbing wash of people. Four minutes max before the next one.

He framed her – this pocket of time with its vanishing possibilities – in his mind.

"What are you doing?" she asked, a frown appearing on her forehead, like corrugated sand patterns after the tide has retired.

"Stealing a perfect moment."

Her eyes glared distrust.

"In my profession," he said, "visual memory is enhanced. I can occasionally take a snapshot. It just seemed a perfect moment. They don't come very often."

"Why stealing?"

Micah shrugged. "I didn't have your permission." And you belong to Katrina. Patches of his recently-aired anger from his debrief with Vince hung like flotsam around him. It wouldn't take much to set them off again.

"Why did you follow me?" he said. He still had a faint thread of hope, though his rational mind said he was wasting his time.

Her face flushed, her hands wrestling each other. "I came here to find out something."

He didn't want to get angry with her – or did he? He wasn't sure. So he let his analyst sense emerge, trumping his emotions, taking in the events so far, and her body language. He calculated what she must already know. She worked in comms as an analyst, and had access to the outgoing data-streams. Her job was checking their integrity, but that meant that there were few checks after she handled the data, so she had the perfect vantage point to find and then delete hidden messages. His assessment conclusion had negligible uncertainty.

"You came to ask me about the simulacra in the landscapes," he said.

"How did...? Wait – Vince doesn't know, does he?" Her voice betrayed more than a hint of concern.

"Not about yours. Though he'll figure it out soon enough."

She looked crestfallen. Micah was feeling fed up, anger at being rejected welled up inside him, heading for the surface. He went on the offensive.

"I saw Katrina's simulacrum in Rudi's landscape, and yours in mine. Rudi's world is pretty ravaged. The Katrina simulacrum wasn't in good shape." He noticed how she became increasingly motionless, holding herself together, barely breathing, not meeting his gaze. He had to be sure. "To be honest," he said, "I don't think she will survive –"

"Stop! Stop it," she said, not yelling, which made it worse. "You're hurting me!"

Micah recoiled. The words cut through him, snapping off his breath. The booster and Lucidium-fuelled angst deserted him, leaving him suspended like a surfer whose wave had just vanished into thin air. His bravado freefell. *What the hell was I thinking! Now is no time to behave like a bastard; like my father.*

She bit her lip, eyes swimming in salt water, but held his gaze, not caring.

"Micah, you have to help her. The real Kat, I mean. I keep having these terrible... She and I ..." she choked off. He closed towards her cautiously, like a child who had hurt his sibling when playing rough, not meaning to cause real pain. He reached out and touched her arm, gesturing to some uncomfortable-looking fixed seats plastered with seedy holo-graffiti. He hoped they hadn't been desecrated by the tramps who slept there. They sat down on the gaudy, unyielding plastic.

She sniffed tears away and stared at the swirling incandescent ads on the opposite wall. "We met at an international dignitaries' function nine months ago – my uncle is the Slovakian ambassador – I'm not usually into girls, but she was so funny, in a dark sort of way. She stole a kiss from me. She changed my world."

Micah felt hollow. But he said nothing, accepting his retribution for how he'd just acted.

"Ever since, we've been seeing each other secretly, up until the launch. We signed a three-year pax agreement before she left orbit." She glanced at him sideways. "You're okay, aren't you, I mean with girl-girl... Oh, never mind. Anyway, about a week before we lost contact, the messages she'd been sending me via the simulacra stopped. But my simulacrum warned me that something was wrong, that someone was tracking both of them down. I didn't know if it was you or Rudi. I was going to talk to Mr Kane. When he was murdered, I was desperate. I knew the danger had penetrated the Eden Mission staff. I didn't know who to trust."

"Did you tell Vince or Louise?" Micah's voice sounded croaky, even to him.

She spat a mirthless laugh. "The Chorazin? They're probably involved. And that Louise isn't what she appears to be."

He cleared his throat. "Antonia, I'll do my best to help you get back in contact with Katrina –"

"Kat, if you don't mind."

"Okay, Kat – and I don't mind at all," he lied, because this was hell. "But I'll need your help tomorrow finding the simulacra, if they're not already decompiled."

"Gladly, I want to *do* something!" Her face lit up. She pressed her hand on top of his. "I hoped you'd help. It means a lot to me." She retracted her hand. He stared at his own hand, making sure it didn't follow hers. Commuters began clogging up the platform.

"One more thing, Antonia. Who made the simulacra? They're not IVS are they?"

"God, no! That would be a sackable offence, maybe even treason. Kat brought them in, actually. They're MI9, believe it or not." She smiled. "I'm not meant to know of course, let alone tell anyone. To be honest I think it was that God-awful Uncle of hers, Lord Beornwulf – he wanted an independent way to keep tabs on her."

The first wisps of air ruffled her blouse as a bubble thrashed its way down the tube, its braking screech getting louder. He stood up. "Tomorrow, then."

She stayed seated as he turned towards the platform's edge. He struggled not to look back. The bubble arrived, a popping sound as its doors opened. Boarding it, engulfed by the sweaty throng of other passengers, Micah caught a last glimpse of her, head hung down, as the bubble vomited out of the station.

He wondered how his father would have handled it. He'd probably have somehow seduced her away from Katrina – Kat – seeing their lesbian affair as a challenge. Seduction had been his father's other forte, so he'd heard. But it wouldn't be his path. He recalled his mother sobbing alone at night, when he was too young to understand, but not too young to make the connection. *Every hero has a dark side*, Vince had said.

His stop arrived. As he and the anonymous crowd flooded out of the station into the constant warm breeze of Kaymar cavern, a flower-seller, who his mom always complained was ridiculously over-priced, called out to him and other passers-by. His father had always brought home red roses for Micah's mom – *afterwards*. Micah bought white.

He paused on the moving walkways criss-crossing the underground habitat towers like an Escher sketch, the fake scarlet sunset putting him in a pensive mood. Vince had said Micah wanted to be a hero. He'd never admitted it before, because he hated his father's hero status so much. But maybe he could be a different sort.

He'd been in close proximity to four people who had died in the space of two days. Something big was happening, involving the Ulysses, Alicians, and IVS, the last surviving Titan Corporation. Some very powerful forces didn't want people to find out what was on Eden. Micah knew he didn't fit the bill of being Chorazin agent or astronaut, but he had a talent for solving puzzles; and that was what this situation needed most – intelligence – rather than brawn or the normal brand of heroism.

When Vince had mentioned IVS finding a ship, Micah's analyst sense had rung alarm bells. He'd been too preoccupied at the time to react, but now he realised it was a key piece of the jigsaw. He quickened his pace to get home to see the news.

He knew the four astronauts were in mortal danger, and if Eden failed, then Earth's future was bleak at best. Suddenly it was all so shockingly real, like falling into ice cold water – the Prometheus, the Heracles, the Alicians, Kane, Rudi, Ben and the Cleanser. He shoved away all thoughts about his father, and wanting to be any kind of hero. This was much bigger than his petty baggage. He needed to help the Eden astronauts, and only someone on Earth could save them. He had to help unlock this puzzle before it was too late. The ship that had been found – that was the key – his intuition screamed it at him. He stopped dead when he saw a vidcast playing on a wall. Others had paused to read it too. <Space ship found by IVS; fast-track mass transport to Eden awaits…>

Micah didn't hear the excited conversations around him. He tried to join up the pieces, but there was still not enough information. He'd need to study the nets, do some research at home. Yet he had the feeling things were accelerating, that there wasn't much time left to solve this enigma. He walked faster and faster through the thinning rush hour crowds, his mind churning over the information he had, trying to make sense of it. By the time he reached home he was running.

Chapter 25

Sighting

Kat listened to Blake and Rashid trade information while the three of them sat inside the cramped, dimly lit remains of Rashid's ship. Rashid was burning ylang-ylang incense, and though Kat couldn't smell it because of her helmet, she followed the tendrils of smoke as they spiralled and congregated beneath the ceiling.

Rashid explained how he had survived there in terms of food and water. The latter was apparently safe to drink, and some of the bushes produced edible, bitter fruit, though it had taken several weeks of diarrhoea for him to adapt. His ship had carried seeds, and he had got some basic vegetables growing by the time his ship supplies had run out. Everything here tasted slightly metallic, though, he said.

"No grain, no wheat?" Blake asked. Kat knew the Ulysses carried a range of basic grains to ensure that Eden could produce wheat or rice or astrasa.

"No. It does not take, it will not grow here. It will need genetic adaptation I believe, if it will ever work at all."

Not good, an Eden where Earth food doesn't grow. She sized up Rashid's meagre, fat-free frame. *And what does grow barely sustains.*

In return, Blake filled Rashid in on the small advances made in terms of space travel in the intervening two years since Rashid had left Earth.

"It is something of a miracle that these technological discoveries have all been made so quickly," Rashid said, "almost as if God is helping us out, after a period of seemingly ignoring us."

Kat noted that Blake refused to be drawn into an ideological debate, though she suspected he had strong religious convictions. It was reasonable to talk about all of this, but it was small talk, circling around the real issues, the threatening ones. She presumed Blake was gaining the measure of the man, letting Rashid relax, listening carefully to the answers, deciding how much to trust him, before he embarked on the really difficult subjects. To her, though, Rashid seemed eminently trustworthy.

Glancing at her air monitor on her wrist, she saw that she had a little over three hours left in the re-breather system, before recycling air would start to get problematic. It was close to two hours journey back to Ulysses, where she hoped Pierre had made some progress.

Blake noticed her glance, and changed tack. "Rashid. The message – I assume from you – told us not to land here. Why?"

Rashid clasped his hands together. For a moment he seemed agitated. His eyes darted around and seemed not to want to look at Blake or Kat, instead fixing on the faded painting of the Taj Mahal. Kat found it odd that Rashid found solace in a structure which had been wiped off the face of the planet over a decade ago.

"Yes, yes. It is indeed my message." His smile faltered. Kat's instincts snapped online: something was wrong. Blake clearly detected it too; his posture shifting, more alert.

Rashid continued. "But now you are here, yes?"

Blake's face hardened. "That's not the point. You implied danger. Are we in danger? If the people of Earth come here, are they in danger, Rashid?"

Rashid got up and walked over to the airlock door, his back facing them. Kat and Blake glanced at each other. Blake's hand was already moving toward his holster when Rashid whirled around, far quicker than Kat would have given him credit for, a pulse pistol in his hand.

"I'm so very sorry. We must wait. It... it will be here very soon."

She couldn't believe it. She started to rise, but a throbbing in her head began, as if someone was banging a gong inside her brain. Her hands clamped to her helmet. She winced as the pounding escalated to a hammering. Through groggy eyes she saw Blake's consternation, but there was nothing he could do, except get shot. She looked towards Rashid through watering eyes from the pain, but he paid her no attention, his pistol trained on Blake.

It felt like small volcanoes were erupting in the centre of her brain, then she heard a noise like a train, getting louder and louder. She cried out, not even hearing her own voice drowned in the relentless, increasing din ricocheting around her skull. She caught a last glimpse through wet, strained eyes, of Rashid and Blake facing each other, and then she keeled over. Lying shaking on the floor, jaw clenched in agony, her eyes fell on the porthole. Through a gap in its curtain, she saw a blood-red flash streak across the twilight sky – an emergency flare from Zack and Pierre. Her brain did the only sensible thing, and crashed into unconsciousness.

* * *

Pierre stood on the top of a hillock, a kilometre from the ship, still in its line of sight, though the light was fading. He surveyed the landscape. He could see maybe ten miles of greyish greenery on one side like fields of lavender, and a vast expanse of desert on the other. It was good to be out of the spaceship after all those endless days cooped up in three small compartments. He altered the spectral filters on his helmet visor to detect anything unusual, something perhaps sticking out against the background. Nothing. He switched to infrared – too bright for the desert – and then ultraviolet. Zero – *nul*, he thought, in French – just unbroken landscape, bushes and trees. The quiet was disconcerting, as if the land itself was holding its breath, waiting for something to happen. The lack of sound and activity reminded him of when he'd visited the now-petrified forest of Clamart, just outside Paris, where he'd played as a child before the War. Like most people, he had only returned there once, and not for long either.

He heard static on his com-link. "… can see something."

He'd forgotten Zack was seeing on a screen what he himself could see, remotely via the micro-camera mounted on his helmet.

"Say again, Zack?"

"Wait a sec; I'm replaying it here in the cockpit. There we go. Try UV again. It was right on the periphery, maybe why you didn't see it. Your current nine o'clock."

Pierre turned to the left, scanning in that direction. He modified the filters again. There it was. A tall, thin object, a hundred metres away. He raised his binoculars but could see nothing through them. He squinted into the hazy distance, without glasses. The object was gone.

"Shit, Pierre. It was there and now it's gone. What does that tell you?"

He didn't like it either. But at the moment it told him very little: too many possibilities, too little data. However, he predicted exactly what it would mean to Zack.

Zack said it for both of them. "We've got company."

Pierre hadn't got a good image of it. He looked again toward the spot and a few large bushes nearby. It had been close to one small tree, but taller than it by a third. He estimated it was three metres high. He hadn't noticed head or limbs and the silhouette was dark, so it could have been mechanical.

"Pierre, get back here. But before you go, launch a red flare. I want Blake and Kat back here, a.s.a.p!"

"Zack, it – if it is indeed an it – will see the flare too."

"Damned right it will!"

Pierre didn't see the logic in that, but agreed to alert the Captain at once. He knelt down and took off his backpack, laying his rifle on the floor. He hunted through the main compartment for the flare gun. He found it, but just as he was about to get up he noticed a long shadow on the ground in front of him.

"Pierre! Look out!" Zack yelled, but Pierre had already leapt sideways away from the shadow and rolled, coming up in a kneeling position with the flare gun pointing exactly at where the shadow must have come from. There was nothing there. His combat training cut in and he swivelled three-sixty degrees; his breath rasping inside his helmet. After a few half turns, he heard Zack's voice again.

"Pierre – listen to me. It's still around there, I've been watching with the viewer, but it moves so fast it's difficult to get a fix on it. Fire the flare now, then pick up your rifle and head back toward the ship. And if I say run, run like hell."

Pierre did one more visual sweep. He still hadn't got a good view of the thing, but it was twice his size, and could move very fast. Yet it was very quiet. Given its speed and apparently effortless movement, he guessed his chances of out-running it were minimal. He raised his arm and fired the flare, all the time circling, looking over his shoulder. The hairs on the back of his neck stood up, each one like an attentive, nervous soldier.

For the next few minutes, Pierre half-walked, half-skidded down the escarpment, the ship still seven hundred metres away. He hadn't turned around once; Zack was scouting for him. Pierre had left the larger bushes behind him, which meant that if the creature came out it would be easily seen. It also meant he had no cover. He'd been on safari in Tanzania once as a kid, and watched cheetahs hunt in the Ngorongoro Crater. They waited in the tall grass and rocks on the edge of open savannah, and right now he felt just like a Thomson's gazelle cut off from the herd, alone and vulnerable.

Suddenly he felt a rush of blood to the back of his neck. He turned and saw a tall black shadow charging down the hill towards him. Without hesitation he raised his rifle and fired three shots at it. It didn't even slow down.

Zack yelled down the comms: "RUN!"

Pierre discarded the pulse rifle and his backpack, and sprinted for the ship. His arms pumped fast as he tried to control his breathing, the way he'd learned at school, to stretch out the dash to the ship. Within a few seconds, he saw Zack limping at the Ulysses Lander entrance, hoisting a heavy weapon onto his shoulder and aiming towards him. He heard a sharp clicking noise behind him, then a bizarre, heavy-footed galloping noise, gaining steadily on him. Pierre lost control of his breathing, and ran faster than he ever thought possible.

* * *

Blake sat, the pistol trained on him, but his weight was on his thighs, ready to spring up if Rashid took his eyes off him even for a moment. He didn't. Blake didn't know who he was angrier with – Rashid for betraying them or himself for being too slow to react at the critical moment. He regarded Kat's crumpled body. At least she was alive. He'd also seen the flare, so he knew Zack and Pierre were in trouble. He had confidence in Zack's abilities to deal with it in the short term.

"We trusted you," he said; although he knew he hadn't really, not yet, he'd just let his guard down a little. But he saw it hit home. Rashid was flustered.

"You can still trust me, Captain. You will see, I just need you to not over-react when it arrives."

Blake decided another approach. He leant back, smiled, and put his hands behind his head, though his abdominals inside his suit were rigid, tensed like a spring to propel him upwards if Rashid reciprocated.

"Now, why on Earth would I over-react? It's not as if you just overcame my corporal and had a pistol pointing at my chest, and were talking of an 'it' arriving without telling me what the hell 'it' is." He stopped smiling, and made his decision.

"To hell with this, Rashid. One of the mottos of my platoon was 'Never be taken prisoner'. Part of our code. So if you're going to shoot me, then go right ahead and shoot." He got up, calmly, as if going to take a walk. He bent over Kat, not approaching Rashid just two metres away.

"What did you do to her?" Kat's face twitched beneath her visor. He spoke quietly to Rashid. "What the hell is going on, Rashid? Talk to me."

Before Rashid could answer, the door opened, and a pulsing electric blue light washed into the room. Blake gaped as an oval object, half a metre in diameter, and about Rashid's height, drifted into the compartment. Its surface at first reminded him of the purple and blue ripples sometimes seen on an oil film stretched across a circular wire frame. Rashid kept his pistol trained on him, his arm not quite steady.

To Blake, the intruder resembled a mirror, but with a fluidic surface, fractal images swirling, almost taking shape, but not quite. He was unable to focus properly on it. Around its circumference was what appeared to be a tube of gold-coloured metal, about the same diameter as a handrail. It hung thirty centimetres above the floor, all the time emitting a faint sound of water trickling, like a small fountain. It stopped next to Rashid, and then oriented itself towards Kat. He realised this had to be alien in origin: not even IVS had anti-grav technology. The implications were overwhelming, but he pushed them aside for the moment, focusing on gathering information, and protecting Kat. But then he saw her body and face reflected in the object's mirror surface.

Just as he reached for his pulse pistol, Rashid spoke up.

"Don't. It won't hurt her. It is trying to communicate with her."

Blake kept his hand on the butt of the pistol. "Did it make her black out?"

Rashid nodded. "It has already been in communication with Kat before, for some weeks now."

"Wait. You're telling me this thing has been reaching across light years of space to my ship?" *The nightmares!* He glared at it, wondering if it had any defences.

"Yes. Because she has a node. That is right, is it not?"

Blake flared. "How the hell do you know that? Not even my first officer…" He stopped. Could it be true – that this thing was interfacing with Kat's internal multimedia bio-chip?

Rashid spoke as if reciting from a list. "Your first officer is named Zack. Broken right leg. Utters profanities far more than is necessary. Sits on the port side. Pierre is science officer, sits behind you."

Blake's face didn't hide his surprise or outrage. "How in hell's name…?" He felt that his ship, his command had been violated. But as he was about to ask, he saw Rashid nod to the mirror-like object, which turned toward him. Dumbfounded, he saw on its surface a moving image of him and his crew as seen from Kat's position in the Ulysses. He sat down, reeling from the security implications. The critical question was whether it was hostile or not. As if knowing that this question would arrive soonest, Rashid began to talk, his voice adopting its previous calm, amicable tone.

"I have asked it its name, but communication is very difficult. It does not speak and can only show pictures of what it has seen itself, or via someone or something it can communicate with. I noticed it, that is, it found me, when I was burying my colleague, Azil. It appeared at the top of the nearest dune, and my immediate reaction was to run inside, get out my rifle and shoot it."

"You missed?"

Rashid laughed, a little too loud. "Oh no, I never miss. But it was close – for me, that is. You see it looks like a mirror, and in many senses it is one. My high powered bullet ricocheted off it. So I tried the laser rifle. As I fired, it turned a fraction, and bounced the pulse straight back at a piece of wreckage just beside me, burning a hole right through it. It was our first meaningful communication, looking back on it. I communicated fear, and it taught me respect."

Blake studied Rashid's eyes; he seemed to be telling the truth. Rashid had not actually lied about anything – yet.

"What about Kat? Why has it done this to her? What does it want?"

Rashid got to his feet. Blake wanted to floor him; Rashid seemed to understand that too, as he approached cautiously.

"I am human, like you," he said, eyes wide with almost religious fervour. "There is a great threat to all of us. But not from this." He indicated the alien mirror. "It has helped me survive, to stay alive, against..." He trailed off. Blake noticed him clenching and unclenching his fist, one of his own habits. His anger at Rashid checked itself. There was something about this man that made him difficult to dislike for very long. He was a tortured soul, a poet forced to be a commando and an astronaut. Blake had seen it before, men like this had been in his ranks during the war, but in his experience they never survived in battles, because they always ended up making the ultimate heroic sacrifice. So, Blake thought, I don't need to kill you, your days are numbered. And then he wished he hadn't thought it at all.

Rashid picked up again. "It helped me survive against... the others. There are beings here. Guardians. Tall, impervious to our weapons, very fast, very dangerous." His hands trembled. He laid his pistol on the floor. Despite Blake's face of stone, Rashid gingerly laid a hand upon his shoulder, which tensed immediately. There were tears barely held back in Rashid's eyes, and his voice was unsteady.

"They mean to kill us all, Captain Alexander. All of us. All humanity. Eden is a trap." He raised his hand to Blake's other shoulder, gripping him hard, and stared wildly into Blake's eyes. "We have to stop them. No matter what it takes. We have to stop them."

The mirror's picture changed, and Blake was shown the enemy. His anger at Rashid dissolved. He recognised true evil when he saw it.

Chapter 26

Choices

Gabriel took a sling-jet, boarding as a business passenger – staff asked fewer questions of first class clients. His fake ret-scan passed flawlessly. The jet arrived early morning in Old Denver, slicing through anvil-shaped clouds, accompanied by lightning cords and strong winds which buffeted the twelve-seater.

A reliable source had told him Sister Esma was due to hold a Chapter meeting at noon. After a short deviation to pick up some gear, he located the once famous Country Club in the oldest part of town, more recently used as a school. The streets were deserted. This quarter of Denver was known for being ultra-religious, full of fanatics, so the Chorazin, civic police and all non-Fundie up-standing folk stayed away.

The dilapidated building, grey and crumbling with age, was no longer in use: all children in the area attended the huge state boarding schools further up in the low-rad Rockies. He entered via an unlocked side door.

Gabriel studied the dust on the furniture-less floor – he stroked some onto his finger and smelt it – synthetic, sprayed liberally to give the impression no one had been here for months. He scanned the interior until he discerned a faded symbol above a wooden floor-boarded stage – three outstretched olive branches, representing neo-fundamentalist aligned Islamic, Hindu and Judeo-Christian faiths. He scoped the floor again, and the beamed ceiling. He needed to get across without leaving any trace.

He fished in his rucksack for the two knife-hooks, then fastened a lanyard around each wrist. Crouching down, he sprung into the air, stabbing both blades into the first wooden beam with a resounding thunk. As soon as they penetrated the wood, he twisted the handles and microscopic barbs speared outwards from the blade. Gabriel hung there like a trapeze artist, swinging his legs. He twisted the right hand hilt the other way, and the knife released. He swung twice more, then pulled sharply on his left arm as he propelled forward and upward, twisting the hilt, releasing the second knife. A fraction of a second later his right hand stabbed its knife into the next beam, and he continued, gathering speed as he'd seen macaques do in Uganda years ago.

When he arrived at the final beam next to the symbol, he stalled his swinging, and pressed on the two lower branches simultaneously with his feet. A click beneath him revealed the outline of a trap-door. He lifted his knees up to his chest and waited. As the door rose automatically, a crossbow bolt shot out firing straight ahead to where an uninitiated would have normally stood. It thudded into the wall beneath his feet. He angled himself, hanging by his left arm, and wrestled the bolt out of the stone. It left a small hole, but there were others already there. He smeared as much of the surrounding chalk over it as he could, twisted his knife-hook and dropped down through the trap door onto the first rung of a spiral staircase.

He primed the bolt back into its firing mechanism, and descended into the darkness below. One way in, one way out: he felt like a man walking into a cage – but the bait was worth the price.

Depositing trip-sensors on the trap-door, he closed it after him, then waited at the bottom, kneeling on the damp concrete in the musty basement devoid of furniture or fittings – nowhere to hide. Pale light strobed through the floorboards above.

Ten o'clock – ample time to reflect, to purify his mind. Important to die with a clear head: he'd seen so many, almost everyone he'd cleansed, die screaming, pleading for their lives or wetting themselves with fear. He slowed his breathing, and slipped into a meditative trance.

He intended to consider the events of the past few days, but as he relaxed, his mind reached further back. He remembered playing with his sister so many years ago, back in the outskirts of Shannon, on the cliffs of Mohar. In his mind he saw the lush greens that were all but gone from that radioactive wasteland, the tragic remnant of the last major nuclear battle of the war – a jewel of an island raked and scorched by a desperate last venting of rage, an attempt at mutual annihilation. The only limiting factor that had stopped both sides unleashing their complete arsenal, had been the unanticipated EMP harmonic shockwave that destroyed all the missiles' and air attack squadrons' guidance systems. It had shut down both armies, even with their supposedly EMP-proof technology. If they'd have continued, the resulting fallout would have breached the Kudoly threshold, triggering a radiation spike, annihilating most living creatures on the planet within six months. Earth wouldn't have recovered.

His mind travelled back to Jenny, his sister, to a time almost in their teens. She was on the swing in the garden. She cajoled him into pushing harder, and he'd worried she'd fall off. Each time she flew a little higher, she shrieked, and her shrill laughing scream merged with the laboured creaking of the mechanical joints. He stopped pushing, and after she realised that no matter what she had said he would push no more, she let her head fall back, eyes closed, the sun on her face, waiting for the swing to drift to a stop. He watched her a long time until she came to rest.

"Why'd you stop pushing?" she asked, eyes still closed, head still back.

He was leaning on the swing-set frame. "I was worried you'd fly off and hurt yourself, stupid."

She opened her eyes and smiled at him in a way that made him uncomfortable.

"I'm invincible, Gabe. Don't you know that?"

He didn't reply. He envied her free spirit, compared to his own dark thoughts. But he worried he would hurt her in other ways. His body was undergoing changes and he found himself looking at his coquettish sister in ways he didn't understand, and didn't trust. Later, as his maturation took its course, he sought refuge from the onslaught of his hormones in other girls at school – his dark looks and sombre moods found him no shortage of willing playmates.

Even at that early age, though, he'd become concerned about world affairs. While other kids talked about the latest music holos, he wanted to discuss politics. At home at supper time he listened to his father rant about the corrupt politicians and the religious clerics, how it was all going to hell, and how Jeannie and Joe Average would pay for it all, as always. His sister and mother managed to rise above it, but to Gabriel, the eldest, it all really mattered, so much so that it twisted his stomach, and people's wilful ignorance and lassitude made him ball his fists and occasionally punch them into doors, and later on, straight through them.

Gabriel surfaced from his reverie and checked his breathing. It was long, deep and smooth, his body perfectly still. Satisfied, he resumed his train of thought, moving forward to when war had loomed across their lives, three years later. He signed up, barely sixteen years old. After psychometric examination he was taken out of his platoon and trained by the fledgling Chorazin Corps – at first shock-troop tactics, later on, graduating to advanced psychological techniques. As the War got longer and dirtier, and the threat of protracted nuclear theatre became more tangible, he was sent deep cover to infiltrate an Alician training centre.

He remembered the school, hidden in the Nepalese foothills. Most of the students had been religious maniacs, as full of fervour as their minds were closed. They were used by the Alician order as martyrs: cannon-fodder, suicide bomber pawns laying out a carpet of blood following the Alician strategists' goals. But Gabriel, like a few others, was seen as less dispensable, more useful than a simple weapon or bomb carrier whose sole aim was indiscriminate carnage. Gabriel undertook full Cleanser training, including Alician religious training and mind discipline techniques.

At first he only paid lip service to the teachers. But after six months without Chorazin contact, he realised he was on his own, for whatever reason – lost, forgotten, cut-off. His Alician watchers began to suspect his motives, so he threw himself into the training. He'd never swallowed the Alician hype, but he found peace in Cleansing. Both sides had trained him to kill, and he surrendered to it, becoming an adept assassin. His skills didn't go unnoticed.

Just after the end of the War, he was sent to Tibet: he and nine other Cleansers, already blooded numerous times, were each to receive one-to-one instruction from a Master. It was an incredible honour. He'd never been so proud.

He met his Master, Cheveyo, and immediately recognised him as the most enlightened person he'd ever encountered. He worshipped the man, did everything he was asked, no matter how difficult, no matter how seemingly pointless, including standing naked, blindfolded atop a mountain overnight.

Then came the shock. Cheveyo took him on an arduous seven day trek into the mountains. After three days they descended inside a glacier, hacking through thick ice for hours in conditions of thirty below, with blinding winds so cold that any exposed flesh was frost-bitten in minutes. For a whole day they ferreted deeper into the glacier's treacherous tunnels. They used head torches as there was no natural light, only the occasional muffled shade of blue, but eventually they arrived inside a gargantuan chamber. Gabriel recognised he was standing on something that was not ice – more like metal. In the distance he saw a squat tower. Shaking with cold and exhaustion, he was led by his Master to the tower's foot and a large hatchway held open by a log of frozen, ancient wood.

The stench from the two rotting corpses made Gabriel recoil even though he should have been used to it. One of them he recognised: a former acolyte he had met a year earlier, whom he'd heard had been killed in training.

Cheveyo led him a short distance inside to what seemed to be a control room, and sat down cross-legged. Gabriel reciprocated so as not to be standing over his Master, who spoke as always: quiet, calm, authoritative. Gabriel listened, intuiting that his life depended on it.

"Before you now is a choice, Gabriel. Choice is man's constant companion. Choices define who we are, what we are, how we live – and whether we continue to live."

The last part hung in the crisp air, within the small cloud of freezing mist that formed from his Master's breath. Gabriel knew better than to interrupt.

"A thousand years ago, a small band of visitors came from another world. They are called Q'Roth." He never took his eyes off Gabriel. 'They fed on many humans, though not the way most humans eat the meat of dead animals. They do not consume the flesh – they draw the neural energy, the bio-electric life force from their victims."

Gabriel stared downward. Only in the past decade had Eastern and Western medicine systems finally met on even ground, confirming with Western techniques the essential bioelectric meridians that Chinese doctors had charted for millennia. This had spawned new research directions into the neural energy signature of the human brain. Although electricity is electricity, as some physicists had put it, whether biological or chemically induced, there were subtle differences related to human, cetacean and primate consciousness. But it was hard to conceive that there were other beings out there, and that this was what nourished them.

"The Q'Roth curried favour with a group of humans they found useful, and set up an Order to await their return. They left ships, like this one here, behind them. They also left certain humans who they genetically altered. The genome persists in very few people. These people have become powerful, physically and politically, through careful, deep, long-term strategies. They are the inner circle of the Alicians, called the Protectors, and they are the vassals of the Q'Roth. Most Alicians, even those higher up, do not realise who they really serve."

Cheveyo drew his Cleanser knife, and laid it before him, the blade pointing at Gabriel. "Even the name, Alicians, is far older than people know. The Protector Regent, their leader for six hundred years, was a genetically-enhanced woman named Alessia. The Q'Roth are dominated by a female queen, and so the Protectors have always been led by a female. Alessia was formidable – it took five Master Sentinels to kill her, and she took four of them down with her in hand to hand combat. After this famous battle, the Protectors secretly adopted the name *Alessians*, in reverence to her."

He paused again. Gabriel appreciated the time to assimilate not the words, but their import. If this were true... He felt nauseous, trying to recall how many he'd cleansed for the Alicians, while supposedly working for the Chorazin. Now, to learn that all this time he'd been used by an alien race...

"The Q'Roth will return. Soon, maybe a decade from now. The inner circle of the Alicians, these Protectors, have been plotting for a millennium, and have become more active in the past hundred years. Many inventions, many discoveries, are scheduled technology releases fostered by key Alicians to bring humanity closer to harvesting by the Q'Roth."

The pieces slotted together for Gabriel. Most Alicians appeared to be of the "robe-and-dagger" fanatic variety, but he'd also seen visitors to the training centre in sharp business suits, from one of the large Titan Corporations' research agencies. He'd also been called upon to cleanse several scientists. The Alicians' outward face was a façade, hiding their inner machinations.

Cheveyo continued. "They increase our internal discord, while avenues of science dangerous to the Q'Roth are blocked from us. The War was triggered by the Protectors, to bring the Alicians out of the shadows just beneath an unstoppable popular force, the Fundies who will unite Eastern and Western fundamentalist ideologies. And the War was halted by the Protectors at the last moment, to prevent catastrophic loss of the Q'Roth food source."

Cheveyo picked up the Cleanser's knife. "I must ask you a question, Gabriel."

Gabriel's eyes widened, lost on this sudden stormy sea of revelation, whose evidence he was sitting on, since this behemoth of a ship buried inside a glacier couldn't have been created by man. He clung to his Master's voice, the only lifeline he had left. The knife was there to delineate choices, he knew. If his answer was wrong or insufficient, he would join his two comrades at the entrance of the tower. His Master would report him as killed during training, and would not be questioned. Moreover, Gabriel knew that he could not physically overcome this man – despite being a good forty years younger – as numerous physical training bouts in recent weeks had made abundantly clear.

"Gabriel – what is the nature of fundamentalism? What choice characterises it?"

Gabriel's brow furrowed; such an abstract question, one he had never heard before. He had to think of the context his Master had used earlier, equating choice with life, and he clearly had to answer differently to the men lying on the floor, their throats bled dry.

An answer struck his mind, dredged up from the memory of a man he had killed – a famous Professor who had been unafraid to die, one of the very few. He had said it to Gabriel just before the cleansing. It now came back to haunt him, but it resonated with a shocking truth. Gabriel didn't hesitate. He trusted his Master, and if he gave him the wrong answer, then he was prepared to suffer the consequences.

"Fundamentalism values blind faith more than intelligence." He remembered the rest of it. "Faith: a blind, deaf and untouchable faith which will hold even in the face of clear counter-evidence."

"Those are not your words, Gabriel." Cheveyo rose effortlessly and walked around behind him.

Gabriel swallowed, feeling his Adam's apple, wondering if it might be slit in two at any moment. "Fundamentalism is about controlling the masses, the herd," he said, hesitantly, and then he understood. "In this case, so the herd can be led to slaughter."

Cheveyo returned in front of Gabriel and sat down, placing the unsheathed knife between them. This time the hilt faced Gabriel. "The Q'Roth want people to leave this planet. We do not know why exactly, and we do not know where – yet – perhaps to their home planet."

Gabriel risked a question. "How do we know these things? Alicians are trained to resist torture."

"The Q'Roth have not been the only visitors to Earth. Another alien, a Ranger, crash-landed here a century after the Q'Roth scouting mission. My ancestors helped and nursed him back to health, although his physiology was more reptilian than human. He detected traces of the Q'Roth's visit, and warned my forebears what was to come."

"From what he could communicate, the Q'Roth have a thousand year life cycle. When they are born, they are utterly savage, violent creatures. They need to feed quickly on sentient neural energy. It acts as a catalyst for their intellectual maturation." Cheveyo paused, looking downcast. "It is not so uncommon in nature, for hatchlings to feed on others so that they may have life." He raised his head again. "But this wanton culling will eradicate humanity – each Q'Roth will consume a hundred souls."

Gabriel realised how weary his Master was. But there was a further question he had to ask. His legs were numb from sitting on the glacial ice, but he ignored them. "Master, you said 'we'. Who is this *'we'*?"

His Master nodded. "We are called Sentinels. We are very few, less than fifty now on this globe hurtling through space, its population oblivious to the raptors out there, and to the wolves dressed in robes at home. We are scattered, fragmented, no longer able to do anything of strategic significance. Once we were stronger, but violent struggles with the vassals of the Q'Roth over the centuries have exacted a heavy toll on our numbers. But we remember, we know and understand the threat, and we look for opportunities. A number of us are hidden within the Alician ranks themselves. And we look for new blood." He closed his eyes.

"My choice," Gabriel said, looking at the knife lying between them. It was an invitation – he could try and kill his Master, or he could join with him. He made no move. "The others – the two lying at the entrance. They did not… believe you?"

His Master, eyes still closed, in a move so fast it surprised Gabriel, sheathed the razor-sharp curved knife; it disappeared into the folds of his sleeve.

"They answered differently."

Gabriel opened his eyes in the dark, musty room – the trip-sensors had detected someone. He heard footsteps descending the spiral staircase. Instinctively he knew it was Sister Esma, and he was sure she was a vassal of the Q'Roth, one of the Protectors, possibly their Grand Mistress herself. If so, she would be very hard to kill, and at the least would almost certainly take him with her. Perhaps he could gain more useful information from her, or perhaps he should simply send her onwards, pre-emptively. *Choices.*

He sprang into a fighting stance. He saw two legs appear, stepping sedately down the last steps. If he was to kill her it must be before she reached the bottom. He made his choice. His throwing knife pierced her chest up to its hilt just before her head appeared. There was a gurgling, and she toppled to the floor, head down. He listened for any further footsteps in case she was not alone, and then approached to turn her body over. Sister Esma smiled at him, her mouth leaking green bile.

"Matthias – or should I say Gabriel – I knew you would come."

His hands whipped around the back of her head and jaw and flicked to snap her neck, but there was no crunch, just a rubbery resistance. Her left hand shot upwards and closed around his throat. With one hand he tried to pry it loose, and with the other he twisted the knife sticking into her chest, but she kept smiling.

"My heart's not there anymore, Gabriel. They moved it a long time ago."

Long fingernails pierced his neck, and he felt toxins surge into his bloodstream, a boiling flush washing through his skull, attacking his brain cells. Brown blotches appeared in front of his eyes like spats of mud. He punched her temple hard enough to smash a normal human skull, but it did no damage. His strength collapsed. He reached down to activate the small grenade strapped to his waist, to kill them both, but her free hand intercepted his with surprising speed. He let go of the hand locked around his neck, yanked out the knife in her chest, and attempted to slash her throat, but his arm seized up, the blade mere centimetres from her jugular.

She continued to hold him above her. His limbs were rigid, unresponsive, and his chest muscles ceased to perform their vital function. Paralysed, and slowly asphyxiating, all he could do was watch her hideous smile.

Chapter 27

Q'Roth

Zack hurled the long range pulse rifle to the ground. He'd managed to hit the bastard square on eight times but it had no effect; the pulse beam reflected off it, hadn't even slowed it down. So he switched to his favourite weapon, the one he'd used in Rome to face down a stealth jet – his 'catapult'. He thanked God they'd let him bring it on the mission – it had taken all Blake's military clout and rhetoric to get the bureaucrats to allow it onboard. But he'd rather go up against another stealth fighter than this. To make matters worse, his leg was sending tremors of agony up his spine. He'd jumped down the steps in his race to save Pierre, forgetting his leg was in a cast. But he dared not take a pain-tab – he needed crystal vision. He felt adrenaline flooding through him, just as it had in battle during the War. Adrenaline is coloured brown, he'd always told his troops.

He hefted the field cannon onto his right shoulder. His left hand gripped the stabiliser on the main body, his right eye glued to the targetter. His right index finger stroked the trigger.

"Sonofabitch!" he murmured. "Run in a straight line God damn you!" He couldn't lock onto the target, despite the creature's size. The cannon had an auto-zoom for moving targets, with superimposed digital readouts of the distance between the creature and Pierre, and between Pierre and Zack. Using a sub-vocal interface he programmed four projectiles – the first an explosive warhead, the second an armour penetrator, the third another explosive device, the fourth a high yield explosive. The last was in case the first three failed – Pierre was already too close to the creature not to be caught in its blast.

Zack studied it while it was still out of range, tearing down the escarpment after Pierre. He tried to ignore what the creature looked like, because that just might make him turn, bolt the hatch and take off. Its blue-black sheen made it difficult to discern detail, and the setting sun was behind it. Still, its long, thin, rectangular shape and its angular, trapezoidal head made it look almost noble when it stood up. But when it ran, it resembled a giant deranged locust – if a locust could run that fast – body bent double and then stretched to maximum with its fore and hind legs lashing out, clawing into the terrain and projecting it forward in seemingly random darts, always closing on its target.

He counted six insect-like legs, the two middle ones folded into its body when it stood up. Each leg was long, thin, and serrated, rose-like thorns the length of a man's hand travelling down the side of each lower leg. If it reached Pierre, it would shred him in seconds.

It dodged left or right more than twice a second, and was gaining on its prey. Zack was thankful at least that Pierre had stopped zigzagging. Smart kid, he thought, knows it's not working anyway, because the thing is so damn manoeuvrable, and it makes it harder for me to zero it. Zack had been waiting for them to come into the optimal range of the cannon. An icon in his sight-glass switched from yellow to green for Pierre, and from red to yellow for the creature. Zack flexed his finger over the trigger, and breathed out slowly so his arm became rock steady: three hundred metres, the creature some thirty metres behind Pierre, closing fast.

He counted the creature's zigs and zags, trying to guess which way it would go next. On intuition, he fired a shot to the right of Pierre – he doubted he would hit the creature; he was gauging the timing. He estimated the projectile took a full second to reach them. A huge boulder some way behind them exploded, sending rocks the size of footballs into the sky in all directions. Neither of them slowed down. Okay, we're in business.

Zack knew there was only one way to hit it. He hoped it wasn't that tactically smart – he would only get one shot at this. Two hundred and fifty metres; fifteen metres between them. He spoke to his microphone.

"Pierre, when I say '*now*', you hit the deck fast and stay down. Don't be late."

The silence from Pierre indicated to Zack his consent – at least he hoped it did. He could hear Pierre's stuttering intakes of breath, could almost smell the panic. Hold it together just a little longer, Pierre.

He waited five more agonising seconds until the separation reading said five metres. It was right behind Pierre, and began to rise up slightly, the two upper legs extending upwards and outwards, ready to slash.

Zack fired and shouted "NOW!"

He fired again.

He held his breath, finger poised on the trigger for the fourth, final shell.

* * *

Blake watched the mirror in silence for ten minutes, jaw muscles tight throughout. He didn't understand all he saw, but enough to appreciate the danger from these beasts – the locusts as Kat had called them. When they stood tall they were sleek monoliths, a diffuse black that made it difficult to focus on any detail. But he made out what might be eyes, though they looked more like blood-red gills, on either side of their heads, and a gash that was possibly a mouth. At first the mirror had shown him just one or at most two, at a distance, clearly on Eden. And then underground – he didn't know where – he'd seen eggs, tens of thousands of them, laid out in neat rows.

The mirror showed him another place. Blake realised he was seeing a different planet, not empty like Eden, but teeming with life. He glanced at Rashid for verification. Rashid nodded, but the dark look in his eyes told him what was to come. An air-brushed violet sky speckled with silver dust hovered over a mercurial city, pastel hues rippling across tubular buildings, conduits, bridges – he wasn't sure exactly what was what. Spider-like residents ambled about the city, drenched in fluorescent hues, on four nimble, hairy legs. He couldn't make out heads. It was difficult to take it all in with the continual, hallucinogenic cascade of colour.

Many mirrors like the one he was viewing now – some oval, some octagonal in shape, others triangular – hovered, interacting in some way with the spiders. Blake guessed the mirrors served the spiders, or at the least the two had a symbiotic relationship.

Occasionally the shifting sands of colour subsided, to be followed by a spectacular reverse waterfall of fireworks into the sky, glowing lights creating night-time clouds of pulsing garnet and amethyst. Blake was mesmerised. The more vistas appeared, the more it was evident that this was a culture devoted to peace and art. Without having heard a word or explanation of anything, he instinctively appreciated this sublime race. But his stomach remained tense, ready for what was to come.

The scene switched back to the sky. Colossal grey ships sank like monstrous snowflakes down towards the mountains surrounding the rainbow city. The spiders and mirrors gathered and watched. Explosions shook the ground, pulverising several of the city conduits. The ships' doors opened and the beasts swarmed out in their thousands, some airborne in small ships. He decided Kat had been right after all calling them locusts. He saw close up, then from a distance, how they killed everything in their path.

Each time one of them took a spider, it hung on for a few seconds with its gash of a mouth, while the spider's colour drained away, then its lifeless corpse was discarded. Blake's knuckles squeezed white, mainly because the spiders mounted no defence, and were slaughtered. Some of the mirrors were smashed by the beasts, many more shattered of their own accord, perhaps when their masters were killed – he didn't know. The view switched to a faraway sweep of the city, grey and smoking, a black wraith of the beasts strangling it like a cancer.

The last scene was of the ground, and then the planet itself, receding, viewed from space. Abruptly the mirror returned to its fluid, non-descript 'face', as Blake had come to think of it. But he found himself still staring. He closed his eyes and the images remained. He'd just watched genocide, an entire species eradicated. His thoughts turned to Earth, and anger rose inside him at the sheer stupidity, the futility of its internal wars, the squandered time, when there were such abominations out in space.

Rashid held out a cup of tea. Blake hadn't noticed him making it. But as he reached for it, Rashid said, "No, it's for her."

Kat was coming round, eyes scrunched against the light. Without hesitation, before Blake could stop her, she released the seals on her helmet, took it off, and dropped it next to where she lay. She propped herself up, took the tea, and gulped it down in seconds.

"Thanks," she coughed, wiping her mouth, and then turned to Blake.

"Sir," she said, eyes wide. "It's been in my head. The mirror. It used my node, re-activated it, and communicated with me. Not for the first time, either. I think it's been in my dreams, hiding in the back of my consciousness for some time, maybe a month. I guess I blacked out this time because of its proximity. The information rate was too intense. Then it slowed down."

Blake interrupted. "Why don't you slow down yourself? Now you've taken your helmet off, I can see you've had a rough ride."

"Sir, my air was getting low, and…"

"It's okay, Kat – bad air seems like the least of our problems right now. Can you talk to it?"

Her brow furrowed. "Not really, but it shows me things that trigger thoughts, sounds, even occasionally a word association. It spent a long time studying my memories, trying to understand me – us. But it's *very* different."

Rashid spoke as if from a distance. "I envy you. It has been my companion here for nearly a year, and yet we have never been able to communicate – except that it has shown me images. Things that at first made me fear God had deserted us, then that there can be no God, and then, a deep hope that God was still investing in our survival."

Kat put the cup down and moved forward and patted Rashid on his leg. "It has wanted to communicate with you, Rashid. I don't know whether it has emotions like us, but it somehow expressed –" she sought the right word "– concern. I think it likes you. It misses its master, that much I do know, and you're the first being it's related to for a very long time."

Rashid locked his gaze on the mirror for a moment, and then turned his back on them to pour some tea for Blake.

"So," Blake said, "what exactly did it communicate to you? From what I've seen, it comes from another planet that was attacked by these beasts. What else?" He understood enough about nodes from one of his nephews' brief experiences to know that the images must already be fading in her mind. The intensity of nodal communication – basically direct-to-brain communication, by-passing the senses – offered perfect clarity at the time, but then ebbed rapidly, like waves lapping over dry sand. He had to get as much as possible from Kat while it was fresh.

She took a deep breath. "Their planet – there's almost no audible language, so I don't know its name – was culled by the *Q'Roth* – the beasts as you called them, locusts as I did. It happened almost a millennium ago. The Q'Roth are nomadic. They travel to distant worlds outside the Grid." Kat held up her hand to stall a question from Blake, and he decided to let it pass, noting a new confidence, an intensity in her that hadn't been there before.

"They feed on other civilisations. They send advance scouts to select and cultivate candidate worlds – some to harvest, others to breed. Their life cycle is around a thousand years. They feed once a millennium in our terms, then they travel and explore new worlds for five centuries, and at last they finally breed. Shortly afterwards almost all of them die, leaving guardians to watch over the eggs for a further five centuries. When the eggs hatch, they need to feed. But they don't eat flesh. What they need is to extract the life force, the bio-electricity, whatever you want to call it –

the psychic energy out of living things. The more sophisticated, the more nourishing. Intelligent races, artistic ones, violent ones, it doesn't matter – it's the emotional and intellectual complexity they crave. It matures them, very rapidly, apparently. They need beings like... us." Kat stopped and stared downwards.

Blake knew the reality of it all was only now catching up with Kat. That was partly why nodes had been banned three years earlier, and surgically removed from anyone who had one. They allowed direct communication, whether from phones, computers or vids, to the mind. The attraction had been immediate, but very quickly had come the brain damage cases, the psychoses, the addictions, and the associated "detachment" murders, caused by a temporary suppression of emotional connection. A mother who interrupted her son in the middle of a node experience, might find herself being calmly strangled by him, while he was meanwhile enjoying a node-based vid or porn scene, or even exploring h-mails. The more the nodes were used, the more the user became detached from emotions and reality. *Nodal schizophrenia*, he recalled.

He hadn't told the other crew members about it because the node had been rendered dormant. She'd suffered an astro-surfing accident that led to a steel plate being inserted in her brain only a week after the node was implanted. The node had unexpectedly bonded with the plate, and couldn't be removed without killing her. He'd have to keep an eye on her from now on. He remembered he'd been given special suppressive medication for Kat, *just in case*, by a Chorazin agent the day before take-off. The agent had never said what it did exactly. Blake didn't trust Chorazin, and had tossed it into a micro-furnace on Zeus I right before departure.

He cut to the chase. 'Kat, where are they in their cycle?'

She sighed. "I'm afraid they're going to hatch soon, Sir. Then they'll need to feed almost straight away."

"So, where are their ships? We could use the ND to take out a few."

"This is indeed the part that I have not understood," Rashid interjected, passing Blake his cup. "At first I was afraid that humanity would come here, and be fed upon. But then, I reasoned, it would simply take too long. It would be at least fifty years, shuttling people here in large transports of a few hundred at a time, if we could manage it at all, before we have an established community here."

Blake nodded. Parts of the puzzle were missing. He stared at Kat, whose eyes were clamped shut, clearly trying to remember.

"This was the hardest part of the communication – because of course the mirror hasn't travelled to Earth. It followed the Q'Roth in a lone ship when they came here, waiting. It's the last of his kind, I think. Its master severed their bond and ordered it to follow the Q'Roth, not for revenge, but to look for opportunities to help others in the future avoid the same calamity. But it thinks – if that's the right word – that this time the Q'Roth are using a different strategy. Humanity *will* come to Eden, and in very large numbers, large enough for a preliminary feed. Then the Q'Roth will travel to Earth, enhanced and better able to fight, for the main feed."

"But where are these ships?" Blake asked, anger stoking up inside him: he needed a target to strike. "And who on Earth would be dumb enough to come here to…" Then he thought he almost understood. "Kat. You said *cultivate*. You said they sent advanced scouts to cultivate other planets. What did you mean?"

Rashid leant forward. But Kat's face became confused, distressed, no longer able to recall the shared nodal vision. Her lips moved but no sound came out. She hung her head. Blake recognised the rapid post-nodal depression symptoms. He laid a hand on her shoulder. "It's okay, Kat. Relax for now."

Exhausted by the experience, she lay back down, and quickly fell asleep.

The mirror sprang to life again. Blake and Rashid observed ten minutes of images, and diagrams. They appeared alien, but had an odd familiarity to Blake. At one stage he recognised the molecule plutonium and a fission reaction. There were also helical structures that could be alien DNA. Then it showed the ND device, sitting outside. Rashid stood up, agitated. Blake thought about it. It had not shown ships. It could not show Earth, since it had not been there. But it had shown clues, the missing links he hoped would enable Rashid to make the connection, while for him it hovered tantalisingly on the tip of his mental tongue.

"Rashid?"

Rashid tried to pace, but there was no room in this small cabin. He sat down again, his fingers agitated. "It is showing us, albeit in an alien tongue, schematics for the neutralino detonator, and also long range communications and surveillance concepts. It also showed more advanced technologies, nuclear weapons, and I believe I even saw the molecular structure for the nanovirus fractal genome that led to the banning of nanotechnology thirty years ago. It is trying to answer your question about cultivation, based on what it has gleaned from your colleague." His eyes blazed somewhere between excitement and shock at the revelation.

"In short, I believe it is saying that the Q'Roth, now that I know their name, have been seeding ideas into humanity, particularly over the last hundred years, guiding us to end up here. I have always marvelled at the fortuitous discoveries that befell us recently. We find Eden, and then discover a miraculous new propulsion approach to bring it within reach. And yet other technological marvels – especially nuclear weapons, genetic engineering and nanotech, have become closed-off avenues, illegal or unable to attract research funding. In short, we have been channelled down a narrow scientific and technological tunnel that steers us to one place – Eden."

Blake felt like he'd just joined a chess match to find his opponent was one move from check mate. He suddenly remembered the red flare. "Rashid – we have to get back to my ship."

Rashid peered behind the curtain, and shook his head. "We must wait until morning. To go out at night will be too dangerous, and Earth needs us alive, to warn them. They must not come here."

Blake remained overwhelmed by the implications – that aliens had influenced human progress. He wondered if they had caused the last war; helped invent the atom bomb even. And then there was the War itself – as an army Commander he'd harboured the conviction more than once that it would irrevocably destroy infrastructure that would plunge humanity into post-civilised chaos, famine, and disease, with massive loss of life. Each time, the leaders, or some battle or event somewhere had pulled them back from the brink. For the first time he wondered if it had all been carefully moderated. A hundred ideas threatened to overload his brain. He banged his fist hard on the small table, upsetting the two tea cups, splashing hot tea onto the floor.

He stood up. "You're right. We sleep here." He looked down at Kat's unconscious frame. "I'll take first watch, you sleep now. First thing in the morning we're taking your comms system apart, Rashid, and it's coming back to our ship." He half-expected some kind of argument, but Rashid nodded his assent.

"I am joining you. If your comrades have indeed been attacked, you may need an extra pair of hands."

Blake cast him a hard look. He went to the hatch, and then turned around. "All right. But let's get one thing straight. You don't ever point a gun at me again unless you mean to fire it."

Without waiting for an answer, he stormed outside and yanked the hatch closed behind him. He knew his anger at Rashid was misplaced, but without warning, everything he believed in was in danger. He'd gone from elation at finding Eden, to realising it was a malicious trap. He'd always fought for justice, and now he found himself, and humanity, in a much larger universe where the rule of the jungle applied.

He sat on the step and stared at the stars. Since a kid, they had been his constant companion, first his fantasy playground, and then his actual territory since graduating as an astronaut twenty years ago. Yet now he pondered how many of these twinkling lights harboured terrible enemies.

Here he was, his first night on another planet, under different stars, after three months of arduous travel. He scanned the sky, and tried to locate the constellation that shrouded Earth, but he couldn't find it, and was too tired to search for long. Instead of jubilation at being there, finally on Eden, he felt the sky and the weight of Earth's survival pressing down on him.

He recalled his wife saying he had such broad, strong shoulders that he could carry the world on them, and that someday he would. The thought of her drew a smile across his lips. "Well, we made it, Glenda. Not exactly textbook Eden, though." He resolved himself. He'd find a way, first to warn Earth, and then to do battle with these creatures.

The hatch opened and the mirror emerged. It paused briefly in front of him. He bristled, then barked at it, "Go check my men!" As an afterthought, he added, "Please. You're here to help us apparently."

The mirror's face flickered purple then became translucent, so all Blake could see was its outline, and through it the silhouettes of dunes and the stars. It drifted out into the desert night and was gone.

Blake sat alone for four hours, thinking about it all, but as usual, thinking late at night when tired got him nowhere. It would have to wait till morning. Rashid came out, looking like hell. He obviously hadn't slept a wink.

"My shift, Sir."

Blake's earlier anger had long since drained into the desert sand; he'd never been able to be cross with anyone for any length of time. Rising a little creakily, he nodded to Rashid, and went inside. He'd been getting cold in any case. He lay down on the still-warm cot of Rashid, seeing Kat had been made comfortable and remained fast asleep. He looked up to the ceiling, and for the first time noticed the artistry of the stars painted on the ceiling, recognising Orion as it would be seen from

Earth, and other constellations, and wondered if Rashid had done it all from memory.

He tried counting the stars to fall asleep, but it didn't work. He couldn't sleep because he still had no target, nothing to fight. And then it came to him – he'd been so focused on the ships, a typical military target, that he'd forgotten the other obvious target. The eggs – he had to find the eggs, and destroy them. He recalled that Q'Roth guardians watched over them. Fine – he'd find out what they were really made of.

While running through combat scenarios, he finally fell asleep.

* * *

Zack watched Pierre dive just as the creature reared up behind him, its forelegs raised high. Smoke and flames erupted on its chest as the missile struck home. The creature staggered back back but stayed upright, just as the second volley punched it off its feet amidst an explosion of white-hot flame. It disappeared behind the cloudburst of fire. Pierre crawled a few metres away, struggled to his feet and ran again, straight towards the ship. Zack watched, counting. All he could see now was Pierre and a column of curdling smoke behind him. He waited to see if the alien burst through the fire curtain, but nothing happened. Still he held the weapon, counting. He set the charge to detonate automatically at two hundred metres, and when he got to a count of twelve, he fired it ten degrees up into the air, then unshouldered the heavy weapon, letting it slump to the ground.

Although Pierre was out of blast range, the shock wave still knocked him off his feet, and pushed Zack backwards so that he stumbled on his gel-cast leg. As he was trying to stand up again, Pierre arrived, panting, and helped him up. Zack noticed Pierre's face streaked with smoke and sweat, his hair matted, singed at the back.

'Thanks... Zack. I... really... owe you one.'

Zack grimaced from the leg-pain. "More than one. Fetch me another pack of armoured heads, and we'll go see what's left of that motherfucker."

When they arrived at the site where Zack had hit it, they couldn't find the creature anywhere. They searched for half an hour. All they found were a few splotches and one small puddle of a thick blue-black oily liquid. Pierre took a sample. Zack surveyed the area.

"That's one tough SOB."

"If we can make it bleed, then we can kill it."

Zack pointed to the small plastic packet in Pierre's hands. "How'd you know that isn't just monster poop you've got there?"

"Then at least we got its attention."

Zack laughed, and nodded to the ship. "It's getting dark – I reckon it'll come around quickly here. Let's get back and seal up for the night."

Pierre picked up his own rifle.

"What about the Skipper and Kat? Do you think they saw the flare?"

Zack's face darkened. He kicked at a rock with his good foot. "I'm betting they did, but they must have their hands full."

"Should we go look for them in the morning?"

Zack shook his head. "We have to stay with the ship. If we leave it, I have a bad feeling it won't be here when we get back."

* * *

Later that night, far away on the hilltop near where Pierre had first seen the Q'Roth, the mirror stood guard over the Ulysses Lander. It had never known emotions, but just once, briefly, its translucent face showed its master, with a body colouring that signified approval. After all this time, it was finally doing what its master had asked of it. And then it showed a Q'Roth dying – their one fatality during the assault on the mirror's home planet, when a power plant exploded. The scene of the dying Q'Roth replayed a dozen times on the mirror's surface before it became once again translucent and calm. The mirrors' masters had been true pacifists, and had never programmed the emotion of revenge. But the mirror had been inside Kat's mind. It didn't fully understand primitive emotions – like anger – but it was a quick study.

Chapter 28

Tarpit

Micah ground his knuckles against puffy eyelids. He'd been working on the data cube for four hours straight, borrowing the newly-installed mil hardware. Initially he'd focused on the thirty minutes when the ghoster had awoken. There were no video images, just telemetry and voice comms, but it had been like listening to a museum-style radio show. He'd been surprised how much scarier it was *not* seeing any images. Just hearing the tension in Kat's voice, contrasted with Blake's raw control, Zack's bravado and gung-ho swearing, and Pierre's clinical matter-of-factness laced with fear – he felt like he knew them. But the ghoster's screaming – he'd instinctively yanked his earphones out when he had first heard it.

The suppressed transmission had been confusing at the end, but it seemed that shortly before Kat tripped the comms virus, they killed the ghoster and the ND was still intact. Micah had pinpointed the time when Rudi had made the switch from real to synthetic IVS-supplied data feed, about two months into the trip. Very slick, he had to admit.

For the last hour he'd been looking at the end of the data cube's storage. Luckily, after Ulysses had stopped transmitting. IVS had let it run and record anyway, in case it came back on-line. There was noise, just the electromagnetic radiation that's ever-present in space. He'd always mocked the idea of silent space – silent to human ears of course, but on the "star waves," as he liked to call them, it was a cacophony of signals from stellar bodies and pulsars – a cosmic Babel.

He searched for Kat's simulacrum, hoping it had been smart enough – and fast enough – to anticipate the Trojan Warp virus. The Alicians – he presumed they had installed the virus – had focused on human detection and response time. This meant that they could put in a more robust virus that chewed up software and really made it irreparable, but this took time. The simulacrum would only have had a couple of seconds, but it was intelligent and worked in micro-seconds. All Micah needed was a keystone – a password – a translation device to unlock the hidden data.

The door opened, and Louise strode in, her usual sleek black top and skirt, but her hair was down today. He wished it wasn't. Since the previous evening with Antonia – even though she didn't want him – he felt he couldn't handle Louise anymore.

"Ah, you're out now," she said.

He cast her a puzzled look.

"You were under before – that machine totally engrosses you, doesn't it?"

"Immerses. We get immersed in it," he said, a little testy.

"Does it increase your grumpiness, too? Maybe you need some discipline, Micah?" She walked right up and leaned over him. "Maybe I should spank you over your desk?" Her glossed pink lips stretched into a smile.

He ignored the rush of blood to his groin, pushed his chair backwards and got up and walked away from her.

"Look, Louise, I'm sorry, this is really hard work, and it's really urgent. I need to concentrate."

She stalked towards him, but not too close. The smile was gone, replaced by a harshness that made him remember she was Chorazin.

"Don't apologise, Micah. It's a sign of weakness. Do what you decide to do and swallow the consequences. Regret, guilt and sorrow – they're all irrelevant. You do look like you need a break, though – or a diversion."

"I need a coffee, Louise. Really." He forced a smile. "I'm close, I can sense it." He tried to stare her down, like a cat and a mouse, but she was the cat.

"You want her, don't you? Your coffee-mate."

"I don't know what you're talking about. She's – she's already seeing someone. She's not interested in me."

"Someone working on the Project?"

"You could say that. Yes and no, actually." As soon as he'd said it, he knew it had been a mistake – he could see Louise latch onto it, like a bloodhound picking up a scent.

"Interesting," she said. "Do you love her?"

Micah flushed. He wanted to deny it: no reply meant it was true, and even he didn't want to believe it, it made him such a fool aside from anything else. He'd made his mind up last night, but only with his brain he realised – his emotions lagged far behind.

She reached down and with both hands smoothed one of her stockings all the way up her leg. "Your loss. Do you have any idea what you're giving up?"

He sensed he was almost off the hook. "I have an idea, Louise. That is, I have a good idea that I have no idea what I'm giving up, but it just won't work. Sorry."

"Good. You've made a decision." She smoothed her skirt back down. "I'm going to send your girlfriend to you. Try to keep your mind on your work."

As she reached the exit, he called after. "Louise, the scars on your back. Are they what I think they are?"

She stopped at the door, her hand gripping its handle. She didn't turn around.

"They used to queue up for me, you know." Her voice wavered. "All hard. I can still smell the stink of their sweat, anticipation, lust, even their guilt – a few of them, anyway. Each time one of them came inside me, I swore I'd kill a man for it, one day, somehow. I never pulled at the chains; wanted to be in good shape to escape later." She paused to inspect her wrists. "When the camp was raided by our side after I'd spent three months in the cages, they captured and rounded up thirty of them, to take them prisoner, interrogate them. I was being shuffled with a few other girls into the air ambulance. I snatched an assault rifle from a soldier who looked sorry for me." She paused and glanced over her shoulder. "He looked young and naïve – like you, Micah. I shot every one of them where it hurts most. Takes quite a while to die that way. Some of the soldiers tried to stop me at first, but the Colonel – a woman – she knew what had been going on there. She ordered her men back. Afterwards, she told me the only way to avoid criminal proceedings was to join the Chorazin. She was sure they'd have me. We took off, then she dropped a clean-up bomb, vaporised the whole base."

Micah hardly breathed. He stared at her back – part of him wanted to comfort her, but the sane part held him back.

"Did you get even? Have you killed enough men now?"

She turned to face him. Her eyes steeled. "Not even close."

Micah swallowed.

"You see, Micah, I saw men, and a few women, do unspeakable things during the War, and ever since. It's human nature, just needs the right circumstances to bring it to the surface. They should all..." She bit her lip. "Micah, you're only the second man to ever say 'no' to me.

Interesting. Not sure how I feel about that." The door swung closed behind her.

Micah slumped into his chair; feeling way out of his depth. *They should all...* He thought of a dozen ways to end that sentence, none of them good. He shook himself, glad that she was Chorazin and not Alician.

His gaze drifted back to the gleaming Optron. He thought of Antonia, the astronauts, Vince, the ship and the sea creature he'd heard about on the nets, and what he sensed was coming. He switched it to power-up again. He needed something far stronger, but decided an ultresso would have to do.

When he came back with his fifth ultresso of the day, Micah found Antonia sitting, hands atop her knees, waiting for him. She was dressed almost identically to Louise, which made him uncomfortable. He suppressed an image of her, instead of Louise, seducing him in the bathroom in Kane's suite.

"Er, hi. You okay?" he asked. Her porcelain face looked ready to crack.

"Yes. Just... next time please could you pick up the phone and call me – don't send that woman to come and find me."

He wondered what had happened, but judged she didn't want to talk about it. He wasn't sure he wanted to know in any case.

"Sure. You need a coffee?"

"No. Look, I assumed you didn't send a Chorazin agent to escort me here to have coffee." She trawled her hands through her hair. "Sorry. She just makes me uneasy, I don't even know why. She looks at me so strangely." She'd been fidgeting with her hands, and promptly folded them, sitting up straight.

He walked up to her, and almost put his hand on her shoulder, but stopped just in time. "Listen," he said, "I have the telemetry from Ulysses – the real telemetry. I've been over and over it a dozen times. I think there may be messages in there hidden by Kat's simulacrum, but I need a key to unlock them. A password, a clue – anything, really – I don't know exactly what I'm looking for. Did Kat give you any key word or phrase?"

She flared for a moment then stared toward the wall. Micah guessed it was because he had mentioned her lover's name.

"I know it may be private, but it could be important..."

She shot to her feet, glaring at him with a face suddenly flushed red, hands on hips. She shouted. "You think I don't know that?" She began pacing. "She's up there, Micah, maybe dead, maybe alive. How can it *not* be important to me?"

Micah stepped back. "Of course. I'm sorry. I didn't mean…"

"Do you love me?"

"What?" *What the hell had Louise said?*

The anger drained from her face.

She turned and paced again. "I'm sorry, Micah, it's not you. It's that woman. She said some things on the way down here. I knew it was lies – why does she do that? But it's just that if you did – I couldn't cope – I couldn't work with you, but we need to, to help, maybe even save Kat and the others."

Micah's face masked the tornado of thoughts in his mind. He nodded. He was still trying to process what had just happened, like taking a fast bend and finding a truck coming the other way in the middle of the road – swerving, just missing the fatal accident, and then driving back in the sunshine again. As if nothing had happened.

"It's – it's okay, Antonia. She's just fucked up. I really like you – I mean, who wouldn't." He searched for a cliché. "Maybe under different circumstances… but you're with Kat, and I'm…" *stop you idiot – you almost said with Louise.* "Just trying to do my job, trying to help you. You and Kat. And the whole crew. And Earth."

He waited to see her reaction.

"Fucked up, eh?" she laughed, obviously not used to saying that word. "You're right about that. I pity the poor schmuck who she is fucking, or fucking with." And as she laughed some more, Micah joined in, without really knowing why. He decided he maybe survived the truck, and was still alive in the car, driving along in the sunshine.

She approached him. "I'm sorry for doubting you." She reached forward and gave him a kiss on the cheek. She stayed there. "Micah," she said, locking his eyes. "May I ask you a favour?"

Anything. Everything. "Sure."

"Would you hold me for a moment? Just a moment. I really need a hug. Kat used to hug me so often."

Silently, they embraced, and he knew who she was thinking of, and he wished Kat could be here right now, and he could take her place on Eden, because the truck had got him after all.

Three hours and a sandwich later, and after at least a hundred ideas for passwords had gotten them nowhere, he noticed her necklace.

"A gift from Kat, just before she left: platinum, gold and silver. Quite unusual, especially since it looks like titanium."

Micah began typing at the console.

"What are you doing? Does my necklace mean anything?"

"We've been looking for a password, but truth is, I'm not sure how I would use a password in any case. But a digital password – that would give me something to look for – the numbers could signify a carrier wavelength."

"What numbers?" she said.

"Atomic weights of the three metals in your necklace. I need to go inside the datastream again."

"I'd like to remain here, with you."

Micah looked at her. "Normally I go in alone."

She stared at him.

"Okay. Just please don't touch anything, no matter what happens."

As he strapped into the Optron chair, she walked over to him and put her hand on his shoulder. "Good luck Micah. And thanks for doing this. I know you're doing your job, but I feel you're becoming a true friend."

He made his face move into what he hoped resembled a smile, and then lay back and keyed in the command sequence. As he slipped into the datastream vista, he called up a digiwizard to enter the atomic weights and search for a construct that might use the base numbers. Within seconds, it appeared – a single silver strand twining around others in the distance.

He flew towards it. Although he'd programmed it to look a certain way, it seemed to have a life of its own. He followed the filament upwards, where it separated from the others. His mind surfed along it as it twisted and curved out into what seemed to be space. He noticed something up ahead, dissolving from out of the shadowy depths of a star-less void, a space that should have been unencoded, and therefore blank territory.

His heart rate ramped up as he realised this was way beyond the capabilities of Kat or the simulacrum – something, possibly alien, had embedded a transmission into the Ulysses data-streaming processing system. It showed up first as a dark planet eclipsing a blood red sun. It grew larger, and he felt himself falling, then accelerating towards its hard, sheer black terrain. He tried to slow down but couldn't. He'd never programmed gravity, and to his knowledge no one ever had – this shouldn't be happening. He began to panic. He imaged the emergency bail-out signal to stop the Optron session but nothing happened. He flailed his arms and legs, uselessly, as he tumbled. The dark, solid planet tore towards him at terrifying speed, and despite it all being illusory, he did what any normal person would do, and screamed.

Chapter 29

Whispers

Vince piloted the Chorazin hover-jet, Louise by his side, as they sailed over dust towns in what used to be Virginia, on the way to New Washington. Vince had always found it ironic that after the War, the key cities, the ones most irradiated, had never been completely abandoned – rather, new versions were grafted onto the original cities' outskirts. It seemed unthinkable to Americans that the seat of power could exist anywhere else. New York was different – completely decimated, the ground turned to black glass in the worst bombing in the War outside of Central Asia and Western Europe.

Vince was a New Yorker.

Seeing the ghost towns triggered reflections about the War. An airbase outside New York – his brother had been stationed there – had been the US home for the infamous World Alliance's Deathwatch drones – autonomous stealth aircraft able to reach tactical targets anywhere in the world and deliver a bomb, atomic if necessary. Way better than suicide pilots, they'd been used to quell numerous uprisings, and to seek and destroy terrorist cells. Prior to the War, the drones had facilitated an unprecedented decade of peace; not a single War nor government overthrown. The world united in its fight against impending environmental collapse, building underground cities following the 2038 heat excursion, and accelerating the World Alliance Space Program, trying to crack warp drive theory to find a second home. The Golden Age.

He veered the aircraft around a slim tornado stretching from the gloomy carpet of cumulus down to the tan desert floor. This area was prone to 'whispers', sudden vortices spearing to the ground below, sucking sand and dust back up into the billowing clouds. There were no people around to be harmed – it was fifty degrees Celsius down in the desert, but they made a pilot's job challenging; one reason he guessed Louise was quiet, letting him concentrate. He should have had it on auto, since the onboard computer could anticipate and react quicker, but they both knew what happened if you relied too much on automation.

Like the Deathwatch drones. He recalled how the fledgling World Alliance became complacent, ignoring warnings. They mistook overt peace and opulence for the real thing. The terrorist cells and groups moved deeper into the undergrowth, biding their time. Anti-government factions waited until they had the key tactical advantage: they learned how to hack through the Deathwatch's firewalls, convincing their AI units that the enemy had annihilated their sovereign races, so the drones started laying waste to their home countries in retribution. In the US, the first twelve nukes detonated were American origin. It took three days to even work out who the enemy was.

More whispers lay ahead, a lattice of lethal natural power.

"We could go above cloud," Louise offered.

Vince retracted the wings by half, and accelerated, slaloming a pathway through whipcords of extreme turbulence. She didn't complain. They broke through, the desert succumbing to scrub land. Cracks in the sky appeared, brutal sunlight lancing down on Dalgleish, one of a string of new frontier towns for displaced Irish, most of whom had emigrated to the US after Ireland had become too rad-saturated for any clean-up to have an effect. Vince respected these Fringers – they'd turned down opportunities to live in the new cities or underground, choosing instead the toughest areas, trying to recreate the emerald isle they'd lost. Doomed to failure in his view, but they were proud folk; their sacrifice had ended the War. He'd seen it the final weeks; it was where he'd learned his greatest lesson about leadership.

The Deathwatch drones were eliminated in the first month of the War, and counter-warfare developed based on focused EMP satellite beams. After almost three years of 'traditional' non-nuclear warfare, save a few sporadic volleys which penetrated satellite-based detection grids, a new delivery system emerged. The 'fly-drones' were so-called because they flew like insects, in sporadic fractal patterns, continually changing direction. New stealth tech gave them a basic immunity to the satellite EMP beams. They took longer to arrive but were much harder to shoot down. Their guidance systems were genetically engineered, and a typical drone's propulsion chassis could push fifteen gee's as it ricocheted towards its goal.

Their target had been the fledgling peace talks in Orleans; there was so much distrust on either side that face-to-face talks had become the only option. The French militia, in Operation Hailstorm, launched three hundred suicide pilots in stealth jets to detonate as close to the drones as possible. Still half of them got through, but the delegates escaped to their next rendezvous in Galway, Ireland. As peace was finally being hammered out, the drones attacked, coming in from all sides. The only way to stop the drones was to detonate nuclear warheads in advance – a nuclear firebreak – taking out the drones before they homed in; the 'mushroom curtain' as it was later dubbed. The final wave of drones required so many counter-nukes that a powerful EMP harmonic wave was created, shutting down all drones and aircraft alike over a five thousand mile radius, switching off war machines from Western Asia to the Eastern American seaboard. Once War had been stopped, few had the stomach to start it up again; all sides were losing. Peace, which had been hanging by its fingernails over a cliff, gained a foothold.

The Irish premier had given the order for the nuclear curtain, and seen it through, enveloping three separate waves of drones. Forty-five per cent of Ireland was engulfed in flame that raged for weeks. The day after peace accords were signed, three weeks later, she put a bullet through her head, her home town and family having been nuked by her signature. Vince had been impressed. He'd thought political accountability to be a lost art.

The ground below transitioned from fringe-towns to the city's sprawling edge. They overflew one of the Goliath-like Fabricators, a massive mobile factory constructed before the War, capable of building small towns in less than a year; the pinnacle of the Recycling Age. He banked the aircraft to circle it, taking a better look. In the past decade since the War they'd been a Godsend; luckily only one of the thirty originals had been destroyed – no government had the resources to build new ones. He glanced at Louise, but she was absorbed, watching the towering 'dung beetle' as kids called them, as it crawled glacially over virgin terrain and deposited squat homes, roads, sewers and other infrastructure in its wake. Vince felt a rare spark of optimism. He levelled out and headed towards the nest of skyscrapers on the shimmering horizon.

He reflected on humanity's moral balance sheet during times of war – ineptitude, betrayal, cowardice on the one hand, and self-sacrifice, bravery, and leadership on the other. He knew that at the heart of the Chorazin was a ruthless professionalism, borne of a mission to ensure that the scales never again tipped far enough backwards to allow humanity to destroy itself. Nobody liked the Chorazin, but most were privately glad it was there. That made perfect sense to Vince. He couldn't see how it could be any other way – people needed protecting from others – and from themselves.

A holo appeared in the middle of the cockpit asking for a security code. Louise tapped in a response, and it dissolved. Several towers glinted in the distance.

Vince chose a flight corridor over the craters where the Pentagon and the White House had once sat. Most avoided this route, but Vince swore never to forget why his mission mattered. He swooped over the renewed suburb of Maryland, the only surviving original district. No one could stay there for more than a month at a time, due to the radiation, despite advances in medical counter-measures and massive shielding around the worst areas. So people worked a month on, two weeks off, out in the country, such as it was, or by the bleached sea. The rich lived most of the year in Africa, relatively untouched by nuclear weapons, and the super-rich and super-powerful lazed in the famed Oasis Hotels in the Antarctic.

The looming towers brought his mind back to the present mission, and to Louise. He'd never known her so quiet.

"How's it going with Micah?"

He noticed her almost shift position, restrain it, then shift anyway. *The complex games we play.*

"He's getting there. Says he can extract more information from the data cube. I'm not sure how, and neither is he, but he's proven resourceful."

Vince banked the aircraft towards the localiser and ceded control to the onboard computer.

"Are you two… getting on?" The dashboard flowed green, signalling it was now on auto-pilot and had captured the approach glide path.

She folded her hands in her lap. "You mean like we used to?"

Vince heard a tinge of bitterness. She'd never forgiven him.   "It's been a long time, Louise. But yes, like that."

"You usually don't take an interest in my methods, just my results."

He checked the docking doors were opening, and then turned to her.

"The stakes are high this time. Micah seems to be a key. I don't–"

"Want him damaged."

"Exactly."

"You want me to stop fucking him?"

"I want you to stop fucking *with* him."

"Already done on both counts."

The hangar doors clanked shut behind them and the craft landed. The engines powered down.

She folded her arms. "Anything else?"

He studied her, remembering the good times, before he'd seen the chasm inside her, a sloping, bottomless pit where nothing other than increasingly violent sex could ever find a foothold.

"Are you okay, Louise?"

She threw her head back and laughed. "Like you give a shit?"

He did, unfortunately, and raised his voice. "I'll be more precise. Are you okay with the Mission?"

Her face tightened. "You mean fighting the bad guys, and all that?" She shrugged. "Gets me out of bed."

She made to release her seat buckle, but Vince placed his hand over hers. "Answer the question, Louise. This is me you're talking to."

She pivoted toward him, brought her face close enough to smell her scent. "Do you think we're making any difference, Vince? Does the bad ever stop? We kill people we define as bad, but for who? Can you name me one of our chiefs you'd trust your life with? A President who isn't corrupt or slave to shady business interests?" She removed his hand, snapped open the buckle, flinging the belt aside so that it rattled against the door.

He tried again. "You know that if we stop for just one day the Alicians –"

"The Alicians, what? At least they have an agenda, they're unified."

Vince didn't know what perturbed him most – what she'd just said, or that she'd said it so openly. He gripped her wrist hard. "If you were anyone else I'd take you down for profiling, right now."

She smiled, easing back in her chair. "You're still sexy when you're angry, you know."

His shoulders tensed; he wanted to slap her face to make her snap out of it. "This is serious, Louise."

She gave him a look he hadn't seen in a long time. "You do care, don't you? I thought you'd buried it – us – years ago."

Vince cursed and let go of her wrist.

"Vince, listen to me, just once. Just listen. Is humanity really worth saving? I mean think about it. If there were an alien race out there, what would they think of us? We kill and wage war on each other, love and torture each other in equal measure. If there was some kind of galactic society, what would they do if they found us?" She touched his hand. "Do you ever just wonder if we're too fucked up to merit survival as a species?"

Vince heard her, but he wasn't listening. He was there to do his job, and he did it well. Until now, so did she. He retracted his hand.

She sighed. She kicked open the door and leapt out.

He watched her go inside, and wondered whether, if he'd have kept their relationship going, she'd have stayed on the rails longer. Truth was she was scarred too badly to ever heal. He'd read her profile years ago – she'd been a 'giver' before the War, a teacher for Christ's sake out in the Congo. In the early days he'd seen some of that re-surface, but now all he saw was a woman with the goodness ground out of her. Working for the Chorazin allowed her to vent her anger, but it wasn't ever going to be enough. He'd have to watch her closely.

As he jumped down from the flyer he recalled one of the Chorazin guidelines about not having relationships with another agent, for the simple reason you might have to kill said agent one day. He stopped in his tracks, remembering the day his father made him – at age thirteen – shoot his own horse after it broke its leg during a cross-country tournament. "Why does it have to be me?" he'd pleaded. "You love him," his father had replied, "so you have to be the one to put him out of his pain." Vince could still see those great wild eyes as he pressed the large bore gun to his horse's temple, stroking his sweaty mane with his other hand, pulling the trigger. The recoil broke his wrist, but something shattered deeper inside him. He'd killed a lot of people in his time, but he wasn't sure he could kill Louise.

"Are you coming or not?" she shouted, holding a door open.

He followed her inside. Time to talk with Senator Josefsson and see what he was really up to.

Chapter 30

Final Mission

"He's awake."

Gabriel heard the words as if through a thick block of ice. He felt as if his outer layer of skin was frozen, as if he was back inside the glacier. He tried to move, but although he could sense his body, it wouldn't respond to his commands. He managed to blink – nothing else worked. He couldn't move his head. All he could see was the ceiling above him – luminous white and non-descript. The sharp tang of disinfectant invaded his nostrils. He heard two voices in the room, one male, and one female. They were close, and from the lack of echoes he knew the room was small, probably an operating theatre: the table he was on was metallic and hard, with several creases and a footrest, so it could tilt in different planes.

The ceiling dazzled him. He felt no pain, but he was light-headed and nauseous. So, he surmised, they had probably not only drugged him so he couldn't move, but maybe they had already performed some sort of surgery.

A face loomed: Sister Esma. From his vantage point, the shadows accentuated her harsh features – the long hooked nose, high cheekbones, and thick but not pretty lips. Eyes like black holes, not caring what they consume.

"Hello, Gabriel O'Donnell. That is your real name, isn't it? So glad you could join us."

He noticed a slight yellowing of her incisors, and there was the smell of something rancid on her breath, like rotting onions. He began inwardly counting his own breaths, to distance himself from her. She was no doubt there to torture him.

"We have been watching you for some time. You seemed too good to be true: top of your class, ruthless with no trace of malice; obedient, fervently religious. A flawless performance."

She moved out of view. He heard metallic stilettos strut around the room. He'd lost his count. The drugs made it difficult. He started again.

"But then two months ago, your Master, Cheveyo, disappeared."

Gabriel ceased counting. She'd stopped moving and talking. Why did she pause? What was the other person in the room doing? Whoever it was, their breathing was slow, concentrated, yet deadened, so he or she was not facing him. The other person was studying something, but what? Was she looking at it too? Then he realised – they probably had him in a psy-net, watching changes in breathing rate, electro-dermal response – the full gamut of advanced lie detection parameters. He began counting his breaths again, trying to keep them smooth, to subdue the reactions. But whatever drug they had given him was making him emotionally labile. He could feel himself over-reacting, on the verge of panic, which he hadn't experienced for a decade, though he'd seen enough of it in his victims' pleading faces.

"We have since determined Cheveyo is one of the last Sentinels. We exterminated most of them over the centuries. You were his disciple, his protégé. He told you about the ships, didn't he?" She hovered close to his face, leering.

"No – he did more than that, didn't he? He showed you a ship! You have been inside one!" She moved away again and laughed. "Such irony! And such control, Gabriel, you hid all this so well!"

Gabriel's heart rate increased. He wanted to distance himself from the emotions, but it didn't work. He fought to concentrate on a deep meditation exercise that would transport him into the recesses of his mind.

"He's using the distance technique." A man's voice.

She appeared above him again, and showed him a scalpel. It disappeared from view and then Gabriel felt searing, blinding pain in his left hand. His breath sputtered. He could not flinch, cry out, or even move his lips, but the pain skewered up through his arm into his head, behind his eyes. She held up his bloodied little finger, severed from his left hand, and waved it in front of his eyes.

"No, Gabriel, that won't do at all." A drop of blood from his finger dripped into his left eye, so that half his vision turned scarlet, hot pain drenching his eyeball.

"Next time you try that, I'll cut off something a little more personal."

His mind reeled with the pain and the frustration, anger and fear; unaccustomed emotions. For the first time in many, many years, he wanted to run, or curl up and hide. He tried to focus on the small filaments of anger lurking in his fear. If he couldn't find his usual dispassionate equanimity, anger was preferable to despair.

"Now, Gabriel, we all know how brave you are. And this must be very distressing for you because we've injected you with negative emotion-enhancers, so I know you're afraid right now. But, you see, I need you alive." She rested her head on her elbow placed on his chest. "Personally, I'd enjoy killing you slowly, here and now. But business comes first. There is one last task we need you to fulfil."

She disappeared from his vision again. Gabriel managed to breathe more slowly. He had to concentrate on her voice, because otherwise the pain in his hand was too much. He had to play this out: the emotional rollercoaster and the blinding pain would pass, one way or another.

"Now, Gabriel, I know what you're thinking. That you will not do one last mission for us. That you would die first, sabotage the mission, kill me, etcetera. But, you know, you will carry out my command, even though it will kill you and many others."

He heard the rolling of small wheels, and then a vid screen appeared above him. It was playing a news pod. He saw a ship, like he'd seen years ago, but in water, the pictures taken from above.

"You see, you'll do it, because if you don't, we'll kill her." The vid changed to a scene with a small crowd gathering around an open hatchway. A young female came into the frame, next to a large-girth man who talked and gesticulated with uncommon exuberance. The scene froze and zoomed in on the girl's face. Gabriel's breath halted, as if he was seeing a ghost – because it couldn't be her. She was dead. She'd been in Dublin when three nukes detonated above the emerald city, flattening it before sucking out the oxygen into a huge firestorm. No one had survived in a twenty mile radius.

"It was filmed yesterday. You know her, of course, though you probably haven't seen her for years. Possibly believed she was dead. Please breathe, Gabriel." She scratched the stump where his little finger should have been, causing him to intake a sharp, jagged breath.

"That's better. Now, where was I? Ah yes, we were monitoring information from this site, and came across her genetic analysis, taken to confirm that both of them were human – since she and the Professor stepped out of something more sublime than human artistry could ever hope to construct – and you'll never guess what, Gabriel. That's right; she's your little sister. Jennifer, isn't it?"

Gabriel could only stare at the picture. He'd been sure she was dead, but it was definitely her. Not-quite-blonde, mousy dishevelled hair, her slight ski-jump nose which she used to say saved her having to give the world the finger all the time, and the bottle green eyes that rarely looked forward, even now, because she never trusted anyone, except him and their father. He couldn't help but notice she looked more cynical than when he'd last seen her thirteen years ago. And, as if to confirm it all, the necklace was still there, the one he'd bought for her fifteenth birthday. He could see the two gold links he'd inserted in the otherwise silver chain after he'd broken it during one of their last, terrible rows at the beginning of the War. He didn't know how she'd survived – she must have got warning and escaped before the missiles detonated. And afterwards, straight after Dublin and the wiping out of his entire family – or so he had thought – he had gone into deep cover. If she had tried to find him, if she'd looked, she would have found no trace of him either.

He forgot the pain in his left hand. A tear built up, and even though he knew it was partly drug-induced, he didn't care. She was the only person who had ever elicited tears from him. For a split second a tsunami of remorse threatened to rise up and engulf him – a crucifixion of angst for the lost time they would never recover, for the life he had chosen, believing her dead and so having nothing to live for. A chasm of regret opened up in front of him, beckoning. But he re-directed his thoughts – she was alive, that was all that mattered.

He knew Sister Esma had him. He would, as she had said, do whatever she asked, to keep his sister alive, though he wouldn't see her again.

"Touching. Reunions can be so tearful. But we haven't much time. Our schedule has been moved forwards by unexpected events, mainly caused by the Eden Mission. It seems the Ulysses made it to Eden after all. We cannot let them send a message back to Earth, and since we can no longer stop them sending a message, we have to make sure no one will be there at the receiving end." She shoved the video monitor aside and leaned over him again. "Which is why we need you to blow up their headquarters." She swept out of view again.

Gabriel's mind raced – could he do it – could he make that trade? But he already knew he would. Of course they could kill his sister anyway, but if he was out for even a few hours, he could try to safeguard her.

She returned with a short needle and thrust it into his jaw; tiny stabs of pins and needles ensued, then fire, and then numbness. His jaw loosened.

"Some good news and some bad news, Gabriel. The good news is we inserted something into your skull. A chemical device with a twenty-four hour deteriorating casing around it. There is no way to remove it or stop it from releasing acid directly into your brain – such a death will be quite ugly, I can assure you, so it is best all round if you are in the building when you destroy it. The bad news is, I'm afraid, that we inserted it twenty-one hours ago."

She leant over him again. "I've released your mouth so you can say yes or no. And if you spit at me I will claw out your left eye with my bare fingers. So, what is it going to be Gabriel? The Eden Mission or your sister?"

Gabriel swallowed a few times, trying to lubricate his throat. There was something he wanted to know, a suspicion he harboured. "What about Micah?"

Sister Esma eyed him, her voice level. "What about him?"

Her look and tone confirmed it. He'd been tracking Micah's progress via a bug in his Optron lab, wondering how Micah had been able to fathom so much of the Alician strategy in only a matter of days. "We know about the intelligence levels, Esma, how humanity is only Level Three; why we're fit for culling by your masters, the Q'Roth."

Her face was stone.

"He's Level Four, isn't he? Must have slipped through your net. You've been killing off nascent next-evolutionists for the past two centuries, whenever you detect them – if you can't recruit them. If a Ranger came now, he'd stop you and the Q'Roth, stop the invasion, because humanity is on the verge of elevation. We'd be protected –"

Her eyes leapt across the room to her colleague, who Gabriel heard stand up – of course, the man probably hadn't known any of this. Sister Esma's right hand whipped out. A flash of silver left her palm, and Gabriel heard the sound of flesh puncturing, followed by a jugular squirt of blood, a groan and gurgling, and a body slumping to the floor. She turned her face back to him. "Now look what you've made me do. He was really quite useful."

"Micah doesn't know, does he?"

She leaned forward. "Micah is in a coma, and I'm going to make sure he never comes out of it." She leant back. "Now, there's no more time for this, particularly for you. And if you contact the Chorazin, I'll visit your sister myself, is that clear?"

Gabriel let it go.

"It's over, Gabriel. The ships will all be found shortly, and it will begin. You and your Sentinels have lost our little silent war. Your generation, so to speak, had its chance, but you squandered it. The Alicians will breed a new era of humanity, on a new planet. Earth's days are numbered, and mankind will be slaughtered, except for the Alicians. But if you do this for me, we will take Jennifer with us. That is a promise, Gabriel. So, what is it going to be?"

Gabriel closed his eyes. *Forgive me, Jenny.*

"Yes."

She injected something into his neck. "I must leave now. We won't be seeing each other again. The package you'll be needing is in the adjacent room. We're fifteen kilometres from the Eden Mission complex. This room is wired for an explosion in ten minutes." She held up his dead finger, in a small transparent plastic bag, for him to see. "A memento." The clacking of her stilettos diminished as she passed through successive sets of double doors.

Gabriel thought about his sister, and how to protect her. There was only person he could trust. His muscles tingled, slowly re-awakening, returning to his control. Within five minutes he rolled off the table and dropped onto all fours. He bandaged his left hand using sim-skin from a med-kit they had left behind, located the package, and staggered out of the room. Two minutes later he heard the explosion behind him. It was a good decoy for him, as it would distract Chorazin away from the Eden Mission itself. He had little time, but there was one thing he needed to do first. He headed to the nearest Net outlet.

* * *

Professor Dimitri Kostakis, with his uniquely persuasive personality, convinced IVS to allow him and his assistant, Jennifer, to be part of the study team for the ship, mainly on the grounds that they already had several days head-start on understanding its controls.

Jennifer adopted a low profile. Dimitri had explained how, when they had been attacked by the creature – which he now described as some kind of prehistoric hammerhead shark – they had dropped to the foot of the ship. He had then used the limited power and manoeuvrability left to traverse one of the sides, where they had found a large flooded open hatchway that led to a chamber where there was air. After they had entered, the hatchway had closed and would not open again, so they had left the capsule and entered the ship. He had no explanation as to why they had no decompression sickness symptoms.

Jennifer had played along with the story, nodding appropriately, adding small details that made the story seem true, whilst leaving the broad brush strokes to Kostakis, so the focus remained on him, and she seemed merely the dumb, not quite pretty assistant.

The truth was they had no idea what had happened: she had been about to jettison the escape hatch when a sharp, rising white noise had made her black out. They'd awoken inside the sphere in a chamber filled with air. As for the hammerhead shark, she knew it was no such thing, and probably as much a relic of Earth as this ship. It had to have been the one to drag them into the ship's hold, for no reason she could even guess at. But she didn't want to be interrogated, mind-probed, or profiled – and her lover's story, which was, in true Dimitri form, just about what everyone wanted to hear, was preventing that, for now, at least.

Dimitri's enthusiasm and brilliance soon had the IVS scientists trusting him as part of the technical team, if not its scientific guru. What they had found out so far was that it was indeed a space-faring vessel with massive storage and accommodation space. The controls consisted of some kind of three-dimensional holographic projection of space, with a means to enter co-ordinates plus a time reference. This seemed obvious to her, since stars and planets in the galaxy are in continual, if slow, relative motion. They had not yet figured out how to use this temporally-stamped destination entry system, and it was here that Dimitri's rare grasp of what Einstein's relativity theory really meant, in practical terms, stood him in good stead with the rest of the scientists. There were also what she guessed were start and stop controls. It was ridiculously easy, aside from figuring out the digital sequence and numerical language, and the temporal referencing system.

But she couldn't believe people who could build such a ship would have made it so simple. Or were all the science fiction books and vids written by tech-junkies, and was this ship exactly how starships would one day be built? Space-flight for dummies? Her instincts rejected it. Something was very wrong. *We're the dummies.*

"Eureka! I've got it, I've found it!" Dimitri exclaimed, one of the few who could get away with using Archimedes' catch-phrase. Her spirits lifted – she still loved it when his sheer genius broke through. She crossed over to him, as did several others, to the console where he and several IVS scientists and technicians had been working for hours. But before she arrived he was surrounded by people, and was too short to see over their shoulders. She didn't have to wait too long, however.

"Jennifer! Jennifer! Where is my wonderful assistant – you must see this!" The small crowd parted to let her through – they all knew her by now, guessing she was his muse. She smiled coyly, buoyed by his loyalty to her. A technician dutifully gave up his seat, and she sat down as Dimitri explained and expounded, expanding his entourage. She watched more than listened, his wild arms flying about in Mediterranean style, his eyes dancing like the child he was, a child of this universe, discovering its treasures while others went about their mundane existences.

He had worked out the digital sequence, not a simple binary code, but a cube-based numeric, a natural logarithm to the power of three rather than two. He said he'd noticed some figures on the console that were, he believed, also cube roots. She saw it now, too, but surveyed the faces around her as she always did, as his protector, to gauge their reaction. The technicians were impressed – those few who followed it only mildly less than those that did not understand, but all were nevertheless carried along by his wild and chaotic explanation. One of them, the IVS team leader, spoke up.

"We'd have spotted it sooner or later, but it might have taken days or even weeks. Well done, Professor." She saw in his eyes no jealousy – that was Dimitri's unique survival trait, to be smarter than everyone else in the room *and* have them thank him for it without envy.

Without warning he pulled her towards him and gave her a bear hug. She succumbed, wishing they were alone, that he would really love her as much as his work, his discoveries. But she understood the checks and balances of their relationship. When he released her she gave him a private wink of pleasures to come – she always rewarded his genius, and his loyalty to her. Besides, one of the female technicians – Italian by the look of her – was young and pretty enough to catch his eye. Jennifer had seen her occasionally staring at him with saucer-shaped eyes when she thought no one was looking, and wasn't going to leave anything to chance.

Four hours later they got the holo-projection to function. She watched closely. Although Dimitri and the other IVS engineers were working it out, it still seemed rather too easy for her, as if the ship itself was trying to help them learn. She wanted to discuss this with him privately, but there was no 'private' while the whole team, including him, pored over the console, making small discoveries every thirty minutes. By ten pm they had achieved something truly remarkable – they had accessed the ship's navigational star-charts and had plotted, in three dimensions, a course between Earth and Eden. Mercifully, the ship had added the required temporal parameters automatically. Champagne corks had popped at that point, and they were all but worshipping her Professor.

She was tired, and during the hubbub, she spoke into his ear that she would be waiting for him in their cabin – one of several hastily installed affairs, an all-terrain tent, inside the ship itself to save time going to and from the surrounding vessels. "Don't be long," she said, and headed off. She left the ship's top control tower floor and descended to find their temporary lodging. They were on a different floor from the others, as they were the only "couple" onboard, so there would be no disturbance. She stripped off and walked naked to the portable bathroom cubicle and stood under the small rain-shower until it ran cold. She cleaned her teeth, chewing the brush as she always did, rather than brushing normally.

She came back to the tent and opened a small personal backpack she'd retrieved from their original IVS ship the day before. She pulled out a burgundy silk negligee and matching panties and put them on. She knew her legs were too short to be particularly attractive, but rather than cover them up, the lingerie she wore for such occasions simply re-directed the eye further up her body, to her hopefully more enticing assets. She lay belly-down on the futon, and adjusted the negligee to give Dimitri an appealing view when he arrived. She planned to stay awake until he arrived, but she was exhausted, and it was so quiet…

A school of hammerhead sharks swam far below her. As she dove closer to them, she noticed they had insect-like arms. They were playing with something which was thrashing around, caught between them. Blood swirled in the water. She heard someone call out her name, his voice gurgling. Except this person shouted "Jenny," and she never let anyone call her that: it had been reserved for someone very precious. The sound kept repeating, and she began weeping; her dead brother Gabriel was being torn apart by the hammerheads. She tried to swim downwards, but one of the creatures held her back. She thrashed to get free, and then the creature shouted her name, "Jennifer!"

She woke with a start, tangled in the folds of her nightdress and in the confused arms of her lover.

"My love – are you alright? A nightmare, just a nightmare."

She looked at him, her face streaked with tears, her voice shaky. "Hold me," she murmured.

She never dreamt. Ever. She curled up inside Dimitri's strong, warm arms, trembling, eyes closed, reaching back towards the dream that had receded into the depths. She called out again and again in her mind to her long lost brother, all the while clutching the locket on the necklace that she never took off.

Chapter 31

Hohash

The mirror travelled in long undulating arcs, weaving between the dune tops, as Eden's mid-morning tangerine sun reached its summit. Blake wound the skimmer alongside, twenty metres to its left, never letting it out of his sight. He hadn't decided if this alien artefact was good or evil; only that it held valuable information on what awaited mankind in the galaxy.

Rashid sat behind him, Kat – unconscious – strapped in at the rear, all of them helmeted to allow communications as the wind whipped by. Kat had blacked out shortly before leaving, he presumed due to the mirror again. But he couldn't delay their departure, especially after the flare the previous evening. The mirror matched Blake's every turn or change in velocity. The journey was becoming hypnotic, and he hadn't had much sleep. He needed a distraction, or else he might just slam straight into a dune.

"Rashid, mind if I ask you some questions?"

"Not at all, I still have eleven months of conversing to catch up on."

"Right. First, how come those creatures – the ones you say you've seen – let you live? And keep your antenna?"

"A good question. I have only seen one of them a handful of times – or perhaps I saw a different one each time. In any case, I was far away and, well…"

"Well what?"

"Well, an old Irish friend of mine once said, if you go looking for trouble, you'll find it. So I applied the reverse."

"You mean you saw where it was and never went back there."

"Exactly."

The wind continued to strafe past them, a distant roar in Blake's helmet.

Rashid spoke up. "Commander, did you ever do something, even by accident, and then worry it might have triggered a catastrophe?"

Blake came out of a long bank a little early. He wondered if Rashid was trying to throw him off the scent. "No. Others might disagree. You?"

"Well, not yet. But, you see, you asked me a question yesterday I have not yet answered."

Blake saw a glint of reflected copper – the Lander – a few minutes away. "The desert wasn't here before. You mean you think you caused it?"

Rashid cleared his throat. "No, no. It's just that when the desert arrived, one of the creatures came to investigate. That was when I rigged the neutralino detonator. If it goes off, it will increase the desertification rate a hundred-fold. This whole continent will become a desert within weeks." He added, in a quieter voice. "I keep a remote trigger with me at all times."

"What do you think caused the desert?"

"I do not know." His voice was subdued.

"Your ship, the Phoenix, is the epicentre, isn't it Rashid?"

Rashid's voice rose in register. "Believe me, Commander, I have carried out every scientific analysis I could, and have no explanation."

But still, your ship is ground zero for the desert. "How fast is it spreading?"

Rashid's voice softened again. "In a year, this entire continent will be desert."

Inside his helmet, Blake bit his lip. The bad news was stacking up: barren soil, hostile aliens, desertification...

The skimmer skipped over the threshold of the desert, small grey-green bushes appearing around them like splashes of spring rain. Blake examined the onboard navigation chart from yesterday – the desert had moved closer to the ship, around thirty metres. He switched back to the more immediate threat – the creatures.

"Rashid, how would they know that you'd rigged the ND to explode, or even know what it is or what it would do to the desert – and why would they care?"

"The first is a most interesting tactical question, is it not? How they would know? But that is almost certainly a mere matter of technology, a trick once understood, soon taken for granted. The second question you raise is the one I believe to be of strategic importance – why would they care?"

They drew closer to the Ulysses. Blake recognised the signs of an explosion on the hillside – a small impact crater, a medium-sized area denuded of bushes, leaving only scorched trees. He gunned the skimmer's engine. A green light flickered on the skimmer console. *About time*, Blake said to himself.

"Zack, do you read me?" But even as he spoke he saw the tell-tale flash of a ground-to-air missile being launched – it raced toward him then veered to the right. *The mirror!*

"Zack – it's friendly, dammit!" He pulled hard on the skimmer to shear away from the missile that had locked onto the mirror's image, since it had no heat signature. In the last fraction of a second the mirror dove low enough to scrape the desert floor, sending a stream of sand up into the sky. The missile missed it by centimetres and slammed into a dune behind it. A mushroom of sand skewed upwards, momentarily blocking out the sun. There was no explosion: Blake guessed Zack had fired an armour penetrator, to avoid damaging the skimmer. He racked through the gears to slow down, Rashid sliding into his back as they decelerated hard. The mirror sped off and vanished into the hills.

"Blake – Skipper, can you hear me!" Zack hobbled towards them, using the long range pulse rifle as a makeshift crutch.

Blake drove the vehicle towards Zack, skittering to a stall, and then unsealed his helmet visor as the vehicle stabilised and powered down. "Some welcome, old friend. What was that for?"

Zack reddened. "Well, you weren't answering the radio, and from here it looked like you were being chased by that thing."

Pierre approached, and Blake got the impression he hadn't shared Zack's opinion.

"Who the hell is this?" Zack looked Rashid up and down, noting the helmet Rashid had just taken off. "Jeez – don't tell me IVS got here first!"

"Introductions later – first, help him with Kat."

But Zack was already there, catching her limp frame, trying to carry her and balance on his gel-cast leg at the same time. Pierre took her from him and rushed towards the Lander. Blake took off his helmet. It was good to be back to his ship. He eased off his ride, and faced Zack. "Tell me about the flare."

* * *

263

Kat's head still swam from the mirror communication; she felt like her brain was full of drunken bees.

"Kat?" Blake said, close to her face, locking her eyes onto his own.

She realised she should respond. She tried at first to signal using the colours, and then remembered how to talk. "Yes, Captain. I'm a little out of it. I've been... somewhere else."

"What the hell's been going on? Is she okay?" Zack asked.

"Will be," Blake replied. "Long story." He nodded his head toward Rashid. "Very long."

She saw Zack squint at her first, then look to Rashid. Zack was gripping the rifle firmly – and then she saw that Blake detected Zack's distrust of Rashid. She was paying more attention to body and eye movements than speech. Her perception had been altered; not surprising, she thought, after where she'd just been.

"It's okay, Zack." Blake said.

Kat listened to the introductions, the words flowing around her like a choppy sea. She heard the contours of each speaker, the rise and fall of the tone, the timbre, and read the emotions underneath all of it. The fear, the aggression, the concern, underlying all of their speech was like ribbons of colour. But they were individually tempered by more subtle hues: honesty and scientific objectivity in both Rashid and Pierre, the tight control-maintenance of Blake, Zack's tough-image exterior that belied his compassionate nature. She focused on Zack's speech. There was something else there, something that didn't belong. She felt like she was watching a foreign vid with alien subtitles. However, the talk of the creature and its attack on Pierre made her snap back into focus on the words, the content.

She sat up sharply. "Now. I have to talk right now."

"Okay, Kat. Go ahead. The rest can wait," Blake said.

No trace of irritation in Blake's voice, she noticed. Good. She saw Pierre get up and activate a recording device. She began.

"Okay – this is going to be a little muddled – I'd ask you not to interrupt if possible, otherwise I might lose track."

"Go ahead Kat, we're listening." It was Zack. Something she meant to remember about Zack; too late – already gone.

"Recording," Pierre said.

She took a deep breath, and reached back into her mind. "I was on the home planet of the... Our-shee-wan; Ourshiwann ... best pronunciation I can give – their mouths are different to ours and they have no tongue.

They don't really use sounds at all, but they have a name in case visitors – I'll explain later – come by. I – I know, because, you see, I was one of them for a while."

"What?"

"Later Zack," Blake said, raising a hand.

"I had four legs, like two of you have seen, no head, and no eyes as such. The senses are around the circumference of the body and the top. We – they – see, or perceive is probably better, three-sixty degrees around them, like a sphere. They communicate in colours that make soft watery sounds." She glanced from Pierre to Rashid.

"It's so beautiful. For a while I was still thinking that way, that's why I've not been saying much." And as if by stating it, she somehow catalysed it back into her forebrain: her vision shifted, colours swimming around them all, rainbow hues, including some colours she knew she shouldn't be able to see. Rashid radiated mauve warmth at her, like a cloud; Blake's earnest face was haloed by a shimmering vermillion shroud, more metallic in tone.

She concentrated. "Listen, all of you. We're not alone. We're on the galactic outskirts, but there are many other intelligent species out there. I mean hundreds, closer in towards the hub of the galaxy."

"You mean you saw them, as well as the spider creatures?" Blake's voice had a sharp edge – it conjured up jagged, stark colours compared to the soft, undulating pastels of where she had been, and would have been considered rude there. But she knew Blake was merely probing to get the information out correctly.

"No. But – you see, I was inside their heads. I had images – in fact yes, I believe I 'saw' some of them, but not first hand. They send their Hohash out in small ships –"

"Hohash – the mirrors?" Blake again. The others were letting him alone interrupt. Kat nodded quickly, feeling nauseous.

"Yes – the mirrors – they sent them out, so they could bring back images when they return. There is something called the Grid. It spans a sixth of the galaxy – not the very centre where stellar density is too strong, but an inner ring, where dark matter density is highest." She was relieved she could remember it, but knew it would fade fast.

"The Grid is a three dimensional matrix, toroidal in shape, like a doughnut, used for superluminal inter-stellar transport. Nodes on the Grid are located near inhabited worlds. Thousands of worlds, Sir. And..."

They all stared at her, tongues of inquisitive purple leather snaking towards her. She shuddered. "Sir – some of them are way, way ahead of us. I mean completely beyond our league."

She felt an inner panic pushing upwards in her throat. Before, when she had been part of the Ourshiwann, their maturity, objectivity and passivity had protected her from the emotional impact of what they themselves had found out. Now, a wave of dread threatened to paralyse her. It was a slippery colour infinitely darker than black, threatening to suck her downwards.

A rapier of red cut through. "Kat, listen to me. You're a soldier. Tell us all of it, no matter how bad it seems to you."

She clung to Blake's voice, and decided to do just that – tell it without pausing to think of the ramifications.

"Within the grid there is an order to things, has been for a very long time, maybe a million years. There's a hierarchy, a sophisticated set of laws and allowable interactions. And a kind of policing agency – Rangers. There are nineteen levels in the hierarchy, but the Rangers only operate within the boundaries of the Grid, and we're way outside it – too expensive to travel so far from the Grid, too uninteresting to bother. Also, they only protect Level Five and above; Level Four species are borderline, and will only be protected if a sponsor race can be arranged. The Ourshiwann were considered Level Four pending a status upgrade to five, but didn't want to leave their home planet and move inside the Grid area. They also refused sponsorship from a couple of nasty races. The Q'Roth – the ones hiding somewhere on Eden – are Level Six, predatory by nature, and culled the Ourshiwann before they could gain Level Five status." She paused.

Pierre spoke, a smooth grey ceramic sheet – but something else under the surface: darker, moving fast, insect-like.

"Kat. What level do you think we would be?"

Kat saw a harmonic rippling across all their colours – it was the question they all now shared.

She cleared her throat. "Three."

Zack slumped back in his seat, a smear of brown arriving then disappearing. "That figures."

She sensed the colours heating up, becoming agitated. But she had to get it all out. "That means… it means that the Q'Roth have a *right* to hunt us. We don't even have the right of appeal which the spiders rejected. It means other species have a right to enslave us or consume us as they see fit. We're effectively seen as animals – for the Q'Roth we're vermin at worst, food at best." Storm-clouds of rusted grey and violet rain swam around her. She closed her eyes. "The Q'Roth also pass through different stages in their thousand year life cycle. At first, when they hatch, they're primitive, predatory pack creatures, relying on a basic feeding instinct. Not food as such, but – sentience, in a way; a kind of emotional and intellectual electro-potential. In Grid Society it's effectively a classified drug. Frowned upon by higher races, but accepted for lower ones as a catalyst for maturation, or elevation as they call it."

"Once they've fed, they change, and go through an intense period, five centuries long; a phase of blinding artistic and technological creativity. But the Q'Roth are mostly valued as soldiers in Grid Society. That's what earns them Level Six status. They mate once, and then most die, leaving their eggs and a handful of guardians. They mean to feed on humanity, to extract the bio-electric energy."

Silence swept into the cabin. She paused to let it sink in, and dared to open her eyes again. The evanescent coloured fresco, this mode of perception, was fading. She wasn't sad to lose it, and examined her colleagues in grainy sepia. Rashid was sitting on the floor, head down, in a loose lotus position – trying to accept the bad news with equanimity. Zack was tight-lipped, looking out toward the desert, seeking out the enemy, no doubt worried about his family back on Earth. Pierre was looking down. Kat couldn't read his thoughts or emotions, but his body language was compressed, she presumed trying to rationalise it all, but struggling to do so. Only Blake was facing her, glaring. Her brow widened with shock: he was angry.

"Anything else, Corporal?" The words came out like the unfurling of a whip.

Kat swallowed, and wondered if she, the messenger, was about to be proverbially shot. "No, Sir – well, some fragments, but nothing that makes much sense at the moment."

Blake stood up. "Now, listen up, all of you. What Kat has just told us is pretty grim. I have no doubt that she has told us exactly what he saw – what was imparted by the mirror – this... Hohash."

She relaxed a little.

"Now, it may be true, it may not. The reality on the ground, here and now, is that we know there are creatures out there that are hostile and damned difficult to kill. There are eggs somewhere on Eden that could be a serious threat to humanity if more of us come here or, God forbid, if the Q'Roth make it to Earth."

"So, we have four goals. First, we must re-establish comms with Earth, let them know we're alive, and what we've found out. Second, we need to gather and take back some proof, because no matter how real this is to us, you all know how difficult it will be to accept without hard evidence back on Earth. Third, we need to determine if the eggs are here, and if we can destroy them before they hatch. Fourth," and he looked around the room, "Fourth, we need to go home."

Kat felt Blake's words wrench her out of her own growing despair, like a glowing silver lifeline hauling her out of a dark pit. Zack and Rashid stood up, followed by Pierre. Kat scrambled to her feet as Blake's gaze met hers, and then the others, one by one.

"Listen, all of you," Blake continued, quieter. "Let's just consider, for one moment, that everything Kat has seen is true. That we're insignificant in this so-called hierarchy – prey, if you will." All eyes were on him.

"Well damn them!" He slammed a closed fist against the side of the hull, its dull thud reverberating around them. "This level three species is not going to lie back and take it. We will fight, and we *will* survive."

A grin crept across Zack's face. "Amen, Skipper."

Rashid nodded and gave a loose salute to Blake. Pierre followed suit, Kat too. She held it for a long time.

As the others left the compartment to make preparations for their tasks, Blake and Kat were left alone. She was trembling.

"Sir, there was something else."

He approached her, eyes sharp. "Tell me."

She took a deep breath. "The only way the Hohash could let me see these things was to connect with its master's memories. Well – you see… I was there when the Q'Roth came. The spiders knew they were coming, and had decided as a group – as a people – to retain their pacifist mode of life through to the end, though it meant they would all die. They had no space-ships themselves, since they never travelled – the Hohash did it for them. They'd resigned themselves to their fate, very much in control of their emotions you see." Kat folded her arms tight around her. "But when it happened – the carnage, the pain – some of them wavered – including the one I was 'inside' – that's why he disobeyed his society's agreement and sent his Hohash out into space."

Her legs shook, threatening to give way. "I – the spider – ran. I ran for my life, when others stood tall and were slaughtered. I knew it would do no good, and I was not alone to run, but suddenly I couldn't accept this fate, neither mine nor that of my species. So I ran in blind fear and one of them chased me. It caught me and slashed at me, cutting my hind legs from under me, then it's mouth bore down on me, sucking my life force away." Her eyes brimmed with the memory of it, but she sniffed the tears back. "Captain – I was killed. I bloody-well died with it. I shared its terror, its grief for its kind."

Blake steadied her, hands on her shoulders. "Kat," he said, "every soldier in battle goes through what you've been through – maybe not as far, for sure. But you're through it, and you're alive. And you'll fight when the time comes. These spiders – noble creatures for sure – while I can respect their culture and their choice not to fight, it won't be our way, I can assure you."

She nodded, and steadied herself.

Blake reached into a pocket in his jumpsuit with his right hand. "Zack told me to give you this when you really needed it." He pulled out a crumpled, folded piece of paper. "Someone gave it to him on Zeus. Said it was to be opened in your darkest moment. He wouldn't tell me who, but he left it with me."

She stared at it. "What is it?"

"I don't open other people's mail, Kat."

Her lungs seemed too full to breathe except in shallow gasps. "Read it out to me. Please."

Blake unfolded it, and read out loud. "Let me see. It says – To Kat– I promise –" He paused, shifted uneasily, and cleared his throat. "I promise I will wait for you, no matter what, no matter how long. All my love. And then it's signed – *Antonia.*"

She gaped at the piece of paper, and then took it gingerly, as if it might break or crumble into dust. Blake left her alone. She sat down, cradling the note in her hands. Zack had written something on the outside in his large scrawl: Happiness is knowing that someone, somewhere, really gives a shit.

* * *

A kilometre away, the solitary Hohash hovered on top of an outcrop, still tuned into Kat's mind. It felt her emotional response – this grieving. It let go of her mind and displayed on its mirror face a churning sea storm, an image borrowed from a painting stored as a memory in Kat's mind years ago. In this image, the mirror stood alone on a small vessel, strapped to the helm, thrashed in all directions by the ravages of the maelstrom, whipped by wind, shaken by thunderclaps. Other boats were also caught in the storm, tossed by the mammoth waves. The mirror, via this image, was finally able to express its anguish at its masters' and comrades' annihilation.

The storm image raged on for some time. Abruptly it pacified, the sea calmed, and the sky cleared. In the image, the Hohash was still on the inundated boat. None other had survived. Beneath the boat, dark shark-shapes circled. But deeper still in the water, on the seabed itself, there were glints of reflected, fractured, mirrored sunlight.

The image on its surface evaporated. The Hohash set off at a fast pace. Like the crew on Ulysses, it also now had tasks to accomplish, and time was running out. After nearly a millennium of biding its time, it knew everything would come to a head, one way or another, in the next few days. And in the brief connection between Kat and Blake, it had absorbed something new, energising – a hitherto alien construct – this time it would find a way to fight back.

Chapter 32

Louise

Vince tried again, but Louise wasn't answering, and her signal had gone off the secure nets. Technically she was AWOL, which meant he should have reported it three hours ago. But this wasn't the first time.

He stood legs astride for balance in the sky-taxi, surveying New LA below. His wristcom pulsed – the fulsome face of his superior officer at Chorazin HQ appeared, looking even less happy than usual. Vince kept his poker face; he'd give her more time. But not much.

"Vince, check Channel 49."

Vince tapped the console and up popped the broadcast.

"Idiot!" This was the only word Vince uttered during the transmission. He watched Senator Josefsson live across America and God alone knew where else as he announced two things. First, the fact that Earth had less than ten years before undergoing a significant, fatal climate shift, a global increase of thirty degrees Celsius. Second, how the recently discovered ships – two more like the one IVS had discovered had been "found" – could take people directly to Eden. He talked about how America, a nation of pioneers that had lost its way, should take the ultimate step and colonise Eden, in partnership with its high-tech Indistani colleagues. Vince wanted to switch it off, but had to see it through. Afterwards, the voice of his superior cut through again.

"Did you know he would do this?"

Vince recalled his and Louise's meeting with Josefsson yesterday. He'd left early, left them alone. She would have got under Josefsson's skin, possibly in more ways than one; he was the type to brag to try and get her into the sack. She should have seen this coming.

"Had I known, I would have stopped him." He'd have to deal with Louise later.

"Recommendation?" His boss growled.

"It's too late to sanction him now, verbally or otherwise – if anything happens to him it will only convince people more. Containment, maybe some of the details. Consequences – what it would mean to move to Eden so suddenly. All the research that's been going on at PsyTech since we first found out about the climate time-bomb. Contingency plans. Smearing Josefsson for what he clearly is – a reckless self-serving hypocrite who doesn't give a rat's ass about people, only his career." Vince smiled. "Or maybe putting him on the first ship."

"Ah, that's something we hadn't thought of; has a certain appeal."

Vince looked down through the brown haze over the sun-baked city of New LA, imagining it emptying as millions across America tried to leave. And then he imagined an extra thirty degrees, or at least tried to. It wasn't pretty.

"We need something else, Vince. Something on Eden. Did you know there is now a desert there?"

"Since when?"

"First spotted a month ago, but they thought it was a malfunction – you know the pictures aren't always that reliable. Yesterday it was confirmed. Growing at quite a rate."

"Sir – I'm guessing IVS must have the same data – yet Josefsson spoke anyway."

"We all know the senator is in their pocket – we believe they may have primed him, but possibly he went off early, so to speak."

"I'm on my way back to Eden Mission now. I'll see what they are making of the desert issue."

The wristcom cleared.

He called Louise: *unavailable*. "Louise – it's Vince, call me after you've seen Josefsson's speech on the Nets." He saw the Eden building approach, and considered Louise's recent behaviour. She usually came through. Still... He sent a coded message to a level ten colleague, Abrahams, to check on Micah at Chorazin-Med. He had a feeling she would show up there sooner or later.

The Eden Mission Complex loomed in front of him. "Take us down to street level," he instructed the sky taxi computer.

* * *

Antonia shifted in the chrome chair, her composure faltering.

272

"So, he just slipped into a coma?" Louise said, continuing the questioning. "How could you tell?" She scraped a chair across the room and sat astride it, leaning forwards on its chrome back. Antonia stared back at her.

"I couldn't at first, but you know, or maybe you don't, that when analysts use the Optron their bodies remain tense. His just went limp."

Louise stifled a yawn. "I'm told that can be quite upsetting." She got up and walked over to Micah's comatose body, and ran her hand down the length of the various drips and devices feeding into and out of him. She stood right next to Antonia, who turned to see Micah. As soon as she did so, Louise first put her hand on Antonia's shoulder, then brushed the back of her hand against her chin and cheek.

"I can see why he likes you."

Antonia blushed, looked away and made to get up, but Louise's hand pressed down firmly on her shoulder. Antonia folded her hands in her lap. Louise walked around right in front of her and lifted her chin.

"Do you care for him?"

Antonia's mouth opened, and then closed. "What... what do you mean?"

Louise let go and walked to her chair, and rested her buttocks against the back of it. "It's a simple question, Antonia. You've known him for some time, you met him on the bubble platform the other night, and now, here you are, at his bedside."

"I – how do you know I – we – we met accidentally on the platform. Anyway, I was just..." she stopped, not wishing to divulge her relationship with Kat. "What does this have to do with anything?"

"People don't just slip into a coma, Antonia. Perhaps you did something to him. Lover's tiff, perhaps?"

Antonia shot to her feet and headed to the holo-window. She tried to recover herself. "This is ridiculous, Louise. Micah and I are just colleagues. I was trying to help recover data from Ulysses. Micah works in telemetry and I work in data processing. It just seemed logical." She remained facing away from Louise.

"You're one poor liar, my girl. You know he's in love with you, don't you?"

Antonia tensed, and blinked hard. She spun to face Louise, eyes glaring. "No he isn't! Where are you going with all of this?"

Louise remained poker-faced. "He says you have another lover, Antonia. You know how pliable men are after they've come. Does this lover want Micah in a coma?"

Antonia's mouth dropped open. Her eyes flicked for a moment towards Micah, shocked that he had told Louise, of all people... *and slept with her*! She stood up. "Stop this right now. You can't just question me like this." She picked up her bag, "I'm leaving." But she didn't.

Louise smiled. "Actually, I can interrogate you anyway I like. Let's see. I'm Chorazin. A key person in my investigation is in a coma for no good reason, and you were the only person with him at the time. In fact my boss would probably reprimand me for not putting you in a holding cell and having you deep-profiled. So, Antonia, you have to give me a reason. A piece of information that will keep me, and my boss, happy for the moment. What were you and Micah doing, what is your relationship with our sleepy friend there, and who exactly is your lover? And you have to give me these three bits of information straight away, or I will arrest you and you'll spend the next three days in an uncomfortable cell. By the time your Ambassador father finds out, you'll be a wreck, and believe me, the Chorazin have impunity."

Antonia lowered herself back into her chair, clutching her bag, and stared at the floor. She didn't doubt this woman – and she didn't want to go to a cell – she'd be useless to anyone she cared about once inside one. She weighed everything up.

"My lover is Katrina Beornwulf, the Ulysses astronaut. I believed Micah could find a way to contact her and the others. I wanted to help. Micah and I are colleagues, that's all. Just before he went into the coma, he seemed to be on the verge of a breakthrough."

Louise walked over to her, and knelt down before her lowered head and spoke close to her defeated face. "There, that wasn't too hard, really, was it?" She walked back to the chair and pushed it against the wall. "Micah's not a bad fuck actually. Inexperienced, but a quick study." She turned to see Antonia's bewildered face. "Don't leave town." She walked out.

Antonia stared after her, then at Micah's almost lifeless body. She raised a hand to her throat, closed her eyes, then leant forward onto her knees, and buried her face in her hands.

* * *

Sister Esma continued the dispatch of orders on the vidcom using a secure line. The chess pieces were all in place. Endgame.

"It has begun… We must move quickly... How fast can the remaining ships be found? Use discovery protocol beta, I believe an MIT scientist is working in the area, he would be a suitable candidate. It must be handled very carefully. Scripts will arrive within the hour for synchronised transmission across G-Net by Fundamentalist leaders. We have rehearsed for this moment for many, many years. The people must be persuaded the ships are gifts from their one true God, whichever one applies to the local population. The ships' apparent simplicity will assist credibility of the message... The message will be a strong trigger – fear, anger and outrage at suppression of information will do the rest. The ships will only take at most a few percent of the population in the first volley, but that will be enough, and the political turmoil left behind, fuelled by tens of millions who will want to go but have to wait, and possibly die, will deliver us the power we have waited for… After? I will tell you in good time. Information is earned, revealed only when needed."

The vidcom cleared.

After, she thought. After the feeding on Eden, and the harvesting here, we – the Inner Circle alone – will be elevated, and will travel to the Grid. Those of us touched by these Gods, those of us who have borne their genetic gifts – the insights, strength, and above all the longevity, want nothing more.

She leaned back in her chair, clasping her hands behind her skull. Galileo, my dear man, you should have listened to me. If you had, then you could have seen with your own eyes what your brilliance had only just managed to grasp – not just the non-Euclidean solar system, but the rest of the galaxy. And Amadeus – at least we will take your music with us, though you chose to remain so finitely mortal. She thought of the people she had known over the past six centuries. Most she despised – her perspective was so different that she no longer thought of herself as human, and found humans – earthlings as she had started to call them, hopelessly bound to this doomed planet – their pitiful, short lives and limited vision, their petty selfishness. Humanity left alone would never rise above itself. There had even been a time when she had questioned the Q'Roth-Alician pact, but the longer she trod the Earth the more she knew the inevitable choice was between culling most and upgrading a few, or culling all.

There had of course been some exceptional men and women – a few. She and others had tried to turn them, most without success. Still – there were five hundred like her, a few even older, roaming the world. They controlled humanity, misguided it, kept it off-balance, bringing it to ripeness for the return of the Q'Roth. Soon – very soon – almost no time at all, this narcissistic civilisation would be eradicated, and they, the five hundred who knew what was coming, plus another five thousand promising Alicians, would have their own ships and a passport to the Grid. A new existence and legitimacy as a sponsored Level Five species. The hierarchy they had heard about would know this new humanity for the first time and would respect it: our next stage of evolution.

The vidcom buzzed, the code indicating her favourite protégé. "Report."

"Micah is in a coma. Antonia doesn't know anything. I'm on my way back to Chorazin HQ. I have a bunch of calls from Vince, which I'm about to take –"

"Don't. I have a mission for you."

"My absence will already have been noticed. If I don't turn up soon –"

"I said I have a mission for you." Sister Esma waited. Anyone else would have apologised profusely for making her repeat herself, but Louise was special, and her silence was sufficient. "It has begun, Louise. I have instructions for you which must be passed face to face. Then you must return and kill Micah." This time the silence which followed was not acceptable. "Is there a problem, Louise?"

"No. I'll be there in ten minutes." The vidcom cleared.

Sister Esma looked wistfully over to a wall where an unknown original by Leonardo hung, secret, beautiful. "And you, too, will come with us when we leave." The drawing showed two people, her and another, standing next to a large grey-black insect-like creature, upright, nearly twice as tall as its human companions. Such stark, uncompromising beauty.

She switched on the vidcom again. After a few seconds a hooded face appeared; silent, tranquil, eyes unseen.

"Start the beacon. Wake them."

The hooded figure nodded, and then cut the transmission.

It was an irony that she and her Alician flock were actually saving humanity: at least the Q'Roth had offered a lifeline, preserving a portion of mankind, allowing it to evolve to its next generation. Other races who stumbled upon Earth might prove less generous. But she had no sympathetic pretensions. The Q'Roth genetic alterations gave their human followers razor sharp clarity over what some would call ethics, and what later historians would call ecological necessity. Survival of the fittest, she had once argued with Darwin. At least he had finally understood, if only for the animal kingdom.

She activated a mosaic of viewscreens showing major channels all over the world, and waited for the announcements. She could feel the tapestry of the manoeuvres and manipulations of a millennium coming together. Finally, all the loose ends had been accounted for. It was not unlike a Da Vinci, she mused – a vivid painting that would flow inexorably from the brushes of the Q'Roth and Alician Protectorate, bright swathes of red on Earth's dusty brown canvas. It was a painting she intended to see once, and then cast aside forever. Perhaps Mozart's Requiem would be fitting music for the end of the world. She began to hum *Dies Irae*, recalling its first performance in Vienna.

PART THREE

BATTLE FOR EDEN

Chapter 33

Final Request

Gabriel gained entry to the Vidsex parlour. He quickly strapped in, inserted his own data crystal, logged on and accessed the net, and faced the redhead again. He spoke with urgency.

"I will be dead within two hours. Sister Esma and her cohorts, maybe the Q'Roth themselves, are finally moving. Louise is the Chorazin double agent."

The redhead morphed into an old man who nevertheless stood lightning rod straight. "It pains me to hear that you are departing this life. But I have also learned they are on the move, and so am I, too."

Gabriel's normally lake-like composure swirled with emotional riptides from the Alician drug. He found it difficult to focus on strategy; he would very shortly no longer be part of it. "I have a final request."

"Speak and I will grant it."

Gabriel swallowed. "I have discovered that my sister – Jennifer – is alive. You've no doubt seen the vids of the ship in the Pacific. She's the Professor's assistant. You may have noticed a family resemblance."

There was a pause. "I will protect her. I was planning to go there next. Now, prepare yourself. Gabriel – whatsoever remains of us after, will meet again."

Gabriel bowed to the figure. His Sentinel master bowed lower. He broke the connection, tore off the temple electrodes, and crushed the crystal underfoot.

He had been preparing for death for the past seven years. Each evening he contemplated the void, to the point where his ego dissolved and all that was left was space, and the intangible sense of something else that remained: spirit, that which was there before he was born.

He had always believed that nothing immortal could have a start – if it did there would be an end too, so whatever would be there after death must have been there before birth, and the ego, all the worries and joys, the personality, was just clothing used for the journey before the return to the nakedness of death. Every morning he had also meditated and acted as if this were his last day on earth.

Despite the clarity such meditation had delivered him these past seven years, he couldn't quieten his soul. There was something in the back of his mind that stirred restlessly.

Finding out that his sister was still alive had unleashed a shockwave of inner turmoil and remorse, amplified by the emotion-enhancer Sister Esma had pumped into him. Futile thoughts arose of lost time, and a different life he could have had, with his sister, or even a family of his own. He had spent most of his adult life invisible to society – no one would weep for him, or even know he was gone. He tried to observe these feelings in a detached way. He dared not let them surface fully now, or else they would overwhelm him: he would crack, his resolve would splinter and he would be useless to himself, to Jenny, and his whole chosen way of life would be negated. He did not relish the idea of being cast into the wilderness at the moment of death – he'd seen it all too often.

Taking a deep breath, he held it for a minute, breathed out slowly, then held his lungs still and empty. His mind cleared. Nothing mattered anymore except the mission. He picked up his bulky bag and headed for the exit. But the aching inside remained, even if subdued. As he moved toward the transit level, he realised there was one thing he could do to assuage this sudden longing, but it was a ridiculous idea – there was neither time nor opportunity.

As he approached the Eden Mission service tunnel, his mind switched into killing mode, as he began to plan how to destroy the building completely, calculating how many guards and others it would take. For the first time in his vocation, he searched for the minimum kill ratio. Now that he was busy again, the inner voice silenced. The brief mayfly flutterings of his ego had ended, accepting his fate, his choices. When he came to the first guard, the blade of his right hand whipped against the man's carotid artery, spiking the guard's blood pressure and knocking him unconscious, rather than crushing it and causing massive brain haemorrhage. He even protected the man's head as he slumped to the ground. Gabriel felt as if a legion of the people he'd cleansed over the years stood behind him, watching, curious, but also anxious to meet him on the other side. He checked his wristcom. Sixty minutes left on this world, in this skin. He moved forward quickly.

* * *

Sandy came in to pick up her things – she'd been given two week's leave, on account of everything that had happened to her. She had a small list, but once she arrived, she screwed it up and threw it in the bin. She hadn't come here for things – she'd come to say goodbye.

Before discharging her, the Chorazin psych had warned her she was off-balance; the trauma of the last two days had raked over old scars, unleashing depression. *Too right, and then some.* The stiff but well-meaning psych had pulled her old files, and given her a fatherly lecture about not getting suicidal again, like the time she'd lost her brother Jake in a car crash on his twenty-first. She'd been driving.

The shrink had shaken her hand and given her some pills to take. They currently inhabited New LA's sewage system.

Sandy felt unclean, like she had black, oily poison lining her gut; everyone she'd ever cared about died violently. She wanted to vomit it up out of her, but it clung to her insides like tar. It made her think of cutting herself again, but that had been a former life, and she didn't want to restart that particular addiction. Anyway, she reminded herself, she wasn't unique – everyone on the planet had lost loved ones violently in the War. She tried to mentally kick herself, to snap out of it. Easier said than done.

She'd had it with the Eden Mission; Kane had been the only reason she'd stayed all these years. She had no idea where to go next, but had made up her mind: she'd leave town. Start over somewhere. Anywhere. Maybe Russia. She spoke Russian, and no one knew her there. But first, she had to say goodbye. She placed her hands on the door handles, took a breath, and entered the office.

The conservative teak furniture was still pretty much where it had been. She went into Kane's office, closed the doors behind her, and strode straight to his desk. She traced a finger over the inner edge. She steeled herself, and turned towards the bathroom, her prison for two days, and looked straight into the dark eyes of the man she'd shot at two days ago.

"You!" She glanced from him to the inner door. He walked over to it and turned the key. She silently cursed Keiji's desire for antique locking devices. Well, at least the assassin hadn't shot her yet. She opted as usual for bravado.

"Come to finish the job? I thought that bitch did you in?"

He stared at her, looked her up and down, taking his time about it, she noticed. He was stripped to the waist, wearing only a pair of tight-fitting black trousers. She couldn't help but notice the menagerie of scars on his upper body. She wondered what the lower half looked like, then mentally pinched herself; the psych had been right, but unbalanced didn't quite cover it. Her dark impulses drove her forward.

"Strong and silent type, eh?"

He strode across to her. She smelt his sweat – it wasn't distasteful. With a shock she realised he'd be about the same build and age her brother might be now, if…

"I was trying to save you, Sandy. Louise is the killer."

She gave out a sharp laugh. "You're Alician, a Cleanser, remember, one of the bad guys."

He returned to the bathroom, fiddling with some kind of device, a green glass cube the size of her daddy's old footstool. She made out the word 'Hextrite' in red lettering on the side. She'd seen enough war-vids to know it was an ultra-powerful explosive, the type that produced a vertical compression shockwave, perfect for collapsing a building while leaving surrounding ones intact.

"Christ, you don't do anything by half measures, do you?"

Still, he made no reply. She went to the door, but the key was missing.

"So, you're going to blow up the building? And take me with it? Or am I coming with you."

"I'm not leaving."

Shit. Despite her mounting fear, her mouth continued on autopilot, with no navigation. "Look. If you're the good guy, let me go."

He fished in his pocket briefly, and tossed her the key. She snatched it in mid air, and looked at the door. Her mind said *"Run, you idiot!"* But she remained. He punched a code into a small keypad and then sat cross-legged on the floor.

"There's an implant in my head. In twenty minutes it will release a violent toxin into my brain and I will die, painfully."

He locked eyes with hers. The effect on Sandy was like being struck by two jet-black lasers. The only men she'd ever been able to love had been completely convinced of what they were about – her father, her brother, Kane; no one else ever measured up. They'd all given her a reason to live. She studied him.

"I haven't made love to a woman for seven years. I have no children to leave behind. I never expected to have any. I'm not exactly a family man." He made an attempt to smile. She could tell he didn't get much practice.

"Is this an Alician chat-up line?"

"I'm not an Alician; they're my enemy." He balanced the backs of his hands on his knees in a meditative pose. "Their inner circle are genetically advanced."

She wasn't surprised; it fit, since they'd eluded capture for a decade, not one ever brought to justice. Genetics had been banned, but that never stopped anybody. She wondered why he was telling her this.

"Three years ago I was infused with an experimental metagenic virus. It doesn't affect me, but my children, if I had any, would be advanced, developing rapidly, becoming as strong as the Alicians."

An explosion deep down in the building shook the room, sounding like a bomb had gone off underwater. The fire alarms shrieked. Sprinklers showered them with a fine mist of cool water. She realised he'd set off a smaller device to evacuate the building. He was an assassin, not a mass murderer. Her feet still didn't budge.

"Go," he said. "Take Kane's emergency drop lift, it's still there. It will get you fifty metres underground in ninety seconds. Then just head away from it in any direction."

But she couldn't. *Stupid bitch*, she thought to herself. *They die violently, remember?* But the irony made some kind of sense to her. This was the kind of pill she needed: serious psychological – and probably terminal – detox. As her decision firmed, all the self-loathing and depression fled like the people pouring out of the building six hundred metres below. Poison needed an anti-toxin; she needed a reason to live. She approached him.

"You finished with that thing?"

He nodded.

"Good – so how long have we got?"

* * *

Vince entered the building just as the explosion shook the floor. He made it inside seconds before the waterfall of glass shards from way above. Panic-stricken people streamed out of every orifice, like termites leaving a collapsing hill. He had to fight against a tide of them to get through the atrium to the central elevators. Of course they'd been inactivated; or rather they would only come down, and not go back up. He knew this bomb must be a diversion. Somebody was still up there.

He came back outside and used his wristcom – "It's Vince – I need a heli-jet with a high entry boarder, and a heat sensor, ASAP. Eden Mission – just head for the smoking building – I'll be on the K-level heli-pad." He checked to see if Louise had called back – but there was nothing, no message even. *Dammit, Louise!* He coded a single word message to Abrahams – *Careful*. He charged up the stairs two at a time, dodging the bewildered people cascading down the stairwells.

* * *

Sandy could tell he was close to orgasm, but she herself couldn't make it. *Damn – I thought performance pressure was a man's problem!* But she savoured the passion, knowing she would relish the bruises tomorrow, as he consistently slammed her back against the wall, his hands cradling her buttocks, her legs wrapped around his waist. She'd all but given up, was about to focus on his orgasm, when she opened her eyes and saw, over his shoulder, Vince's slim, sweat-drenched figure dash into the room. Against her better judgement, and without her consent, her body started to wrack itself. Vince lowered his weapon, and perched on Kane's desk, waiting. *Bastard*, she thought, but she began to come, as did the assassin. She grabbed his face and pressed her mouth hard on his, wrestling with his tongue as their bodies collided, her contractions squeezing hard around him, before he shuddered and slowed down. He remained inside her as he recovered his breathing, and his black eyes burrowed into hers.

"Thank you," he said.

She saw his eyes focus inwards. He lowered her legs to the floor, her dress dropping back down, supporting her still-trembling body. He snatched the locket from around his neck and placed it in her open hand, sealed her fingers around it. She saw Vince move toward them, pistol raised. And then, without warning, the assassin's face hardened, and his breathing froze. Eyes wide, he fell backwards, as if in slow motion, and crashed to the floor. She remained at the wall, arms at her chest, clutching the locket, as his rigid body convulsed on the floor. A sickly black and purple bruising erupted around his face, thickened blood dripping from his mouth, nose, eyes and ears. His body shook several more times and

284

then froze. She didn't look away; but she bit down on her knuckle till it bled.

Vince stood over his body. "Fast-acting toxin. Looks like metracide alpha. It'll corrode his entire…" He glanced up at Sandy. "Never mind. Nothing I can do."

She remained where she was, as Vince moved over to the cubic bomb.

"Jesus!" He grabbed her wrist and wrenched her away from the scene. Her legs were too weak to run, so he stopped and heaved her over his shoulder in a fireman's lift. She didn't resist. Her body went limp as they hurtled through the corridors. Smashed windows revealed a narrow, five metre long air bridge to the side entrance of the heli-jet, hovering still as a humming bird, six hundred metres above the ground. She closed her eyes as Vince sprinted across it with her still on his shoulder. She opened them again as she was thrown into a seat. Vince yelled at the pilot. "Ditch the bridge, leave now!"

She watched the world fall away from her through the porthole window as the heli-jet plunged in reverse mode. The Eden Mission building shimmered and buckled, a shock wave rippling down its upper glass exterior before thousands of windows shattered, and a colossal burst of flame swallowed the tower. Glass spattered in all directions like hail. The heli-jet reared up and began to spin, dropping like a stone towards the ground, until the pilot regained control and veered away between two other skyscrapers.

She noticed Vince staring at her, concerned, but also glancing at her bloody right fist, where she still held the locket. She drew her knees up to her chest, her feet on her seat edge, and folded her arms around her shins. She wasn't going to give it to him. He got up, took off his jacket and placed it around her shoulders, then sat back down opposite her, and gazed out of the window. She hadn't even realised she was shivering; her body felt numb. Her mouth, her constant companion, was silent. She realised something.

Her voice sounded husky, even to her. "What was his name?"

Vince turned back to her, his eyes measuring, judging probably. She didn't care.

"Gabriel O'Donnell, according to the DNA scan we took last time."

She closed her eyes, one hand drawing the jacket closer around her, the other hand, still clutching the locket, on her belly. From deep inside her, lost in the chopper's whirring, she whispered to the sky above her. "I hope you find peace, Gabriel O'Donnell." She had the feeling the world around her was unravelling. "Say hi to my brother Jake for me. Maybe I'll see him sooner than planned."

Chapter 34

Eggs

"You think he's hiding something?"

"That wasn't what I was saying, Sir." Pierre wished he hadn't started this.

"But your data show the desert began when Rashid landed. His ship the Phoenix appears to be ground zero." Blake folded his arms.

Pierre had to admit he didn't have a good explanation – yet. But he could feel he was close to working out the puzzle of the desert, and maybe of Eden itself.

"I need more time, Sir. There may be another cause, or his landing may have –"

"Time's a luxury we don't have. He's hiding something, Pierre. I'm going to question him."

Pierre found himself blocking Blake's exit. He held his ground. "Let me talk with him first – scientist to scientist." He saw Blake was about to say *No*. "Fifteen minutes, Sir, that's all I'll need."

Blake's eyes narrowed. He checked his wristcom and headed back to the cockpit.

Pierre let out a long breath, and then descended the ladder to Eden's grassy surface. The tide of emerald green light that flooded over the pre-dawn land nearly made him miss the final rung. The jewel-like blaze tumbled over the mountains in the direction they called east, splashed over the desert and the Lander before shifting to aquamarine. Just as his eyes adjusted to the soothing colour, a blood-orange dawn burst forth.

"Now, that was cool," Kat said, momentarily rising from her lightweight field chair – she'd been studying a pad. "Is that normal?"

"Yes," Rashid said, as if he'd just witnessed a holy apparition. "It lasts only ten seconds, but it takes my breath away every time I see it."

Pierre surveyed the scene. Kat had a pulse rifle next to her, and on her lap a graphite pad the size of a dinner plate serving as a radar monitor with a half-kilometre range. She faced the hill to the North, the direction the Q'Roth guardian had come from before. Rashid sat cross-legged on a cushion from one of the bunks, facing Eden's sun. Weaponless, he looked serene, a neo-native of Eden. The nearest scrub-like bushes to the ship were fifteen metres away, cadaver-grey in the first kindling of dawn.

The daylight warmed his mood. Dawn occurred faster than on Earth, the night-day cycle being twenty-two hours. There'd been no sighting of the guardian during the night. Kat and Rashid had spent hours late into the evening trying to make the comms system work, but there was a scattering effect on Eden – they could contact the remote link on the Ulysses mother-ship still in orbit, but nothing beyond – the compressed radio pulse simply dispersed, like a drop of oil hitting water, once it left Eden's neighbourhood. They would have to try from space itself, or at least from a high orbit.

That had left the tricky question of whether Ulysses' life support system would work for five people instead of four. He'd established that Eden's atmosphere was benign – whatever the additional element in the Eden biosphere, it was inert and could be extracted by Ulysses' nano-mesh filtration system. But the ghoster attack had wrecked the spare capacity of the air processing system. Blake had pressed him on the matter the previous evening in private.

"Sir, we could take five – but if anything goes wrong or breaks down, the situation will become critical for all of us in a matter of hours."

"What about putting Rashid in stasis? I seem to remember you considered quarantining me in stasis for the return trip."

Pierre swallowed. "I've reconsidered that, Sir. Trouble is, the stasis pods have all been configured for our individual physiologies, and the software to adapt to someone new was deleted by the virus."

"So, one of us goes into stasis instead of Rashid. You volunteering?"

Pierre studied the floor.

"I thought not. Find another solution, Lieutenant, that's an order."

Pierre remembered his current mission – he'd already lost five minutes.

"Rashid," he said, "Good morning – can we recap from last night's discussion?"

Rashid nodded, but less enthusiastic than a minute ago. Pierre didn't blame him; they'd gotten nowhere discussing it into the early hours; he'd felt like they'd been knocking their heads uselessly against a dam. He sensed Blake was right, though, that Rashid had a clue buried inside him, probably not one Rashid consciously recognised – at least he preferred that explanation than that it was outright deception.

Pierre began where they'd left off. "The Q'Roth – let's assume that's what they are called – don't like to set foot in the desert. The desert wasn't here when you arrived, whereupon it spread fast, and is continuing to do so."

Rashid stared towards the desert.

He continued. "From the samples I took yesterday, the desert is the residue of a wave front that is consuming everything in its path. Furthermore – and this is the difficult part, it appears to devour everything at an equal rate, irrespective of density or molecular construction – rock, grass, bush, soil, leading to a perfectly circular desert."

Rashid nodded slowly. "Yes. Something does not make sense, and I have been unable to work out what, even after all this time."

Pierre recalled how his father, fingering his grey beard, used to set puzzles at the dinner table, testing him. Pierre rarely solved them, and even when he did, there would be some rebuke about how long it had taken. Nevertheless, he considered that this form of mild dinner-time torment might tease out the answer here. He took on his father's airs and graces, a little unnerved how easily they came to him.

"Rashid – when faced with a conundrum, it is usually because a piece of information is wrong, or missing, or because an assumption is incorrect."

Kat, who had remained disinterested until now, cocked her head, and stared at Pierre. He wasn't sure, but Pierre thought he detected a wry smile. Rashid maintained his orientation to the desert, washed in ruby light.

"Rashid – I believe that if you can give me the missing information, then I can make the correct inference." He gambled. "Rashid – you're hiding something from us, aren't you?"

Rashid rocked himself upwards first into a squatting position, then stood up and bent double, palms on the ground, then flexed upwards, very straight like a soldier on parade, and turned to face Pierre square. He spoke nervously.

"It should not have mattered. Such a small amount."

Pierre kept his face serious, and his mouth shut. He did not meet Kat's gaze. The dam cracked.

"You see," Rashid said, "we had many months in the craft, and before I had been assigned to the Phoenix, I was working on an important exobiological study." He paced around in a slow circle, hands behind his back, addressing the bushes and rocks as much as Pierre and Kat.

Pierre noticed that Rashid's hair was looking ragged. He clearly hadn't slept. *Guilt.* He cast his mind back to the leading edge of that research field a few years ago. A comet had been intercepted and they'd found something… *Merde!*

"Proto-matter," he said, incredulous. "You brought proto-matter *here?*"

Rashid halted mid-step, nodded once, and then continued his circle, quickening his pace, hands wrestling behind his back.

Kat piped up, glancing from one to the other. "Dumb question time. Proto-matter?"

Rashid turned to her, eyes suddenly bright, and began gesticulating. "It is the clay, the building blocks, the very stuff of stars! It is the beginning of everything!"

Pierre cut in. "And extremely reactive. And normally never let out of a sealed laboratory environment. How did you get it past IVS bio-screening? I'm assuming they didn't know you took it on board."

"A space-ship is also a contained environment," Rashid emphasized, using his hands to make the shape of a ball. "And – if you must know – it was in a ceramic capsule in my teapot."

Kat laughed, but Pierre couldn't believe it; it was so irresponsible. "Rashid – what happened – I don't believe you let it loose here intentionally."

Rashid squatted on the dusty ground. "That is the problem, the conundrum as you put it. I do not understand it. I finished my experiment five months before we arrived, and I successfully oxidised all of the proto-matter. The lab equipment on the Phoenix was first class, and it was still contained. Until…"

Pierre held onto his patience – though he'd lost track of time. He hoped Blake wouldn't come out to interrogate Rashid right now, or the information might retreat again.

"… Azil attacked me. When he sent the Phoenix into a spin, many things were loose and the reacted proto-matter container was smashed. But still – it was completely oxidized – an inert dust, it should not have reacted with anything."

Pierre examined him. He knew Rashid was, like himself, an avid scientist, and that his feelings of guilt had blinded him to the obvious.

He chose not to corral him towards the answer like his father would have done – he wanted to help him arrive. This was no game or after-dinner lesson now, the stakes were far higher.

"Rashid," he spoke softly, "it didn't have to react with anything, did it?"

Still Rashid could not cross the inferential chasm which Pierre had already vaulted. Kat chipped in.

"If it wasn't reactive, Pierre, how could it cause a desert?"

He turned to her. "Where does the desert come from?"

She shrugged.

"Look around you, what do you see?"

Without looking around, she answered matter of fact. "Trees, rocks, grass, bushes, lakes in the distance, and an orange desert. And a side of you I've not seen before."

Pierre cleared his throat. "What do *you* see, Rashid?"

Rashid surveyed the terrain.

"I see a virgin world with no animals – I see a land that looks fertile but is sterile. It should be our new home but it is not – it is alien. It is – *a fiction.*"

How apt, Pierre thought. Rashid had finally accepted what he must have unconsciously suspected for months. But Kat stood up, annoyed, propping the rifle against the chair.

"A fiction? Come on guys. Can I please join the party? What on earth's that supposed to mean?"

Pierre's legs felt weak; he'd just discovered what he was standing on, what this planet was. "It means," he said, "that this world has been created – most likely terraformed by the Q'Roth. Made to look like Earth – like Earth was."

Her voice lost its edge. "But why?"

Rashid sagged. "A trap. A beautiful snare. A whole planet used as a lure."

She focused on Pierre. "And the desert? How does that fit in?"

He said nothing, letting Rashid answer – he needed the catharsis after such a long time in denial. Rashid dug his hand into the soil, lifted it up, and spoke as it fell through his fingers. "My proto-matter was inert. It could not cause a reaction. But it could act as a catalyst. When I crashed here, the dust was scattered. One of the first things I did was to bury Azil. His body decaying, with even microscopic amounts of the dust as a catalyst, must have triggered a terraforming reversal or breakdown – a cascade effect dissolving the terraformed matter back into its original state. It means Eden was a dead world centuries ago, a barren desert planet."

Pierre watched Rashid's downcast face: he'd lost so much. It was a wonder he'd survived at all. "You shouldn't feel bad, Rashid. It's the one piece of hard evidence that must by now be visible all the way back to Hubble IV. People will start questioning this planet's true nature. After all, little point leaving one desertified planet for another. I'm also betting it saved your life."

Rashid regarded him quizzically, and then his brow broadened, another piece of the puzzle locking into place. "The eggs. Yes! The Q'Roth do not wish to risk contamination. They do not know if it is inert or not, only that it should not be here. Perhaps they are merely guardians, not scientists. They avoid the desert."

Pierre observed the cloud lift from Rashid, not unlike the transformation of the dawn minutes earlier. But the moment was jarred as out of the corner of his eye he saw Blake leap down the steps from the Lander as Zack, behind, tossed the shoulder cannon down to him. Blake mounted the weapon and aimed it at Kat. "Get down!" he bellowed.

Kat froze, but Rashid rugby-tackled her from the side, allowing Blake to fire.

Pierre didn't bother to check what he knew must be there; instead he dove for Kat's pulse rifle. He rolled and came up into a kneeling position to see their nemesis – the one that had chased him – at the edge of the scrub. He flicked the rifle into free-flow and held the trigger, squirting a jet of white-hot laser at the guardian, twenty metres away. Another solid pulse burst joined Pierre's – Zack's he presumed. The frenzied roar of the weapons made him crouch closer to the ground. He pulled harder on the trigger.

The creature had been stopped by the blinding ionised jets, but didn't disintegrate as it should do, its roar drowned in the grinding din, four of its six legs or arms flailing at them. Zack's beam tracked upwards, finding its vocal system, and the roar stalled. The pulse rifles began to overload, their jets stuttering. Blake's shoulder cannon charges pounded into its chest again and again, blasting them all with scalding shock waves that blew Pierre's hair back. He locked his knees into place with a determined fear – to turn and run would be fatal. He held on for another few seconds till the creature, shrouded in sheets of flame and billowing smoke, its skin glowing red hot, turned and galloped back up the hill.

"Cease-fire!" Blake commanded, and the noise stopped abruptly, leaving a ringing in Pierre's ears. Bushes all around them were either blackened or on fire. His skin tingled from the charged ozone all round them, feeling as if ants were crawling over his flesh. He lowered the rifle, careful not to touch the sizzling muzzle; the entire cartridge was spent. He got up and walked over to help Kat and Rashid up. Zack, clutching the ladder rungs with one hand to stabilize him, checked all around them with the heat-sensing binoculars. "Clear, Skip, it's heading back up the hill, moving damned quick, too."

Kat shot Blake an embarrassed look. But Pierre had been senior officer outside; he knew what was coming.

"So, Pierre," – Blake's voice was barbed wire – "tell me you weren't discussing the weather."

"No, Sir. We've worked it out. It's cleared up now." He gave a slight nod of his head towards Rashid, to convey that Rashid was not a risk to them. He felt Blake's stare for a while. Blake then addressed Kat.

"Corporal – the radar was *on*, wasn't it?"

She looked accusingly at the monitor; Pierre worried she might put her foot through it. "Definitely."

Blake shook his head. "Zack, stay out here and keep watch." He paused, glancing at Pierre. "And Zack – issue Rashid with a pulse rifle. I want this scrub cleared another thirty metres from the ship, so we have a few more seconds' reaction time."

Kat butted in. "What if it attacks at night? If our radar can't see it…"

Blake held up a hand. "Change in tactics. We're not waiting for it, or them, to come here anymore. We're going on the offensive. Pierre, you're with me." He climbed the steps and disappeared into the ship.

* * *

Pierre trudged along after Blake, his sweat absorbed by the chameleon all-terrain suit, his back-pack jiggling around on his back despite having pulled the straps tight as they'd go without chafing his armpits. They jogged their way up the escarpment in the tepid afternoon sun. He kept having to look down to ensure he didn't trip over the small rocks peppering the grassy hill; which meant he had less time to scan for the creature. Each time one of the black-leaved trees loomed ahead he cocked his head sideways a moment to check nothing was hiding behind it, although the trunks were not really wide enough, and the trees themselves were barely taller than he was. They looked like beech. The artistry was impressive, even if something had gone awry with the colour rendering; he had no doubt anymore that the Q'Roth had visited Earth at some point in the past. He shivered inside his suit as a bead of sweat evaded the absorbent lining and coasted down his spine.

His breathing was laboured keeping up with Blake; he realised he should have exercised more during the twelve-week trip, as Blake had done. Blake was pulling away again. Pierre nudged up a gear, pushing his front thighs down harder to lengthen his pace.

The five of them had all agreed they needed to take back tangible proof to Earth. The only discussion, such as it was before Blake made the executive decision, was what constituted evidence. Blake and Zack had already pre-agreed it, Pierre was certain. Although the others said it was too dangerous, Blake's final argument – that it would have to be something clear enough to convince himself if he were back on Earth – had won the "debate."

Pierre hadn't treasure-hunted eggs since a kid, but there had been no three-metre tall guardians before, and this felt more like Russian roulette. Rashid and Kat had taken the skimmer to go back and rig the Phoenix neutralino detonator with a 12 hour silent timer, to accelerate the desertification process, since its effects would be visible to Hubble IV – so that even if something happened to all of them, the people back on Earth would hold back from approaching the planet.

Pierre tried to ease the tension out of his shoulders, but it was difficult: last time, he'd been sprinting down it in high gear in the opposite direction, as if he'd been immersed in Kat's nightmare. Still, the logic was clear – Blake believed they were near the eggs. Otherwise, they would have been left alone by the guardian. Pierre must have been very close, causing the guardian to come out to kill him.

He was impressed by Blake's stamina as they breached the tree-line. He just kept going, not pausing or looking around while on the move, not even stopping to wipe off the sweat. He never tripped, although he didn't seem to watch the terrain.

They'd taken a circuitous route, in order to approach the position where Pierre had been attacked from the rear, rather than taking a direct assault, and had reached the upper escarpment. Blake slowed to a halt, slung off his backpack, wiped his brow and pulled out his flask of water. Pierre caught him up and slumped to the ground, retrieving his own water container.

'Five minutes,' Blake said, remaining standing, hands on his waist as he scanned the horizon.

Pierre winced. His thighs reprimanded him for the relentless pace of the past hour's trek. As he placed his backpack on the ground, he noticed Blake glance at it.

"I see you've slung your knife commando style, like Zack."

Pierre recalled the ghoster encounter. "Well, I wouldn't be much of a scientist if I didn't learn anything, would I?"

"You think only scientists learn? Military engagements are the toughest teacher there is, and you only get one shot, sometimes not even get that."

He sighed. That wasn't what I meant. Can't you see when I'm trying to build a bridge?

"So tell me, Pierre, have you learned anything from its blood yet?"

He took a swig of tepid water before answering. He wanted more, but resisted.

"Nothing conclusive: hyper-dense molecular structure – the Lander auto-lab is still trying to break down its genetic code. Not from Earth, though. Its DNA, if that's even what it is, is very different."

Blake smiled. "Well, that's a relief, I suppose."

Pierre was always a little nervous when Blake smiled at him. For one thing he wasn't used to it, and for another, it usually preceded something ominous.

"You trust Rashid, Pierre?" Blake's eyes bore into him.

There was no way to lie, but this time he didn't have to. "I trust him enough to take him back with us, if that's what you mean." He wasn't going to pretend this was idle banter, and knew that Rashid's life – or to be more precise his ticket home – hung in the balance.

Blake spared a little water onto his self-cleaning kerchief and wiped his forehead with it, then the back of his neck. "Still, he concealed quite a few things from us. Not to mention he pulled a pistol on me."

He wanted to head this off straight away, and took a gamble. "Sir, we all hide things, don't we?"

Blake's hand slowed down a moment, before slipping the kerchief back into a pocket.

Pierre pressed on. "I wasn't there when you were in the remains of his ship, but my understanding is that he was ensuring you heard the truth – as he believed it to be – from the Hohash. He probably thought that if he didn't have you under a pistol, you'd have blasted it as soon as it came within view."

Blake remained poker-faced. "You like him, don't you? More your kind than I am, I mean – or Zack for that matter."

Pierre cringed inside – he hated this type of discussion. No logic – all gut feeling and impressions. "Sir – all I know is that he would be the first one to volunteer to remain here if we decided only four could go."

"I'll remember that." Blake closed his flask tight, stashed it in his backpack, and picked up his weapon. "Shall we, Lieutenant?"

Pierre got to his feet, suppressing aches he hoped would disappear after ten paces, only to resurface more assiduously the next time they stopped.

They lay prone on a ridge, surveying the area below where he'd been earlier, and where the guardian had first been sighted.

"What's our plan exactly, Sir?"

Blake put his binoculars down and gave him a smile that seemed genuine this time. "Zack's going to get its attention, and then we're going into its lair."

Pierre regretted asking.

Ten minutes later, Zack charged up the escarpment on the skimmer, yelling as he came. Pierre strained to hear the words in the breezeless air, and then didn't bother, as they were more colour than content, the word "motherfucker" serving as the general refrain. "Why does he do that?"

Blake was tracking it all through his binoculars. "I remember a cadet asking him that very question, so I'll tell you what Zack told him. He said the difference between a yell and a scream is simply a matter of who starts first, you or the enemy."

Pierre dismissed the idea as the sort of nonsense you tell cadets to make them trust you. He scanned to see where the guardian would come from. Blake spotted it first.

"Two o'clock, three bushes in a triangle, a small tree to the right." Blake said quietly, then with a flick of the microphone, "Zack – he's in your ten o'clock."

They watched as Zack headed right for the creature. Pierre actually thought he was going to ram it, but a second before contact, Zack flipped the skimmer one-eighty, catching the guardian in a focused jet stream, and accelerated away in the opposite direction. It followed in hot pursuit. *God, it was fast!*

"Not so smart," Blake said. "Let's go."

They stole down the hill using as much boulder and tree cover as possible. In two minutes they reached the place where the Q'Roth had emerged. A gaping hole loomed before their feet: a downward channel about a metre wide, and three high, descending into darkness; a ramp to hell, Pierre thought. Blake pulled out his torch and fixed it to his rifle. Pierre copied him, with less practised movements, and followed him inside.

As they jogged through the channel that was far taller than they needed, it only reminded Pierre of their size relative to the creature. The passageway was clearly not natural – the walls smooth, uniform, and dry. There was a strange smell of rancid citrus fruit. Worse was the noise their footfalls made, echoing both backwards and forwards into the tunnel. *If there was another guardian inside…* He gripped his rifle tighter, and checked he could reach the knife handle in his backpack.

It felt like venturing down the oesophagus of some sleeping leviathan. They continued two full minutes descending into the hill at a steep incline – it was going to be tricky getting out of there – it wouldn't be a fast exit. The thought occurred to him that Blake might be on some kind of one-way ticket, armed with as many explosives as he could carry. Pierre didn't want to think that he might end here, inside an alien burrow. He tried to concentrate, praying for an end to this nightmarish corridor that was playing havoc with his nerves, and hoping that Zack was still infuriating – and therefore occupying – the creature.

Blake skidded to a stop in front of Pierre and held out his arm. Pierre managed to stop just in time, on the edge of a precipice, as they entered a cathedral-like chamber. Sharp cracks stabbed the silence, as small rocks they had just pushed over the edge tumbled to the bottom, landing within a couple of seconds. Tardy, deeper echoes told him the vastness of this subterranean cavity, the torch beams dissipating hopelessly in the dark void. Blake put down his rifle and extracted a stubby pistol from his backpack. He lifted his arm and fired a magnesium spike flare upwards into the middle of the cavern. It found purchase in the massive domed ceiling, illuminating the cavern in a ghoulish twilight.

Pierre looked down below, across the plain stretching out before them. "Eggs," he said, a hollow feeling in his stomach; eggs, as far as he could see. But they had been cruelly misled by the Hohash image. It was almost a joke. Steal an egg, they'd decided. As if they could put one in their rucksacks. Pierre recalled that when Blake had seen the Hohash image, there had been no frame of reference. He gazed at the nearest row. Each egg was twice the height and width of a man.

He switched into scientist mode, to allay the welling-up of fear. He cleared his throat. "They must hatch fully grown. Makes ecological sense for a predator."

Blake crouched on the solid-rock floor, and tossed a pebble over the side of the small cliff. He pulled out a navcon from his backpack and swept the surrounding area, before the light from the flare dimmed. When it sputtered and died, it felt worse to Pierre – not seeing the silent arrays of eggs, yet knowing they were there.

"The navcon has ninety-five per cent of the image," Blake said.

They both retrieved and donned their goggles, and switched off their torches, plunging themselves into abyssal darkness. Pierre flicked a switch on his goggles and instantly could see pretty much what he'd been able to see in the fullness of the flare a minute before, whichever way he moved or turned his head. Pierre recalled this gadget had come close to getting the Nobel Tech prize. He reckoned it should have won.

He activated his transponder, so the navcon could map their relative positions and overlay them onto the recorded scene, stopping them from bumping into each other. Peering over the edge again, he saw the eggs – large and rugged-looking, sitting upright. Of course he was seeing where they were, and was assuming – hoping – that nothing was moving down there.

Pierre heard Blake remove his goggles briefly, so he did too, flicking his torch on.

"Motion sensor," Blake said, lobbing a small device back into the tunnel behind them. He then took out a self-burying eye-bolt, placed it on the rocky floor, touched the two-second primer, and stood back. With a sound like an underwater gunshot, it fired itself into the stone with a reassuring thud. He attached the auto-feed wire system to the eyebolt via a karabiner and replaced his goggles.

"Wait twenty seconds, then follow."

He swung himself smoothly over the edge and abseiled down.

Pierre counted to twenty, attached his own auto-descent system to the wire, and replaced his goggles. He backed toward the edge. He thought he heard something, a distant rumbling, coming from the entrance. Uselessly, he looked toward it, but of course the goggles could show no movement. He leant back, bent his knees, and kicked off, propelling himself away and down the cliff-face.

A shrill electronic whine, rising in tone, made him misjudge his descent, and his knees smashed into the cliff face, stinging with pain – the motion detector had sensed something approaching, fast. The whine was drowned out by the creature's roar, and it felt to Pierre as if the whole chamber vibrated. He pressed the freefall button on his harness and dropped faster, but was suddenly yanked upwards. Pebble-sized rocks pummelled his head and shoulders.

"Cut the line!" Blake shouted from below.

In disbelief Pierre looked upward and saw nothing, then raked his goggles down and managed to switch on his torch – the creature was hauling him up. He could see its trapezoidal head, the blood red breathing slits writhing on its black-blue face. The creature's roar made Pierre's hands freeze, clinging to the cord.

"Pierre! CUT – THE – LINE!"

He rose rapidly in jerks, a metre at a time, the creature's forelegs feverishly pulling up the line, like a spider reeling in a fly. Pierre could hardly breathe, as his right hand flailed behind him groping for the knife. His head bashed against the cliff face knocking his torch from his left hand as he tried to protect himself. He knew he had only a few more seconds. His outstretched right hand fingers brushed across the hilt and he gripped it with all his might. Another yank pulled him up almost to the ledge. With a yell not far short of a scream, he whipped the knife above his head and severed the line, feeling a gust of air as a claw lashed past his face. He freefell, hurling the knife sideways so he could lock his elbows around his neck and head, the creature's howl of fury chasing him as he tumbled into the darkness below.

Chapter 35

Confession

Micah forced apart leaden eye-lids. It felt like prizing open an old, soil-encrusted coffin, from the inside. For a moment he thought he was suffering déjà vu – he expected to find Louise leaning over him, and Vince there as well. But instead he looked up into the doe-brown eyes of Antonia. Their gaze locked for a moment as he detected a flicker of passion, and he dared to wish... But she pulled away and slapped his face. Hard.

"He's awake," she stated, her voice taut.

Micah felt four individual fingerprints stinging his cheek. He tried to sit up but his muscles weren't talking to him. For the second time in a week he momentarily feared he'd become paralysed. But he tried to calm himself – Antonia wouldn't be so harsh on him if he was. He could no longer see her, but another body, plumper and with features that should ideally be kept in the dark, loomed into view. Must be the nurse. She muttered in a Spanish dialect he didn't recognise, and fiddled with tubes he guessed were connected to him, moving her garish moon-face closer to his. He tried unsuccessfully to shrink into the pillow.

"You wake now?"

Micah always wondered why people said such obvious things. He decided he was too vulnerable not to humour her. "Yes."

She smiled, though he wished she would stop, at least with those teeth.

"You hungry?"

Micah thought about it. "No. How long?"

The face pulled back. She inspected the drips. "I get doctor, he explain everything. Eh! Que pasa? What *that* doing there? Bien, doctor must have reason." She seemed to be talking to herself. She leaned conspiratorially closer, her breath causing Micah to suspend respiration, and whispered louder than most people talked. "She mad with you." And like a sped-up eclipse she receded, revealing normality again.

I already worked that one out. He was about to sigh with relief when Antonia appeared above him. It didn't help that he felt drunk, tense and sentimental all at the same time – he wondered what they were pumping into him. Then he remembered – the booster – it had worn off. What had the doc said? Depression, emotional rollercoaster, best if you lay low for a couple of days, stay away from sharp objects and people you love...

"Antonia... Don't hit me again," he said, meaning it. Her face hovered, as stern as she could muster, he guessed.

"Slap. I slapped you. Hit and slap are different. Trust me."

He did. "Why? I mean why did you slap me?"

She shook her head in disgust and strode out of is line of sight. He heard a few steps and then nothing.

"Antonia – are you still there?" Silence. Micah could hear his heart pounding of its own accord, the faint sound of air conditioning, and a bubble from one of the many drips that were stopping him from feeling hungry and, he imagined, suppressing the pain. He couldn't quite remember how he got there, wherever "there" was. But the Antonia situation seemed more pressing. His thinking was confused, like an old style radio receiver that couldn't quite tune in.

"You and Louise. You've been – fucking. That's the word she used."

Shit! He knew the only way out was full disclosure. Well, partial disclosure at least. His head was swimming. He hadn't felt this bad since the morning after he turned eighteen. But as well as the physical withdrawal – like his insides had been raked out, mashed, and then glued back in – his emotions were haywire. He was brimming with self-doubt and self-loathing in equal measure, his life amounting to a heap of pathos. And a cliff-drop of sadness – he'd not felt this way since his sister Cindy, his only real childhood companion, was killed, and he stood at the funeral without a coffin, as she'd been ashed... His mind was all over the place. His head wasn't swimming, it was drowning. He tried to focus, to reach the surface. What had Antonia asked him? It wouldn't be good to lose track now. Thankfully, he remembered.

"Actually, she kind of..." he knew it was going to sound lame."She kind of pushed me into it. She's quite forceful, in the physical way, too." His brain succeeded in applying brakes to his mouth. He stared up at the ceiling. Maybe it would conveniently collapse right now. He imagined her face appearing there, moments before he experienced the difference between hit and slap. But her voice speared towards him from across the room.

"So, you're telling me now she raped you? That's just another sick male fantasy, Micah. You disgust me!" Her heels clopped over to his bedside, her face swinging into view – eyes hard, nostrils flaring.

"She knows about me and Kat, Micah. You told her I had a lover – well, I don't know how much you told her, but she forced it out of me. I trusted you, took you into my confidence, and you led that – that Chorazin bitch – to my deepest secret. What were you thinking?"

Good question. He tried to distance himself from this – he'd crossed a line, more than one, screwed up. But more importantly, he'd hurt her. His intestines wrapped themselves into a tourniquet. He didn't know what to say, but decided platitudes were better than nothing.

"I'm sorry. Believe me, Antonia." He meant it. He wanted to wake up again, somewhere, anywhere else, with the past few days erased.

She scrutinised him, then vanished from view again. "She threatened me with interrogation – deep profiling." Her shrill voice filled the small room. "She could put me in prison – you know how they work. And you placed me in that position. All so you could... so you could... fuck... that whore!"

The fact that he was sure she never swore was acid on the blade. He somehow knew she was not looking at him. A swell of remorse swept through him. This was booster-withdrawal-aided, but knowing that didn't help matters. But a part of him mounted a silent defence – he *had* been seduced by Louise, and he loved Antonia, yet she didn't love him. But another part of him, a cooler, more collected part – the analyst – asked himself why he had told Louise?

"Micah, I only told you because of Kat. I thought you agreed to help her, to help us?"

He gave up his internal self-defence. Somewhere in the back of his mind he saw his father shaking his head in dismay, disappointed with him yet again. Everything that had happened over the last few days surfed over him; the booster wasn't there anymore to buoy his confidence. His lips began to tremble so he forced them together. He felt a stinging in his eyes. *Not now*, he thought, *that's the last thing I need*, but the emotional storm sought release. He squeezed them shut, too late.

"She's up there, Micah!" she continued, in full flow. "Light years away, risking her life for all of us, and you don't – you don't give a shit! This isn't a game you know."

He heard her approach. He wished his neck would damn well respond, so she wouldn't see the tear burning a trail down his cheek. He sensed her standing right next to him. All he could hear was his own jagged breathing.

A cool finger touched his cheek. He felt the wetness between his face and her, a kind of amniotic connection. He squeezed his lips tight, his eyes still closed – if he opened them now, and saw sympathy or even empathy… He never wanted her to see him like this, like the small boy his father still taunted him from his grave that he would always be.

Cotton wool dabbed at his face, his eyes. The transitory vortex of self-pity and angst blew itself out, and he regained at least a fumbling control of his breathing. Sniffing once, he opened his eyelids, still wet from the inside, fearing what he might see. But her face had mollified. He saw a degree of confusion there, but at least the anger was gone.

"I'm – so – sorry, Antonia." The words came out naked. His own voice sounded foreign, the analyst switched off. "You have no idea. No idea what I've been through these past few days. And I'm trying, trying really hard," he sniffed again, and she dabbed at his cheek, "to save them all. And I would never – ever, do anything to hurt you. As for Louise – I honestly wish none of it had happened. It was you, Antonia, I –"

Another voice cut across the room. "Well, well, finally woken up, I see."

Micah stopped dead. Antonia whirled out of view.

"Why are you wearing that? Where's the doctor?" Antonia shouted.

There was a dull sound followed by a rustling.

Micah frowned. "Antonia?"

Louise loomed into view, a deadly calm expression that outdid Antonia's stern look any day of the year.

"What have you done to her?" Micah tried again to move, but nothing happened.

"You men are so dreadfully predictable, so pathetic. She doesn't love you, Micah." Louise flickered a smile. "Don't worry; your platonic friend is just KO'd for a short while. She was beginning to sound whiny, don't you think?" Louise perched herself on the bed next to him. "The question is whether to let her wake up or not." She paused to allow it to sink in. "And that depends on you, Micah. You see, I'm willing to make you a deal. Your life for hers."

Micah gaped at her. 'W-what do you mean? Why would you kill either of us? You're Chorazin… we're on the same side. Vince –"

The suddenness of the fist rocketing into his solar plexus was almost as much a shock as the blinding pain that occurred a second later. He couldn't breathe for a good twenty seconds, even as the nausea churned deep in his gut. At last he sucked in some air, as if through a straw.

"Vince isn't here. As for the Chorazin, you could say I just tendered my resignation. I'm playing for the winning side."

Although she glared down at him, there was still something, Micah thought, a strand of possible redemption in her eyes. "Then why," he rasped, "why did you, you know...? I thought you –"

Her face hardened. "You thought what, Micah? Don't think you know me. You haven't even scratched the surface. Vince and I were an item for two years, but he barely understands what I'm capable of."

Micah didn't doubt it. He recalled Rudi's devastated Optron landscape, wondering if that was what it was like inside her, ruined beyond redemption.

"First things first," she resumed, "do you love the Slovakian waif lying unconscious on the floor?" She arched her eyebrows as she waited for the answer.

Micah was nonplussed. Could she be jealous? Ridiculous. Idle curiosity? He did his best to nod in the affirmative. He coughed, at long last getting serious air back into his lungs.

"I want to hear you say it, Micah, loud and clear."

"Why? What does it –?"

"Just between you and me."

Micah swallowed. He'd been on the point of confessing to Antonia when Louise arrived, though he had not been sure the words would ever have come out. Perhaps it would be good to say it to someone. Anyway, Antonia was knocked out on the floor...

"Okay. Yes, I love her. I've loved her from the first day I saw her."

"And yet you are going to try and re-unite her with her astronaut girlfriend?"

He scrutinised Louise. He didn't know what game this was, but he saw no other option for now than to play along. *She's probably going to kill me anyway.*

"Yes. I – I know she loves her, not me. I... I want... Well, I know you won't understand, Louise, but if she's happy and I'm not, then it's better than nothing." It sounded pretty sad even to him.

"I'll give you this, Micah, of all the losers I've met in my time, you have to be the most self-acknowledging of them all. A shame. I had my eye on you, you know. Thought you showed promise, that maybe we could save you. Would have been a lot of work, but... Never mind, your choice."

He detected a shift – whatever the something he'd seen in her regard for him before, was gone. She placed a thumb and forefinger on either side of his neck.

"Here's the deal. You tell me what you found out during your Optron run of Rudi's data crystal, and then I kill you. But she gets to wake up."

He looked at her incredulously. It was one thing to think someone might kill you but quite another to hear it from them, so cold, so matter-of-fact. But he recognized she was serious; he'd seen that look in the assassin's eyes too. Her right hand closed around his throat, thumb on one carotid artery, fingers on the other. Her other hand brought a pulse pistol into his line of sight as she waved it in what was presumably Antonia's prone direction.

"How do I know –?"

"That I won't kill her afterwards? Well, I've been undercover long enough, I've enjoyed my – sabbatical, let's say – at the Chorazin, but the agenda is moving faster now, and I've been recalled. Frankly, your little friend is inconsequential, and what she doesn't know won't hurt her, or in this case, won't get her killed. It's just between you and me, Micah. I like to make my business personal."

Micah knew he'd die, but he could save Antonia. It was something. "Okay," he said, voice firm.

"I want all of it, Micah. You lie for an instant, I'll kill you both, her first. And I'll see it if you're holding out on me."

Micah did his best to nod. Since waking he'd been aware that something had been downloaded into his brain during the Optron accident. It hung in his mind like a wrapped parcel waiting for him to access it, and he had the feeling it wasn't good news. Shutting out the external world, he switched into recall mode. He let the words pour out.

"When I crashed in Rudi's landscape, I blacked out, but it downloaded memories that weren't mine; I still don't know how... I saw partly through the data-stream hidden by the Kat simulacrum before it was destroyed by the virus, partly through Kat's own eyes, and also through something else's the rest of the time, what or who I have no idea. I witnessed the ghoster attack from the cockpit screens, which is where Kat was at the time, and her actions, which triggered the comms virus. I also saw what I believe was one of her nightmares, but it was very clear – she was being chased by a blue-black creature, a giant insect with six legs." Micah felt Louise's hand on his neck flex when he mentioned the creature. "Then she woke up, and I saw Zack through Kat's eyes, and then Pierre." He paused. So much had been downloaded. This was way beyond Rudi's expertise, or anyone else's.

"Resume," she said, flat.

He realised she was encoding it in her memory, word for word, maybe even the intonation – he'd seen the technique before, some analysts could do it – so she could relay it later. He continued; he couldn't afford to interrupt the flow. "Then, there was something else. It was very different, and I don't think it was seen by the crew, but by someone, or something more like – well, not human, at any rate." He flicked open his eyes to look at her, but she was just staring at him, and for the first time she looked somehow alien to him – or rather, she was looking at him as if he were an inferior being. He felt a chill run through him, as he grasped the truth about Louise. Her hand twitched, reminding him of the deal. He closed his eyes.

"It was somewhere else. I mean not Earth, nor Eden. This set of images had been lodged in the datastream before it finally disappeared, before the Kat simulacrum was disaggregated by the virus. It was a city – a beautiful city, with spider-like creatures..."

Micah re-counted the whole scene of the destruction of the planet, and then the scenes of the eggs and the two guardians on Eden. He stopped.

"Anything else?" Again, a flat, distant tone. *"Anything else?"* she repeated, squeezing his neck so that he felt a throb of blood pressure in his skull.

Micah thought about the old story he'd heard when he was a kid – A Thousand and One Arabian nights – but he had nothing more to tell, and Louise only wanted facts, not stories. "That's it."

She stood, fishing for something from a black doctor's bag, while one hand remained on his throat. Micah knew he had very little time. Since witnessing the creatures and the other-planet incursion, he'd been trying to put all the pieces together: the ships, the creatures, the Alicians. He had to ask. A name had been encoded in the message.

"These creatures – the Q'Roth –"

Her hand tightened around his throat. "Don't speak their name, Micah."

He coughed. "They're on Eden, but they're coming here, aren't they?"

She produced a syringe filled with a blue liquid, and spoke while she inspected it, tapping it with her second finger. "Some people go to Eden;

there is a first feed – a booster if you like, and then they come here for the main course." She stabbed the syringe into one of the drips above his head, her thumb poised on the plunger. "They're going to eradicate this pitiful, fatally flawed species, and crush this planet – but the best, with humanity's weaknesses genetically ironed out of us, will survive, start afresh. No more wars, Micah, no more injustice and corruption, no more hurting each other or our new planet."

She gave him one last look. Then she closed up like a fan. "Goodbye, Micah. This won't hurt, you'll just go to sleep and not wake up. But if you make a sound, I'll crush your vagus nerve and leave you to asphyxiate slowly."

Micah wondered what he should think about in his last few seconds of life.

He heard a loud popping sound. Hot blood rained down on him, a deep cavity appearing in the centre of Louise's forehead. He watched with a mixture of shock, revulsion and morbid fascination as she continued to stand for a second, a coin-sized cauterised hole above her right eyebrow, so that he could see charred brain matter inside, the smell of barbecued flesh assaulting his nostrils. She slumped out of his line of sight. He coughed as some of her blood trickled down his throat, and squinted painfully as more of it seeped into his eyes.

Vince, panting, appeared over him, sweat on his forehead.

"Christ that was close. I damn near ran all the way from the set-down point, once I found what she'd left of Abrahams. Had to down three of our own to get through the false security ring she'd placed around this ward." He caught his breath. "You okay, Micah?" Vince wiped most of the blood out of Micah's eyes with a piece of bed-linen.

"You killed her?" Micah said, still trying to come to terms with what had just happened. It was yet another obvious statement, but he needed to have it confirmed.

Vince paused and looked down at her, as if surprised at what he'd just done. "Reflex," he said. "No time to think about it. She was about to kill you, and believe me the girl would have been next." Vince tugged some of the tubes out of Micah's arm. He barely felt the pain.

"One of these drips is a neuro-muscular blocker – shouldn't be here – no doubt Louise inserted it yesterday – that's why you can't move."

Micah looked up at Vince, trying to gain his attention. "Vince – she wasn't going to kill Antonia – she knocked her out, so she didn't hear any of the stuff I got from the datastream."

Vince shook his head. "Antonia wasn't knocked out, Micah. Louise used a curare-based stun needle on her – she's been paralysed but conscious the whole time. Believe me; she was going to be killed straight after you."

Micah's mouth opened. Then it closed.

"I'll bring her round in a moment," Vince said. He moved close to Micah and whispered. "She must really like you, kid, looks like she was so worried about you she's been crying."

Micah nodded absently. His head felt heavy. Vince injected him with something and he immediately felt his muscles again. Vince helped him up into a sitting position.

"Stay there. Don't move." Vince pulled Louise's body to one side. He seemed to Micah to feel no remorse about killing her, but he decided, with Vince, you'd never know. Two more agents appeared at the door. Vince nodded to where Louise lay,

"Take her for autopsy straight away." As they manhandled her body, he added, "Hey – take it easy with her, for Christ's sake."

Micah observed the scene, surreal to him, as Louise's blood-drenched form, so full of life a minute ago, now a flaccid corpse, was hefted out of the room.

Vince stooped over Antonia, now in a chair facing Micah, and gave her an injection. Micah could see her half-glazed eyes, her face immobile and soft, no muscle tone. But her cheeks were stained. She stared in his direction. Micah didn't utter a word. He'd said more than enough already. Besides, he had no idea what she was thinking. But while everything else was being cleaned up around them, she never once broke his gaze.

Chapter 36

Sentinels

It had been a bloody day. Sentinel Master Cheveyo and his small team had racked up a death toll of twenty-six in the past twelve hours since he'd spoken to Gabriel – to secure transport, steal IVS identities and a nuke, and gain access to the IVS-found ship. They'd also cornered, questioned and then executed one of the Alician Inner Circle. The interrogation hadn't lasted long – the woman had almost wanted to tell Cheveyo how he and the rest of an inferior humanity would perish. He now understood the Alician-Q'Roth strategy. He did not know how many Q'Roth ships there were, but he was going to make sure at least one of them didn't return.

Cheveyo came from an Order that had been in existence almost as long as the Alicians, since the time a reptile-like Ranger had crash-landed in the Himalayas. Wounded, he'd been rescued by the local tribes people who worshipped all manner of animal gods. The Ranger later led them to the Q'Roth ship hidden beneath the glacier, where he knew he could get supplies to repair his own small craft. He – or she – took pity on the people of a doomed planet, and helped them understand the storm that was coming. The one thing the Ranger had impressed upon the original ten Order members, nine hundred years ago, was that when the Q'Roth came, it would be fast, the onslaught relentless.

He and Ramires, his last disciple, had replaced the Chief and First Officer of an IVS cargo ship laden with supplies. They stood on the bridge, Cheveyo at the helm, although the vessel was automatically piloted. They had just left the safety of Truk Lagoon, a natural shelter against the typhoon which had been hampering efforts to get near the Q'Roth ship, but was now dying down. Heavy rain pattered the ceiling as their jetfoil skirted over giant, lumbering waves to reach the site by nightfall.

Ramires interrupted his teacher's reflections. "Master, do you –"

"Do not call me that – not here."

Ramires, fifty years Cheveyo's junior, nodded at once, respectfully. "I understand the plan only to a point. We can board the Q'Roth ship – but the key – we do not have the key."

Cheveyo watched the rolling of the horizon, the spray spattering the bridge windshield, and found it calming. "The key will arrive. They want the ships to go to Eden – they serve no purpose if they remain here."

"I see," Ramires said, though Cheveyo detected the hint of doubt. That was good. He had never wanted acolytes to follow every word – that was the Alician way. A blindly obedient mind was useless to the Sentinels.

"Our paths must separate: you will head back to your part of the world, to the ship that was found yesterday."

Ramires was about to protest, but Cheveyo held up a hand. "We are very few now. I do not know if any other cells of the Order have survived the recent Alician purge."

Ramires frowned. "But what if –"

"What if?" Cheveyo rounded on him. "Have you learned nothing from me all these years? What if? That is the realm where resolve founders on the rocks." He handed Ramires a flight chip and a metallic object that looked like a thin metallic torch.

"Your apprenticeship is over. When we dock, take the IVS jet back to Manila, steal another and fly direct to Cocos. From there you are on your own. Board the ship by whatever means possible, and ensure it is appropriately loaded."

Ramires stared at the thin metal cylinder cradled in his hands. He bowed deeply. Cheveyo knew Ramires' apprenticeship was ending prematurely – in truth he was not ready. But they were out of time.

The resurrected ship reared up on the horizon, growing larger as they crested each Pacific swell. Cheveyo had been inside one beneath the glacier, but had never seen one in its massive entirety. Charcoal in colour, it looked like a metal cake with triangular portions missing, a tower extruding upwards from its middle. He did a quick mental calculation of how many people it could carry, and didn't like the number. The huge, matt object had a distinct 'other-ness' about it, as if superimposed digitally onto the seascape. Barely moving despite the weather, and with the sun behind it, it resembled a barren volcanic island. The waves lashed against it, as if nature abhorred this harbinger of Earth's destruction.

As they grew nearer, he noticed that no sea-birds landed on it, or even approached it, instead remaining in flight or resting on the dwarfed flotilla of IVS ships rocking slowly in the Q'Roth ship's shade. He was reminded by something his Master had once told him: nature's instincts are less easily fooled than human intellect.

The disconcerting aspect was that eighty per cent of the ship was still underwater. He presumed this vessel was identical on the inside to the one he had explored numerous times over the years since a child. He closed his eyes and visualised the conning tower, containing several rooms that controlled the ship, with a surrounding spiral ramp accessing all levels except a central core beneath the tower. This area was believed to house the engine that no one except the Ranger had ever seen.

Each of the seven main levels of the ship beneath tower level had a ceiling four metres high, forming a honeycomb of interconnecting rooms of various shapes and sizes. One of his childhood friends had gotten lost in the ship under the glacier; it had taken three days for the Order to find him, perished from hypothermia.

He now knew it would take people to Eden, but return full of strengthened Q'Roth. For a moment he wondered if people would really board such a behemoth – it was like persuading sardines to climb into a tin can. But rumours already abounded that people were flocking to the new-found ship encrusted in one of the Willow Pattern Mountains of Guilin, China, and another in Central Australia. The promise of Eden, and the current plight of humanity, had worn people to the point they could overcome their better judgement and see salvation in a vessel so hideously bleak.

As the autopilot steered them towards the docking barge adjoining the ship, they were boarded by officials to have their papers and cargo checked. Ramires turned to his Master of the past fifteen years, his face locked down to show none of the emotions Cheveyo knew churned on the inside.

"Die well," was all Ramires said, the obligatory Sentinel farewell, and without awaiting a reply he left to find the small boat that would take him to the IVS command ship.

Cheveyo smiled as he watched his last surviving student leave. I was wrong about you, Ramires; your apprenticeship is over. Live well. It would be good if at least one of the Order survives.

* * *

Jennifer squatted on her haunches in the makeshift bedroom she shared onboard the Q'Roth ship with Dimitri. Alone, having just finished an advanced karate kata, sweat glistened on her brow, the breezeless air clinging to her skin. She never showed this side of her character to Dimitri. She paused before the final kata in the series, recalling a conversation with him.

"I love the way you outsmart people, Jennifer – you see through the words to what they are really thinking, and you cut them up marvellously. Even people who are more intelligent than you" – she'd inwardly winced – "you outsmart, staying several steps ahead of them. It really annoys them!"

Yes, she'd thought at the time, that's why I never get invited to parties, and have almost no friends. But she recalled the rest.

"I have had beautiful girlfriends, models… But I prefer you, your mind – and of course I love your physical assets, but it's your mind I love. That will never fade."

She stood motionless remembering how she had felt: getting what she had wanted, but with barbs attached. Was she that unattractive? She launched into the seventh and final kata with renewed energy, finishing with a heartfelt *kiai* shout that managed to dredge an echo from the dank, dark walls.

She headed for the makeshift shower in the room next door, walking along the floor of the ship that was the same mouldy mottled grey as the walls, and was like dead skin to the touch. The walls seemed to suck in sound. Although space heaters had been installed on two floors to house the thirty or so engineers and scientists working aboard the ship, as well as aircon units to protect the bio-computers they were using to understand how the vessel worked, nothing seemed to allay the relentless cold. The lack of corners anywhere on this ship, giving all the rooms an oval feel, made it seem like an insect's lair; or maybe a nest. She turned the shower to very hot, scalding the sweat from her body.

She dried off and donned a purple IVS jumpsuit, and went to find Dimitri. But as she neared what had been designated the main control room in the tower, she heard raised voices. Not listening to the words, instead she searched for Dimitri's signature Greek accent. Sure enough she found it – his was the only voice that remained quiet, though she was sure he was infuriating the other engineers. She peeked into the room.

"Hell, Kostakis," Hendriks, the Chief IVS Engineer, shouted. "For the love of God, we can't just throw the damned switch! We don't have a clue what will happen. The simulations –"

"Simulations?" Kostakis threw the straight-standing, balding man an incredulous look. "Simulations you say? Listen to yourself. You might as well run a sex-vid – it would just as likely be a reliable simulation of this ship's engines! We have not even found the engines yet." He fingered his goatee, shaking his head in dismay. "Hendriks, my dear fellow, do you know the difference between an engineer and a scientist?"

"You mean besides the fat salary and the female students?"

Hendriks had clearly had enough, Jennifer thought, as she edged into the room – when people get really angry, that's when they speak their mind. She watched the two men hold their ground in the face-off, six other engineers around them trying their best to melt into the background.

Dimitri bridled at the insult. He smiled broadly. "Yes, besides those things and other... perks." He paused to let the reversal take its full effect. "It's that you engineers approximate, that's all you ever do, and you always stay within your limited paradigm. You never try to understand anything first, or embrace something truly new – something alien!"

Hendriks thwacked his hand down on a small metallic table. "Well, the way I heard it most scientists believe in data, analysis and prudence – you want to switch this thing on and that's your whole fucking experimental paradigm – trial and error – a bit of adventure! Crap! You want the glory without the hard work, and that's the approach of a charlatan, not a scientist!"

Jennifer darted towards them as Dimitri's bulk closed on Hendriks – she'd never seen him violent, but no one ever talked to him that way either.

"Gentlemen – please." She parked herself between them with her small frame and muscular arms. "If I may suggest, it seems to me we need some division of labour here. We have to get the engine online and figure out the navigation system before we try to go anywhere, to see exactly where we'll end up, whether we'll hit any stars en route, and to know how to get back."

Neither of them looked down at her; they stood like two boxers before the first round, anxious to throw the first punch. Hendriks broke gaze first. "Ging, Wu, Araceli: you work with the Professor on the Nav system. I want a protocol by nightfall, not a fucking roulette system. Garrett, Cintati, Sokolov: you're with me."

Jennifer lowered her arms, and turned to her lover, his barrel chest heaving. She could see he'd been bruised this time. After a few seconds, he stopped glaring in Hendriks' direction and at last seemed to notice her. His face metamorphosed. He beamed at her, holding out his arms. "Thank you, my dear Jennifer. What would I do without you?"

She took his hands in hers, and started walking towards the navigational console. As she led him there, she caught a glimpse of an older man who had been standing just outside the room. He turned away, helping another three men lift a large crate onto a levi panel, manoeuvring it down to a lower level. She noticed that despite his age, he seemed to be stronger than the young men. Something about them wasn't right – but it would have to wait.

Two hours later, an uneasy truce hovered in the control room. Slow but measured progress was being gained by both teams, and a light chatter permeated the room, signifying a cessation of hostilities. Jennifer decided to see where the men with the crate had gone. She hadn't felt like asking Hendriks.

Descending to the foot of the tower, to what appeared to be a smaller control room whose function they had yet to ascertain, she walked in alone, wrapping herself in the silence, wondering how long this vessel had lain at the bottom of the ocean, empty, waiting. The engineers had had a real hard time dating it, since nothing stuck to it, and they couldn't even dent the metal. On being pressed, one of the engineers had stated that it was somewhere between a thousand and a hundred thousand years old; that was the best he could tell.

The absolute quiet she revelled in was punctured by the sound of fast, furtive footsteps. She remained still in the darkness as three people in rain gear slipped past the entrance heading down to the next level. She waited ten seconds and then sidled out quietly to follow the trio at a distance.

She was surprised how quickly they moved. She was tempted to try and catch up but her wartime instincts stopped her – it could be a trap – they were probably waiting quietly to see if anyone followed. She froze and held her breath, and began counting. When she got to thirty, the muffled sound of steps on the ramp below her resumed, descending further. Only when she reached sixty did she breathe in, slowly. Adrenaline surged, reminding her of the hide-and-seek med-evac runs she'd made in the ruins of radioactive Dublin, evading hunter-seeker robots.

The idea of going to get help surfaced and then submerged, partly because she knew she would lose them if she did that, but mainly because she never relied on anyone, not even Dimitri, not since she'd lost her family to the War.

She ran her hand over her right trouser pocket – the small stiletto knife she always carried was still there. Taking off her shoes, she continued barefoot. The floor in the second main level was clammy. A sheath covered all the metallic floors, walls and ceilings, like transparent linoleum. It gave everyone the creeps.

At the bottom, she saw the three figures receding into darkness across a vast chamber the size of a football field. The illumination was sporadic, cones of mustard light cascading downwards every ten metres. Jennifer knew she could follow them as long as she stayed about fifty metres behind, keeping between the circles of light on the floor. After a few minutes, she saw them approaching the opposite wall. Squinting in the half-light, she tried to see where they were going, wishing she had night goggles. As far as she could remember from her brief and futile foraging excursions when trapped inside the ship before it surfaced, there was only a blank wall. She struggled to see them at all, then realized they had vanished.

When she arrived at the wall, she looked for an opening, a crack, anything – but the wall and floor were seamless like the rest of the ship, as if the vessel had been hewn out of one piece of metal – or grown in some way. But where did they go? There was only one thing for it, she decided. She went to knock on the wall – and nearly stumbled straight through the holographic image as her hand disappeared. As she stared at her arm cut off at the elbow, someone grabbed her wrist and yanked her through the illusion – despite herself she shut her eyes and tensed up. She hit the ground hard and found herself staring up at the three people she had seen earlier, but they looked different now, standing proud, haughty, and it came to her instantly – Alicians.

"It's her," a woman said, her voice scornful. "The one they told us about."

Jennifer didn't like the sound of that. She'd seen enough in the War to recognise killers. She made as if to get up, in a way that would allow someone to kick her if they wanted to, and at the same time eased the stiletto out of her pocket. She hoped they would want to inflict pain before shooting her, or else she was dead meat. Looking small and defenceless had its peculiar advantages, she had learned since being bullied at school

– it brought out the worst in people, they just couldn't let an opportunity go by to kick someone when they were down.

"Kill her," the woman said, accompanied by, as she'd suspected, a boot aimed at her face. Jennifer ducked back down and the foot met not her face, but the stiletto, which pierced the heel up to the ankle as cleanly as a syringe. Jennifer hoped the scream that followed was loud enough to attract attention. She launched herself upwards and head-butted one of the two men in the groin just as he drew a pulse pistol. He made a deep grunting noise as he toppled onto her. She hadn't anticipated it well enough, and his weight collapsed onto her, pinning her down. Even as she wrestled for his pistol, another foot kicked it aside.

"I said kill her!" The woman's voice was shrill and full of rage. Jennifer considered her options and decided there was none other than dying. She heard three rapid swishes and then several heavy thuds, and what sounded like liquid squirting and then trickling onto the floor. Suddenly the weight of the man on top of her was removed, and blood gushed over her torso. Her hand was next to the head of the woman, its eyes frozen in shock. Two other heads lay on the floor, eyes gawping, mouths agape. The only man standing was the old man she had seen earlier. He didn't look at her. He scanned the room. An electric blue sword-length blade hung from his left hand, a torch from his right.

He flicked something on the hilt and the blade disappeared. She stared up at him. "Nice weapon." She glanced at her stiletto, protruding out of the dead woman's boot. "Wanna trade?"

"Get up, Jennifer, time to go."

She struggled to her feet, almost slipping in the blood. "Everyone seems to know me, but I don't know anyone. It's like being at a surprise party, only the surprises aren't very pleasant."

He knelt over the dead woman and snatched an ankh pendant from around her neck.

"Souvenir?" Jennifer asked. "Trophy?" She retrieved her stiletto, with a slurping sound.

"I bring bad news."

She managed one laugh. "Bad news? You mean this is good?"

His glare silenced her mocking tone.

"Gabriel sent me. He is dead."

Jennifer staggered, almost tripping over one of the heads. "What? He's... What are you talking about? And what do you know about my brother?" Visions from the previous night's nightmare re-surfaced.

"He's gone, Jennifer. I spoke to him yesterday, but Alicians – like these – killed him."

She balled her fists, sensed the blood rushing to her head. "Why are you doing this? Who the fuck are you, anyway? My brother died in the War years ago. He was a hero, he was –"

"Grimelda."

She paled. "What... what did you say?" her voice was uneven, her legs weakened beneath her.

"He told me that he once called you by that name, to annoy you. It usually worked. You broke his nose on the lake with an oar. He said he never told anyone you did it. He sent me to look out for you."

Her body trembled. She felt herself lose control, the rage boiling inside her. "Liar!" she screamed at him. "Bastard liar!" She lunged at him with the stiletto. He caught her hand in a vice-like grip and pinned it in mid air, centimetres from his neck, his eyes stone calm. With her other hand, and then her feet and her knee she attacked him, landing hefty blows that would have brought anyone else to the floor in agony. But he stood, taking it until her wrath wore itself out. He shook her by her arm.

"He only found out you were alive yesterday. He loved you. You were the only one he ever loved."

She was silent except for her serrated breath, her head bowed. He still held her stiletto hand. She let the stiletto fall. He released her, and she sank to the floor, head clasped in her hands.

"People are coming from the tower," he said. "We will talk more later. Gabriel had a mission. The war is not finished against his enemies – our enemies. You will see me again." He let go of her hand and vanished through the holographic wall.

She was drenched in someone else's blood. Dimitri's voice boomed out, calling for her, frantically shouting her name. She listened to him call her name several more times before she got up and walked through the holo-wall.

"Over here!" She brushed away tears, not caring that she smeared blood in their place. "I'm over here!"

Later, alone in their cabin, she told Dimitri everything. He implored her to leave the ship, but she refused. It was two in the morning and she was still wide awake. Dimitri was dog-tired, but refused to sleep.

She felt as if she'd just noticed she'd lost a limb. The worst thing was, if that man was telling the truth, and if Gabriel had only found out she was alive before he – died – then he would have been as warped as she was now. All that lost time they could have had together.

She had often thought their relationship mirrored that between Caligula and his sister – without the incest – a blood-bond intensity that surpassed any other relationship. She closed her eyes and tried to feel his presence, but couldn't. It was like a sound you didn't notice until it was switched off. All these years she had drawn confidence from him, maybe because at some unconscious level she knew he was still alive, and now he was gone.

Dimitri, his eyelids bloodhound heavy, stirred and squeezed her again, his bear-like paws wrapped around her unresponsive body. It didn't comfort her, but maybe, she thought, it was stopping her going over the edge. But it wasn't – she grasped that it was actually holding her back from dealing with this. She pretended to sleep, and sure enough, a few minutes later Dimitri began to snore. She eased herself from his loosened grip and slipped outside their tent.

She went to the lower control room, inhaling deeply the moist air. Now at least she could be alone with her thoughts. And with her brother. She sat on the cold floor and fingered her necklace. She didn't need to look at the picture inside of her brother – she knew every line and hollow of his face. "Gabriel," she said, "I never told you how –." Her neck prickled. She sprang to her feet.

"You!" It was the old man, right behind her. She hadn't heard him enter, and had just suddenly become aware he was there – she had a suspicion it was only because he'd allowed her to. Although she didn't trust him, she wanted to know more about him, and her brother. Anything he could tell her would be hard currency.

He squatted, tracing a circle on the floor with the hilt of his nano-sword – she'd thought they were an old War-myth – etching a pattern on the surface that was like a tarpaulin stretched taut.

She squatted too, studying his features: grey hair, clear complexion, white moustache and beard, and sandalwood eyes – she hadn't noticed until now. They accented his composure. No matter what this man did on the outside, she knew he inhabited the eye of the storm on the inside. But she wanted information, facts to paint over the vacuum of ten years of lost connection with Gabriel.

"My name is Cheveyo."

"You trained my brother, didn't you?"

"My best pupil."

"Assassin?"

318

"Cleanser."

She was both stunned and proud – it was rumoured only one in twenty survived the training. "Many enemies?" She didn't take her eyes off him for even a moment.

"One snake, many heads."

She made an effort to play out this game – using statements, not questions – to be equals. He was not *her* teacher. And she had the feeling he would only accept fiercely independent-minded students in any case.

"But the snake is still alive."

He carried on drawing patterns.

She felt a new sense of purpose – Gabriel was back somewhere in her universe again, part of her life, defining her as he used to. All the past ten years: of failed Chorazin entrance, of being a student biding her time – squandering it – loving a man but having to hide part of herself – the real her – to keep Dimitri – all this suddenly dropped from her, like cinders.

"Who do I kill?" she said, cold-blooded, slipping effortlessly back into Dublin gang-mode.

He met her eyes head on. "You think you are smarter than you are. That is a danger."

She bristled. "I *am* smart! It's not just my studies. I saw you earlier. You didn't look right, something was out of place."

"You think you notice things others do not."

She wanted to get up; her thighs hurt, but she knew that would somehow be defeat. She was in some kind of interview, and if she failed, this man, the one link to her brother, would be gone. But she knew she *was* smarter than other people.

"I see things others don't."

The reply was instant, which annoyed her, because she was stuck following his script, which wasn't how it usually went.

"All others? The men I was with, for example?"

She was about to snort with contempt, and say *well, of bloody course!* Then it dawned on her that she had been tricked.

"Ah," he said, "progress. What really happened this afternoon, Jennifer?"

She concentrated, suppressing the burning sensation in her thighs. She had missed something – no – she had been misdirected. She'd focused on him alone, not the others. But they were normal – weren't they? Just some guys lifting a crate. *The crate - what was in the crate?* It crystallised in her mind.

"You've loaded a nuke on board!"

He rose as easily as if gravity was suddenly working in reverse, but did not extend a hand to help her up as she followed suit. He put his hand under her chin, and held it there. "What was I doing just now?"

Instinctively her head tried to move downwards to see what he had drawn, but the hand under her chin was iron.

"Nothing I do is without purpose, Jennifer. Nothing anyone does is without meaning. You must observe, and you must perceive – foreground, background, the threads between. You do see more than others, but your ghosts get in the way." He let go of her chin. For once, she knew she'd met more than her match.

She had to redeem herself. "How long have we got?"

"Where would you like to go?"

"That little time, eh?" She pursed her lips for a moment. "To the snake's lair."

She grinned – it was the sort of game she and Gabriel would have played – should have played, together. He had been playing without her for a decade, but now she would finish his hand. He would watch from somewhere, maybe applaud. *God, how she'd missed him.*

Cheveyo flicked his eyes downwards. She looked at the pattern he had been drawing. It was a kind of insect, one she couldn't identify, and next to it the ankh.

"The enemy." She understood; it all fitted together. "The owners – the true passengers of this ship."

"You are indeed smart. Gabriel told me that once – intuitive almost to the point of prescient. But knowledge divorced from action is academic. Are you ready?" He held up the metal ankh taken from the dead woman's neck. He walked over to the console. "The people upstairs would not have been able to start the engines. They do not have the key. Besides, upstairs may control navigation, but here is the real control room. If I activate the engines from here, the destination is already pre-set." He held the ankh above a groove in the console. He waited for her reply.

"Shouldn't we wake the others first?"

"What do you think they will do?"

The engineers would take control and delay launch. "Dimitri was right, after all?"

Cheveyo laid a hand lightly on her shoulder. "Professor Kostakis is usually right, even when he doesn't know it. That's also why he loves you – your certitude. In fact he has it, after a fashion, but despite what that man said, Kostakis is a scientist, and is bound by a scientific approach. It sometimes slows him down from his true destiny."

Jennifer wondered how and why this man knew so much about Dimitri as well as Gabriel – the only two men she'd ever loved.

"It is time," he said.

She tried to swallow, but her mouth had gone dry. Still he held the key, waiting.

"We're going to Eden, aren't we?" She struggled to believe it.

He smiled. "You are ready. Take a deep breath." He offered her his hand. As she took it, he dropped the key into the slot.

Chapter 37

Detonation

"We must go faster!" Rashid shouted through the helmet intercom system. Kat was already edgy enough. They had only just out-run the last shock wave, which had sent a mushroom of scorched sand high into the Eden sky, but they knew another worse one would soon come, as the neutralino detonator unleashed a series of discharges, each more powerful than its predecessor. Sweat trickled into her eyes as she swerved the skimmer around boulders at top speed. Her forearms and shoulders ached, but she continued to follow the Hohash mirror, twenty metres ahead, as it threaded an optimal escape route through the terrain – it meant she could drive as fast as her reactions permitted. A click interrupted her as Rashid activated the comms-link.

"Fifteen seconds until the next pulse. This one will send out high energy radiation. We must find shelter – the large boulder up ahead and to the right – stop on the leeward side."

Kat braced her arms and back, and let go of the throttle, triggering a descending high-pitched engine whine, shoving Rashid's body forward onto her as they braked. She veered the skimmer in a steep turn to the right. The mirror also turned, marking a wider arc. As she tucked the skimmer in a final tight twist toward the opposite side of the boulder, she caught sight of the pre-flash of white and purple, back where the Phoenix had been. She ploughed the skimmer over the sand like a surf board, as it juddered to a stop, but she misjudged it, and they bounced off a small dune hidden behind the boulder, knocking them both to the ground as the skimmer skittered away, sputtering to a halt.

"Right against the rock. Cover your eyes!" Rashid shouted.

Kat had no trouble complying, scrambling toward the boulder's sheltering stone face. She curled up on her knees, face down, forearms across her visor, trying to bury her head in the sandy floor, to save her retinas from melting.

A hissing roar rose to an ear-splitting crescendo, even through her helmet. Kat knew it was the sound of the sand vitrifying and splintering, sending deadly shards up into the air. It was followed, not like last time by a sonic boom, but by a screeching that made Kat imagine banshees hurtling over them at great speed. Part of her wanted to take a look – she'd seen remote images of a neutralino detonation, but they'd always been optically filtered. Apparently, so a few now-blind people had said, it was one of the most spectacular sights ever, since it ionised the air and everything in its reach, casting out a luminous rainbow of metallic hues whipping like laser-wire through any unfortunate atmosphere in its wake – a scouring aurora borealis at ground level.

She recalled that the first 'small' test detonation six years ago in Alaska had not been sufficiently far away from population centres, and hundreds of Eskimos had gone blind. The scientists had also failed to predict the amplification effect underground, as the detonation had collapsed subterranean habitats hundreds of miles away. As the static-charged wind battered against her suit, she squeezed her eyes shut further. She recalled how they'd got into this.

They'd been heading out to the Phoenix, and were only ten minutes away from it when she'd copped a blinding migraine. Within seconds she brought the skimmer to a halt, and staggered off, unable to see. She fell to her knees and could barely hear Rashid's increasingly alarmed questions. Then she saw what the Hohash was transmitting to her through her node.

"Rashid! There's another ship next to yours."

"From Earth?"

She saw a small black ship, insect-like in shape with a large glass canopy in front, on six spindly legs. A single Q'Roth guardian emerged, carrying a long pole with a small box at one end – she presumed a weapon.

"No – Q'Roth." It was hard to talk; the transmission hammered inside her skull.

"Kat, you must tell me everything you see. Everything!"

She narrated the scene as the Q'Roth walked – no crawled, or whatever – around the site, and then entered the single surviving module – Rashid's home. The view shifted to the ND device and a digital display with three green lights shifting to reds. A figure of six-zero appeared, then it read five-nine, then five-eight...

Rashid pulled Kat to her feet and steered her over to the skimmer. Her headache vanished and her vision returned.

"Kat – listen to me – I have no idea how, but the Hohash has activated the detonation sequence. We have only fifty seconds before the initial discharge. Are you fit to drive? I have never driven a vehicle like this."

She drove for her life. The first, tightly-focused detonation had merely been felt as a pressure wave behind them. She managed to control the skimmer and surf it out.

But since then, despite the increasing distance they put between themselves and ground zero, they had already taken shelter twice behind a land mass to avoid being shredded by the sand-blast effect, or microwaved from a cocktail of lethal radiation.

Kat had not only received visual images from the Hohash, however. Just before it disconnected from her, there had been a fleeting emotional burst. It had wanted revenge, to kill a Q'Roth, a slayer of its masters. Having seen the guardian's ship, undoubtedly armed, she was glad the mirror hadn't wasted the one device they had which could destroy one of the aliens. Up to now, it seemed the Q'Roth had been ignoring Rashid and the Ulysses, probably out of contempt – they weren't worth bothering with. That had changed. They'd gotten the guardians' attention.

Rashid tapped her on the shoulder. It had passed – until the next one. She got up and witnessed the desert dunes to the sides of the boulder, shimmering like glass blisters. Behind them, back toward what had been Rashid's camp, a corona of sky around the boulder flickered a halo of violets and deep blues, as if somewhere in the distance hell was throwing a party. She had a bad feeling this particular party was just beginning. But she knew they were past the worst of it; they could outrun it now, and it wouldn't reach the Lander. Lifting her visor, she gathered some saliva and spat onto the desert floor. It sizzled. "Let's get out of here."

* * *

Blake stared upward at Pierre being reeled in by the Q'Roth warrior.

"Pierre! *CUT – THE - LINE!*" He fired his second flare, as Pierre managed to slice through the taut wire. The flare stuck in the rocks just below the creature, so it wouldn't be able to see them unless it jumped down. Blake prayed it couldn't fly. He ran towards Pierre to try and break his fall but he didn't make it. As Pierre hit the ground he crashed straight through it.

"Pierre!" Blake ran toward the hole, but the entire chamber shook, and he was knocked off his feet. The shaking was severe – it reminded him of the San Fran quake of '34, the mother of all US earthquakes, the one that finally brought down New Bay Bridge. He rolled away from the cliff bottom just in time as rocks tumbled down. The noise rose to the point he couldn't distinguish anything. In the last moments of the light, several eggs toppled over and rocks from the domed ceiling crashed to the floor. A second before the light failed, he saw an overhang that looked as solid as anything could be. He dove underneath it, tucking into the crash position with hands clasped over his head. The bone-shaking continued for another minute. He knew this wasn't a Q'Roth protection system – it clearly endangered the eggs.

At last it ceased. Coughing from all the dust, he realised it was either a nuclear device or the neutralino detonator had gone off early; if Kat and Rashid had been in the vicinity... He had to focus on his and Pierre's survival now, and the reason they had come here – to steal an egg – though he clearly had to re-think that strategy.

He crawled out from the overhang as the avalanche of rocks eased off. His vid imprint of the chamber was useless, so he fired the third of his four flares, set to low-burn, into the domed ceiling far above him. In the granite twilight it offered, he craned his neck and strained his eyes towards the ledge, but couldn't find the creature. He stumbled over loose rocks to where the hole had been. It had narrowed in the quake.

He froze as he recognised something a few metres away, buried under a large rock – the creature, refreshingly immobile and in a mangled posture, like a nightmarish cubist painting. Maintaining a safe distance, he shone his torch on it. A large pool of the blue-black fluid they assumed earlier was its blood gathered about its head.

"Mortal. Well that's good news. Stay dead, you sonofabitch!"

He stumbled through the debris and the snowstorm of dust that smelt like coal falling all around, returning to the hole that the ND-induced earthquake had sealed to a crack no more than a fist wide.

"Pierre, can you hear me? Pierre!" He waited. He thought he heard something, but it was difficult to tell. At last the rocks settled through the chamber. After a few moments he heard a voice, depressingly far away.

"C-Captain! I'm down here – my leg's broken in at least two places, but I'm alive. It's not a compound break, but some internal bleeding. I've travelled pretty far, quite a ride. I believe this was a passage once, very steep. Can you hear me?"

Hell! There's no way I can get to him through solid rock. "Yes Pierre – I can hear you, but you sound distant. Have you taken the trimorph?" He thought he heard a shaky laugh.

"Very much so."

Blake was grateful these latest drugs didn't impair mental functioning like the old pain-killers, though the initial shock-negating euphoric effects had evidently kicked-in.

"Is there light down there – can you see anything?" There was no reply. Blake worried he might have blacked out. "Pierre – can you hear me?"

"Yes. Yes, I hear you. Some light. The passage carries on down from here. Can you get a rope to me? The hole might just let it fall down to where I can reach it."

Blake had to decide whether to tell Pierre the truth or not. "Pierre – do you see another passage, another way up?"

Again a pause. "Hole closed up?"

Blake remembered who he was dealing with, and respected Pierre's intelligence. He shouted back down the crack. "Afraid so."

"How's our alien friend up there. Maybe you'd better get out of the chamber."

"Dead, as far as I can see." Blake looked around. Several eggs had been smashed. An odour like rotting salmon reached him.

"Captain. There's only one way out here. The passage going further down – that's where the light is coming from. I think I'll check it out, while I can still crawl."

Blake's heart was thumping. 'Pierre – wait.' He fought hard to think of a solution, but knew there was nothing he could do, at least not alone. He heard a clicking noise from across the chamber. The ceiling light was beginning to fade, so he couldn't see what it was. "Pierre – just wait there a few minutes – I need to go check something out."

"Sure."

Blake guessed that the trimorph was not completely blocking the pain. That meant Pierre was trying to occupy himself to take his mind off it. But Blake needed to know this place was secure so he could come back with help. He moved over to one of the taller-than-him ruddy-brown eggs and inspected it. There was an intermittent vibration, and a dull scraping noise. The shell wall was opaque, but Blake's torchlight highlighted dark blue veins the size of his forearm just beneath its thick gnarled surface. The egg shivered again. *Almost hatching time.* He walked over to one of the eggs smashed by ceiling debris. The remnants of the egg revealed the crushed body of a fully-formed Q'Roth – there were some minor differences to the guardians, but it was obviously mature enough to hatch. He and the others, especially Pierre, were almost out of time. He jogged back to the gap, careful not to trip on the loose rocks.

"Pierre – you still there?"

A small, hollow laugh. "I went for a stroll but I'm back again."

Blake guessed Pierre had taken the entire trimorph dose. He decided to give him the whole picture. "The hole is almost sealed, and it's solid rock – I'm not sure we can get through it with the tools we have here. And the eggs – they're close to hatching." Blake bit his lip during the inevitable pause.

"What's the bad news?"

Blake stared up the cliff face and vidded it, just before the light sputtered out. He put the goggles back on.

"Sir – I'm going to see where the light goes. The ND – I'm guessing it went off – the desert will grow really fast now. You should get off Eden while you can, and warn Earth from orbit." His voice sounded far away, weak.

Blake looked down at the small fissure, and felt a sharp pang in his chest. His right hand began to tremble. He made a fist with it and squeezed it hard with his other hand. *Shit! Don't make me do this!* Various scenes flashed through his mind – his last encounter with the General; his private parting with his sick wife Glenda; the speech he'd made before departing Zeus I. So many reasons to do as Pierre had stated: the mission; *mission before men*, his creed since he'd enlisted. And he'd never once failed in his duty before – never. But the memory that kept intruding was of his dead son, Robert, the last time he'd seen him alive, back on the ranch, laughing in the sunshine atop a combine harvester, and then lying dead in a pool of blood in Kurana Bay. He'd always feared the day would come when he could no longer make the necessary sacrifices. He recalled the General's words about why he'd been picked to lead the Ulysses. But then he remembered his mentor's earlier advice at his wedding, to consider the options and then follow his heart. Blake made up his mind. His right hand stilled. He bent forward and bellowed through the crack.

"Pierre! You listen to me, real good. Are you listening?"

An uncertain "Yes, Sir," filtered through the gap.

"I'm not leaving Eden without you. Do you understand?"

"Sir – nice of you to offer, but we both know –"

"Have you ever, *ever* known me to lie?"

Silence.

"So, you go down that passage, you follow the light, and look for another way out. But if there's nothing, you crawl your ass back to where you are now in six hours. Have you got that?"

"Oui… Yes, Sir." Pierre's voice was taut.

"One more thing. I'm going to drop my trimorph kit through the crack and see if it gets to you. I just need to wrap it in something to make it roll better. I'll stick a strobe on it to help you find it." After a minute he had arranged the small package and dropped it through the hole.

"Okay, it's on its way." Blake waited. He heard the first few bounces then it was quiet.

"I see it… *Merde!*" Pierre laughed. "It's bounced right down the passage toward the light."

"Well, you now have some motivation to crawl in that direction. You'd better get going."

"Yes, Sir… And thank you, Captain."

Blake stood up. "Thank me later. Get going." He looked round through the vid-vision goggles, then down at the hole, and sighed. Probably two metres of solid rock, he thought, and a whole host of hungry Q'Roth stirring in their eggs, and a near-radioactive desert heading this way. And if he's bleeding internally he'll go into shock, lose consciousness and die. And I may have just lost Kat, too…

But as he began climbing the ledge, he thought of his promise to Pierre. Had he made it in the heat of the moment? Would Zack persuade him that the mission – warning Earth – was the priority? Would Kat, if still alive? He realised they wouldn't – if he said they must leave, they would follow his orders; and if he said they wouldn't leave without Pierre, they'd stay. He knew what their preference would be. He prayed that Glenda, and the General would understand the choice he'd just made.

But the one whose comprehension mattered most was Robert. He paused on the rock face. "Sorry, son. Duty's second now. A little late for you, I know." He took a breath and resumed, climbing faster.

As he neared the top, clambering upwards more by feel than using the navcon imaging system which was now hopelessly incorrect, he imagined being court-martialled for jeopardising the mission. He almost laughed at himself. Why on Earth – no, why in *hell* was he worrying about a court-martial? He'd most probably be dead in the next twelve hours.

Chapter 38

Kidnap

Micah and Sandy killed time in an anonymous beige waiting room, failing to find a comfortable position on the worn leather chairs lining two of the walls. An old-style wooden ceiling fan creaked just fast enough that he couldn't be sure how many blades it had. In the high-ceilinged room, it failed to stir the air with conviction, serving little useful function other than distraction.

Sandy had chosen a seat on the opposite wall from Micah. He welcomed the space. He and Antonia had been separated several hours earlier, and he'd debriefed Vince on what Louise had confirmed about the ships – the coming invasion. Despite a muted shouting match behind closed doors between Vince and a doctor, Micah had been given a second booster. Micah hadn't protested; after what he'd seen via the Optron, a small risk of long-term infertility paled insignificantly against the prospect of an imminent invasion – he needed to be working at full capacity if he was to survive.

Sandy was oddly quiet – he didn't know her that well, but enough to recognize that some extreme event had come to pass. For the first hour she'd been wearing a ragged dress, then she'd left for half an hour and come back in a hospital gown, and then an hour ago they had given her some Chorazin clothes. Unfortunately, the sight of a woman in Chorazin uniform reminded him of Louise. He hadn't dealt with any of the conflicting emotions about her sudden death – shock, grief, anger, loss, and hate – but the over-riding emotion was relief. He'd stepped briefly onto a roller-coaster without any safety nets, and was lucky to still be breathing.

Two other issues swamped his mind: the Antonia situation – or, rather, non-situation – and the revelation that the Eden Mission building was now a heap of charred rubble and glass.

The booster had helped him straighten his thoughts, but he needed to talk to Vince, who'd promised he'd be back in an hour, four hours ago.

Sandy spoke up, without looking at him, eyes staring straight ahead at the wall.

"Did you know Gabriel?"

He thought at first she meant someone at work. Then it dawned on him, because he'd overheard Vince use that name. "The Cleanser?"

She nodded.

He shifted in his seat. "Well, not really. I mean the time I spent with him wasn't exactly social, if you know what I mean."

She didn't smile or nod, just sat, leaning forward, hands on her knees, eyes fixed on the blank wall. A nurse came in and knelt down beside her. She whispered some things that Micah couldn't hear, mainly because they were in Spanish, which Sandy evidently spoke fluently. The nurse handed her a small folded slip of paper and put her hand on her shoulder. Sandy whispered *graçias* as the nurse rose and left.

Micah decided to risk the question. "What's going on, Sandy? If you don't mind me asking."

"I know he wasn't obviously a good man – you know, assassin, and all that. But did you feel he was – that he followed a code, that he had..." She swallowed. "Honour?"

Micah sensed the need in her questioning. "Well, he was professional, that's for sure. He was a Cleanser – it's the toughest training system in the world, so I'm told – well, by the vids, you know – but I suppose, yes – he seemed highly disciplined. I knew that whatever he said, he would do. He had complete control over me to be honest, and I don't think he could have done that if he wasn't completely in command of himself." Micah leant back. This was all a little weird. He'd seen Gabriel in action, and it still made his blood run cold.

Sandy stood up and walked to his side of the room and sat down, a few seats away, and stared at him. He noticed her eyes lacked the full-on self confidence he had seen there before.

"I'm carrying his child, Micah. He made me pregnant just before he died."

Micah was glad he hadn't been drinking anything – he would have choked. Once he got over the shock, his first instinct was to ask her if she would have an abortion; the current laws would grant it in a second, as they would assume it was non-consensual. He realised that she had placed him, for whatever reason, in the role of judge and jury, right here, right now. She locked him there in that gaze, demanding an answer.

Somewhere inside his brain, the booster-energized neurons connected in a way that enabled him to see what she needed to hear.

"You cared for him, didn't you? I mean, in that moment?"

She lowered her gaze. "Can you care for someone you've just met who was trying to kill you a couple of days ago?"

His mind instantly switched to Louise, then he backed up – Sandy probably didn't even know Louise was dead. But it was ironic – he and Sandy, right now at any rate, had a lot in common.

She continued. "There seemed such sadness in him. He took lives, I know, but … Oh, I don't know Micah. It's stupid. Forget it."

Micah stood up and walked over to her chair, then squatted in front of her, his face level with hers. The words came out of their own accord.

"You could keep it, you know. It would be like a second chance for him."

Her eyes tore at his, and for a brief moment he glimpsed beneath the front to the vulnerable person hidden beneath. He wondered if he should try and hug her or place his hand on hers – he had so little experience. He thought she might cry, but instead she sniffed, nodded, pulled her knees up to her chest, and cradled her shins. He got up and sat on the chair next to her, staring at the opposite wall.

Neither of them said another word.

Micah listened to the rhythmic swishing of the fan to subdue the clamouring thoughts of the impending Q'Roth invasion, and drifted off, oblivious to the fact that Sandy's sleepy head rested on his shoulder.

Micah's consciousness flicked on at the sound of harsh footsteps approaching. He glanced at his wristcom – two more hours had passed. Sandy was already awake. Vince strode in carrying a backpack and a small black book – an actual book. Micah detected a momentary hesitation in Vince's step as he saw him and Sandy side by side, but had no clue as to whether Vince thought this was good or bad. Nor did Vince start with an apology for being five hours late.

"We need another Optron, Micah. Where can we find one?"

He pondered for a moment, his head still clearing. "NLA Tech – they have one. It's more experimental, but it works on the same principles. MIT's is better but further away."

Vince lifted his wristcom to his mouth – "NLA Tech – twenty minutes, tell them to get it ready… Well, wake them up then!"

He turned to Micah and tossed him the backpack.

"Put these on."

Micah opened the bag to see it contained a grey Chorazin uniform. He nearly dropped it onto the floor. Then he just shrugged. Why not? He stood up and was about to head for the door when Vince stopped him.

"Change here, we don't have time. She's seen you before and I'm not interested."

Micah frowned but shifted to the side of the room to change, as Vince turned to Sandy, who had not even acknowledged him yet.

Vince said something to her in Spanish. Micah wondered if he was the only person in NLA who didn't speak Spanish.

He saw her face raise, defiant. "Si,' she said. It was clear to Micah that Vince didn't approve, but he nodded acceptance, and held out his hand to ask her to stand up. Micah was fumbling with his new underwear, and just at the critical moment, they both turned to him, and watched inappropriately, Sandy folding her arms, head cocked to one side.

"Is the booster working properly?"

"I'm not sure," Vince replied. "That doctor was disagreeable. He may have slipped him a placebo."

Micah, underpants now in place, snapped back at them. "Pack it in, will you?"

Once dressed, Vince gestured for Sandy to stand next to Micah, while he began searching for something on his wristcom.

Sandy leaned over to Micah, and whispered. "Such a fuss over a little thing."

He gave a short laugh. "Glad to see you're feeling better. And yes, the booster is working fine, thank you very much."

"Don't hit on pregnant women, Micah. Bad form."

"Okay you two.' Vince broke in, "Put both your hands on this book and repeat after me."

"What?" Micah said. "You're not serious!"

Vince's poker face invalidated Micah's remark. "Listen up, both of you. Louise was an Alician agent. I have a serious security breach, and since most of my people reported to her directly, I'm swearing you both in. The few people I do still trust are carrying out more demanding orders, if it makes you feel better. And before you ask, you have no choice, I've been granted additional temporary powers under the National Security rules."

Micah fidgeted, while Sandy stood resolute, accepting it already. A thought occurred to him. "Did you swear in Antonia too?"

"Not a placebo after all," Sandy murmured.

"As a matter of fact, yes."

"What's her mission?"

"Not your concern. Now, can we proceed? There's a matter of some urgency to take care of."

Micah knew he had some bargaining power. It was probably his last opportunity, and he needed to put something right. He straightened up.

"I want my father's jacket."

Vince flared. "Now it's you who can't be fucking serious. Stop screwing around and get on with it."

Micah folded his arms. "You need me, or we wouldn't be here. And you need me much more than you realize. What's more, you need me voluntarily, for due process I suppose. I want the jacket."

"Do you have any idea how difficult that's going to be?" Vince's forearm muscles flexed.

"Definitely not a placebo." Sandy said. "And Vince – do you know how beautiful you are when you're angry?"

"Christ!" Vince closed on Micah. "Why? Why is it so important – or are you just trying to screw me over here?"

Micah stood his ground. "Because – and it's not the booster, Sandy – it's because I never got a chance to understand my father, nor him me. We parted on bad terms – shitty terms if you must know – and he's long dead now. So, when I die in the next few days, which is pretty much my conclusion on the future for all of us, I want his jacket, the only meaningful part of him I have left, on my back."

Sandy's hand moved to touch Micah's. She jutted her chin at Vince. "Do it, Vince. Impress me."

Vince clenched his teeth, turned, and kicked a metal stool right across the room, clanging noisily against the wall. A nurse appeared at the doorway, but evacuated after a withering look from Vince. He put his hands on his hips, breathed out heavily, and then smoothed down his Chorazin tunic, and lifted his wristcom to his mouth. While he spoke he glared into Micah's eyes.

"It's Vince… Get me the Secretary of State... You heard me... Yes, now... Well, interrupt him."

While they waited, Micah felt another presence in the room. He knew it was in his head, but it didn't matter. Maybe somewhere he'd at last gotten his father's attention and approval. It was ironic, just as apocalypse was approaching, he felt for the first time he knew who he was, and that his life was coming together. Better late than never.

"Yes, Mr. Secretary, good evening... Yes, I realize that, Sir... I completely understand, Mr. Secretary. It is indeed, Sir, an urgent matter of national security..." he glanced at Micah. "In fact, Sir, we're talking global security..."

It was midnight by the time they arrived at the NLA Tech lab. Three sullen-looking technicians awaited their arrival. Micah now understood why he and Sandy had been given the uniforms. If they'd been civilians, cooperation would have been anything but civil. Instead, Micah found he could simply give orders, and the techs complied, albeit with mutterings trailing after them. Luckily, Professor Partridge, the Head NLA analyst, was on leave, since he knew Micah and would have blown his cover. As it was, the technicians, once they started following his orders, began to be more than a little curious about how a Chorazin agent knew so much about an Optron.

Vince returned. "Are we ready?"

Micah played the role. "Yes, Sir!"

"Okay, everybody non-Chorazin out. Now."

There were half-hearted complaints and warnings about this not being a toy, etc., but Micah reckoned they wanted out as soon as possible anyway.

Vince turned to Micah. "Your jacket is en route."

Micah nodded. "What are we waiting for now?"

"We're bringing someone in. You're going to link with him so that he sees what you saw."

Micah's eyes widened. "Wait a minute. You can't do that! Is he an analyst? If not it could fry his brain!"

But even as they spoke, two Chorazin agents bustled in, pushing past Sandy, dragging a handcuffed, hooded man. They deposited him on a chair and pulled the hood off. He was gagged and unconscious. Micah recognized him. His mouth dropped open.

"Good God! That's Senator Josefsson! Vince, you're out of your mind!"

"Perhaps," Vince said, his composure unruffled. "But this senatorial sonofabitch has stirred up a real hornet's nest, and if what you told me is true, we have to try and get people's attention, so they understand what's really going on."

"I won't do it. It would be the equivalent of torture!"

335

Vince moved very close to Micah's face. "Listen to me carefully, Micah. He knows who kidnapped him. If you don't convince him, then either we let him go and we'll be arrested for treason shortly afterwards, or I kill him. Which option do you prefer?"

Micah couldn't believe he'd been manipulated again by Vince. His intense unease about using an Optron on a civilian – a Senator, no less – alchemised into anger. "You set me up! You knew I'd have no choice, you bastard."

"Your choice of words is a little rich, coming from someone who's only just re-discovered his father."

Before he realised he was even doing it, Micah threw a punch at Vince, but Vince caught it inches from his own face, not even flinching in the process. He spoke quietly in Micah's face, while Micah's chest heaved. "We're wasting time. You told me an invasion is coming. The world is defenceless and not even aware of the danger because we have no credible mouthpiece. Now, either you were bull-shitting me, or else the ends certainly justify the means. Your Dad *was* a fucking hero, not a comic book one, a real one who got the job done by doing what mattered. Now I can't make you do this. So you decide what type of man you are."

Micah's nostrils flared, he pulled back his fist. In his mind, his father stood behind Vince, waiting to see what he would do. Would he run away, or see it through. Micah faced off Vince for ten seconds then glanced over to Sandy. She nodded to him, biting her lower lip. He walked over to the Senator.

"Can we at least untie him and wake him? I need to ask him some medical questions in any case."

"No. We untie him afterward. Make your best medical guesses. Get on with it."

Micah managed to make the link, so Josefsson saw, or rather, experienced the downloaded scenes from the Ulysses, including the strange transmission from somewhere else – Eden, and another planet conquered by the Q'Roth, he guessed. Luckily Josefsson was a wily politician – it meant his intellectual faculties were resilient enough to withstand the process. They woke him up and untied him. He was helped off the Optron chair into a seat facing Vince. He came back to his senses with a vengeance.

"Vince! You motherfucking asshole! You did this to me! I'll see to it that they throw away the key and leave you to rot in some shit-hole cell in Salvador."

"Undoubtedly, Senator, but first, there is the matter of world security."

Sandy fetched the Senator a glass of water. He drank greedily, not caring that half of it spilled down his tux. He slammed down the glass afterward, cracking it. You mean that 'show' I just witnessed? What sort of brainwashing techniques have you people been cooking up, eh?"

Micah moved between Josefsson and Vince. "Sir, it's no hoax or show. What you saw happened. And the fate of that planet is the fate of Earth unless we act quickly."

Josefsson snorted. But as he downed a second glass refilled by Sandy, Micah could tell that although he was trying to deny it, it was sinking in. The Optron after all fed impulses straight into the cortex – no mediation – it was direct, untarnished communication. It had the ring of truth.

Micah continued. "Senator, Sir, these ships popping up all over the planet – they're programmed to go to Eden. When people get there they'll be slaughtered. Then the aliens will come here and finish the job. They'll harvest the human race."

Vince took up the lead. "And you, Sir, have been pushing people into those ships. The first is already missing, but in the past twelve hours a further fifteen ships have been discovered around the globe, and they keep finding more. Terribly convenient, isn't it?"

Josefsson pursed his lips, his bushy eyebrows meshing above bleary eyes.

Vince drove onward. "There is also a conspiracy on Earth – the Alicians are involved. Probably not all of them, but the aliens couldn't do all this on their own. And Louise – my assistant you met yesterday – she was one of those conspirators. She was killed earlier today. The preliminary examination of her corpse revealed genetic alteration beyond anything our scientists can manage." He pushed her med-pad across the table.

The revelation about Louise clearly had an effect. Still, his anger was evident. "What the hell exactly is it you want of me?"

Vince nodded to Sandy, who had been primed for this moment.

"Senator Josefsson. You've already spoken to the people once. Speak again. Tell them of the danger. And explain to the President – and to IVS – what they are up against. And even call on the Fundie leaders."

Josefsson squeezed his large hand around the empty glass. "But even if I do what you say, there's no proof. You can't link the whole nation up to that God-damned machine! A pronouncement like that will ruin me, and we'll probably fail in the process."

"But Sir, so many of the people trust you," Sandy said, holding eye contact, "like I do. You speak to the people, for the people. And if they do listen, then you will be the one that saved humanity from a disaster of biblical proportions."

It moved more smoothly from that point. Thirty minutes later the Senator was en route back to his office, scheduled for a network-wide announcement at 08:00, followed by a meeting with the President.

Vince, Sandy and Micah headed back to Chorazin HQ, where they could get some sleep. Micah had finally got his Dad's jacket back. The ice between him and Vince had thawed, but only a little.

"Do you think he'll do it?" Micah asked.

"Oh, yes, he'll do it. But the question is whether he was right about not being listened to. And even if he is, will it be fast enough to prevent a substantial exodus?"

Micah winced. Vince needed to know the whole content of the message.

"Vince," he said reluctantly, "there was something mathematical in the transmission."

"Mathematical? An equation?"

"Exactly. Or more like a geometric plane, but one I recognized immediately from my math theory. Only a mathematics-trained person would see it, or its relevance."

"You're being obscure, Micah. What was the message?"

"I believe it was from the alien race, or their messenger. It was an exponential expression."

Sandy spoke up. "Micah, we're all tired. Speak English, please."

"Okay. Well, we think in linear terms, when we think of time."

"Please, Micah, no Einstein at 2am!" Sandy implored.

"No – don't worry. It's just that nature itself often works in logarithms, exponential – that is, accelerating – events. Think of a baby for example – oops – well, anyway, the rate of cell growth is exponential, otherwise how could a single ovum and sperm produce anything in nine months."

Vince sighed. "Your point, Micah?"

"The point is that these ships have been here for a very long time. Alicians have been steering us toward this point. The rate of convenient discoveries themselves has been increasing, including the rather obvious one yesterday that miraculously allowed scientists to locate these ships. Everything is accelerating towards the end. The equation is represented by a theory known as catastrophe theory, with a definable end point."

"The end being invasion," Vince said.

"But we've got a chance now, don't we?" said Sandy. "Tomorrow, or rather later today, the Senator will go public, and –"

Vince broke in, his eyes set. "Micah's right, Sandy. Even if Josefsson does a perfect job, the political process will be slow. And we're still not sure we can defend against an invasion force if it comes. You said it was mathematical. That means you could use the equation to predict how long we've got."

Micah leant back against the wall of the Chorazin vehicle. "I was afraid you were going to ask that. Yes, that's why the transmission held the equation. Whoever or whatever sent it understands the planning, the timing of the planned Q'Roth incursion. It wants us to be able to react before it's too late. So I've been plugging events into the equation, doing a rough calculation in my head. The booster helped, as I can visualize more clearly the slope of the catastrophe curve we're riding, so to speak."

"How many weeks do we have left, Micah?"

"Three days. Maybe less."

All three of them sat quietly for a while. It was Vince that finally spoke.

"We need a contingency plan."

"What sort?" Micah asked.

Vince spoke into his wristcom. "I want a jet to Cocos Island, fuelled and ready for three passengers when we arrive at CHQ in ten minutes."

Sandy spoke sleepily. "A last beach holiday before the invasion? Vince, you really know how to treat a girl."

Micah ignored the sarcasm. "What's in Cocos?"

The corners of Vince's mouth lifted a fraction. "A ship."

Chapter 39

Sabotage

Kat squatted on her haunches, watching things go from bad to worse outside the Lander. Zack kicked at a large stone with his good leg. "We can't leave him there, Skipper", he muttered. Kat noted that Rashid faced away from them – it wasn't his call, and he'd accept whatever decision was made.

"Well," Blake said, "just before I arrived, I believe you were asking a pertinent question, Zack."

Zack raised his eyebrows.

"Why haven't they blasted us to ashes already? I saw thousands of eggs down there. Most of them about to hatch. I think they've been ignoring us so we can be bioelectric food or whatever for the first hatchlings. My guess, however, is that just recently we've pissed them off enough that they've decided to get rid of us. I am certain there are other Guardians on Eden – I can't believe there are only two of them for a whole species. Probably a network of egg-nests all over the planet, like this one.'

Rashid pitched in, "This has also been my suspicion."

"Which means our days are numbered," Zack said.

"More like hours, old friend. We took out one of them with the ND – but that was it, we've nothing left that's going to be much of a threat, especially if they have airborne ships here." He nodded to Kat and Rashid. "Prepare the ship ready to leave."

Kat waited for Zack to speak, but he said nothing. Rashid looked downward. So she seized the initiative. "What about Pierre? We can't –"

"I'm not leaving him behind," Blake stated. "Now, get the ship ready. Move to it!"

Kat hesitated, and then drifted toward the ship's ladder. As she reached the first step she noticed that Zack hadn't budged. Good – Zack'll talk some sense into him! Rashid came over to her and tried to usher her up the first rung, but she planted her feet firmly, listening.

"I won't do it, Skipper," Zack said, quiet but deep. "Ain't going to leave you two here to die – to be vaporized or carved up by those motherfuckers."

"Zack," Blake dropped his voice, "you know you have to go. We must get a message back home. Things are coming to a head, I can feel it. There's not much time."

Kat strained to hear what Zack said next.

"But for him? You've left men behind before. It seems like there's nothing you can do. You're throwing your life away. Hell – ask Pierre, he'd tell you himself!"

"He already did. I can't explain it. I've made my decision. There's a chance, a slim one. And you're right – I've left plenty of men behind before. I'd like to say I remember all their faces. Truth is I don't."

Zack lifted and then pile-drove the butt of his pulse rifle into the ground.

"Then we'll wait for you. You try and get him out. We'll wait. Hell, I can even take off and land one more time if necessary."

"But you can't go into orbit and come back. You need to send the message, hit the ND and get the hell out of here. That's an order, Zack."

Zack raised his voice. "You give me just one good reason why I should follow that order. Just one. You can't court-martial me out here, and I'm your only goddammed pilot."

Blake looked up to the sky, bit his lip, then took a step toward Zack, and whispered something in his ear. Blake moved away afterwards, but Zack stayed where he was, ear cocked, as if the words Blake had whispered still echoed inside his head. Suddenly, Zack whirled around and came up behind Kat and Rashid.

"What are you two still doing here? Captain gave an order. We're leaving." Kat and Rashid parted leaving the ladder open as Zack limped towards it, seized the rails and heaved himself upwards, clanging the rifle on every rung. Kat glanced back at Blake, but his back was turned. Rashid again put his arm on her shoulder, and this time she climbed into the ship.

Kat found the cockpit oppressively quiet. Blake's seat was empty, with Rashid perched at Pierre's science console. Blake had taken an assortment of weapons and supplies outside – they could last a month at most, if he and Pierre were really careful. If Pierre wasn't already dead. If several miracles intervened. *Fuck this plan!*

Blake's voice crackled through from outside via com-link. "Okay – good luck all of you. Tell them… tell them everything."

The screen showed Blake moving away from the ship's lift-off zone. Her stomach felt like a tightening knot. She couldn't contain it any longer. "Zack, we can't leave them here!"

Zack threw switches, tapped at touchpads. Low, grinding whistles slowly ascended their scales. Hydraulics hissed and clamps thudded, adding percussion to the orchestral tuning that signified the pre-flight engine warm-up.

"Zack. What did he say to you to make you leave him here?"

"Back off, Kat. Don't push me."

But she felt like her stomach was in freefall. Blake had been her anchor throughout this mission, and she realized for the first time that she had some undefined feelings for Pierre. She searched for something to stall Zack. She found it. It was dirty, below the belt, but once they took off, that was it. No turning back.

"What are you going to tell his wife, Zack?"

Rashid gaped at her. Zack's hand froze above a switch. She saw his huge shoulders heave up and down several times. Suddenly Zack's harnesses flew open and he launched himself upwards and swung around to her position. Kat hit her own harness release and was half-way up as she met Zack's left hand. It swatted her back down and pinned her against the seat. She saw feral, white rage in Zack's eyes, as his right hand found her throat. Yet she was defiant. Her voice croaked. "How long do you think we're going to last without him? We haven't even taken off yet, and we're literally at each other's throats. Earth has its message. The ND and the desert are as plain as Jupiter's red dot. He needs us. They both do!" Her words choked off as she ran out of breath.

Zack's hand eased off.

She coughed, massaging her trachea, getting some oxygen back into her lungs. As soon as she could, she continued.

"He needs you, Zack. Now more than ever." She stopped there. There was nothing more to say. She didn't know what Zack might do next; maybe kick her off the spaceship.

Zack manoeuvred himself back into his seat. His fingers lingered on a panel above him that glowed red.

"Rashid – check your instruments. See any problems?"

Rashid called up various displays. "Oh. Yes. The solenoid is –"

"Fried. Abort take-off. Do you concur?"

Rashid nodded vigorously. "Most definitely, I concur. Take-off would be fatal, I am afraid."

Kat watched, confused, as Zack and Rashid powered everything down. She coughed. "Zack... So... we're not taking off?"

He kept his back to her. "Not unless you want to become a human meteorite. Go outside and start setting up a defence perimeter. Rashid – you go explain to Blake we're stuck here for at least six or seven hours. That's how long it'll take to fix it. I suppose it's lucky for us it's one of the few parts we carry a spare for."

Kat made it outside in record time. Blake ran over to her.

"What the hell happened? There had better be a damned good reason!"

Rashid dropped down the ladder. "Captain, the solenoid in the thruster power centre fused – we would not have been able to dock or achieve a stable orbit. Luckily the pre-flight checks found it."

"Dammit! But it was fine earlier." Blake turned away to look at the hill-top, toward the cave.

She scrutinized Rashid, but he avoided her gaze, and spoke to Blake. "There must have been a power surge as we started up," Rashid said. "These things happen, and your ship took quite a few knocks on landing."

During that last sentence she thought, but couldn't be sure, that Rashid's left eye twitched. But at that moment, Zack emerged from the ship hefting a toolbox down to the ground.

"We're here another six hours at least, Skip. Why don't you take Kat with you while Rashid and I finish the repairs? We don't need her here."

Blake gave his friend a measured, questioning stare. "You'll be pretty vulnerable out here."

"You mean it'll be safer inside the cave?"

Blake managed a thread of a smile. "Point taken. You want Kat here and Rashid comes with me?"

Kat's eyes flicked sideways to Zack, but he replied directly to the open toolbox, where he fished for all manner of tools.

"No, Skip. Too much testosterone for my liking. She's developed the killer instinct. Might come in handy where you're headed."

Zack stooped under the Lander's hull, reaching towards an underside hatch. When Kat turned back to Blake, she encountered a penetrating stare, as if Blake hadn't really looked at her, hadn't noticed her, for a long time.

Blake said quietly, "What was that all about?"

She shrugged. She didn't feel like talking.

"Okay, Kat. Bring an extra rifle and your night goggles. I've already got the explosives over there in the bushes."

She walked to the ship to get her gear together, not once looking in Zack's direction. Just before departing with Blake, she noticed the ground was redder, and the bushes were fewer. The desert had arrived.

Zack and Rashid removed the plating, after twenty minutes of difficult coaxing, revealing the brown carbonized solenoid. "Hot damn!" Zack said. "Well, I guess I'll leave the rest to you, Rashid. I'm gonna' go patrol the perimeter."

"Zack, you honour me with your faith in my maintenance aptitudes. But I would indeed benefit from your assistance."

Zack, though, was already heading away from him, limping badly, using the pulse rifle as a crutch again.

"Nonsense, Rashid," he said, without turning around, "you'll do just fine. Besides, we had a saying back in the War – he who breaks it, fixes it." Zack drifted away, whistling tunelessly.

Rashid dared say no more, and focused on the rather tricky job of repairing his handiwork.

* * *

Deep below the surface, Pierre had reached the bottom of the steeply sloping corridor, carved through solid rock, leaving a scalloped effect on smooth walls. He'd found Blake's trimorph kit, and tucked it into a side-pocket for near-term use. But he was mesmerized by a dark blue metallic console, its stand extruding upwards from the floor like a plant's stem. Small lights sparkled across its flat, translucent upper surface. He heaved himself up to see the controls. It was obviously built for a Q'Roth, as it was so tall; he felt like a small child trying to gain access to an adult's kitchen table.

The controls on its upper surface were large, and he had no clue how to activate any of them, or even if they were controls at all. Some looked like baroque joysticks, with spindles jutting out in shards; others were like oval pushbuttons pulsing with a dark backlight. The whole console was the colour of deep ocean water. The centre-piece was a large vertical control resembling a double-stacked punch-ball – the type a four-handed boxer might use. Pierre decided not to touch it. There were recesses that looked as if the Q'Roth "feet" or hands, from what Pierre had seen of them, could fit into them.

But it was the displays that interested him. He wasn't sure, but one of them appeared to show a cross-section of Eden, from the external crust to the centre of the planet. Thin lines, like tendrils, drilled down from the surface to the central molten core. About half were light blue, the others a ruddy brown.

"I'm betting you're the terraformer control panel," he said to the display. He then noticed another display to the left, on the far side of this inner cave. He dragged his self-splinted leg – he'd used a strut from his backpack – over towards it, grimacing with every step, and studied a mosaic displaying thousands of tiny silver beads winking in unison. Here and there were a few blobs of red. He presumed it was a health monitor for the egg chamber lying a hundred metres or so above him. There was also a thick horizontal line underneath the bead layer that was silver along almost its entire length, except for the very end.

"Egg timer; almost cooked." And with the weight of that thought, the dull throbbing from his leg washed over him, and he crumpled to the floor, moaning with pain. He rolled over onto his back, and lay there panting through gritted teeth. He glanced at his wristcom. Three hours since his fall, so three hours left before Blake returned. He had zero idea how he would climb the corridor, or even get upright again. Ideally he should wait and conserve the trimorph, but he was worried he would black out, and if that happened he would die there for sure.

Taking out the small canister, he broke the scal roughly, held it to his mouth and inhaled. Immediately his head felt lighter, as if on a soft silk cushion, as the pain flushed away. It was tempting to lie there. His leg, which had felt a moment earlier as if there were ground glass inside it, began to feel like warm cotton wool, but he heard a beating noise deep inside his body. It was the pain, held at bay for now; it would return soon enough. He propped himself up against a wall, careful not to injure his broken leg further, now that pain receptors could no longer warn him.

He stared back to the corridor where he had entered. From his current perspective, he noticed two things. First, another corridor leading upwards – so, there was another route down there. But it was the second structure that captured his attention: a large church-like door made of a slate-grey metal. He had a sneaking idea of what lay behind the door. He had to make his choice quickly – he could go back up 'his' corridor or he could take the new one, or he could try and see what lay behind the door. He recalled how his mother chided him when he was younger and first accidentally created nitroglycerine, blowing up their garden shed. "Curiosity killed the cat! " she'd said. He never really understood that quaint aphorism until now. Heady from the trimorph, he tried his best to put on a Cheshire cat grin, and crawled towards the large metallic door.

When he got there, he pulled out a phial from his jacket, containing what looked like a swirling liquid of iron filings. They shimmered in the dim lighting from the console. "Hope you were right about these, Dad." He took out a syringe and extracted a thimbleful, and injected it into his neck. An ice-burn feeling shot from his throat to his head for ten seconds before dissipating, and his vision blurred temporarily. He was glad he'd just taken trimorph.

While his head was clear, he unholstered his pulse pistol and discarded the pulse charge from the handle, inserting the half-full phial in its place. He snapped the handle closed, and switched the pistol mode to "Monopulse". One shot. He took a few deep breaths. "Okay," he said aloud, "time to make some new friends." He activated a pad on the side of the wall next to him, and the door slid open revealing a cavern.

On the floor in front of him was possibly the last thing he expected to see: a human skeleton, and a date etched into the ground: *1756 anno domini*. He shook his head in disbelief – someone had arrived here more than three hundred years earlier. In the distance, as a backdrop, was the largest ship Pierre had ever seen. But the skeleton's left arm pointed to a much smaller craft, green in colour, and in front of it stood a Hohash; except it wasn't the same one they'd met earlier. Pierre lowered the pistol and slid to a seated position, back against the door, as the pain reasserted itself. "Papa," he said, "you really should see this."

Chapter 40

Warriors

Rashid hung underneath Eden's rocket boosters via a trapeze system of uncomfortable wires, occasionally pausing to wipe the sweat off his brow. He'd been working for three hours straight. It was dark, and the halogen lights necessary to see the wiring detail basted him as if he was on a rotisserie. He thought Zack would have come over to check how he was doing, or even to help him but, truth was, he had no idea of Zack's whereabouts. Rashid was lit up like a Christmas tree right now, just in case any Q'Roth guardian happened to be passing by and wanted some target practice. Maybe that was it, he thought, perhaps Zack was using him as bait. It made sense, but it would be nice to know, to be asked, even. *Enough – work! Undo what your momentary caprice has done.* Having scolded himself, and wiped his brow one more time, he carried on with renewed fervour.

An hour later, he finished the job and re-sealed the external plate. As he disentangled himself from the trapeze harnesses, he became aware of another presence.

"Zack! Is that you?" He couldn't turn his head yet in the right direction. "If you want an apology please don't resort to scaring me – just ask!" There was no reply. He got his legs free, and twisted his torso and legs out of the wires. "It's finished, you know." He fumbled and dropped his torch. Rashid was limber, but after so much time in a contorted position, he had difficulty getting to the ground and then upright. He fell out of the trapeze, hit the ground hard, and groped for the torch, crawling out from under the ship. He caught a glimpse of something golden. He clambered to his feet, and saw that it was the Hohash, standing upright, a few inches from the ground, a short distance away, facing him. Zack stepped down gingerly from the ship.

"I thought you were outside," Rashid said, more than a little worried.

"Getting some sleep. You woke me."

Rashid doubted both these statements, but did not pursue it. "Look, over there."

Zack pointed a substantially larger flashlight. "Ah, your friend is back." And then, it seemed to Rashid in jest, Zack continued, addressing the Mirror. "No ND's here – up there!" Zack grinned, pointing the flashlight upward. Rashid didn't appreciate the humour. Of all the crew members he'd like to be left alone with, Zack was last on the list.

Rashid saw something stir in the mirror. He was seeing a world, Eden, with their side in the night time. "Look!" he said.

"I see it." Zack replied, in a measured tone.

Rashid saw Eden getting larger, very rapidly, so that now it filled the whole of the mirror.

"Rashid!" shouted Zack.

"Yes, I'm watching," he said, a little irritated.

He suddenly felt Zack's hand clamp down on his shoulder. "No – *up there!*"

Confused, Rashid tore his eyes away from the mirror and followed Zack's other hand to see a huge silhouette of waxing darkness etching itself into the sky, first rippling, and then blotting out the stars. Zack limped back to the space-ship entrance and clambered up the ladder. Rashid followed, chased by a bow wave of wind crushing down on him. Zack plucked Rashid's relatively lightweight frame inside as he slammed his fist on the button to emergency-seal the door.

The thunderclap arrived less than a second later, rocking the ship. Rashid was sure it would roll over, or worse, be crushed underneath the descending craft. But the sonic booms and after-shocks abruptly ceased. They both lay inside the airlock, Zack gasping from the effort and the pain in his leg. His cast had split open. He swore continuously until he had managed to wrench it off.

"Is that wise?" Rashid asked, but got no reply. "Thank you, in any case," he added, still on the floor, "you just saved my life."

"Help me up, then," Zack groaned, searching for his pulse rifle, "my leg's suing for divorce right now."

Rashid manoeuvred himself under Zack's shoulder, steering his heavy form past the weapons and spacesuit rack into the cockpit. The screen showed swirling clouds of dust. Zack groped inside a compartment and stuck a low-dose trimorph patch on the side of his neck, while Rashid switched screen views to check to the rear, but all around them it was the same. He left it on front view, which was where the radar showed the ship had actually landed, about half a kilometre away, in the forested area. Several minutes later, the dust cloud settled.

"Where have the stars gone?" Rashid said. Although he knew the answer, he couldn't believe how tall and wide this ship was. Yet the evidence was there: it occluded nearly a fifth of their forward view. He glanced back at Zack, but found he had his elbow over his eyes, his jaw clenched closed.

Rashid went to get another trimorph capsule from the med-cabinet. "You need to take more –"

"No," said Zack, breathlessly, "can't fly with that stuff."

Rashid hated to watch people suffer needlessly; he'd seen too much during the War. Real pain twisted people, and too often soldiers avoided painkillers only to die shortly afterwards anyway, no longer themselves.

"But you cannot fly if unconscious, or in agony." Rashid said, as he considered administering the dose anyway – Zack was in no state to resist. Rashid was beginning to respect Zack, even if he didn't like him.

"I know my limits," said Zack. "Any more and I'll be more liability than help. But you do the extra-vehicular stuff from now on. And no more fun and games, Rashid."

"Agreed. I will go and investigate."

"Wait. Listen up. While you fixed your own sabotage, I rigged up the micro-fusion reactor." He pulled out a black makeshift pushbutton ensemble with a key inserted. Rashid backed away from the detonator.

"You're a soldier, right?" Zack sputtered. "You damn well know what to do if we're caught here. We take out as many as possible when they come out of the cave, or," he jabbed a finger toward the viewscreen, "off that ship!"

Rashid abhorred the very idea of suicide, even if for a greater cause – his native land had suffered a plague of it just before the War. But he knew Zack was right, even if he doubted whether he could activate it. He didn't want to waste effort arguing right now, so he took the small metal box.

Zack's breath was ragged. He gripped Rashid's arm hard. "Turn the key; lift the lid; press the button; instantaneous; one kilometre range around the Lander." His face contorted with pain, eyes rolling up under barely opened eyelids. Then he slumped again, exhausted, his chest heaving. His arm let Rashid go.

Rashid noticed a glistening trail of blood trickling down Zack's leg. He traced it to a bloody piece of white bone protruding through the side of Zack's upper right thigh. He made sure Zack was firmly in the seat, with his head on the head-rest, then he picked up a large dose trimorph ampoule, snapped it open and whisked it under Zack's nose. After a few seconds, his body went completely slack.

It took twenty minutes and all of Rashid's field-medic training to retract the shard of bone back under the skin, plaster the hole with anti-septic sim-skin, and splint the entire leg. There was little else he could do, except haul Zack's bulk to a cot and activate a stasis field.

He felt as if he was back in the war he had thought long behind him. He stared at Zack's bulky features under the already-frosting glass.

"Sleep well. I cannot yet call you friend, but if I activate this button, we will have plenty of time to get to know each other in the after-life." He walked to the weapons rack and put a pistol in his belt, two grenades in his jacket, and slung a pulse rifle over his shoulder. Night goggles hung around his neck.

As he opened the hatch, he added to himself. "Why does everyone forget that I am a pilot, too?" But he knew that tonight different services were required. He had been a commando before, holed up in the Nepalese highlands. It was not a skill one forgot, no matter how he'd tried. Sealing the hatch behind him, he slipped silently into the night, heading toward the large Q'Roth ship.

* * *

Kat was jittery, and for good reason. As she circled the perimeter of the vast egg chamber, with Blake far away on the other side walking in the opposite direction, not a minute went by without a cracking sound shattering the pregnant silence. They had no idea how quickly these eggs hatched, and whether or not they would emerge ready for fighting, but both knew they were on borrowed time.

Blake's voice cut through on the radio. "Anything, Kat?"

She turned towards where she thought he was, eight hundred metres away on the other side of the chamber. They were both searching for another way down to where Pierre lay. They had decided that it seemed logical, or at least plausible, that there would be more than one way out of the cave, and more than one way down to whatever was below. They'd already confirmed that the direct route Pierre had fallen through was impassible, even for the Q'Roth. Blake had used a special long-lasting magnesium white flare, impaled in the centre of the domed chamber some fifty metres above them, to give a basic low level lighting, preventing them from stumbling over rocks every other step. The relentless maze of upright eggs, each one three metres high, trickled piano-like arpeggios down her spine.

"Nothing yet, Sir."

"Okay, keep moving. If there's another entrance it's bound to be on the perimeter. And keep your eyes open. If you see one hatching, do what I plan to do – discharge your entire pulse rifle into it and run like hell."

"I read you loud and clear, Sir." She wondered if Blake was trying to comfort her. They'd discussed the possibility of trying to trigger a massive cave in, but their small charges wouldn't be nearly enough. They also considered trying to blow up a few eggs, but since they estimated there were close to half a million in this chamber alone, that would also be futile. Blake had rigged most of the explosives up to the single entrance tunnel they had found so far, which might stop the young Q'Roth getting out for at least a short time. But they knew that everything they had thought of so far was like building kids' sandcastles and moats to stop an oncoming tide. When these creatures started hatching, they would be unstoppable.

Something snagged her attention. One of the eggs looked different. She realized it was because there was light reflecting from it. Not daylight as such, but a pale, cyan, electric glow. She heard a low hum, looked behind her toward the outer wall, and saw a Q'Roth scout ship enter the chamber. She crouched, her back to one of the eggs, and watched, careful not to move.

It was not a big craft. It resembled a giant fly, with two oval-shaped glass bubbles at the front for a cockpit, and small, mobile turrets on each underside. After the front end, the rest of the craft tapered to a point several metres behind, like a helicopter. The craft had six jointed legs that cushioned its landing as it settled onto the rock floor. Two Q'Roth stood in the front part of the ship. Kat saw how much like insects they were, their abdomens consisting of ribbed circular sections that looked very tough – and their legs were barbed. But the trapezoidal heads with their blood red slits on either side rendered them demonic.

She called to Blake before the ship had fully powered down.

"Captain," she shouted in her loudest whisper, in case their sensors could pick her up. "A small ship's arrived just thirty metres from my position. Do you see it?" The engines were almost quiet, and there was a hiss as the two glass-like domes, each sheltering a Q'Roth guardian, unsealed and retracted. "Radio silence!" she barked, before Blake had a chance to reply. Muting the radio, she hid behind the egg.

She had no idea what sensory capacities the Q'Roth had, but she was betting they could see in the dark, probably by infra-red or some kind of sonar – there had been no natural or artificial lighting in here, so clearly there was no need for light, even for the hatchlings. She also suspected they had advanced motion detectors like many evolved predators, so she remained very still, out of their line of sight, her right hand on the pulse rifle trigger, the left on the grenade pin. She closed her eyes, trying to listen. It sounded as if they were moving toward the centre of the chamber, scampering softly through the egg rows, muffled drum beats of claws on rocky ground.

A series of fast clicks came in a short burst. Simultaneously she felt the vibration of her wristcom. With minimal body movement, she turned her left wrist towards her face, and touched a small button once, for back-lit illumination. She read the message in red LED: *Stay down. Have found second corridor to lower level. Try to get back to ship alone.* Kat pressed the acknowledge key.

Just as she was deciding what to do, a bone-thumping crack knocked her forward, nearly making her drop the rifle; the egg she was leaning on was starting to hatch. But the two guardians were still not far enough away. Reluctantly she sat back against the splintering shell, pressing her weight against it, digging her heels into the ground. The Q'Roth footfalls paused. She held her breath, then mouthed *"Shit!"* as they changed direction and headed her way.

Her palms were clammy; she hoped they couldn't smell her sweat, her fear. Still she hadn't moved, and wasn't yet in their line of sight. Her breathing came in short rasps, high up in her chest – she tried to slow it down, but had no effect. Her hands began to shake. At that point she felt her wristcom vibrate again. She risked a glance at it. It said simply. *Cover your ears.* Kat stared at it, then, just in time, clapped her hands over her ears as an explosion at the far side of the chamber boomed across the cave. She guessed Blake had just sealed the other entrance. Echoes reverberated half a dozen times all around her. She took her hands off her ears to crawl around the other side of the egg, seeing both Q'Roth, only five metres away, stood up on their two hind legs, facing the direction of the explosion. From her perspective they looked like deformed, giant locusts. They dropped down and galloped back to their craft, zig-zagging past several eggs with astonishing speed and precision. Within a matter of seconds they were onboard. The engines powered up and the craft lifted off, soaring across the egg-field towards Blake.

Her shakes increased. She had to get moving, but before she could get up the next egg crack not only threw her away from the egg, but cut her as well. She stared in disbelief at the dark blood oozing from her thigh, and then gaped at the egg shell – what was left of it. A full third had come free, and two praying mantis-like legs were hanging outside of the shell – one of them had a spray of her blood on its barbed edge.

She felt paralyzed as the young Q'Roth, almost full size from what she could see, writhed inside, cutting itself free of an inner mucous membrane with thick blue fibres, like giant veins. For a moment it stopped moving, and Kat pushed herself away on hands and buttocks – it was staring at her. It cocked its head, and the two sets of three slits on either side of its face glowed. Her hands reached for the rifle but, aghast, she saw it was at the foot of the egg. The creature turned its head, followed her gaze, and then in a split second one of its free legs stamped down on the rifle, pulverising it.

A bead of cold sweat ran down her back. The moment she had dreaded had arrived. The nightmare, all those times on the ship, was finally real, and there was nothing she could do, absolutely nothing. The creature lifted its head and emitted a piercing high-pitched whine, as it kicked another part of the shell way. Kat found herself on her feet, running full-out toward the second entrance, ricocheting off several eggs that had also started vibrating. She didn't look back. She had no need. She knew it would chase her all the way back to the ship. She ran blindly through this second, wider entrance tunnel, guided up its slope by faint starlight at the other end. She pulled out the two grenades with both hands. Without breaking step, she put them to her mouth, bit down on the pins and yanked them out, then tossed the grenades over her shoulders, leaving them to tumble back down into the burrow. She spat the pins out into the night air.

The shock wave from the two detonations caught her just as she reached the cave exit, throwing her off her feet. Coughing, sprawled on the ground, she donned the night goggles, which cast everything in a ghostly green. She tried to listen above her own hammering heart. And then she heard the unmistakable sound of relentless, galloping footfalls echoing up from the soot-black corridor. She grunted as she launched herself upright and ran downhill at top speed, dodging between bushes and rocks like a wild animal. She prayed that Zack would be there to save her, although in the nightmare Zack was always too late. And for the first time, she remembered something she had forgotten about every single nightmare on her trip to Eden – a small but now significant detail; they had all taken place at night.

Chapter 41

Night Flight

Micah hardly slept on the four hour diversion to Cocos Island, near Honduras. He watched Sandy occasionally emit small snuffling noises, her nose twitching, cat-like. He envied how some people could doze so soundly, anywhere, anytime. Even Vince indulged in power-napping on and off, interspersed with a range of calls – none of which Micah had been party to. For several of them Vince had switched to Spanish, and for one in particular, he had used an Eastern European dialect.

But he must have dozed off for at least a short time because he was woken by a vid-call to Vince. Half-awake, curled up in an executive jet sleeper seat, cranking open his eyelids a fraction, he saw Vince turn away across the aisle and whisper, "What do you mean her corpse is *missing?*"

Micah revisited what he had experienced during his access to the data crystal. It was still confusing, and he had the feeling that this was due to the involvement of a second alien intelligence. But it was slowly becoming clearer, like frosted ice melting. Something from the destroyed spider race was left over, still active. That could mean an important ally, if communication could be established. But whatever it was, it probably resided on Eden, and it would take months to get to it. Unless...

He tried to figure out the logic of the ships. They were on Earth, empty for a millennium, undoubtedly destined for Eden. And then what? Would they come back? With new passengers? It didn't quite make sense to him. But then, why should alien sense make human sense? The counteraction needed was either to keep the ships here in the first place, or else to make sure they didn't come back. His intuition told him that the heart of the problem lay on Eden, where the astronauts were. There were only four of them, but maybe they were still alive, maybe they could help. He wondered if they knew what was going on; had more of the pieces to the puzzle. But there had been no communication now for a week. Although the Eden Mission complex had been destroyed, other deep space tracking stations would have picked up transmissions had any arrived, and it would have been all over the nets.

Vince looked up from his wristcom, and sat up sharp. "Three of the ships have left, the one in the Pacific, one in China, and one in Australia."

"Already? But how?" Micah couldn't believe, despite his predictions, that things were now moving so quickly.

Vince flicked a switch on his seat and a rippling holonet unfurled from the ceiling. Seconds later, as Sandy stirred from her slumber; all three of them watched a WNN reporter describe the event with – for once – adjectives and superlatives that barely did it justice. One second the ship was there, and the next – it was as if it had been edited out of the picture. There was suddenly a Biblical-style basin in the ocean where the ship had been – no take off or ascent – it had simply disappeared, whereupon the waves crashed into the chasm left in its wake, and the aerial video picture rocked so much it was difficult to see anything, except several IVS ships foundering like toys in a child's bath when the plug had been pulled.

The scene moved to another reporter interviewing one of the land-based IVS scientists, who admitted they still knew almost nothing about the ship, or how it worked, or how to activate it. The vid cut to the first reporter, and to a clip of the MIT scientist, Professor Klebensky – a well-known rival of Professor Kostakis – who had discovered how to locate the alien ships all over the world only a day ago, via a satellite-based spectrographic sweep for the ship's unique metallic molecular signature. The reporter stated that he had been found dead in his apartment an hour ago, with no further details available. The image switched again to two dozen other ship sites worldwide. Security had been intensified due to the flocking of tens of thousands people all around them, spurred onwards by Fundie leaders worldwide proclaiming that God's transport to Eden had finally arrived, with an added incentive in the message that the ships could carry only so many people – first come, first served.

Josefsson's speech played out next, followed by a clearly well-rehearsed counterpoint from the Fundies – the Alicians never broadcast themselves – who proclaimed that this was nothing more than US imperialism all over again, trying to stake a claim to Eden first.

Micah sighed. "We under-estimated them. They were already prepared."

Sandy rubbed her eyes. "Of course they're prepared Micah – from what you and Vince have told me, they've had a few centuries to make all sorts of contingency plans."

"She's right," Vince said in a low voice, "and for over fifty years people have learned to distrust politicians, especially American ones. Did you notice anything about the ships' locations?" Vince rewound the news vid to the world map WNN had displayed for a few seconds showing the location of the ships.

Micah stared at the picture. "Good grief!"

"What?" Sandy asked. "Looks pretty random to me – nicely dispersed around the globe."

"No," said Micah. "They're all in rad-green or yellow zones. That means –"

"It means," interjected Vince, clicking off the screen, "that the Alicians supporting these Q'Roth have been orchestrating world politics and pulling strings for a very long time, even within the military, probably on both sides during the last War."

Micah pulled himself upright in the chair. He felt like a novice up against a chess grand master. "So, what do we do?" His fingers tugged absently at his hair; to have come this far, even through a nuclear war, only to end up as growth hormones for an alien race.

"Time for a shift of tactics," Vince said. "Micah, IVS have analysts, don't they?"

"Er, sure. Including one of ours until recently." He wished he hadn't said it. He found it hard to believe Rudi's demise had been just a few days ago.

"Good." Vince was already typing using a holo-keyboard. "I'm going to send IVS all your data – with the key – so they can see what you and Josefsson saw."

Sandy spoke up. "I thought IVS was the enemy?"

"We only have one enemy right now," Vince said. "The aliens, together with the Alicians working for them. IVS are lean and pretty powerful – wolves – and they're not subject to the bureaucracy of political machinery. Besides, they've been trying to claim patent rights over the ships, all of them. They'll never win that of course, but the legal process could maybe stop any more ships from leaving, or letting people enter them."

For the next half an hour, Micah and Vince worked together to download and transmit the datastream via satellite to IVS. Minutes after the first compressed data-packet had been transmitted Vince got a call from IVS in Mumbai. He put it on speaker, so they could all hear the gravelly voice at the other end.

"What game are you playing now, Vince? And what on earth did you do to my Senator?"

"No time for fencing I'm afraid," Vince replied. "Get the data to an analyst who knows what he's doing, fast, and then see what he says. It's the data you gave to me two days ago – check the parameters, there's been no tampering, it just needed an analyst with the key to find the hidden datastream. And remember what IVS said during the War about the best motivation to build a team." Vince cut off the call.

Sandy raised an eyebrow.

"Common enemy," Vince said.

The auto-pilot's synthetic female voice instructed them to take their seats for landing. Micah wondered if anything they did now was simply already way too late. The enemy's last pieces were locking into place. Check-mate was almost upon them, maybe already here. He felt a chill, and zipped up his jacket.

Chapter 42

Mongolia

Sister Esma breathed in the chill, Mongolian mountain air in the last surviving cold patch on the planet, in a room that barely kept out the sub-zero winds and blinding snow. Not even the Alician scientists had predicted this strange weather phenomenon, an ice blue eye in the swirling inferno which slow-baked Earth.

She'd spent fifty years in Tibet a long time ago, and had learned the secrets of slowing and deepening her breath, even of creating heat through special breath-hold techniques. Each lean outbreath produced its own fleeting fog, which she studied as if it were an ice-sculpture. The art of patience, she had learned centuries ago, was not in doing nothing, but rather rested in finding natural art in the smallest details or events, no matter how evanescent. It was also in counting down, measuring the progress, even if glacial, to an anticipated event. She had been counting her outbreaths, and had reached three hundred after three hours. It was time to wake them, time for humanity to meet its nemesis. Eleven of her most trusted, scattered around the globe, were about to play out a similar ritual.

While she was wrapped in furs, the frail-looking, head-shaved man in front of her wore only a simple robe. Although he had only arrived ten minutes ago, he was already shivering violently. But the pale light in his eyes and their religious fervour were unmistakable. She drew a stretched sliver of the rarefied air into her lungs and spoke forcefully, shattering the silence.

"Do you make this sacrifice willingly?" It was hardly a question – rather, the beginning of a brief and terminal ceremony.

He bowed deeply. She nodded to the two other men in the room. "Bind him."

He did not resist as they tied his wrists behind his back, and shackled his legs with a heavy chain. His eyes radiated uncompromising faith, and an unspoken promise that the chains were not necessary, that he was a willing sacrifice.

Sister Esma knew better. "Proceed. Your time of glory is at hand."

The two thick-set, oily-skinned men each lit a flaming torch, and lifted up the dust-ridden carpet to reveal an oak trapdoor. They strained to heave it up, their groans under its weight competing with the screeching of its age-rusted hinges. They propped it open and led the man down the steps. Sister Esma followed.

The undulating, narrow passage was redolent with an ancient odour of decay, mingled with the acrid smoke from the flaming oil torches, casting hideous shadows on the crudely carved tunnel walls. The young man did not falter, but his two guards walked nervously. *You should indeed be afraid*, Sister Esma thought. She pulled out the deep blue diamond-shaped amulet that had been inside her clothing since Alessia herself had passed it to her five hundred years ago. It shone dully, and she bathed in its warmth – it had never felt old, or cold, and now seemed to glow in anticipation, as if it knew.

After a ten minute descent, the close air felt warmer, and Sister Esma saw flecks of sweat on the guards' faces in the flickering flame-light. They stopped at a landing before an oval metallic door. Although everything else about the tunnel reeked of centuries lost, the door had no rust or other signs of corrosion or age.

"Aside!" she commanded, and all three made way for her. She pressed her amulet into a central, diamond-shaped recess. This time there was no creaking of hinges, it withdrew soundlessly into a recess on one side, with only a faint hissing of equalizing air pressure, and the crackling of the torches as they found a fresher supply of oxygen.

"Follow," she said, and walked into the dimly-lit, circular chamber, some fifty metres across and ten metres high at its apex.

The guards scanned the area apprehensively, no doubt trying to figure where the grey, morgue-like light was coming from, but soon all eyes were on a central pedestal, surrounded by a circular stone plinth some ten metres in diameter. On the pedestal stood a three metre high egg. It was russet in colour, but not smooth – blue veins wormed around its opaque external surface.

"Douse the torches." She pointed to a small stone font full of black water. The guards hesitated, both glancing back to the dark corridor behind them, knowing that once wet, the torches could not be re-lit.

"Now!" she said. Failing to obey Sister Esma was always fatal, so they both sidled up to the font and thrust in the torches, which sputtered and hissed, then expired. The robed acolyte swayed faintly, muttering indecipherable prayers. He had that beatific expression, Sister Esma considered, of one who was about to meet his maker, though without having fully appreciated the travel costs.

She recited a litany in a long-forgotten tongue, her accent thick, her syllables guttural. The guards shifted nervously. Abruptly she stopped, and prostrated herself three times in front of the egg. She stood up, glowing with pride, and approached the acolyte.

"Do not be afraid. Your sacrifice will free this Soldier of God, and you will shine in the afterlife, a saint, never forgotten." Her lips sketched a smile.

He bowed in return. She pulled out a small push-button device, flourished her long fingers with their black-painted nails, and pressed down with her thumb. A humming started, rising in pitch, ascending to a high squeal. The guards placed calloused hands over their ears. After a full minute the crescendo broke. Silence flooded back into the chamber, punctuated only by the guards' heavy breathing.

She led the acolyte to the smaller pedestal in front of the egg, and tied a rope securely to the shackles around his feet. She turned him to face the egg. Even as she glided back to the edge of the plinth, the first intense crack fractured the dense air, its echo catapulting around the chamber, causing both guards, and even the acolyte this time, to flinch. The guards turned toward each other, whispering, but Sister Esma paid no attention. As the second crack shattered a lower part of the egg, the acolyte turned round briefly to Esma, who nodded calmly.

The third crack revealed a black serrated leg, with a main joint half way along its two metre length. It lashed out and harpooned the young man's right thigh. He screamed as the creature dragged him closer. The young man fell and again turned to Esma, wide-eyed. Only his faith, now punctured by doubt, kept him from screaming again. A nice touch, she thought – she hadn't actually expected such ardour.

She remained serene while one of the guards ran forward and fished out a torch, trying haplessly to light it. The other glanced to and fro between the egg and the corridor behind them. He bolted for the corridor. A fourth crack disintegrated most of the front part of the shell, revealing the creature's dark, blue-black head. It had two pairs of three diagonal slits on each side of its face, sweating a viscous, scarlet fluid. The top of the head curved smoothly upwards at the edges, ending in two points at either side, as wide as its shoulder-sections. The lower edges of its head tapered down toward the neck, giving it the overall shape of a rectangle that had been stretched down at the middle, like the silhouette of an open book. She smiled. *Such noble symmetry.*

The creature's head rolled back and emitted a deafening, high-pitched roar, and one of its middle legs seized the stiff, simpering body of the acolyte, another leg easily slashing the rope that secured him. It looked at first as though the head collapsed backward, but in fact a huge mouth had opened below the slits, and gaped wide revealing pitiless blackness inside. The acolyte's head was thrust into the yawning hole. As the creature's jaws clamped down on the acolyte's cranium, a terrible sucking noise reverberated across the chamber. The wretch's body kicked and thrashed violently, held in an immovable vice-like grip, and then went limp as a rag doll. The guard who had been trying to light the torch, gave up and, whimpering, crawled over to Esma, kneeling before her, his head on the floor protected by his arms.

The creature, with a single swing of its powerful neck, tossed the spent corpse aside and burst from the remains of the egg, roaring. In one bound it leapt down before Esma, towering a good metre above her. She did not flinch, but held up her amulet before the young hatchling. She made a sharp clicking noise with her tongue, and pointed to the quivering object at her feet.

The second guard ran blindly through the coal-black twisting passage, arms out-stretched in front of his face. He heard his colleague's blood-curdling single scream. Then he heard a strange distant galloping sound, getting louder, closer. He sprinted as fast as he could, bouncing bloodily off endless, catacomb-dark corridor walls, unseeing eyes wide with fear.

Chapter 43

Cocos

Micah and Sandy lay flaked out against curiously cool plazsteel crates at the side of a makeshift airfield. It was only 8am and Micah was already sweating. He glanced at his wristcom which displayed the temperature as forty degrees Celsius with eighty per cent humidity. They both observed Vince, twenty metres away, stripped to the waist, glistening with transblock, wearing baseball cap and shades. He shouted into his wristcom, and barked orders to scurrying Chorazin and assorted military personnel. Helicopters and small swing-jets landed every fifteen minutes, some discharging cargo, some picking up crates like the ones they had been told by Vince to stay with. At least someone had leant Micah and Sandy a couple of baseball hats to shield them from the scorching sun.

Micah glanced down at his forearms, the first streams of sweat forming in this natural sauna. He hoped they would be somewhere else, at least properly shaded, by midday, preferably by 9 am.

"He's quite sexy, don't you think?" Sandy quipped, "All that testosterone barely under control? We need a man with balls right now. A man of action, instinct. He seems to qualify."

Micah never understood – and guessed he never would – what turned women on and off; to him it was all a lottery with infinitesimal odds of winning.

He shrugged. "If you say so. I'm not sure about the 'barely', though. He always seems to be completely under control. Even now he's just using the form of anger to achieve results."

"Have you forgotten about her yet?" Sandy's non-sequitur came unwelcome at him. "You know, that bitch, Louise."

Micah levered himself up, hobbled and hopped a few paces on the blisteringly hot sand, gazing out over to the dazzling, choppy sea, and the horizon blurred by heat haze from the runway tarmac. He found a cool patch in the shade of one of the crates, and stopped. "Yes and no." He didn't want to go there. "You forgotten Gabriel?"

She took it in her stride. "Unlikely. He left me a going-away present." She tapped her belly with an index finger. "Still, according to you, I won't get to open it."

He had nothing to say to that. But her banter was preferable to imminent reality.

She nodded in Vince's direction. "Do you know what muscle-man over there has planned?"

Micah could feel the booster in him demanding action of some sort. So he raised his eyebrows then strode over towards Vince, standing at the water's edge. It was like taking a stroll in a frying pan. He tried not to run, and mercifully a small crystal clear cool wave washed over his toes. As he neared Vince he slowed down. Vince was giving an Oscar-winning impression of anger.

"Well, then I expect we'll both see each other there shortly!" He snapped off the call, shot a glance at Micah, and added "asshole" to his wristcom. "They won't give me high-end nukes. Needs to go through congress for fuck's sake, and the President is out of reach. Sonofabitch!"

Micah flinched. "Nukes? You want to take nukes to Eden?"

Vince stopped perusing the various transport operations, and walked up close to Micah. He removed his sunglasses, his blue eyes blazing into the back of Micah's skull.

"Sure – I thought you were with the plan. Nuke them before they arrive here. Got a better idea? If so, I'd like to hear it."

Micah faltered. "I just thought… you know, we were going to go on a rescue mission or something."

Vince cracked sweating knuckles. His face was sombre, but all the same, Micah was sure he was laughing at him.

"You mean rescue the four astronauts, and bring them back so they can get killed on Earth rather than on Eden. Remind me, what's your job title again?"

Micah realized that although he'd been chewing it over for hours, the result wasn't up to much. *Still, nukes?* "Maybe there's some other way," he said weakly.

"Well, if there is, I'm all ears. But you said we had at most days. We don't even know how long these ships take to get there. So maybe by the time we arrive they'll all be gone. But if not, I intend to give them a New York handshake."

Micah felt dazed. Before, he'd played the Delphian messenger predicting imminent doom and calamity. Yet at this moment, as it became reality, he found it difficult to accept, and even harder to respond appropriately. He reckoned this was the Alician and alien gambit all along. Humanity would simply not react fast enough. And Sandy was right – they needed someone ballsy to get a fight going.

"I'm coming with you," he launched, expecting an argument.

"Of course you are. And so is she." Vince nodded to Sandy.

Micah was surprised. "You're taking a pregnant woman?"

"She'll be safer with us." Vince replaced his sunglasses and turned back to supervise the others.

"Where's Antonia?" it came out of the blue, from undefined emotions, but Micah was worried he'd never see her again. Vince, without turning, plucked a sat-phone from his belt and tossed it over his shoulder to Micah. "For Christ's sake, call her – hit star and then '3'. But make it quick, we're leaving."

"We know how to take off?" asked Micah, only just catching the phone with slippery hands.

"IVS came through – the ship they 'lost' had stealth cameras throughout, hooked up to an external relay and satellite telemetry, so they could analyse everything back in Mumbai with only a few seconds delay. They saw how it was launched, and sent a schematic of the key we need, on a secure net feed. It's being replicated onboard the ship right now."

Micah was surprised. "Why are IVS suddenly being so cooperative?"

Vince lifted his cap and wiped the sweat from his forehead. "You know, I asked them that. They said it had something to do with suppressed news in some remote village in Outer Mongolia. A massacre of some sort by a wild creature; same again in Venezuela, similar story in Transylvania – that's where Antonia is, by the way."

Micah grimaced.

Vince shouted to him while still using his hands to direct people. "They're here, Micah. They're already fucking here, some of them at least, and IVS are shit-scared about it, as we all should be. So, make the goddammed call, because with or without you we're leaving."

Micah walked ankle-deep into the water. He got straight through to her.

"Hello?" she said.

He paused, momentarily tongue-tied by the sound of her voice. He had no idea what he wanted to say. Well, that was a lie; of course, he knew exactly what he wanted to say. He just had no idea what he would actually say.

"It's me, Micah."

"Oh, Micah. Thank God you're still alive."

Micah's eyes closed in relief that she wasn't mad at him.

"It's chaos here, Micah. We're holding back thousands of people trying to board one of the ships. I've seen one of them Micah, the creatures, from a V-jet in the mountains – a half-dozen or so of them are loose here. They're unstoppable, and they just keep feeding on people, sucking the life out of them, ignoring everything else. The Alicians have spread rumours that Earth isn't safe anymore, that devils have arrived to cleanse Earth, and the ships are the only escape. Listen – it's really bad here – I have to go. Take... take care, and... Micah?"

He could hear only her words; all other sound around him disappeared. "Yes?"

"I'm sorry I doubted you. And thanks. For saving my life. Vince said you're going to Eden – is it true?"

"Yes." He swallowed. I love you. "I'm going to find Katrina, make sure she's safe. We'll bring her back, I promise."

It was hard to hear the sounds at the other end of the line. Sea-water lapped around his feet. Vince appeared and snatched the sat-phone from him.

"Antonia, this is Vince, we've got to leave right now. Good luck, and whatever happens, don't get on that ship!" He clicked it off and stormed away.

A gentler hand touched his shoulder."Micah, it's time," Sandy said, her voice softer than he'd ever heard it. He let her lead him to the heli-jet.

Micah stared out the window and saw the crates they had been sitting on hanging from another chopper a hundred metres away. He shouted over the din of the rotors.

"What's in those crates we were sitting on?"

Vince grinned. "Level-two nukes. Secret Chorazin supply. Not grade-one, but close. Smaller, easier to deploy. Less range, but they'll reduce anything within the blast zone to molecules of hydrogen and oxygen, and then burn very brightly."

"Good," Micah said. "Let's toast the mother-fuckers."

Vince and Sandy exchanged glances.

Fifteen minutes later they saw the ship, floating in the ocean. Micah couldn't believe how vast it was. And then he recalled what Vince had said, that some of the aliens were already here. He spoke to Vince.

"What other weapons do we have?"

Vince leant forward and patted him on the shoulder. "Glad to have you back on board, Micah. As well as twelve tactical nukes we have air-to-ground fusion missiles, and around a dozen swing-wing and VTOL jets already onboard, tooled up."

Micah noticed that for the first time Sandy was sitting between him and Vince, whereas up till now she'd kept Micah between them. Figures, he thought to himself. The world's ending, and I'm going to be left with my mother, if I'm lucky. But he laughed at himself. All these years he'd always felt sorry for himself. Never really even saw it. One of the things his Dad could never tolerate.

Sandy passed him something. "You nearly left this behind, Micah."

It was the jacket. Despite the heat outside, he put it on.

Vince slapped a hand on Micah's shoulder. "It's a good fit."

* * *

Vince checked that everything for living had been placed inside on the second main deck, including makeshift sleeping tents, as well as kitchen and chemical bathroom arrangements, and three International Rescue Packets, as large as old train freight containers, usually reserved for rescue missions for flood and disaster-hit provinces. But his priority had been the military hardware on the first deck, which now resembled a weaponry convention, or possibly a future war museum.

The mil-support had found a way to open a larger hatch on this upper deck just underneath the conning tower, allowing them to lower helicopters and the VTOL aircraft inside. Stealth fighter aircraft sat waiting, like birds of prey.

In the larger upper control room in the conning tower, a nav and comms hardware console had also been installed, set back a few metres from the Q'Roth machinery, so that two military controllers could co-ordinate sorties once they landed, via multi-band radar units to be deployed outside the tower once they arrived. Vince and the military Commander Enrique Vasquez, a tall, one-armed man with a shock of short-cropped white hair and oil-black eyes that dared anyone to stare at his sleeved stump, had both agreed that they would need to 'hit the ground running' once they arrived, though neither knew how long that would be. Vince was playing the hunch that these ships in some way moved infinitely faster than their own space-craft. When anyone asked, he replied 'a matter of days'. He was guessing of course, but he understood the importance of authority and morale.

He'd been speaking on and off with the Chorazin chief scientist assigned – a real pain in the ass named Gorman – who kept saying he had no idea how it worked, how long the trip would take, the dangers of acceleration and deceleration effects, etc. In short, he said they might all die as soon as they figured out how to start the engines, or whatever powered the ship. In the end Vince offered him a trip back to Cocos. The scientist squirmed a little but remained on board.

Vince had at least been able to download advanced news bulletins that announced strange disturbances in six different locations worldwide, sparking worldwide panic. Seven ships had disappeared so far, including one near Beijing with fifty thousand Fundies aboard, and another one in Brazil, similarly stocked with human cargo. Antonia with her Balkan political connections through her father and his Chorazin men there had managed to keep the Fundies out, but blood had already been spilt. IVS had seized control of another ship buried in Rajasthan's northern desert, and were stockpiling food and weapons, guarded by their own elite paramilitary security force. Josefsson was using his political muscle to good effect, but the Senate was divided and the President wavering. Now that one or two pictures of the aliens had hit the nets, more politicians were lining up behind Josefsson.

But there had been a complete news blackout in Central Australia after a ship that had disappeared near Ayers Rock had apparently returned six hours later. Qahuru, the capital of Central Australia, a desert that had been reclaimed following the irradiation of both East and West coasts during the War, had gone eerily quiet, despite its million-strong population.

Vince balked at the news. He knew the Alician bastards had played a cool, calculated game, and all the cards were stacked against humanity. The United Nations had been disgraced and abandoned twenty years ago, and since then there had never been anything approaching a world federating organization capable of orchestrating a concerted response to a global threat – the New World Alliance was a bureaucratic sham. *We've been reduced to tribes.* Worse still, after the nanovirus epidemic and then the nuclear holocaust, national governments were extremely reluctant to use dwindling supplies of the latter, and the former had all been dismantled years ago, so Earth's defences were feeble. Even the orbital satellite high-powered laser system was useless, as it was intended for rogue meteorites that might one day approach from outside, not an enemy who could simply materialize in the heart of a city. Vince had to admit that mankind was in no state to stage a decent fight.

His bosses had their hands tied up with politics, but at least now he'd been granted temporary authority to act as a relatively free agent and coordinate whatever resources he could muster. As well as five military flight teams and support personnel, he had a small staff from the remnants of the Eden Mission to try to rewire, or whatever the equivalent was in alien terms, the automatic guidance system, based on the downloads IVS had received from Kostakis' team before they'd disappeared. The steps they made were shared instantaneously with IVS, Josefsson and Antonia. Vince grit his teeth at the bitter irony that his most critical allies were now a handful of civilians he had only met that week, a self-serving politician, and the most ruthless commercial corporation that ever existed.

He flipped open a small radio that broadcast to the whole ship via an installed public address system in the tower and levels one and two.

"Okay, people, what say we leave?" As he snapped it shut, a klaxon blared out inside the ship. Vince beckoned to Sandy and Micah to follow him, as people started running around, and hatches snuffed out the external noise of the sea.

"Come on," Vince said. They made their way to the second, lower control room, which they now knew to be the real control hub. Vince nodded to Vasquez, positioned at the main console. A military corporal gave a stiff salute to Vince, ignoring Micah and Sandy despite their uniforms. Vince appreciated that the man could tell the difference.

"All ready here, Sir," he said.

Vince saluted back. Like many Chorazin, he had been in the army in the last war, and had no problem in either giving orders to military, nor, for that matter, having them carried out respectfully. He picked up a microphone, and switched it on. "Okay, everybody, we're initiating take-off. I suggest you hang on to something." He looked over to the anxious-looking Corporal who held the metal ankh key.

"Do it," Vince ordered.

The man held his breath, and then dropped the key into the slot.

Nothing happened. They waited. He looked nervously at Vince.

"Again."

He tried several times – he pressed it, jabbed at it, and added some creative permutations, all of which had no effect.

"Damn!" Vince picked up the microphone. "Okay, people, stand down. We have a minor technical problem."

He turned, sighing, to the scientist, Gorman. "Any ideas? And saying 'I told you so' is seriously not an option right now."

Gorman shifted from one foot to the other. "We made the key based on appearances, because all we had was a brief shot of what it looked like. But it might need to be a specific material, or have a magnetic code, or a host of other things."

"And I don't suppose you'd have any idea where I can get one?" Vince asked, laconically.

But before the scientist could try to figure out a suitable reply, someone else spoke in a Mexican accent from the shadows at the back of the room.

'You need this," the man said.

They all turned to see a tanned mid-twenties man with black moustache and pony-tail. He wore a standard khaki military uniform, but one without any insignia. He was holding up a grey-blue ankh key. He was also wet through. Nobody had noticed him until now.

The Corporal and two other service-men both leveled pistols at the man, who did not flinch, staring at Vince.

"Who the hell are you? And how did you get onboard?"

"Does it matter? Here is the key you need. I had to kill a lot of Alicians to get it. We can chat later. We must go. Now."

"What's the sudden hurry?" Vince feigned nonchalance.

"Check your perimeter sensors."

"Watch him," Vince instructed the Corporal. "If he moves, make sure he doesn't again." He turned to another console on which several Chorazin screens were mounted. An officer began searching different external camera angles, and then halted. "What the ...?" the ensign said. But Vince knew what it was, and it was swimming fast toward them, curving through the water like a shark. He turned to the wet-through man.

"Can it open the hatches?"

"You bet. It's called a Q'Roth. You're in its ship."

"Okay. You can explain – later." Vince picked up the microphone. "Everyone – dress rehearsal over – hold onto something."

He walked over to Ramires and snatched the key from his hand.

He strode back to the main console and slammed it into the recess. As he did so, everything froze and became mercurial. Shades of silver tinged every facet of the equipment, every line and crack of every face, the eyes, the pores, all their clothes and every surface. He had the feeling that they were outside of time while the universe moved beneath them, or rather moved outside the ship.

Vince didn't breathe – it wasn't that he couldn't, but his brain told him it would be a really bad idea.

Chapter 44

Nightmare Run

Jennifer sucked air into aching lungs. The fear of breathing in liquid vanished, or, rather, was overcome by the desperate need to inhale anything. Despite a faint sensation of vapour entering her lungs, which she decided was probably psychosomatic, the dread of drowning in liquid mercury proved erroneous. Even so, she bent forward to regain her breath. She heard coughing down below.

Within two minutes Dimitri swept into the control room along with several other technicians, half of them still dressed in their sleepwear.

"How long?" she croaked in Dimitri's direction. He looked at his chronometer, and shook his head. "According to my watch, no time has passed, but we cannot rely on anything mechanical, since all movement froze. I had the definite sense of suspension of time, like being encased in glass. My thoughts simply paused. A fascinating sensation!"

Jennifer could see his excitement, while everyone else appeared closer to panic or nausea. Still, the others were all engineers and scientists driven by curiosity, and soon were poring over the monitors, and the recess that held the key.

She walked right up to Dimitri so only he could hear. "Were we really in some kind of liquid?"

"I do not know." He beamed. "This is such an adventure! A liquid would make sense, as it is irrepressible, so it would be a good dampener for any accelerative or decelerative effects, but there is no trace of residue. I think perhaps it was a perceptual illusion, a side-effect of the mode of transit itself."

She nodded. Then she remembered her companion. "Er… Dimitri – this is Cheveyo – he's the one who saved me from the Alicians. He had the key.' She turned to the Sentinel Master. "Cheveyo, have you actually travelled in one of these before?"

The man she addressed seemed to be listening for something. Finally he spoke, as much to himself as to them.

"Good. We may yet have enough time." He raised his voice, attracting all within listening range. "The aliens who built this ship – the Q'Roth – have not yet awoken, but they will. When they do they will storm the ship and kill everyone aboard. We cannot stop them entering. If we try to hide outside they will hunt us down. Once they have feasted on us and drained our energy, they will fill this vessel with newly hatched Q'Roth and make the trip back to Earth, to harvest the population. There are some fifty ships on Earth like this one. Each one can transport a hundred thousand Q'Roth. Each Q'Roth will extract the bio-electric life energy of hundreds of humans, and live from it for a thousand years. All humanity will be consumed."

The full stop after his last word was like a silence grenade. Many mouths hung open, and all smiles at having survived the transit vanished. Even Dimitri gaped at him. Jennifer spoke. "Tell us what to do."

"Try again," Hendriks said, as Dimitri and the makeshift crew attempted to send them back to Earth. The key went back into the recess but nothing happened. There were mutterings and more than a few moans from the now-dressed crew; all thirty people who had been onboard squeezed into the smaller control room.

Eventually Cheveyo spoke, unperturbed. "It is as we believed. Long ago, one of my predecessors took a ship but never returned. We assume there is one key for coming here, and another for the return journey."

Jennifer studied Cheveyo. At the moment, she assumed, only the two of them knew there were nukes on board. He had clearly come here with a more or less empty ship, depriving the Q'Roth of a food supply, and was going to blow up the ship before it could be boarded, or, more likely she realized, just as it filled up with Q'Roth. His implacable gaze met hers. It seemed only minutes ago that she had agreed on a pact with him to replace Gabriel on this mission, but now it meant her own and her lover's death. There had to be another solution.

Dimitri perked up. "I refuse to believe these ships can only go to these two locations. It's absurd!"

Cheveyo nodded. His strangely accented voice radiated throughout the packed room. "I agree. But no one has ever been able to unravel the guidance system or its controls."

"We should go outside." Jennifer's small voice, in contrast, flew through the room like an arrow vanishing into bushes, not finding any target. Only someone else's authority could enable it to stick.

"She is right," Cheveyo said. "Here, we are corralled sheep awaiting slaughter. Out there we stand some chance."

Jennifer doubted he believed that, and wondered what game he was playing. But she knew that if they all stayed, they would die, and morale was free-falling into the abyss by the minute.

Some of the men began nodding, agreeing with Cheveyo, forgetting who had suggested it first. Jennifer was used to it, and right now didn't care. Urgent discussions and plans unfurled, and three groups were quickly formed, under Cheveyo's implicit authority.

"The engineering team must stay here with the Professor to work on the guidance system. I need a volunteer – you," he pointed to a man who Jennifer had not seen before; she was certain he wasn't a technician. "Take four people and move some of the larger crates outside to create an external perimeter and defensive position."

Jennifer was impressed – he had a confederate onboard, who was now being instructed to prepare the nuclear devices. At least, she thought, he's off-loading them, so there is a small chance we can escape if we can find out how to operate the ship.

As Cheveyo reeled out instructions, she noticed how no one saw fit to interrupt, or to question the orders' logic. They just needed someone to take charge. Right now, any plan would do.

He continued. "Last, I need five volunteers to come with myself and Jennifer to search for the Eden astronauts."

Gasps of surprise echoed around the room. Things had happened so quickly, that even Jennifer had not been thinking of any humans already there. She quickly assessed the odds of finding them as negligible, but had to admire the skill of this man, for the mere mention of the Ulysses crew, a team of military men, had an almost instant effect on the people – they now had hope and purpose – paper-thin if any of them thought about it, but, she witnessed, they didn't, and it was enough to galvanize them into action.

Volunteers stepped forward from the ranks quickly. Jennifer instinctively picked out the young attractive woman who'd been eyeing Dimitri – Sophia her name badge said – to come with Cheveyo's team. She didn't feel like leaving her behind, just in case.

The planning was minimal and simplistic in reality, but it kept the pack from panicking and running off blindly in all directions. People formed the three groups, some already heading toward the lower levels to get to the ground access. The only problem for Jennifer was that Dimitri had been designated to stay inside. Before she had time to talk to her lover privately, Cheveyo pulled her to one side.

"You must leave him. He has the mind of a genius – maybe he *can* unlock the ship's secrets. Your immediate path lies with me. If the enemy still sleeps, there is a chance we can inflict harm while they remain vulnerable. Besides, if you want you can run back here and be in time to die with him."

She glared at him but then realized he wasn't being sarcastic – just matter-of-fact. She walked up to Dimitri and leant forward, whispering in his ear.

"If they come, I'll be here. Please find the riddle of these scrolls; I know you can do it."

She kissed him gently on the cheek. But he pulled her towards him and embraced her openly in front of everyone. His big arms almost crushed her and conversation around them slowed. Polite coughing ensued. She closed her eyes, memorizing the feel of his skin, his still-sleepy smell, the pulse in his neck under her palm. Abruptly he let her go, and the full weight of his colossal intellect turned and hammered down on the instruments in front of him. She gazed at him a moment, remembering the first time she'd seen him lecture, and savoured the moment.

Cheveyo turned to leave, and she and five others followed him out of the room, the noise returning behind them like an onrushing tide. They headed wordlessly down the spiral walkway, following Cheveyo, to what end Jennifer didn't know. As they neared the lower exit, she clutched the locket with her right hand and intoned inside her mind, *watch over us, Gabe.*

* * *

Rashid was half way up a small tree, at the edge of the forest which the ship had all but flattened. He surveyed the behemoth through night goggles, but with no obvious heat signature, it wasn't possible to discern much detail – cold hard metal, no obvious openings or suggestions of where a door could be. After half an hour of observation, out of desperation, he fired a red flare above the craft to illuminate it. A couple of minutes later, with the parachuted incendiary spiralling down, he saw a crack open in one of the places he thought the door should most logically be, at the base in the middle of one of the ship's sides. He had to lean forward precariously on the edge of the branch to aim his pulse rifle. He still did not know what might come out, human or Q'Roth. As his finger hovered over the trigger, the branch creaked, then cracked and snapped beneath him, and in that instant, the rifle fired. As he fell forwards and down, a tougher branch slammed into his head and shoulder. He landed on his back on soft, mossy ground, blood oozing from his nose. He felt as if someone had just punched him in the face.

"By all the Gods, this is not the time for such foolish accidents!" He sat for a while, gingerly pinching the cartilage at the top of his nose to stem the flow, and then tried to mop up the blood with his kerchief. Struggling to his feet, he wanted to know if he had hit anyone when the rifle had fired, but if the occupants were Q'Roth, he decided he had better get back to the ship. He jogged slowly; his vision blurring from the semi-concussive blow. He knew he must be in shock from the fall, and would have to rouse Zack. Things were going downhill rapidly. He ploughed his way through the trees, stumbling occasionally, to the edge of the desert that had now encompassed the Lander. It was then that he realized the fusion detonator had fallen out of his jacket, and must be lying at the bottom of the tree.

* * *

Kat ran despite the pain in her lungs, but she was losing her bearings – yet her only hope was to get to the Lander. Then a red flare lit up the night sky, and she saw the Lander glint beneath it. *Thanks Zack! You're a bloody marvel!*

She ran in fast but long strides toward the flare, like in her marathon days. She needed to pace herself and not become short of breath when close to the ship. At least out here with the low level heat signature of the vegetation, and now with the flare itself, she could see better with the night goggles so she didn't trip over small rocks or bushes.

The unmistakable sound of a pulse rifle crackled in the distance ahead of her. She hoped Zack and Rashid weren't under attack. A second later, coming from some way behind her, she heard the pounding thuds of the young Q'Roth. It had obviously stopped when it had come out of the cave, probably getting its own bearings on this new planet, lending Kat a precious head start; but now it had resumed the hunt. Kat shifted gear to a sprint. She ran as fast as she could, ripping past rocks and shrubs, twigs and leaves whipping her face and outstretched arms, stinging her flesh. She knew from her nightmare that even though she thought this was her top speed, she could, and would, run faster before it was over.

She launched her last parachute flare so as to light up her way, not even stopping to do it, and tossed the small flare gun aside. She'd already shed most of her gear in order to run faster. A branch she hadn't seen clipped her night vision goggles and knocked them off her head. She kept running. She could hear the pounding on the ground less than thirty metres behind – it reminded her of the sound of a train: steady, rhythmic, a confident predator running down its prey, patient enough to wait for her to slip, slow down or make a mistake, or simply for the difference in their speed to close the gap. Kat pumped her arms harder.

Unlike her nightmare, she found she could channel her fear. She darted onwards, grazing bushes and dodging rocks by miniscule margins. She knew the creature was a matter of metres behind her now, as she glimpsed the top of the Lander up ahead – that meant the shrubbery would disappear and it would be open savannah in a few seconds. Mouth open and drawn back, eyes wide, arms pistoning furiously, she girded herself for the last sprint, thigh muscles burning, chest expanded, trying to take in more air to propel herself further, knowing that this would be the Q'Roth's chance to accelerate too. She might just make it. *Be there, Zack!*

* * *

Rashid lurched groggily around the cockpit. He activated the stasis re-animation sequence, but it would take another five minutes for Zack to come around, unless the pain woke him first. The perimeter radar showed a group converging on the Lander, obviously coming from the ship. He knew Zack must have a back-up detonator for the fusion reactor, but he had no idea where it was.

"Wake up, my friend, I hate to admit it, but I need you!" Rashid realized that having found companions after eleven solitary months, he didn't want to die alone.

He sealed the airlock and prepped the engines, though he saw it would be another ten minutes before lift-off was possible.

He was staring at the viewscreen facing the forest and the ship, trying to see the first signs of the advancing group, when the perimeter alarm went off a second time. The display showed two new figures moving fast towards the Lander, not coming from the newly arrived ship, but from the hills. With a sickening feeling in his stomach, he realized it was a chase scenario – a hunt. It had to be Kat or Blake, with a predator clearly gaining ground. He searched the cockpit and the second module frantically, but there were no heavy weapons left – the 'cannon' was depleted, and Blake had taken the smaller rocket launcher.

For a moment he considered staying put, but dismissed the idea – it was not in his nature to desert a comrade. In any case, he doubted it would take the Q'Roth long to break in or disable the ship. He figured he might as well die doing something his ancestors would be proud of. Grabbing his pulse rifle, he checked the magazine was fully charged, and headed for the airlock. He kicked the emergency release and leapt through the hatch, coming down faster than planned, landing heavily at the bottom of the stairs. He knew the knock he had taken in the tree was still affecting him, but he had to try to save whoever was coming. He then heard Kat yell a single word, *"Zack!"* A shout not far short of a scream.

Rashid knelt down to get a more steady aim, and then observed the scene unfold in slow motion. The flare was nearly down, casting a macabre light on the rapidly approaching figures. He could half-see Kat's face as she tore free from the bushes into the stretch of desert between her and the Lander, straining with every step, contorted whether through fear of imminent death, or pain from the exertion – or both. The creature was just behind her. Rashid saw the raw power in the beast, never before having seen one hunt. Even as he raised his rifle, he knew he had no clear shot, and they were too close together for him to use the rifle in free-flow mode. He watched helplessly as one of the creature's legs spread out sideways and then swept at Kat's back leg. Her forward momentum propelled her headlong through the night air, before she crashed down into the dust like a wounded gazelle brought down by a lion.

He fired two rounds as the creature pinned her down with one of its claws. He fired again three times in quick succession, barely gaining its attention. Kat struggled desperately to get free, while the creature pressed her into the ground. A shrill shriek burst forth as the creature raised two of its legs into the air, and Rashid knew it was about to take her life. He fired one more time before the rifle was knocked out of his hands and he was thrown to the floor. He looked up to see a short girl, a fierce look in her eyes. Confused, he turned back towards Kat to see another figure run towards the creature, shouting a warrior's death-cry and brandishing a blade of blue fire.

Rashid watched the man – suicidal it seemed – leap from the ground as the creature swung its two raised legs at him. The man rolled in mid-air, and Rashid could not tell if the legs hit him or not, but as he landed in the dust behind the creature, it was stilled. Its legs wavered once, twice, and then its legs buckled as it split clean in two, the top half falling backwards, the front half toppling over Kat.

Rashid jumped to his feet, following the girl, who was already sprinting toward the scene. She ran to the man in the dust, he ran to Kat. Three other men followed Rashid and, as he arrived, helped him heave the steaming, stinking carcass of cauterized black intestines and dark blue blood off her back. Without turning her over, Rashid knelt and patted her hard on the cheek.

"Kat, Kat! Can you hear me?"

She groaned, and appeared at best half-conscious. Rashid checked her back and neck for any obvious breakages but found none. "Support her head and get her back to our ship!" he shouted to the other two men. They hesitated.

"Now!" he shouted, and they jerked into action, lifting Kat carefully. Rashid glanced over to the girl kneeling next to the other man, who was sitting up, carrying a short silver cylinder. Rashid recognized the tell-tale electric blue of a nano-blade before it vanished into its sheath, as the girl helped the man get up. Blood was weeping from a line of six gashes across his stomach where the claws had caught him.

Rashid intercepted them. "You are a Sentinel, aren't you?"

The man spoke with obvious difficulty. "How do you... know of us?"

Rashid considered his priorities. He turned and jogged to catch up the other men and Kat. As he reached the hatch, Kat was coming round.

"You're alive! Kat, you survived your nightmare." He laid a hand on her shoulder. She looked like she'd just aged ten years.

She stirred. "Rashid!" she panted, "Nobody's more surprised than me. But I feel like a house fell on me. What happened? Where's Zack? He killed it, right?"

"Later." He checked her over, seeing if she could get up. With some effort, she spread her feet and stood on her own. She stared toward the mass of the creature some twenty metres away, but said nothing.

The girl and the man arrived, as did two more men and a woman. Rashid felt the warrior's eyes boring into him, but it was the girl that spoke.

"Sorry I pushed you by the way, but I didn't want you to shoot our stunt-man here. My name's Jennifer."

Rashid looked her up and down. "I'm Rashid. You pack quite a punch. But... you came in the ship? The Q'Roth ship?"

She nodded. "There's about thirty of us. But what about you? You're not one of the Ulysses astronauts. Where are the others?"

Before he could think of where to start, Kat piped up. "Rashid. I need to talk to you a moment – alone."

He crouched down, noting the hooded look in her eyes.

She did her best to whisper. "The Q'Roth will be coming, Rashid. That wasn't a guardian – that was a newborn. They'll flood down this hill. We have to take off."

He stared at her, and then up towards the hill, then addressed Jennifer.

"I'm afraid we are all in terrible danger. The hatching has started. There are likely to be thousands like that one coming this way very soon." He glanced at the warrior. "Even your nano-sword will not help us this time."

"What are we supposed to do?" said the young woman who had stayed in the background until now, a trace of an Italian accent. "We can't take off! Let us come with you!"

Before Rashid could answer, Jennifer cut in. "Sophia, they can't take us. It's a four-man craft, at best, if I'm not mistaken. We should go back to the ship and make a stand there."

Sophia turned on her. "You gotta' be crazy! We're – what did he say?" She pointed to Cheveyo, "corralled sheep! You can go and get eaten with your boyfriend if you like. This ship could damn well try and take us!"

Rashid smelled rising panic in the air. These people, he realized, were not trained astronauts or military, they were civilians. With alarm he noticed the woman was armed with a pistol. Without warning, it was out and she was waving it around.

"Listen, I'm not going to die on this fucking planet. I'm getting on board, and anyone tries to stop me is cooked meat". She backed nervously toward the steps.

Rashid noticed that the warrior was too far from her to do anything, and was bleeding heavily in any case. As she reached the bottom rung of the ladder, still aiming the gun at them, a hand dropped down from inside the ship, and pressed something silver onto her neck. Her body sagged and her eyes rolled upwards. The hand from the ship caught her neck and held her, and a strained voice shouted. "Well for Christ's sake somebody take her, she ain't as light as she looks."

Rashid turned to Kat. Sure enough, just after two men took her slack, anaesthetized body, Zack showed himself.

"Anyone like to tell me what the hell is going on?"

Before they could answer, the long range perimeter alarm sounded off. It rose in pitch, indicating multiple incursions.

Rashid took control. "Prepare for take-off, Zack – they're coming." He turned to the others. "I'm sorry. We can take one, no more, or else we cannot lift off."

Jennifer spoke for all of them. "We understand. Take her." She pointed to Sophia. "I for one don't want to be caught while trying to carry that bitch's body on my back, and try as I might, I can't quite bring myself to leave her as a distracting morsel to slow them down."

Rashid nodded. "Good luck." The small group turned to leave, breaking into a jog, led by the warrior, evidently in severe pain. Together with Kat he hoisted Sophia onto the ship.

"For the record," Zack said, "she's with you guys, 'cause my wife don't tolerate any hanky-panky. And you both look like shit, by the way." He dragged his bad leg off to the cockpit.

Rashid was relieved once they retracted the ladder and sealed the hatch. They dumped the girl in a stasis pod and he activated it, then he joined Kat in the cockpit where Zack was already strapped into Blake's seat, shivering, a side-effect of rapid stasis exit, and no doubt the pain in his leg. Zack shrugged, and held up an empty trimorph phial.

"Don't feel a thing. Come on, Rashid – let's see if you can really fly."

"Stasis, my friend."

"After take-off, not before," he retorted.

Rashid sighed, and strapped in, trying hard to ignore the perimeter alarm, which instead of individual beeps was now a steadily rising whine.

Zack addressed Kat. "Blake and Pierre?"

Rashid, sitting in Zack's usual seat, turned around as the engines started their pre-burn. Kat shook her head once. "They're in the cavern, but by now hundreds of Q'Roth have hatched."

Zack stared resolutely at the control panel in front of him, his jaw set.

Rashid needed to focus on their imminent plight. "How close are they, and how many?" he said to Kat, who was studying the perimeter radar screen. It was still not yet light enough to see very far, although dawn was approaching.

"At least a hundred, maybe more… the first ones are just about to arrive."

"Then to hell with the pre-checks, we go now!" Rashid waited a fraction of a second to see if Zack objected, but Zack pushed back in his chair and folded his arms.

"You're in the chair," Zack said.

Rashid punched a final key sequence and the roar of the thrusters shook the entire ship. At the same time, there was a loud bang as the first Q'Roth hit the side of the ship.

As he eased forward on the engine throttle, Zack shouted above the din in the cockpit. "Toast them, Rashid. A spin take-off should do the trick."

Rashid bit his lip and rammed the engines full throttle, thrusting him back into his seat as they tore away from the ground, then squeezed a side-bar on the joy-stick, causing the Lander to rotate as it ascended. It was a well-known illegal war manoeuvre, spreading a curtain of flame over a hundred metre diameter beneath them, and scorching their hull. *At least this may give our new friends a little time.* But as they struggled to take off, feeling Eden's gravity pulling at them, he thought of Blake and Pierre being consumed by these monsters. He heard a roaring scream and felt a clunk as something tore off the side of the ship, and they catapulted upwards. Now he had to focus on only one thing – *warn Earth.* He glanced over to Zack, who was drifting in and out of consciousness, having far exceeded the safe trimorph dosage.

"Should we put Zack into the stasis chamber?" Kat asked.

"No – I may still need his advice while I'm trying to dock with only one thruster." He concentrated on the nav track to find the orbiter, and noticed a new alarm on the central pilot's panel. The young Q'Roth who had tried to hitch a lift had inflicted damage before being incinerated.

Kat spoke as Eden fell away beneath them, and the grav unit kicked in to dampen the acceleration effect. "Rashid, the thought that Zack would be there ready to save me; it somehow kept my fear from overwhelming me. But in fact he wasn't there for me."

"That is the beauty of friendship, the beauty of faith, of hope."

"But –"

"You're alive. Without that trust in him, you would not be. That's what matters: the bonds between us. That is what makes us strong. Now, we've little time. Go and prepare a stim for Zack."

She complained. "But that's dangerous, he –"

"The Q'Roth damaged the last manoeuvring thruster when we took off. I'm not sure we can dock without it. The stim, please."

As Kat unstrapped and headed back to the second compartment, Rashid thought to himself, looking over to Zack's unconscious frame, *in fact, my large friend, it is time to see if you can really fly as well as I have heard.*

Chapter 45

Plan B

Micah fell to his knees and dry-retched as the pseudo-liquid evaporated. He gasped several times and coughed so hard he could feel the bronchioles straining in his lungs. But he was relieved – he'd been sure he would drown. He noticed that only three men remained upright, Vince, Commander Vasquez and the new arrival. Everyone else was bent double, or on all fours. Vince still had a gun pointing at the drenched man.

"Name?" Vince demanded.

Micah was impressed that Vince spoke so clearly, as if unaffected by the transfer.

"Ramires," the man said. "I knew Ralph. A good man, and a former partner of yours, I believe. Very clever, managed to infiltrate the Alicians. He died uncovering the secret of that key."

Vince's trigger finger flexed. "For all I know, you killed him."

Micah got to his feet, though his throat still stung from the coughing. All eyes that weren't still watering were on the face-off. Ramires was equivocal, a non-mocking smile spread under his black moustache.

"If that's what you believe then pull the trigger. Otherwise we had better get moving. And I could do with some dry clothes."

Vince's pulse pistol remained fixed on its target, his arm steady. "Where are we?"

"You know where we are. They *will* come. Soon."

Micah moved over next to Sandy. He thought about trying to intervene, but she put a steadying hand on his elbow.

Vince lowered the weapon, and picked up the microphone to the PA system. As he clicked it on, there was a brief whine to gain everyone's attention.

"Okay – listen up everybody. We're on Eden. We're here to stop an invasion. Centre of Ops is tower level four. We have five airborne units prepped, so we spread out in cardinal directions, one stays here in reserve. I'm handing over detailed military operations to Colonel Vasquez."

He passed the microphone to the Colonel, who set about issuing crisp orders as if he'd been born doing it. In amongst them, he sent an orderly to find some dry fatigues for Ramires. Vince walked over to Micah and Sandy.

"The rest is up to the military guys for now, you two need to stay out of their way. Vasquez is a good tactician – my CO in Black Ops more than once in the War."

Sandy cocked her head at Vince. "You're actually going to take orders from someone? This I have to see."

"Dream on. I'm still in charge overall, but he'll get them on the move – he's more up to speed on the hardware and mil-ops than I am. But we need to work on Plan B."

"How to get home?" Sandy asked, momentarily distracted by Ramires unceremoniously stripping naked on the other side of the room.

But before Vince could answer, Micah surprised himself and them by answering.

"No. How to escape from both Earth and Eden." As soon as he'd said it, he wished he hadn't, because he knew it was right. It was booster-enhanced lucidity, enabling him to make an inferential leap. But he needed to unpack it.

"Look, Vince, Sandy, we're stuck in the Alician's game, and they've been moving our pieces for centuries. What are our real chances of winning or even surviving? Earth is going to be in dire straits, maybe doomed." His gut tightened, as if only now catching up with where his mind was headed. He rushed on, needing to get it all out while he had the mental clarity. "And Eden is a trap, a Q'Roth nest. We have to get off their chessboard." Something from his last Optron experience surfaced. There had been a presence there – alien – but not malevolent. And then the realization shook him: the Q'Roth – this wasn't the first time; humanity was just next on their list. Which meant… "Another planet! There must be other planets. We have to find one!"

Vince stared at him hard, and then turned to Ramires.

"*Is* there somewhere else?"

Ramires paused as he buckled his belt. "Rumour has it. But we have no maps, if that's what you mean. We also understand from our one off-worlder encounter centuries ago that it is a vastly advanced place near the inner ring of the galaxy."

"Meaning?" Vince asked.

Ramires put his tunic and jacket on, and zipped it up. "You eat meat, I presume. Many do because it comes from animals that we consider unintelligent."

Micah had understood this implicitly during the Optron feedback from the alien presence. He jumped in. "You mean that there are intelligences vastly superior to our own, so we'd be in serious danger."

Ramires' nod was solemn. "We've never had a credible 'Plan B' as you call it, not for centuries."

"Great," Vince said flatly.

Micah stared hard at the ground, concentrating. Suddenly his mind broke through.

"That's it! Of course!"

Vince folded his arms.

Micah beamed. "We need to find a planet the Q'Roth have already been to, one they've already… harvested."

Sandy butted in. "But Micah, there won't be much left of it, will there?"

"Doesn't matter. It'll probably be deserted, but it'll be safe. The Q'Roth would have no reason to go back, and other races won't be interested."

They all stared at Micah for a while, before Vince cleared his throat and spoke.

"Well, Micah, as plan B's go, it's a long way from what I'd hoped for, but at the moment I don't have a better one. You work out a way to find such a planet. Vasquez and I are going to introduce the locals to hell while we can. Ramires, care to join?" He and Ramires walked over to Colonel Vasquez.

Sandy stared at Micah. "You know, a few days ago when you breezed into my office demanding to see Kane, I thought you were a complete nerd."

He dared a smile. "And now?"

She grinned. "Well, let's just say I think I've seriously underrated how useful nerds can be." She touched his shoulder, her smile fading. "Find a way to this other planet, Micah. I have a bad feeling we're going to need it."

He needed more time to think. There was still more information embedded in the Optron message, he was sure of it, and location would be an obvious thing to encode; he just needed to find a way to decrypt it. He glanced at the Q'Roth controls and displays around them – probably the location of former vanquished planets was sitting in a navigational

387

database in that very room, but it could take weeks to begin to understand their technology and how to search it.

He turned and gazed out the porthole at the night sky, abruptly flooded with stark halogen lights as the bay doors opened, and the first jets rolled out, wings already folded down. *These men are sharp.* He heard the first engine winding up.

As the glaring lights revealed trees, rocks, bushes and grass, he had a hard time believing it was Eden; it looked so much like Earth. He surreptitiously pinched his left arm with his right hand.

Sandy stood next to him. "I don't blame you. But we're not going to wake up."

The jets lifted off vertically, one by one, hovered for a moment, then pitched their noses down and raced forward, piercing the night-time shroud at the edge of the lights' range. He wondered how many would return. *We're desperate, fighting for our very survival, the right to live.* Then he corrected himself – rights are irrelevant out here. That's one of the lessons we have to grasp on this steep learning curve, if we don't fall right off it. He turned to Sandy.

"We haven't been awake for centuries," he said. "That's the problem. And now it's too late."

An hour later, as his gaze followed one of the last aircraft disappearing into the pre-dawn sky, he noticed an oddly-shaped mountain. He hadn't been able to see it before, but now its silhouette was just visible as the first inkling of sunlight edged its way down the mountain's side. He recognized it – he'd seen it in the datastream, from the other side of the desert. Whoever – or whatever – had encoded the hidden Optron message could be there, and maybe the Ulysses crew too, if they had survived. He made up his mind, and turned around to Vince and Vasquez, locked in discussion with the last of the pilots.

His words scythed through the chatter in the room, with a conviction he'd never felt before. "Vince. Colonel Vasquez, I need a plane and a pilot. Right now."

All eyes in the room fell on him, and all conversation ceased.

"Plan B," he said.

Sandy arched an eyebrow. "That jacket really does suit you, Micah."

* * *

Jennifer and the others heard the roar of the Lander as it took off, three hundred metres behind them. She glanced over her shoulder to see it streaking into the dawn sky. They were making good progress but Cheveyo was clearly on his last legs, though he uttered no complaint. Abruptly he stopped, and collapsed into a seated position against a tree trunk.

"You – all of you," he gasped, "go back to the ship – Jennifer, I need a word."

The others looked at him and then at her. She could tell they didn't want to leave him but they didn't want to die either. She turned to the rest of them. "Go – I'll catch up."

One of the men hesitated while the others turned and ran towards the ship. She made a mental note to remember his face – someone a little braver than the rest.

'What about –" he began, pointing at Cheveyo.

"Just go," Jennifer replied. "Tell them we need to leave imminently. *GO!"*

He nodded and ran to catch up the others. She knelt beside Cheveyo and inspected his wound. It exuded a sickly green puss, the blood congealing into a jelly-like substance.

"Their blood is poisonous – when I cut the creature in half, some drops sprayed into the gashes it carved into me. Very careless – I must be getting old."

She saw him try to smile. "Is there anything I –"

"No – I have very little time. There are things you must know." He moved his closed left fist over to her hand and opened it. She saw a metallic object, and recognized it as an ankh symbol, but with a different hue – a lighter aquamarine – to the one that had brought them here. She took it.

"I removed it from the creature's chest. They are somehow born with them, so any one of them can launch the ship for the return journey. You must take the ship back to Ireland, if your man has unlocked the navigational secrets. Ireland is still radioactive, which means the Q'Roth will not want to land there; they are newborn, after all, and no creature is impervious to sub-atomic radiation. Coordinate an exodus from there: collect as many people as you can. Then leave Earth and don't look back.

Head to the stars." He coughed more blood, but was too weak to move. She wiped it from his lips with her sleeve.

He continued, and she read the urgency of death in his eyes. "Tell Yori – the man who will be the last one waiting for my return, to set a three-minute timer to detonate the devices here on Eden, and that I am gone. He is preparing the nuclear devices even as we speak. He will follow your orders from now on."

A dark wave of pain crawled across his face. She'd seen a lot of fatal wounds in Dublin – he should be dead already.

"Listen carefully," he croaked. "The Alician inner circle has for centuries controlled scientific advances for their own purposes; releasing certain inventions, drawing us down blind alleys for things we should have invented; releasing diseases, starting wars. They also experimented with genetic engineering."

"You must save your breath –"

"This is not a history lesson! We, too, performed limited genetic manipulation – only a few individuals – to upset the Alician timetable. Some of humanity's geniuses have been our greatest work. Kostakis."

She recoiled. "Dimitri? He's been altered?'

Cheveyo's body convulsed. He ground his teeth against the pain. Then his chest locked, and she knew he could no longer breathe in. Even in the darkness she could see the blue tinge of hypoxia setting in. He spoke fast, the energy failing in his last words.

"Keep him alive, Jennifer. And you, you stay too much in the shadows. Now is your time. Hendriks will try to take control of the ship, but he is not a leader, and will vacillate. You must take charge. Take the data crystal from my neck, and the nano-sword." There was no breath left. He mouthed his last words silently. "You said you wanted it."

His eyes glazed, and his neck went slack.

She reached forward and closed his eyes. "And I was just getting to like you. Do you know how rare that is?" She took a deep breath. "Tell Gabriel I miss him, but I'm still in the fight." She snatched the data crystal from his neck, grabbed the nano-sword, and sprinted toward the ship.

Chapter 46

Eagle Down

Blake knelt by the opening of the crevasse, its entrance plunging into darkness. He hoped it led to Pierre; if not, he'd thrown his life away for nothing. He prayed the explosion he'd rigged at the chamber entrance had enabled Kat to make her getaway, that she at least would make it back to the Lander, and they could warn Earth – if there was still time. For him there was only one way out, but he waited. She had said the Q'Roth had a small craft – that would give them a huge advantage; he suspected it was armed and would take out their Lander once outside.

He hefted the compact rocket launcher, the one Zack had nicknamed "shotgun", onto his shoulder, flicking a switch to arm the heat seeking missile. The targetter picked out a small craft zipping across the tops of the eggs, several of which were splintering and beginning to hatch. He was unable to make out much detail, as the mosquito-like craft was still several hundred metres away. He had only one shot – he and Zack had cooked up a 'dirty' bomb, taking out half the missile fuel and replacing it with rocket fuel. It would act like a Molotov cocktail, but burn much hotter. He waited until the craft was level with him, and fired.

The missile streaked cross the cavern towards its target, but was intercepted. It must have been a young Q'Roth, just hatched. Their reactions and co-ordination must far exceed humans, he thought, as it leapt up right in front of the small ship and took most of the missile's blast force. The cavern exploded with light, making him squint and raise his forearm in front of his eyes, the incandescent body of the newborn Q'Roth hurtling to the ground like a meteorite. He was as shocked as he was impressed: these Q'Roth were going to be powerful infantry if that act was anything to judge by. He didn't relish the thought of fighting them on an open battlefield.

The sharp sound of a high pitched engine announced the craft as it accelerated through the curtain of flame engulfing the Q'Roth martyr and a handful of nearby eggs. It was heading straight toward him. Blake tossed the empty weapon to the floor, unshouldering his pulse rifle which he gripped in both hands in front of him, and stared at the gaping hole before him. He drew in a deep breath, and then leapt into its yawning mouth.

He hit the ground, rolled, and launched into a sprint, bouncing off the walls of the steep winding tunnel; each time he fell he managed to roll and come up running, continuing downwards. There was no choice: relentless stamping thuds echoed behind him. He had the impression it was only one, as if that made a difference. The creature could obviously run down this tunnel fluidly. If he fell and paused too long it would be on him. He realized that for the first time in his career, he truly understood what 'retreat' really meant – he'd usually been distanced, the strategist giving orders. Despite his many combat years, fear threatened to make him stumble. But he kept Pierre in his mind – that was his mission now, to save him. The fact that he was leading the Q'Roth down to him was secondary. First, however, he had to get out of the damned tunnel.

He rounded a bend at high speed, to find that the tunnel split into two. Just as he was thinking *"which way?"* Pierre shouted a single word.

"Left!"

Blake veered left without slowing down, grazing the wall with his shoulder, pushing off it with the butt of his rifle. A few seconds later he noticed that the tunnel was getting lighter, which meant he was approaching an opening. Blake focused on the ground five metres in front of him, as he'd been trained to do years before, anticipating every bump and rock. His fleeting hope that the creature would turn right was crushed as the creature roared, in the same corridor, two seconds behind.

The tunnel widened into a small room, the outstretched body of Pierre lying prone and facing him, a pulse pistol in one hand, the other hand supporting it. *Idiot, that won't even slow it down!* But it was too late, the slope left no way for Blake to decelerate even if he'd wanted to. Pierre didn't budge an inch as Blake ran straight towards him and leapt into the air, diving over his body towards the wall behind. As he flew through the air, he primed his rifle and tucked his head down for a crash-roll. He hit the ground hard, heard Pierre's gun go off, and rolled up into a braced position, his back slamming into the wall, rifle ready to fire.

As he levelled his weapon, the creature was already hurtling towards him, two legs outstretched – he didn't even have time to look at Pierre. Blake kicked off with his left foot and dived right, as the Q'Roth sailed into the wall. Its body pounded the solid rock like a battering ram, sounding like a tank smashing into a cliff face. Blake fired four times before he realized the unthinkable – it was already dead. He stared in disbelief. His pulse shots had hardly made a mark on it, but he watched as the creature's exterior crumbled and bubbled. In seconds, the smooth, laminated skin became corrugated, rotting flesh. He dashed over to Pierre, who had his head propped against the opposite wall. He was staring at his pistol, breathing hard, in bad shape.

Pierre spoke in pain-spiked gasps. "Glad... just one... shot."

Blake squatted down in front of him. He lifted the pistol from Pierre's yielding hand, and opened it to reveal the empty glass chamber. He looked back over to the Q'Roth, a putrid smell like burning flesh exuding from the imploding corpse.

"Nannites?" Blake said. "But how? Our ship was screened completely before we left." But it didn't matter – it was good news: nannites were extremely effective against the warriors. Problem was, Earth had banned them years ago.

Pierre's breathing grew more laboured. He lifted a hand and pointed to his head.

Blake shook his head. "Inside you? Your blood?"

Pierre nodded.

Blake thought about it for a moment, trying to remember the details of nannite-human contact. "But you should be dead. In fact you should be – well, like that.' He pointed to the rotting corpse, then changed tack. "Okay, you can explain later. Can you stand?"

Pierre barely nodded, and Blake took one arm and lifted him onto his feet, keeping Pierre's arm around his own shoulder.

"Which way?"

Pierre pointed down a short tunnel to the right, then back to the warrior. "Sir... metal object... on its chest... important."

Blake propped Pierre against the wall, and walked cautiously over to the corpse. Blake took out one of his small knives and carefully pried a small blue ankh symbol off the fizzing mass, not wanting to touch any of it. He took out a cloth and wrapped it up, then discarded the nannite contaminated knife, its blade already browning with rust.

"Got it."

"Surprised you... came back." He began coughing.

"Save your breath, Pierre. I came to rescue you, that's all, but I need you conscious, ideally with an idea of how to get us the hell out of here."

Pierre coughed again, a trickle of blood issuing from the corner of his mouth. "Take the little one," he said, and then slumped unconscious.

Blake struggled under Pierre's full weight, unsure what he meant, until he turned the corner and saw the vast cavern in front of them, and the massive metal ship. He then saw the much smaller jade green ship, saucer-shaped, its hatch open. But the human skeleton stopped him in his tracks.

He lay Pierre on the ground, and bent down to inspect it, finding a small dust-covered journal next to the body. There was an ankh sumbol on the front cover. He picked up the book, read the last entry, and noted the date. He could scarcely believe it: three centuries of a silent war with the Alicians, the "vassals of the Q'Roth". He wanted to find the nearest Alician and tear him apart with his bare hands. He raised his rifle, flicked it into free-flow mode, and aimed at the larger ship in the distance. But while his finger hovered in front of the trigger, he thought of Glenda: she'd always said that anger was the last resort of an unintelligent man. He didn't fire. She still needed him, was depending on him; they all were back on Earth. Right now they needed him to think.

He submerged his anger, and focused on strategy. The Alicians and Q'Roth had clearly been planning and orchestrating humanity's demise for a very long time. Could he and others really derail their plans? He recalled what General Kilaney, had told him one day: "Toughest lesson to learn for a man like you, Blake, is when to retreat and re-group, because one day you'll face a choice between fighting to the bitter end, or retreating but surviving to fight again another day."

A rumbling noise, like the sound of hundreds of horses galloping, intruded on his thoughts. He heaved Pierre onto his shoulders and headed for the open hatchway of the green ship.

* * *

Micah wasn't used to flying in a military jet, and several times thought he was going to throw up onto the back of the pilot's seat in front of him. They raced over Eden's terrain, skimming above hills and forests in a cloudless sky. They'd checked a relief holo-map relayed by one of the reconnaissance sorties. Micah had recognized some of the features. There was the desert that had clearly expanded on a massive scale, and there had obviously been some type of explosion or earthquake – possibly both – that had altered the topography. Vasquez told Micah he suspected it was due to a high energy detonation, judging from the concentric rings in the silicated central part of the desert. It crossed his mind that the Eden Lander had blown up. But Vasquez said it resembled the aftermath of a neutralino explosion, though it made no sense for them to have brought the ND down from orbit. Micah guessed it must have been the IVS ship they'd figured had come to Eden.

He had déjà vu, as if he'd been here before; the Optron message had evidently lodged the information in his subconscious, though he had no idea how. He was sure they were near to where the Eden crew should be. They flew a spiral search pattern from the foot of the small mountain, around eighty kilometres from their own ship. They got a radio message from Vince.

"This is Base. We just picked up an orbital signal. The Ulysses mother ship is still up there, and the Eden Lander is en route. We're trying to establish contact. Eagle Three has detected an enemy ship three hundred klicks south. We need all fighters back here."

Before Micah could speak, he heard a click and the pilot's answer.

"Roger that, returning home."

In that moment Micah caught sight of something out of the corner of his eye just as they began a hard bank to the left – a glimpse of black: it looked like the conning tower of another ship as it encountered the first rays of Eden's sun. Micah spoke to the pilot. "Hey, I just saw something back there. I think it was another –"

"Hold on!" the pilot shouted, banking hard the other way; the violent manoeuvre slammed Micah's helmet into the plazglass canopy. Shrill alarms erupted in the cockpit, clanging loudly. He was trying to figure out what was going on when the pilot came on line.

"Command – Eagle Five is under fire, repeat we're under fire!"

Micah tried to turn around to see what was behind them. An electric blue arc swept narrowly above his head. The jet jerked down so hard that Micah momentarily lost his breath, his internal organs pushed upwards by the G-force. They passed over a clearing and a chill ran down his spine: a mass of blue-black animals charged towards where he thought he'd seen another ship. As he and the pilot raced thirty metres overhead he caught more details of the creatures, several hundred of them, in the early morning light. Some of the creatures, without breaking step, rotated their heads upwards towards him; instinctively he wanted the pilot to go higher.

The jet banked left and then right, heading away from the ship, and accelerated forward so fast that Micah's cheeks and brow were sucked backwards. The pilot wheeled and rolled the ship as Micah tried to stay in one piece, the deadly blue arc getting closer with each sweep, homing in on them.

A sizzling slash of electric blue fizzed through the cockpit in front of Micah. The pilot's body transformed into a flaming corpse. Micah panicked as the jet pitched downwards, a forest looming ahead. His hands groped around his seat, desperately seeking the eject lever. Just as the jet began a somersault, he found it and pulled hard. There was a roar of noise as his head was squeezed down by the sudden wind, pile-driving his head into his shoulders. He gripped the edges of the seat as he shot upwards, and then sickeningly downwards, cart-wheeling through a dizzying alternating vista of trees and sky, until the parachute opened and his chair righted itself. He watched as another blue arc sliced through the jet, cleaving it in two. It disintegrated into myriad fireballs hurtling into the forest.

He rocked under the parachute, and caught sight of the Q'Roth ship passing overhead – resembling a helicopter but moving parallel with him. He was close to the tree-line and made the decision. He had no idea where the courage came from – he just knew he had only seconds to escape. He held his breath and thumped the parachute release buckle on his chest strap, and launched himself towards the tree canopy.

* * *

Kat's face was incredulous. "Are you seeing what I'm seeing?"

Rashid re-checked his instruments. "It cannot be! There are low level fighter jets down there!"

"I'm picking up radio transmissions," she said, "but they're still garbled. Probably short-wave radio, or XHF – *military!*"

Although Kat was still shaken-up from the chase, she worked furiously on the comms console to try and break through. "Come on!" she said, punching the panel with her fist. "I can't make it out, Rashid, but I heard something, and I'd swear it was English." She glanced over at Zack who still hadn't come round despite the stims injected into him five minutes earlier. *Please, wake up Zack!*

"We must dock," Rashid said. "Then we will have more chance of communicating from orbit."

"How long till then?"

"Fifteen minutes," Rashid said, but Kat could hear the uncertainty in his voice.

She was staring at her comms screen when black dots began to appear. She tried to speak to Rashid but her own voice sounded far away. She shouted, louder, as her vision blackened, and all the noise in the cockpit became muffled. She heard a faint voice, that of Rashid, as if from another room, growing fainter.

"Kat! Can you hear me?"

She had the sensation of floating, barely aware of her body. She realized it must be the node, but it felt different this time. Rashid's voice was gone, but another voice, somehow familiar, was growing louder. *What was it saying?* She tried to figure it out. Then it cleared.

"Open your eyes!"

Yes, she thought, *my eyes are closed*. With a supreme effort of will she opened her eyes, and saw not Rashid, but Blake. The image was very clear – Blake was standing in front of her and Pierre lay unconscious, in odd surroundings. He was talking directly to her.

"... hope you can hear me, there's not much time. Kat – repeat this to Rashid and Zack. I'm communicating through a Hohash connection. I can see through your eyes, and you're seeing via the Hohash; it's here in this craft. Pierre and I are both alive. We're in a spider ship. You must tell Earth that invasion is imminent. Nano-weapons and nukes are the only defence – I know we have almost none of the former and the latter doesn't help Earth either, but it's that or nothing. Stay in orbit for now, this place is swarming with Q'Roth. Tell them Kat. And tell Zack *Omega Kappa*. Repeat it all now, say it out loud so Rashid can hear!"

She recited everything to Rashid, dully, listlessly, like a poem she didn't understand. Blake nodded throughout, and at the end seemed to relax. Then he said he was going to break the connection. Kat didn't react, just continued to float. She closed her eyes again, and began to fall, hearing a noise like an aircraft landing on her head.

She snapped awake, gasping for breath, standing straight up, nearly hitting the ceiling. "Bloody hell, that was weird!" She leant against the bulkhead behind her console, her head throbbing, her body tingling all over.

"Easy, my friend," Rashid said, re-taking the pilot's chair. "Calm yourself. That was quite an experience you just had. You saw Blake, did you not?"

She felt as if she'd been possessed. It reminded her of some of the bad trips she'd initially had with the node. "Yes. Blake, and Pierre too, unconscious. Looked in pretty bad shape." She dropped back down into her chair.

"They were in some kind of ship, a small one. And – oh shit, I remember now. There was a human skeleton there, laid out on the floor, and…" She appreciated the value of the detached node state, as the scene flooded back to her.

Zack coughed and swivelled his chair around to face Kat.

"Goddammed difficult to get any sleep around here. I've been listening, Kat, most of it, anyways. What was the rest?"

She was relieved to have Zack back. "I could also see past Blake outside the ship. There were Q'Roth, hundreds of them, streaming past. A few were trying to break in."

She watched the blood flow back into Zack's face, the former sleepy facial tone setting into an iron-hard grimace. With a grunt he heaved himself out of the Captain's chair, poised above Rashid.

"Out," he commanded.

"Zack," Rashid protested, "you are not fit, and the manoeuvring thruster is damaged… We could all die!"

"Then we die. This is taking too fucking long. You're an okay pilot, but this is war. I'm going to show you emergency docking like you've never seen before."

Rashid acquiesced under Zack's intense stare. Zack fell into the chair, and strapped himself in. "Hang on to something, this is going to be rough."

Rashid got in Blake's chair just in time. Kat felt herself thrust backwards as Zack fired the engines at full power. After a minute of fast, silent running, automatic collision warnings began to shriek. Zack's good foot permanently disabled the auditory alarm system. He shrugged. "It was getting on my nerves."

Kat trusted Zack, but as they spotted the bright dot that was the mother ship, and it quickly mushroomed in size before her eyes, she began to wonder just how late he would leave it to apply the brakes.

* * *

Jennifer ran all the way, thinking of her new mission and mantle passed onto her by Cheveyo: return to Earth, pick up people, and head to the stars. Everything was moving so quickly, she felt breathless. Was the demise of Earth so likely, resistance so futile now that the only recourse was escape? She had only met Cheveyo yesterday, she realized, and her world was already spinning out of control. And yet she'd seen a Q'Roth warrior, travelled in their ship to Eden in the blink of an eye – they were clearly way ahead technologically, and they had the Alicians on their side, presumably ready to tear Earth down from within. She needed Dimitri's counsel, to anchor her. He would know what to do – especially now she had learned that he'd been genetically advanced. But Cheveyo had told her that she was the one to lead. He clearly had more faith in her than she did.

She arrived at the four-crate perimeter to see a lone figure there. "Yori – Cheveyo is dead," she said, short of breath. "Do we have radio link to the control room?"

The scarecrow-thin Japanese looked at her suspiciously, then, seeing the nanosword tucked in her belt, appeared to come to a decision. He nodded, holding up a small hand-held device. She took it, and pressed the call button, causing a brief crackle.

"Hello? This is Jennifer. Hand me over to…" she paused as she thought about it. "Give me Hendriks, quickly."

A gruff voice came on at the other end of the line. "Come inside, we'll close –"

"Listen to me very carefully," she interrupted, almost shouting. "They're coming. Now. Have you figured out the navigation system?"

"Well, yes, in a limited way. For Earth at least, we can select destinations, roughly."

"Set it for Ireland, Dublin if possible."

"But Dublin –"

"Is irradiated, I know, but it means they won't follow us there. Set it now. We're timing the nukes to go off in three minutes." She nodded to Yori, who pulled out a pad and started tapping into it.

"I'm coming up with the key to start the engines."

"Nukes? Now you just wait a goddamned minute!" Hendriks shouted.

Yori showed her the pad.

"The nukes are set, Hendriks, and they can't be unset. Fix coordinates for Dublin. Do it or we all die! And close the outer doors, I don't want to take back any uninvited guests!"

She clicked off the transmitter, turned to Yori, and they bolted inside, seconds before the doors began to close. She wondered if they could reach the control room, seven floors up and inside the central part of the ship, in three minutes, when Yori headed left towards an electric buggy.

"One of the engineers brought it along," he said, with a wafer-thin smile.

As they jumped inside, the tyres screeched and they sprang forward, zipping across the lower floor towards the ramp. They careened up the spiral walkway at speed, so she had to hang on for fear of being thrown out, with one hand clutching the ankh. Yori at one point grabbed her waist to haul her inside. Abruptly they shrieked to a halt. Hendriks, along with some other men, stood in her path.

She noticed some kind of artifact that looked like a large antique mirror, propped up against the wall. Kostakis was staring at it, and then turned to catch her eye. He flicked his head with an expression of concern toward Hendriks and his men.

"Who put you in charge?" Hendriks demanded.

She knew she had to do this right. She thought of Cheveyo. *What would he do?*

"Listen, there's two minutes till the nukes go off. I have the key to get us out of here."

Hendriks unfolded his arms and wagged his finger close to her face. "Who gave you the right? Give me the key!" He spat the words.

"Stand down, Hendriks. I called you just now because you're a man of decision and logic. Don't prove me wrong."

A man called out from behind Hendriks. "Sir, there's something approaching us on our perimeter radar."

Jennifer held her ground. *Blink, you bastard.* Still he blocked her path.

"Sir," the radar operator said. "There's one ahead of the rest. It's... he's human, Sir, no doubt about it. The others aren't, and are closing fast."

Shit!

Hendriks' lips warped into a crooked smile. She noticed her new associate, Yori, draw away from her, leaving her standing alone.

"So," Hendriks said, "you want us to leave him to die here? Playing Miss God today, are we?"

She stopped trying to play Cheveyo – he'd told her it was her time, so she had to be herself. "Listen, you idiot, if we wait, they'll get in, and we'll *all* die!"

Hendriks spoke to the two heavy-set engineers next to him. "Hold her, and take the key. Open the –"

He didn't finish the sentence. As the two men went to grab Jennifer, she reached for the nanosword to find it was gone. She stared in disbelief as a blue line sliced through Hendriks' neck. His eyes registered surprise, then his head toppled forward off his collapsing body.

Everyone froze, staring from Hendriks' cauterized headless corpse to the young Japanese man holding the nanosword, its blue blade pulsing.

"Your instructions, Jennifer?" Yori said.

She swallowed. Hendriks' two men retreated inside the room. She called over to the radar operator. "Will he make it? How close behind are they?"

"He's ninety seconds away but they're closing on him, and the doors open and close on a thirty-second cycle."

Everyone stared in her direction, while she focused only on Dimitri, who was looking at her as if he had just worked out that he did not really know her at all. She realized the feeling was mutual, given what Cheveyo had just told her. She parked it.

"Do you trust me, Dimitri?"

"With my life," he answered.

She threw the key across the room to him. "Everyone take a deep breath." She nodded to Dimitri. "Do it."

* * *

Micah sprinted for the ship, trying to ignore the pain in his legs and lungs. The creatures weren't that far behind – he didn't know exactly how far, and he didn't want to know. He had a gash across his face and his left arm was badly sprained, but he'd been lucky with the fall.

Through the trees he caught tantalizing glimpses of the huge black metallic ship in the early sunlight, and at one point saw the open doors at its base. His heart raced, and he ran faster – *he was going to make it!* He didn't shout, he was too breathless from running. He reached the edge and burst through a thick patch of bushes, the monstrous ship looming up in front of him. But the doors were sealed.

"No! No! Wait, wait for me, damn you!" he yelled, and sprinted across the last hundred metres of the clearing towards the towering ship. He heard a rumbling sound. "God, no, please God, no, don't do this to me!" But half way across, there was an ear-splitting thunderclap and he was whisked off his feet, sucked towards where the ship had been a second before.

He landed on the hard ground in a sirocco of dust, and then the roar of wind and random static discharges dissipated. He looked up, and struggled to his feet. He could hear a growing noise, a stampede in the bushes behind him, and then a shrill screaming of alien rage. He glared up at the empty sky in disbelief. "Bastards! You fucking bastards!" He stared around as if drunk. It was then he noticed the nuclear devices. He ran over to one and read the digital timer: ninety-three seconds. He wanted to punch the sky, but all he could do was squat down, put his fingers in his hair and pull hard. "Fuck! Oh fuck!" He looked back to where he had come from, and saw the leaders of the herd of Q'Roth burst into the clearing behind him. He turned and ran blindly into the sliver of forest at the other side of the clearing, toward the desert, sweat streaming down his face and back.

Chapter 47

Battle for Eden

Blake recoiled into a defensive stance as a young Q'Roth warrior whip-lashed two legs, praying-mantis-style, at one of the craft's portholes. But the thud sounded distant, and the ship did not rock, nor was the window even scratched. Blake forced himself to relax. The freshly-hatched Q'Roth from the upper cavern had tried to break inside, but Blake had sealed the hatch after he'd brought the skeleton in – he didn't know why, he just didn't want to leave it where it had been in this God-forsaken place.

Since entering the single-room, saucer-shaped ship, the trickle of warriors had grown into a stampede of thousands pouring past like horizontal metallic rain with claws. The young Q'Roth raced along like pack-animals driven by the need for food, following their instincts towards the huge underground ship he knew would take them to Earth, where they would feed.

Since enabling him to contact Kat and the others, the Hohash had remained inert. Blake tried to read the faint ink on the parchment journal written by the dead man. Thankfully, he had written in English – even if it was a little archaic. Blake presumed he had churned out the whole thing in the last days of his life.

It confirmed most of what he already knew about the Q'Roth. The man had belonged to a sect calling themselves "Sentinels", and had travelled there alone in one of the large ships. What had stunned Blake had been the apparent instantaneity of the voyage.

"... Copernicus was right, after all. The stars slid beneath me as I was bathed in a silver liquid that left no trace. I have spent the past twelve days traversing Hades, seeing not another soul, except when I see myself in a mirror which shows me horrors worse than I can imagine. I have tried to break the devil's eggs, but I grow weak and cannot inflict even a scratch on their surface. Alessia was indeed evil to deal with these creatures. I have seen one, atop the hill. My only solace as death approaches is that I will not see one again. It is difficult not to feel that we are doomed to feed these monsters, and that God has forsaken us. I pray that when the time comes, there are those who can rise above our petty human failings and unite to defeat such a gruesome enemy."

Blake closed the book, and held his thoughts silent for a moment, in memory of this Sentinel, yet another fallen unknown soldier.

Pierre had been right about the terraforming, because according to the journal, when the Sentinel had arrived in 1756, the volcanic land was still settling, with violent purple dust storms and no vegetation. It meant no food and, more importantly, water too alkaline to drink, so the man had died as soon as his supplies ran out. He'd had neither a way to take the large ship back to Earth, nor a way to open the Hohash craft. This raised the question for Blake of how Pierre got it open.

The new information Blake got from the journal concerned the secret order known then as the Pentangle of Alessia, and the conflict between them and the Sentinels. Blake had to stop reading several times, as the impact of the brief journal weighed heavy upon him – the discovery of a secret war enduring for centuries, the plotting to sell out Earth as a bio-electric supply – it was unbearable. He gazed at the skeleton, wondering how many Sentinels had met equally unknown, unacknowledged fates – and wondered if any still lived.

Pierre stirred, his eyes flickering open. Blake sat on his haunches next to him. "Pierre, can you hear me?"

Pierre grunted, and then coughed, holding his arms over his chest and ribs to limit the pain.

"Pierre – how did you get in, and how do we get out of here?" He eased Pierre up against the inner wall.

Pierre looked out of the window. Blake followed his gaze – the number of Q'Roth ebbed, and the stragglers no longer seemed interested in them, probably for fear of being left behind.

"They can't get in," Pierre said. "The spiders, the masters of the Hohash mirrors, were cleverer than believed."

Blake nodded, but added "What's going on, Pierre. You never avoid direct questions. Tell me, before you..." Blake didn't want to finish sentence. He had committed himself to saving Pierre, but he seemed in bad shape, and now he assumed they would both die, joining the Sentinel on the floor.

Pierre tried a short laugh; blood spilled from his lips. Blake noticed how cherry red it was – highly oxygenated. But that didn't make sense; it was as if Pierre was healing.

Pierre confirmed his supposition straight away. "I'm not going to die, Sir. And I'll tell you everything now. It won't take long, and then I'll see if I can get us out of here. You remember my father? You said you met him. You clearly didn't like him – why?"

"Listen Pierre, this isn't the time –"

"Yes it is. It's important – and in fact we do have time. When I arrived I tripped a power-up signal. The ship has been dormant for five hundred years, it will take a while to come back on-line, so we're not going anywhere until it activates."

Blake shot Pierre a hard look, and then nodded. "Alright. Aside from being arrogant, thinking that he was better than everyone else – smarter – your father blocked us from doing genetic engineering research. The enemy had ghosters and we had nothing, and people like your father used fear, bigotry and sanctimonious arguments that left us at a disadvantage when it came to genetically-engineered enemies."

Pierre nodded. "What if I told you he did perform genetic engineering experiments, and was successful?"

Blake steepled his fingers. "Well, to be honest, I'd find it pretty hard…" Then it hit him, from the inside, as if he'd always known it. "You?"

"You're looking at one of his experiments," he said, with more than a hint of bitterness.

He noticed Pierre had omitted the word "successful," and the tone implied the reverse. Blake understood – he would never for a moment have wanted a father like Pierre's – an obsessive workaholic scientist, rudimentary on the emotional scale. There would be little chance to be seen as 'successful' in such a parent's judgement.

He searched Pierre's eyes, to see if he was telling the truth. But it all fell into place: the scientific brilliance at such a young age; the dispassionate nature that signalled a lack of empathy, a well-known side-effect from early genetic manipulations; the fact that Pierre had been close to death, yet seemed to be getting stronger. And of course the ability to store nannites in his body without being devoured by them from the inside. He remembered the argument he'd had with Pierre's father all those years ago at a military science convention. The man's passionate defence of a moratorium on genetic engineering – it had all been a smoke-screen protecting his own experiments.

Pierre pressed on. "I didn't know why I'd been genetically changed until after my father was assassinated. After the funeral, a man introduced himself to me – he said he was a Sentinel, and had known my father for years. He told me about the Alicians' genetic experiments, and that my father was involved in counter-warfare, working for the Sentinels. His violent opposition to "genning" was to keep the Alicians from finding out about the real work going on."

Blake studied Pierre. He saw him very differently now. Perhaps this was why he'd never liked him: there was something of a ghoster in Pierre, something unnatural. That was unfair, but maybe somehow he'd registered it at an unconscious level.

"My father completed a dozen experiments. I don't know who the people were, but they're out there. We'll live longer, be brighter, and our immune system is reinforced by nannites hidden in the endorphin system. They're undetectable except via nannite probes, themselves illegal."

Blake didn't like finding this out about Pierre. It felt like he'd had a spy aboard his ship.

"So, what was your real mission?" he said, coolly.

"To be honest, there wasn't one. The Sentinel never made contact again. I asked my mother before she died, and… she didn't actually deny anything, just told me that my father had done everything to protect me, including keeping me in the dark about certain things. After her funeral, I signed up for the Eden Mission. I'm still a scientist at heart, Captain, and a soldier."

Blake was reassured by that last word – he hoped Pierre was telling the truth. Time to get back on track, he decided, just as a low humming began, and a soft shimmer of light emanated from the ceiling.

"So how did you get in, and how do we leave?"

Pierre smiled. "The Hohash let me in. One of them was down here when I arrived. It showed me a set of movements on the pad outside and the door slid open. It then activated the ship and awoke its compatriots, and then left."

"Its com… How many are there? Where did they go?"

"There were five, and they all left except this one. They can communicate with each other, it seems. I don't think the Q'Roth ever got into the ship."

"So, how do we leave?"

"Where do you want to go, Sir?"

"Outside first," he said, pointing upwards, "then back to Earth to join the fight."

The ship rocked, and there was a dull rumbling from outside. Blake walked carefully over to the viewport. "It's gone – the ship is gone! Back to Earth?"

The corners of Pierre's mouth dipped. "Afraid so. It seems the idea is that people come here first, so the Q'Roth get stronger before the major onslaught, but I think everything has gone off early – their plans have been upset by our arrival, and possibly on Earth, too – so they'll go there direct in any case."

Pierre's brow furrowed. "I expect that's why they elicited the help of the Alicians – the Q'Roth work on longer timescales, and with most of them incubating, they don't react well to last-minute changes. The Alicians could help with precision timing, and adapt to developments. Yet they always had a back-up plan. That's why there are some ships already on Eden as well as on Earth. Still, it means they'll be weaker to begin with, which could be an advantage. But this ship we're in is more of a scout ship – I'm not sure it can move as fast or as far as the Q'Roth ones."

"I'm guessing no weapons, either?"

Pierre shook his head. Blake recognized a despairing look in Pierre's eye.

"You don't think Earth is going to make it, do you?"

Pierre winced. "Well, Sir, when I studied the Q'Roth panels in the antechamber, I found one indicating other nests on the planet – sixty in total. So how shall I put this? The soldier in me wants to go back and fight. The genned scientist in me, however, thinks that all the bravado in the world won't make any difference."

Blake folded his arms, tight-lipped, as Pierre continued. "This is a tactical situation, Sir. So, you tell me – when you're caught between an inner enemy wrecking your infrastructure and destroying morale, and an outer enemy who has superior weaponry and infantry – because we both know that's what it will come down to – what do you do?" Pierre held up a hand to stop Blake interrupting. "If you say we go out in a blaze of glory, I will gladly follow your orders, but what if there's nothing left after that blaze? Is that sound tactics?"

Reluctantly, Blake knew General Kilaney would agree.

"Also, Sir, as for Eden – I checked their terraforming control system. The terraforming is pretty unstable – it was never meant to be anything other than cosmetic. The degradation has already begun, particularly with the arrival of the desert, itself accelerated yesterday by the ND explosion. A few years, maybe less, and this whole planet will revert to barren rock."

The mirror flushed in a rainbow swirl of reds and greens, and the craft lifted gently off the cavern floor. Blake's vision diffused, as if everything he could see, including Pierre and his own reflection, was coming apart, de-molecularising, until there remained only a swirling soup of particles and a rushing sound like a waterfall. Abruptly, all the particles slammed back together into place, and Blake found himself in the craft, above ground outside, under the morning sky.

They hovered, noiselessly. Blake turned back to Pierre, who was trying to stand. "Are you okay? Did it understand me?"

"Wow, Sir. That was… incredible!" Pierre's eyes shone, despondency replaced by wonder. "Do you realize what just happened?"

Blake stood his ground, waiting for the answer to his second question. He caught Pierre's eye.

"Sorry, Sir, I don't know. I think the mirrors are trying to understand us. You pointed – I think they understand colours and movements better than words. I'm not sure they can process sound."

Blake was about to try something, when he spotted a lone human figure from out of the viewport, running full pelt, leaving a sliver of trees for the open desert.

"Who the hell…?" But then he saw why he was running so fast: a herd of Q'Roth, less than thirty metres behind, were gaining on him.

"Christ! We have to help him!" Before Blake could do anything, a fast jet came straight at them and launched an air-to-air missile. Blake instinctively dove away from the viewport, and a fraction of a second later the craft leapt sideways to dodge the missile.

He struggled to his feet. There were no chairs or consoles in the craft, little if anything to hang onto. There were a few handles and green vine-like wires hanging from the ceiling, but no furniture.

"You okay, Pierre? That was close – and if I'm not mistaken, friendly fire!" But as he turned he saw Pierre had been thrown sideways against the bulkhead, and was unconscious.

The jet banked and dipped to strafe the chasing Q'Roth with low level attack fire. Although it knocked down twenty or so, the others just leaped over them, continuing the chase. After a tight loop the jet made a second pass and launched two cluster bombs that soaked the Q'Roth in a deluge of white-hot flaming napalm. Blake held his breath, only to see most of them galloping out unscathed.

"Sweet Mother!"

The jet then left the scene – Blake assumed it was low on fuel, knowing it was the right tactical decision, but one the man below would have a hard time understanding, now only twenty metres in front of the Q'Roth front line. The man was tiring, struggling, and occasionally stumbling in the sand.

Blake turned to the mirror, and pointed to the figure outside, jabbing his finger at it. He then ran to the door and pointed at that too. The craft spun around as the door opened. He was nearly thrown out by the centripetal force, but managed just in time to grab one of the green "vines" hanging from the ceiling. He remembered these craft were built for the mirrors, which had independent mobility. He glanced over his shoulder to check that Pierre hadn't rolled towards the open hatch.

As the craft stopped spinning Blake caught sight of the man.

"Get inside!" he shouted.

The young man gaped, and then with a desperate grunt darted over to the hatch and launched himself in, clutching Blake's forearm. Once he was inside, Blake signalled with his two palms to the mirror to close the door.

"N-nuke!" the man gasped, pointing behind him. "Detonating… Now!"

Blake swivelled back to the mirror and threw both arms out in the opposite direction to where the young man had been pointing, and was thrown backwards as the ship accelerated away. Three seconds later all three of them were hurtled to the back of the craft, pinned there as the ship shifted into high gear to outrace the nuclear blast-wave, catapulting them upwards. He blacked out.

* * *

Vince piloted the lead Sarth missile at a distance, using a virtual immersion "head-can" as the mil called it, bulleting across the desert. While he remained back at base, the neural interface allowed him to steer the C6-laden dart just above the dune-tops, caressing Eden's skin, zeroing in on the latest Earth-origin Q'Roth ship arrival. A black scab formed on the horizon. He clicked on zoom.

The swollen image resembled an animal carcass engulfed by ants. "Damn, too late – again," he muttered, knowing Vasquez and the controllers back at base could hear every word. Not that it was necessary

– they saw everything via the slave screens. He was pissed off – each time a ship landed full of human cargo, the Q'Roth began harvesting within minutes. He zoomed in further. People flooded out of the ship, dazed and bewildered, then fought to get back inside, eyes and mouths wide in panic, scrambling over each other upon seeing the Q'Roth warriors swarming towards them. He zoomed out, suppressing a well of anger.

He rapped a control to relay coordinates to two tandem missiles, and the pair of piloted F-39s trailing behind with their nuclear payload. He signalled the attack pattern to the base controller with a single word: "*Delta*". The "*D*" stood for *destroy* – he judged it was too late to save the people; instead he had to make sure the ship didn't take this particular Q'Roth hive back to Earth. A letter flashed in his left field of vision, "'*S*", meaning *Save*. This was the third time Vasquez had disagreed with him. *Okay, we'll try it your way.* He ramped up the acceleration for all three missiles, scratching across Eden's flesh.

His recon system auto-zoomed onto four smaller Q'Roth ships buzzing like flies around the feed – he'd seen similar ones around the last ship too. A blue band slashed in front of him, missing him by metres. He sent a command to stutter his engine thrust, making it harder for the Q'Roth to get a fix on him. His vision auto-compensated – but that was because he was there virtually – the F-39 pilots couldn't use this trick, so he had to take out the smaller ships. But there were four of them, and he only had three missiles. As if on cue, they lifted off, accelerating towards him in a square defense pattern. He picked the nearest one and went to maximum speed, transmitting the command "frag-mode", as he spiralled through blue beams latticing the sky. He pummelled into his target too fast to make out any expression of the Q'Roth pilot.

His vision leapt to the second missile, scorching in from the East. He dipped low to avoid a web of azure fire. He saw that his first missile had found its target – a plume of flame billowed mid-air, the wreckage of the Q'Roth vessel fire-balling to the ground. Better, some of the explosive fragments had scraped another one, not destroying it, but sending it to the ground like a swatted fly. He swerved his missile to the right, attracting another ship away from the transport, breaking their defense formation.

His vision snapped to the third missile – the second must have been hit. He shrugged it off; he'd distracted the ships, allowing the two fighters to roar in from the West ten metres above ground. He watched their high-energy pulse lasers strafe the rear edge of Q'Roth warriors, slicing a hundred out of existence like a razor clearing stubble.

The remaining two Q'Roth ships disengaged from Vince's missile and pursued the fighters. Vince was about to take one of them out when he spotted the source of this particular Q'Roth horde. A steady stream of warriors hemorrhaged from their underground nest into Eden's noon sky faster than blood from a slashed artery. He didn't give it a moment's thought: he broke off his pursuit and swung the missile full throttle into the cave's mouth.

He saw white. He tore off the head-can – no more missiles.

"Christ, Vince," Vasquez shouted, "you just sentenced those pilots to death!"

Vince muscled past Vasquez to the screens relaying video from the two fighters. Most of the people on the Q'Roth transport were already dead, thousands of Q'Roth warriors scurrying over the mound of corpses to get inside the ship, to head toward Earth. A screen relaying live video from the first pilot blanked. Vince snatched the microphone from the military controller handling the second fighter.

"Take out the ship – do it now, you're dead anyway!"

Vasquez pushed next to him, seizing the microphone, but offered no counter-command. They watched the screen in silence as the fighter banked hard enough to make the controller flinch. The transport grew large in front of them as the jet aimed straight for the main hatch, a red light indicating the nuke was about to detonate. The screen flashed white.

"Yeah, I know," Vince pre-empted Vasquez, "another hero. You should be proud. Medals all around later. How many Eagles left from the second wing?"

Vasquez's lips squeezed to a white line. "Four."

Vince eyed him, recognizing the look. "Want me to fly one? I can, you know. I'm a bit rusty, but –"

Vasquez grimaced. "What are your orders?"

Vince scanned the intel around him. Three quarters of their screens were blank; almost all of their info-drones shot out of the sky. He tapped a control and the holomap folded out in front of him, revealing Eden's major continent in beige relief. Blue flags highlighted Q'Roth nests, yellow ones transports arrived from Earth, and red ones transports that had arrived with human freight, swapped for Q'Roth warriors, and vanished back to Earth. *Too much red!* The inbound ships had been programmed to land on top of nests.

Vasquez nodded towards the Southern section. "Turnaround time's getting quicker. They know we're here so they're boarding fast as they can. Latest one was thirty minutes."

He made up his mind. "Change of strategy. We nuke them as soon as they arrive." Vince spoke to the map, pointing. "We send our fighters to these blue flags – we know transports are going to arrive there soon. If the fighters get there before the transports, they nuke the nests. If the transports arrive, they nuke them too." He held up a hand, raising his voice, shouting so everyone in the room was clear. "The fighters go in hot, nukes armed, so if they're shot down, they detonate; if not, they bomb the ships as soon as they find them."

Vasquez blanched. "What about the people on board? We're soldiers for God's sake, not butchers."

Vince rounded on him, ignoring the fact that Vasquez was a head taller. "Your job is to protect humanity, contain the threat on Eden, maximize survival back on Earth. We can't help the people here, they're dead either way. Give the command!"

Vasquez faced off Vince. "We'll meet in hell, for sure, Vince."

Vince didn't blink. "I have a condo there waiting for me. You're welcome for tea. Now give the fucking order, Colonel."

Vasquez bristled. He nodded to the controllers.

* * *

Blake awoke first, rubbing his head where it had slammed into the hull. It was getting dark, so he figured he'd been out for at least eight hours. He shook himself, furious for the loss of time, but he guessed none of them had slept much in the past forty-eight hours. He glanced at Pierre and the young man's unconscious frames; they looked restful. The lad reminded him of his son who would have been about the same age had he lived. *Well, Robert, I finally put men before mission.* Despite the grogginess, calmness swept over him. He went straight to the viewport. The ship floated a good ten kilometres above Eden's surface, where an ugly, broiling smoke-grey mushroom illuminated the charred landscape.

Blake regarded the volume of the nuclear mushroom since detonation, and judged it to have been either a large nuclear warhead or perhaps a cluster of devices. It would leave a scar on this part of the planet, not to mention significant fallout. He couldn't help feel sick at heart at the thought of how quickly humanity had left its ugly trademark signature on Eden – no matter that it was in self-defence.

He heard the young man awaken, and helped him to his feet. Pierre lay unconscious in the corner, and Blake decided to let him wake up in his own good time. The young man looked bedraggled, but he held out his quaking hand towards him. Blake took it firmly.

"Captain Alexander!" the young man said. "My name's Micah Sanderson. Sir, it's an honour. You've no idea. You've always been one of my heroes, Sir, but now – well, you can imagine, no one comes close anymore. Thanks for saving me back there."

Blake smiled, putting his other hand around their handshake, the way he'd learned in Africa a long time ago. "You're welcome, Son, most welcome." As he stared at Micah, Blake had the feeling he looked familiar, as if they had met before. He brushed it aside, it was so unlikely.

Pierre woke up, and massaged the bruise on the back of his head. "I dreamt there was a nuclear explosion." He glanced at the others and frowned. "Not a dream then."

Blake and Micah squatted down to help Pierre into a seated position. The mirror interrupted them – it flashed a few times, settled, faced Blake, then revealed a bald-headed man, intense eyes, staring at all of them.

"That's Vince, Sir,' Micah whispered quickly, "He's leading the… er… rescue mission."

Blake stood up and turned directly to face the figure in the mirror. "You must be Vince."

Vince stared back. "You have the advantage, Sir. No – wait – I take it back. You're Captain Blake Alexander. I'm very pleased, not to say relieved, to see you alive, Captain. And… I see we have a mutual acquaintance."

At that point another face, tear-stained and female, pushed its way into the frame. "Micah? Micah! Oh, thank God! I said I'd cut his balls off if you were killed, and he just ignored me!"

Blake's head pivoted for an instant to raise an eyebrow at Micah. "Ma'am, he's fine, but I need to talk to the one in charge, please."

Blushing, she scuttled out of the picture again, muttering something none of them could hear.

"Vince, are you in contact with Earth?"

"That's a little complicated, but essentially, yes. Your crew on the Ulysses were to send a message, but of course it would take days to reach Earth. However, it appears one of these mirror contraptions travelled back on a ship to Ireland, led by a girl and a professor, and we've been in contact for the past few hours, connecting via them. It's not pretty back there, Captain, and it's been a hell of a day. A total of thirty ships have left Earth for Eden, most people boarding them to escape the Q'Roth already on the loose since yesterday – the Alician propaganda machine has been running flawlessly. We've had jets scan a three-thousand mile radius over the past few hours, and seen the carnage left from twelve of the ships – hundreds of thousands of human corpses, limited firefights, and nineteen ships already headed back to Earth. It's chaos back home, nearly a million Q'Roth on the rampage, and that's the ones we know about. As you can imagine, communications are a mess. At least five governments in desperation launched a nuke each, but they killed more humans than Q'Roth. The Chorazin and IVS are trying to make firebreaks around Q'Roth zones using small-yield fusion bombs, but more ships keep landing, avoiding the irradiated areas. As for us, we're pretty much out of hardware and ordnance here."

Blake interjected. "Nannites – they're susceptible to nannite attack."

Vince shook his head. "Alicians took out the few remaining nannite med and mil research centres in the first wave of coordinated attacks early this morning."

Blake squeezed his fists hard enough that the fingernails dug into his flesh. So much had happened, so fast. But he was thankful for the way this man was delivering the news – not letting his emotions get in the way. It helped – he shut down his own feelings and reactions, knowing he had to remain in control.

"Thank you, Vince. I'd like to talk to my First Officer. Can you connect us?"

Vince turned to someone off-screen, and a voice came on against a background of crackling static.

"Blake! Is that really you? My God, Kat, Rashid and I thought you were buried up to your eye-balls in Q'Roth soup!"

Blake knew he needed to stay cold at this point – Zack was the only person there who could make him emotional, if he let him. He hoped Zack would understand.

"Major, did you expedite Omega Kappa?"

There was a pause. "Affirmative, Sir, via a coded transmission through Vince's mirror – Kat worked out how to do it. We just need co-ordinates."

Blake looked down to Pierre.

"New York," Pierre answered, softly.

Blake stared at his science officer for a moment, considering the larger picture. He reflected that military ops always relied crucially on intelligence, and right now he had the best intelligence the world had to offer sitting before him. He turned back to the mirror scene.

"Zack – New York."

He heard a low whistle. "Okay, Skipper, if you say so. I'll get on it straight away and await further instructions. It's sure good to hear your voice again. Zack out."

Vince had only been half-listening during this brief exchange, talking quietly with someone off-screen. Blake assumed he was getting reports from the jets carrying out recon or battle ops. Vince, hearing Zack sign off, turned to give Blake his full attention again.

"May I ask – Omega Kappa?"

"We take care of our own," Blake said. "It'll be a rendezvous point for the evacuation in North America – New York is still irradiated so the Q'Roth will avoid it."

Vince nodded. "Family." He looked sideways again.

Blake noticed that Vince wasn't calling him "Sir" anymore – the question of who was actually in charge here was still undetermined.

"What's the status of your operations?" Blake asked.

"All Q'Roth ships are now outbound. We don't think any more ships are incoming – the ruse is undone, though it may be too late. Here, we've launched all of our nukes and managed to disable six ships and four nests, but that seems to have precipitated a mass excursion to Earth. Some other ships might be arriving on the other side of the planet, out of our recon range."

"Has an international war council been convened?"

Vince shook his head. Blake knew what that meant. The Alician strategy was not merely technological but political – lack of trust after the last war left Earth divided and conquerable.

Blake made his mind up. "How many mirrors do you have?"

Vince frowned. "There are three here, they arrived a few hours ago. Why?"

"Take them back to Earth – to New York. Can you navigate these ships?"

Vince nodded. "The ship in Ireland learned enough, so they can instruct us via the mirrors."

Blake nodded. "We have the ignition key, we'll bring it to you. Send word ahead to anyone trustworthy for immediate evacuation and command personnel extraction. When you're there try to raise any other ships not under Q'Roth or Alician control. If you find any, the mirrors go to them – it will be the only way we can communicate." He glanced at Pierre. "Then, if it looks like we're losing, we all come back here and go – elsewhere. This planet is unstable – it will revert to desert in a few years according to my science officer, and could well be the next stop of the Q'Roth once they finish up on Earth and realize some of us have escaped."

Blake could hear mutterings behind Vince. Pierre was right; fighting might only delay the inevitable. They needed a back-up survival plan – leave, in order to avoid letting all humanity perish.

Vince nodded once. "Yes, Sir. We'll have our last two fighters back here in twenty minutes – I'll re-route one to fly near your location so you can follow it. I presume you're coming back with us?"

"My crew and I are staying here. That way my science officer can work on our destination, and I can co-ordinate operations from Eden orbit. Micah will rejoin you."

Vince looked satisfied in more ways than one. "Understood, though you might wish to discuss the destination with Micah – he has an idea." He broke the transmission link.

Blake turned to Micah. "Where should we go?"

Micah walked up to the Hohash and ran his fingers over its smooth outer edge. Blake was surprised: it had never occurred to him to touch this alien artifact.

Micah looked mesmerized. "Can this communicate?"

Blake was intrigued. "Yes, in a manner of speaking, with one of my officers."

"Katrina," Micah said.

It sounded more like a statement rather than a question. "How did you know?"

Micah shrugged, and turned to face Blake. "Lucky guess. I need to talk with her before I go back."

Chapter 48

Omega Kappa

General William Kilaney coughed and spat blood for the third time. The lieutenant who never left his side offered him her kerchief. He accepted it, nodding a thank you. She opened her other hand, three trimorph capsules in her palm. He shook his head, and leaned forward in his bridge command chair, staring into Zeus I's viewscreen.

"Is the next batch ready?" he bellowed to his Tactical Officer.

"Thirty seconds, Sir."

Kilaney grimaced, counting eight mushroom clouds churning over former North American cities. He'd advised the President against the Tac-Nuke general order, but it was done now, and she wasn't around anymore to worry about it – High Command had been taken out as soon as a Q'Roth ship had landed at Napa. It was his game now, and he preferred a rifle to a shotgun.

"New targets?" He suspected the answer, but wanted to fire the orbital missiles on fresh ships, rather than areas where the Q'Roth had already begun their cull.

"Negative, Sir. Still holding at fifty-five Q'Roth ships, based on our joint intel with IVS."

"Fire when ready. Usual protocol – target the most recently landed ship not issuing Micah's code."

He wondered how long it would be before the enemy attacked his operation on Zeus I. He'd already destroyed five Q'Roth ships, though the human toll had been extensive – the Q'Roth always landed in densely populated areas. He reminded himself of his mission – to firefight the enemy, giving the four refugee-laden ships enough time for their escape. He turned to his lieutenant. "Get me the IVS CIC – what's his name again?" He disliked having to deal with that infamous magnate, but War had taught him long ago that the enemy of your enemy was an ally, at least during battle.

"Shakirvasta, Sir. Coming through on Line 1."

Kilaney spun his chair to face a vid-screen. It crackled, then out of the scribbled fuzz a man appeared, seated behind a plush desk, somehow looking dishevelled yet composed, a lighted cigarette poised in each hand.

"General, so good to see you're still in the game."

Kilaney heard a shrill klaxon, indicating six missiles had just fired from Zeus I towards their next target – that's how many it took, and they had to strike at exactly the same moment to penetrate the Q'Roth ships' hulls. "What's your status?" he barked.

Shakirvasta took a considered drag, exhaling before he spoke. "Not particularly good. We've lost a million infantry in the last hour. Frankly, all they do is slow the enemy down, and not by much."

Kilaney winced – how could Shakirvasta state it so coldly? At least the man had a cool head.

"General, we're witnessing a change in Q'Roth tactics. The ones who have tapped sufficient human sentience are becoming more strategic, liquidating the few military bases not already sabotaged by the Alicians."

Kilaney thumped a fist on the arm of his chair. "What about the Brazilians, and the Indonesian Navy? We lost contact with them half an hour ago."

Kilaney saw the screen image jump, knocking ash off Shakirvasta's nearly-depleted cigarette. Shakirvasta glanced at something off-screen, then his eyes flicked back to Kilaney.

"There's another type of Q'Roth ship, as we suspected, a medium-sized destroyer, skimming our oceans, dropping hunter depth charges. They're working from the bottom up. Efficient, I must say." He discarded his used cigarette, and without looking, supplanted it with a fresh one. "That disposed of the Indonesian Navy, and I'm sorry to say the Brazilian air force has been neutralized."

Kilaney sank back in his chair. "What – all of it?"

The image jumped again, and Kilaney thought he heard someone shouting the words *"Now, Sir, please!"* Shakirvasta nodded, whether to Kilaney or the man shouting, took a final drag and stubbed out his cigarette, replacing the unlit one in a gold case. He looked naked without his cigarettes.

"There are some smaller craft as well, using some kind of beamed weapon. Very maneuverable, unfortunately; they sliced through the Brazilian fighters easily as a hand through a holo."

"Sir," the Tactical Officer called out, "Sir, we're detecting an unidentified vessel approaching fast from low orbit."

Shakirvasta cut in, rising from his chair, hands planted on his desk. "General, sounds like you have company. I'm afraid we're dealing with adult Q'Roth now. I have to go. I'm in the Tower, and, well as you're about to see, it's time to leave. The game's over, General. I'm instructing our ship to depart for Eden to join Blake and the others while it still can. I suggest you do the same. Good luck." Someone grabbed Shakirvasta's arm and he disappeared from the screen.

Kilaney watched, and then understood. Behind where Shakirvasta had been sitting, the sky shifted violently. Mountain tops slid into view, followed by the tops of more mortal skyscrapers, then the bustling city beneath: the Mumbai Tower was falling.

He'd realized a day ago they could not win this battle, but now the full impact of the loss of his world seeped through him like bitter poison. He gathered himself. "Hostile on viewer."

The vessel resembled a giant mechanical crab, vectoring towards them at terrific closing speed, grappling arms extended. "Fire at the damned thing soon as it's in range. Everything we've got!" He turned to his aide. "Get me Micah."

The lieutenant blurred into motion. "Just audio, Sir."

He coughed blood again, this time using his uniform sleeve. The attack ship erupted in a billowing white-hot cloud of flame, quickly snuffed out of existence, revealing the target completely unscathed, tearing towards them.

"Micah, things are going bad. Looks like I won't be making it. Tell Blake... tell him it's lost here. The four ships must leave now, that's an order. We'll fight here to the end, but –"

A spider-web of lightning crackled across the Ops room, as the space station shook, throwing him out of his chair. The room darkened except for the strobe of electrical discharges sizzling plastic, ozone and charred human flesh into a pungent acrid cocktail. It stung his eyes, and left a taste like rust in his mouth. He coughed heavily, but stayed down till the emergency relays kicked in. As the fizzing sputtered to a stop and a pale light flickered on, he got halfway up to find his lieutenant's half-burnt face next to him. A single trimorph capsule nestled in her lifeless palm. He swallowed it, closing her eyes.

Breathing through the folded kerchief, he squinted through layers of smoke and flame-licked shadows. He was the only one left alive. With a metallic snap, fire-suppressant gas jetted from the ceiling, cooling the air and dousing the flames, evacuating the smoke through vents. He staggered back into his chair.

He heard thumping, hammering noises getting closer. *We've been boarded.* He reached for his pistol but it had been knocked onto the floor somewhere, buried in the debris. Four Q'Roth warriors thundered into the room, circling him. He stood, as upright as he could manage. They didn't approach.

"What in hell's name are you waiting for?" He shook his head, and spat blood on the floor. He wiped his lips on the kerchief, then dropped it next to his lieutenant's twisted body. His left ring finger slipped inside the pin of the high-yield grenade strapped to his waist for this eventuality, and with his other hand he slammed the Zeus I auto-destruct control. It had a thirty second timer, but he had no intention of staying around that long.

He realized he'd spent too many years as a General, sitting in a chair, sending soldiers to their deaths, the last four years steadily rotting from cancer. Life had been crap in recent memory, but death would give something back to him – he'd die as a soldier, on his feet. "You're coming with me, boys." He pulled out the pin and charged at the nearest warrior.

* * *

Micah sat facing one of the Hohash mirrors. He felt he'd aged ten years over the past three days. The bad news on the nets had just kept getting worse, and now there was no news, the airwaves transmitting a static far worse than silence or screaming. He'd waited an hour since the General had been cut off. Zeus Orbital had fallen from the sky like a blazing meteorite.

The massive ship doors closed as they readied for the trip back to Eden. Four ships – that was all – his in New York, captained by Vince, one in Dublin run by a young girl and a professor, one near Mumbai run by IVS, and one in the Andes, led by Senator Josefsson. Twelve thousand people, out of four billion.

Initially, Blake and Vince had been worried that they would have people banging and clinging onto the hulls as they left, but few made it to the irradiated evacuation sites. The Q'Roth easily shot down most transports trying to get there. After initial nuclear attacks, the Alician High Guard had seen to it that Earth's diminished nuclear arsenals were incapacitated, and eradicated nano-tech facilities. An estimated five million Q'Roth were scattered over the globe, each one killing several hundred people a day. Locusts. They'll leave nothing, and then set the world alight, ready for future terraforming – re-cycling the planet.

He knew the most powerful weapon against humanity had been the confusion caused by the reversal from unbridled hope of instant transport to Eden, to nightmarish reports of rampaging alien monsters, and then to terrifying global carnage. Everything had happened so quickly. Many survivors still had no idea what was going on – it was blind panic. And it had all been planned that way. Most people were easy targets, some found in churches or subterranean habitats, others fled to the hills, a few even sought refuge underwater, which didn't stop the Q'Roth – they turned out to be amphibious and fast swimmers.

A small number of human stragglers might survive for a week or so, but the Q'Roth would eventually track them down – they perceived human bio-energy the same way sharks could smell blood over large distances. Other animals were left untouched, except the rare remaining dolphins and whales, whose bio-electric energy also seemed to be refined enough for the Q'Roth menu. People could hide in irradiated areas for a few weeks, but then the rad-poisoning would finish them off. It was over. *Endgame*. Time for a few pieces to escape from the chessboard.

He held up a picture of Blake, and the mirror instantly came to life, revealing the off-world leader's gaunt face. Micah had already given him the bad news about General Kilaney.

"We have as many as are coming. We have as much food and medical supplies as we could gather, plus generators, some livestock – pretty much the manifest you asked for. There's really nothing more we can do here." He hated saying that – he sounded like a politician.

"Thank you, Micah. We'll see you all soon."

The connection broke. Blake's face had seemed to brighten, obviously relieved that he would see his wife again. It hit Micah how ironic it was that he'd been rescued by Blake – again. He wondered if he would ever tell him what he'd known of his son, Robert, before they were captured and held at Kurana Bay. He remembered, a lifetime ago it seemed, being bundled into the chopper by Zack and Blake with the others during the rescue that night. When the news had come out, and there was no mention of Blake's son, Micah's analytic skills did the math – if Blake didn't want it known, Micah wasn't going to be the one to go public on it. He and Robert had been the only two from their group taken to Kurana Bay, dumped with other captives, so it had been easy to keep it quiet. Someday, though, he'd raise the subject with Blake.

Maybe.

Sandy entered the room, interrupting his reverie. "Micah, you have a visitor." She escorted a strained-looking Antonia.

"Hello, Micah," she said tentatively.

He flashed a weak smile. They'd seen each other a few times since she arrived yesterday evening, but since then they'd avoided each other. He knew why she was there. He picked up a picture of Kat, and the mirror flashed various colours before her taut face appeared. *We're all ageing too fast.* He gestured for Antonia to sit down as he left his seat facing the mirror. Antonia paused as she passed Micah, her hand touched his arm, and she kissed him on the cheek. "Thank you. For everything," she said, softly.

He nodded stiffly and headed to the door where Sandy was waiting, without a glance backwards. Sandy hooked his arm in hers and they walked out of the room.

"I hear you located the planet?"

Micah shrugged. "It was a team effort – Kostakis had worked out the nav system, and Kat had access to the Hohash. The coordinates were in the data stream, I just couldn't find the temporal reference, and then it hit me."

Sandy cocked an eyebrow.

"When I was using the Optron to analyse that data stream, just before I went into a coma, I was falling towards a planet. I know now it was the spider planet. But no one ever programmed gravity into an Optronic environment, I mean not real gravity. So I worked out the gravitic constant for the planet and –"

"That was the temporal reference."

He smiled. "Kostakis ran it through the nav system and sure enough it indicated a planet at those coordinates. Since then, the mirrors have shown us images – five hundred years old, of course, but there should be water, and topsoil. The inhabitants didn't put up a fight, so there was little destruction, and no reason to terraform the planet after the culling. It'll take two or three weeks to get there, though, even with these ships."

She stopped him, faced him. "Nice work, Micah."

He looked her in the eye, then shrugged again.

"You're not wearing your father's jacket."

"No. Pierre wanted it to extract the nannites – Vince has him working on a weapon, just in case we run into the Q'Roth again, or they come looking for us."

She looked at him sideways.

"Okay," he said. "I let it go. There've been a lot of things I've let go of in the past few days. It was my father's jacket, not mine."

"I'd say he'd be proud to have you wear it."

Micah shrugged, and smiled. "I know. Really."

"Come on," she said, linking arms again, "I know a feisty old lady who's been raising merry hell about not being able to see you!"

Micah rolled his eyes, and a smile bubbled up from the depths. She held his arm tightly as they walked along the corridor.

Chapter 49

Exodus

Blake had all the Hohash mirrors synchronized, as he prepared to give the final orders. All twelve-thousand people drew together in the four ships to see and hear, via holo-screens, the words of the man who'd shouldered the responsibility for the decision to desert Earth. At the allotted time, silence fell across Eden, interrupted by a few baleful cries of infants and the whimpers of distressed pets. Josefsson had wanted to address the gathering, but Vince dissuaded him. Blake hated giving speeches, but the Eden Mission shrink, Carlson, had insisted it was necessary for morale before they set off. Blake was thankful that Micah had helped him prepare it.

He waited a few moments, with eyes firmly shut as if in prayer, and then broke the hush in a loud and clear voice. "We leave now, with heavy hearts, knowing all is lost for Earth, and that even as we say farewell to Eden, the final embers of our civilization are being extinguished. We could stay and fight – and die with our compatriots, our fellow men and women, friends and lost loved ones. The angels would applaud – and weep at our sacrifice."

He raised his voice. "But it would be foolish, the end of humanity. We are now the last hope of the human race, a small flame taken from those dying embers that will evade the Q'Roth, and seek to burn brightly elsewhere." He paused, letting it sink in.

"We've learned a very hard lesson these past days. We won't be so easily surprised or betrayed in the future. We'll seek knowledge, allies, find a new home, and raise a stronger human race, one fit to meet with our galactic cousins on equal terms. This will be a hard, long road. But the fact that we have escaped at all, shows our worth. I want each and every one of you to recognize that worth. If ever you have doubts, or become dismayed, or second-guess this decision today, know this – that as the last people on Earth die out in the next few days and weeks, they will have only one hope as the light fades from their eyes – that some will escape – that *we* will escape, and will carry on the human race. And…" he paused – he had been debating whether to say it or not, but felt he had to – it was part of his own humanity. "And that one day, we will track down the Alicians who betrayed us, and avenge our fallen loved ones, and perhaps in a little less than a millennium, we will search for and find the next generation of Q'Roth nests and exterminate this galactic plague of locusts." Throughout all four ships, thunderous clapping and foot stomping erupted, together with a murmur rising towards a cheer. Before it reached its crescendo, Blake held up his hand, and the clamour abated.

"We must be careful. We must never again make the mistake of hubris, of arrogance, of not thinking ahead. We must be strong and wise, but also clever and cunning. We will never forget our heritage, where we came from. Nor will we allow ourselves to be absorbed by other species, to disappear. We are Humanity, and we owe it to the people we have left behind, all those who have been slaughtered these past few days, to make that name a proud one in this galaxy. So I say this to you all – and it is not a lie or a politician's ploy – I say it because I mean it, and I believe it. This is not the end – this is a beginning. Now, everyone, prepare for transit. Our path awaits us"

Blake met Micah on his way to the Control Room. "How'd I do Micah?"

Micah grinned. "You're a natural; Josefsson looked worried."

Blake smiled. "I've heard a lot about you, Micah, these past few days. You seem to have a gift for seeing things, how they unfold. Are *you* worried?"

Micah's grin stalled. He was glad Sandy wasn't around to hear what he was going to say. "We've done all we can; each captain has a separate flight plan, unknown to the others, and the routes aren't direct, so even if we're followed, it won't be obvious where we're headed."

"I hear a 'but' coming."

Micah laid a hand on a Q'Roth control panel. "The threat won't come from the Q'Roth. They've fed, why should they care if a few of us escape? The Alicians, though, they will care. We'll be like poor relations to them – an embarrassment."

Blake pondered for a while. "Micah, you're an analyst, so I want your prediction that they'll come after us, and not give up till they find us. What are the odds?"

Micah matched Blake's level gaze. "More than fifty per cent. We haven't seen the last of them."

Blake nodded, heavily. "One more thing, Micah. I want you to work with me. I want you on my team."

Micah couldn't speak for a moment. His mind flashed back to the poster of the four astronauts in his old office. "Of course, Sir. Er... Captain. What do I call you, actually?"

"You're a civilian, so 'Blake' will do fine." His smile widened. "But then 'Sir' sounds fine, too, now that you mention it."

Five minutes later, Blake gave the final order, and four massive ships vanished from Eden's surface, abandoning Eden and Earth, and the last struggling human survivors, soon to be eradicated. There had only been one logical direction for the four ship captains – Blake, Vince, Rashid and Jennifer: the spider world. Perhaps there they could learn more before they headed towards the Grid Society Kat had spoken of – going straight to the Grid itself might well be suicide, as that was almost certainly where the Alicians would be headed. The Hohash mirrors had conveyed to Kat that the Q'Roth were nomadic, and would continue out into the spiral reaches rather than back toward the Grid or the spider world.

He had given a rousing speech because it had been desperately necessary for morale, but he was a military commander and, like Micah, had grave doubts concerning their survival prospects, even in the first year. But he didn't think he had lied – it *was* a beginning, another chance.

The air around him snapped into a silvery liquid, as one more thought lodged into his mind, hanging on a gossamer thread. *Eden.* Twice now mankind had fallen from Eden. Once by their own natures, and now tricked by others. He wondered if there was indeed a third chance, or if the real lesson was that there was no such place as Eden, and wanting it, dreaming of it, only made humans weaker. But even time-frozen in a mercurial sea, he could feel his wife Glenda's hand in his – he'd reached out for her just as he'd given the command. For him at least, Eden was there in those two hands touching. So, while everyone else was just barely holding their breath, praying for the transit to end, Blake could have remained like that for a very long time.

Sister Esma looked up from the star charts laid before her. "I see you are up – is that wise? The genetic re-sequencing is quite fragile in the first few days. The cerebral DNA was barely sufficient. How much do you remember?"

"Everything. Absolutely everything. Anyway, I had to get up out of that ward – I never cared for hospitals – I died in one recently."

Sister Esma studied her protégé. The Q'Roth surgeon had said there might be side effects. "Some humans have gotten away," she said. "We did not predict that. The fighting on Eden was also unanticipated, though the Q'Roth losses were negligible. They are, after all, a collective species. The nourishment here on Earth has been very strong for them – the anxiety levels of the population were at fever pitch, making the bio-energy more powerful than they could have wished for."

There was no reply, despite a lengthy pause. Sister Esma continued. "We're heading for the Outer Grid tomorrow. It will take more than thirty transits, and we need to recharge after each one, so it will take four weeks in total. We will be sponsored by the Q'Roth for Level Five status, and will be allowed limited Grid access. We will be given a new planet, and we will found a new civilisation."

Still no reply. Sister Esma waited, patiently. Clearly something was troubling the younger one. Eventually, she spoke.

"What about those who… killed me. Did they escape?"

Sister Esma let out a short, single laugh.

"My dear Louise, you will live a thousand years. They are Level Three. They will not survive long. What does it matter? Billions have died here in the last four days."

"I understand that – and I am grateful that you regenerated me. It's just – personal. They killed me. I would like to repay the experience. And if – I say only if – they somehow survived – they could become a nuisance to our new civilization."

Sister Esma stared out over the floor of the cavernous ship, housing the five hundred Inner Circle and another five thousand shortly to be genned, the next evolution of humanity that would amount to something significant, taking its rightful place amongst its galactic peers. She knew, however, that there was a possibility that Louise was right, even if her motivations were personal. But Louise's judgment was clearly clouded – the genning hadn't worked fully, or else hadn't settled yet. Sister Esma knew what that meant, though she did not allow her face to betray her thoughts. "What do you propose?"

427

"That I take one of the long-range Q'Roth attack ships, and four nukes. One for each ship they stole."

"Alone?"

Louise's lips broadened. "A small crew – a young man and woman should do."

"Very well. Pick two consorts and I will speak to them before you leave. The Q'Roth have also given us four Hunter Class ships – you may take one. We will be able to track you and communicate between transits, unless you fall too far behind, and we will give you our flight plan." Sister Esma smiled, knowing the last part was a lie – it would be too risky. "You will have two weeks, three at most to rejoin us. Do not be late."

Louise nodded and left. Sister Esma watched her stride away. A shame. She made her decision in an instant, and called over one of her most trusted. "I want you to insert this into the engine core of the long range attack ship chosen by Louise."

The man looked at the glass phial she had handed him. His brow furrowed.

"Nannites? But within a few weeks they will degrade the…" His words dried up under her arctic glare. "Of course, Excellency." He shuffled off.

She cast her gleaming, six hundred-year old eyes over her people, the next generation of Humanity, the apogee of man's intellectual abilities shorn of all weaknesses and social inhibitions. How wise they had been, all those centuries ago, to throw in their lot with the pure and vigorous Q'Roth, ascending the evolutionary ladder. Nothing could stop them now from assuming their rightful role in the galaxy, not as feeble, erratic human clowns, but as a new race of masterful Alicians.

Two Q'Roth joined her and gave her the news. She picked up a microphone. A shrill whine made all stop what they were doing and turn to their leader, flanked by the magnificent warriors.

"I have great news. Earth is finished, the old humanity is no more. Shortly, all life will be extinguished." Cheers erupted from all around her, and a chant began: "Alessia, Alessia…" She beamed, letting the chant rise, then held up a hand.

"From this day on, we are all Alicians. This is our time. Prepare yourselves, we leave in one hour. The galaxy awaits us."

Chapter 50

Epilogue

The Ranger closed down his recording system. His hooked claw stroked the Bartran slave-mind's back ridges. He watched Exa-Grid Spiral 4A Mono-System 82435 Sol 3 on the multi-view screen, all life eradicated. Species 195 <<Q'Roth>> had moved on. The Bartran purred.

This had been a routine covert inspection, following the filing of a complaint after a previous incursion. Species 195 had followed protocol, although they should have filed in advance for sponsoring a new species, and the atomic and nanotech capability of the indigenous species had not been entered on the original incursion manifest. The sponsored escapees would behave according to the dictates of their Q'Roth benefactors, but the other refugees were an unquantified variable.

His claw slid into a hole on the Bartran's back, and the purring ceased instantly. He thought – *encode message to Ranger Grid Sub-Commander 423.* The Bartran's mind became fluid, stretching across the galaxy. The Ranger began:

ENCODE: *UNSPONSORED SPECIES: UNCONTAINED: GRIDBOUND: ORIGIN SPIRAL 4A: IDENT HUMAN: TRANSPORT SP195 SHIPS [4]: PREPARE COUNTER-MEASURES PROTOCOL 32E>*

GSC 423: ACKNOWLEDGED – PROTOCOL 32E INITIATED.
ENCODE: *REQUEST INSTRUCTIONS>*

…

GSC 423: PURSUE.

The Ranger removed his claw, and tapped twice on the sticky console. His ship vanished.

Lightning Source UK Ltd.
Milton Keynes UK
UKOW021408051211

183232UK00011B/100/P